Praise for William Shaw

'Grips the reader by the throat and never lets go' *Independent*

'A contender for thriller of the year' *Sun*

'A superb storyteller' Peter May

'A first-rate police thriller' C. J. Sansom

'A gripping story, impeccably researched' *Guardian*

'A thrilling plot, recreating all the political tension of an explosive time' *Figaro*

'A superb, flowing writer . . . always intelligent' *The Times*

'An elegy for an entire alienated generation' *New York Times*

'The question of why a killer kills is always central. William Shaw delivers a perfect motive' *Spectator*

'Sensuous storytelling . . . Shaw goes from strength to strength' *Daily Mail*

'William Shaw makes his sentences sing' *New York Daily News*

'Astoundingly good' Elly Griffiths

'An emotional intensity found only in the very best crime fiction' *Sunday Times*

William Shaw has been shortlisted for the CWA Historical Dagger, longlisted for the Theakstons Crime Novel of the Year and nominated for a Barry Award. A regular at festivals, he organises panel talks and CWA events across the south east. His books include the acclaimed Breen & Tozer crime series set in sixties London and standalone bestseller *The Birdwatcher*. He worked as a journalist for over twenty years and lives in Brighton.

BY WILLIAM SHAW

The Breen & Tozer Investigations

A Song from Dead Lips

A House of Knives

A Book of Scars

Sympathy for the Devil

The DS Alexandra Cupidi Thrillers

Salt Lane

The Birdwatcher

SALT LANE

William Shaw

riverrun

First published in Great Britain in 2018 by riverrun
This paperback edition published in 2019 by

riverrun

An imprint of

Quercus Editions Limited
Carmelite House
50 Victoria Embankment
London EC4Y 0DZ

An Hachette UK company

A CIP catalogue record for this book is available from the British Library.

PB ISBN 978 1 78648 658 5
EBOOK ISBN 978 1 78648 659 2

10 9 8 7 6 5 4 3 2 1

Typeset by CC Book Production
Printed and bound in Great Britain by Clays Ltd, Elcograf S.p.A.

For LaLa

PROLOGUE

1995

WE ARE WATER.

That summer afternoon, as dragonflies hovered above them, the boys played in the long grass while Mum painted the words in big letters on the side of Royale.

'There,' she said, stepping back.

'We. Are. Water,' the older boy read aloud.

'That's right. We are.'

'No I'm not.' He touched his own bare arm; it didn't feel like water.

The woman smiled at her young sons, green paint on her hands, and laid the paintbrush down on the can. 'We are made of water,' she said. 'Like water we go everywhere. However much they hold us back, we still flow.'

The boy nodded, though he didn't really understand. His attention had already moved on; a big hairy caterpillar was crawling up his brother's leg.

'Nothing can stop our flow,' said the man called Deva, squatting near the boys on the grass and blowing a cloud of white smoke out through his nose. 'We are water. We are elemental. We seep through the cracks.'

'Right,' said the woman, smiling at Deva. 'Elemental.'

He grinned back. The boy watched them, wondering if Mum preferred Deva to them now. They had only met Deva for the first time two days ago when they had arrived on the site. Deva had looked at Mum, perched behind the wheel of their Land Rover, smiled and said, 'You can park it next to me if you like.' He had pointed at a big bus, windows covered in fading curtains; the sign on the front of it read: *Heaven*.

At the back of the bus there was an enormous bed, big enough for loads and loads of people to sleep in. The boys had been allowed to sit on it while Deva and Mum had manoeuvred Royale back and forth into place, putting bricks under her to keep her steady.

Now Mum is in that bed with Deva, and the boys are alone in the caravan. But the wind comforts them, rocking Royale on its axle in the dark.

'Royale rocks, Royale rolls
Royale carries the royal three.
Royale rolls, Royale rocks
Across the wide and empty sea.'

The two boys chant the words in unison.

It's a caravan though, really, not a boat. They know that.

It's just a rhyme Mum made up, but for the two small boys, it has magical power. She got the name Royale from the badge on the front, fixed between the two grab handles. The royal three is the boys and Mum; not Deva. He's not one of them. Never will be. Hope not, anyway.

Royale. Mum loved the sound of it so much, she always calls their caravan that. *Royale is my ark in which I am queen, and you are my princes. Together, we are Royalty, roaming Albion under the protection of the White Goddess.*

The two children are alone in bed in Royale, but their mother is just a few yards away even if she is with him, and the familiar buffeting reassures them that everything is OK. They are in the right place, in the top bunk, snuggled warm under heavy blankets and coats that smell of sheep and cigarettes, chanting the rhyme like it's a spell to protect them. There is a stove, made from an old gas bottle, fed with wood pillaged from skips and copses, and it keeps them warm enough, even in winter.

This is home. When they stay with their gran in her brick house with carpets, banisters and a bathtub, it seems too solid, too stable, too orderly. They can't sleep there. The quiet of the place is sinister. It's as if the silence there is full of monsters and demons, ready to pounce.

It's noisier here, but that's what they're used to. Noisier than most places they've stopped. Outside, they hear men shout and argue. On a windy night like this the dogs are restless, barking. The trees creak, still heavy with fluttering leaves.

But wherever they park up, by the side of a road, like here, or off in some field or wood, they know that here within Royale it's always safe and cosy, rocking in the breeze. They're never anywhere for very long. People in suits and uniforms always come and move them along, but nothing bad can happen in Royale.

So they are both lulled to sleep in the gentle rocking, arms around each other.

They wake only briefly when the caravan is filled with unexpected light and warmth and the stink of hot petrol. And now the shouting around them is louder than it has ever been.

'Fire!'

'Fuck.'

'Fucking fire.'

Royale is burning. Their castle is vanishing. And in the abrupt blare of brightness, the two boys cry out, holding on to one another, heads peeping above the blankets, suddenly afraid. But only for a little while.

It is how the fireman finds them, arms still around each other; two pale bodies under burnt black bedding. It is a sight he will never recover from.

ONE

The day the woman who claimed to be his mother arrived at the door, Julian Keen was killing Nazis in the spare room. He didn't even hear the bell.

'Can you get it, darling?' Lulu called.

He had no idea, as he thumbed his PlayStation controller, that the woman at the door would change his life for ever.

At that moment, he was outside Castle Wolfenstein, climbing the wall by the lift shaft, and he knew from previous experience that if he didn't kill the Nazi at the top within seconds, he'd be shot and have to go all the way back to the castle entrance again.

'Get what?'

He had spent the afternoon in the park pushing Teo on the swing, then spent the last half hour reading *The Gruffalo* to him, twice. She should know by now, this was his me-time. Tomorrow morning he would be back at work; why shouldn't he spend just a couple of hours on a Sunday evening playing games?

'Julian? Didn't you hear it? The doorbell.'

'Can't you get it?'

'I'm making dinner.'

He wasn't sure how much of the story Teo actually understood, but Lulu was convinced that the more you read to them at this age, the smarter they'd be.

'Julian?'

It would only be someone selling cleaning equipment. Those young men with bad tattoos and lean faces who came round every week, box full of dusters and brushes tucked under one arm, dubious-looking ID held up in the other.

For God's sake.

The Nazi had shot him anyway, sending him plummeting back down the lift shaft; the screen dimmed. He hadn't been fast enough. He sighed, stood, put down the controller.

He heard it now, the doorbell ringing. 'Coming,' he shouted, irritated, pushing back his chair and setting off down the steep stairs.

Their flat was a duplex; first and second floors. Three bedrooms. Two bathrooms. Magnificent views of canal from big glass windows. Use of swimming pool and gym. He squeezed past the buggy and his new bike. 'Yes?' he said, yanking open the door.

He saw and smelt the old woman simultaneously.

It was warm, late summer, yet she was cocooned in a dark men's overcoat, greasy at the cuffs, frayed at the collar. Her face was filthy, the lines on her skin crusted black. The air around her was infected with the sharp scent of the unwashed.

She moved her head to one side slightly, as if examining him.

He returned her look, puzzled. 'What?'

Her mouth opened, but nothing emerged.

She was scared, he realised; and, equally, he was too, because there was something frightening about homeless people. She was old and dirty and would want something from him.

It was a crime that such poverty existed in this modern city, but it was also impossible to know what to do about it. Maybe that's what was so disturbing; the sense of not knowing what was to be done.

'Look, I don't know what you want. I'm sorry,' he said, and firmly tried to close the door.

'Who is it?' Lulu called from upstairs.

But the door wouldn't shut. He looked down and there was a threadbare shoe in the way. Dimly, Julian registered that it was a blue Converse, the kind of thing a teenager would wear, comical on a woman her age. Just before he had swung the door to, the old woman must have thrusted her foot into the gap. The thin shoe can't have been much protection. It was a thick door, heavy with security features. The weight of it must have hurt her, he thought.

When he opened it, she was standing there weeping dirty tears.

'I'm sorry,' he said. 'But you shouldn't have . . .'

She was mumbling something.

Was this some attempt to extort him? Would she claim that he had assaulted her? It struck him that it might be some kind of scam. There might be more of them. They had heard stories of a barrister – or a journalist – being stabbed to death on his own doorstep. Hadn't it been on the news? He looked past her into the darkness of Canada Street, more afraid now, but no one moved from behind the rows of cars. She was alone.

'What are you doing, Julian?' Lulu was at the top of the stairs now, above the baby gate, a glass of Gewürztraminer in her hand.

In spite of himself, Julian leaned towards the woman, trying to catch her words. And finally heard what she was saying.

He was so shocked by the five words she spoke, he took a step backwards, recoiling.

'What's wrong, darling? Has something happened. Shall I call the police? Julian?'

But he just stood there, open-mouthed, looking at the old woman, who was weeping on his doorstop.

'Why did you invite her in?' demanded Lulu in whispers.

'Because she said . . .'

I am your mother, Julian.

'You told me. But it doesn't make any sense.'

They were in the kitchen. The woman was sitting in the living room on the orange Eero Saarinen butterfly armchair, waiting for the cup of tea Julian had said he would make her.

'You don't even have a mother,' Lulu said. 'Your mother is dead.'

He was in weekend clothes – jeans and a sweatshirt. In a slate grey skirt, Lulu always looked like she was dressed for work.

'She is dead, isn't she? Your mother?'

Through the open door, Julian peered at the woman. She was perching uncomfortably on the edge of the designer chair, looking down so that he couldn't see her face.

'I mean. I was told she died before I was adopted. But what if she wasn't?'

Lulu was behind him now on tiptoes, attempting to examine her. 'I don't think she even looks like you. Did you see the scab on her face? It's revolting. She's just trying it on. Or sick in the head or something.'

'Probably,' said Julian.

'You're upset, aren't you?'

'Well, obviously. Yes.'

'Tell you what. Ask to see some proof.'

'What sort of proof?'

Behind them, the kettle roared.

'I don't even understand why you're making her tea.'

'I couldn't really offer her wine.'

'Don't be ridiculous.'

He went to put a teabag into a cup. Lulu remained at the door. 'She's probably got lice. I'm going to call the police.'

'Don't,' said Julian. 'Not yet.'

'But she can't be your mother. It's not possible. She's obviously mental or something.'

'Keep your voice down. She'll hear you.'

Julian realised his hand was in front of his face. It took him a second to realise he had been chewing the skin on the side of his thumb, something he hadn't done for years.

TWO

They were in the downstairs ladies' washrooms, facing the row of sinks. 'It'll be fine,' said Constable Ferriter. 'You just have to read out what they've wrote on the card.'

'We had television in London, too, you know,' answered Detective Sergeant Cupidi.

'Right. Obviously.' Her junior officer pouted into the mirror. Cupidi was still new around here; the young constable was just trying to be helpful. 'What is it then? Are you nervous?'

Behind them, a toilet flushed. 'Nervous? No.'

'I would love to give it a go, being on telly. So why don't you want to do it, then?'

Ten minutes ago the Kent Police press officer had announced it would be better if a woman did the piece to camera, so Inspector McAdam had suggested his newest officer do it, the woman who had joined them from the Met: Sergeant Cupidi of Serious Crime.

'In London nobody knows who you are,' said Cupidi. 'It's different round here.'

Ferriter ran a finger across her neat eyebrows. 'What's the point of going on telly if people don't recognise you? Half the fun. Your daughter will be proud.'

'You don't know my daughter. Besides. I'm supposed to be at home. She'll be wondering where I am.'

Ferriter smacked her lips together. 'Want a lend of some of my concealer?'

'Concealer? Why?'

'I could have a go at your hair too, if you like.'

'Jesus. It's an appeal to the public to identify the body of a dead woman.'

'I know. But there's nothing wrong with trying to look nice.'

Alex Cupidi frowned at herself in the mirror. What was wrong with her hair? 'I do look nice.'

'Yeah,' said the young constable. 'Course you do. That's the spirit. See?'

A fist banged on the door. 'Ready for you now, Sarge.'

Cupidi paused, ran her fingers through her hair, and looked at herself again, conscious of the younger officer's critical gaze. For a second, she imagined she saw not herself, but the dead woman looking back.

'What's wrong?' said Ferriter.

As if the glass were water, and her face was floating below it, just as the corpse had been.

She blinked. Opened her eyes again.

The man from the Marine Unit, in long waterproof waders, hands beneath the pale body floating in the dark ditchwater, preparing to lift her out. The long greying hair swirling about her white-skinned face, as if it were her own. She shivered. She felt suddenly old.

'Sarge?'

'Coming.'

They had set a camera on a tripod facing the sign that said *Kent Police*. A man from the BBC was trying to clip a mic to her lapel as she mouthed the words, written on the board that someone was holding up next to the camera.

'You don't look well,' whispered Ferriter. 'Want me to have a word with the DI?'

'I'm fine. Who even wrote that?' She pointed at the board.

'It's from the press office.'

'There's only one "t" in *requesting*.'

'You don't have to spell it out loud, just read it,' muttered the BBC man, who had moved to stand behind the camera. 'We'll cut from you to the artist's impression of the victim. Stand a little to your left . . . Do you mind crouching down a bit so you're in line with the sign?'

'Won't that look stupid?' At 5' 11" she was tall for a woman.

'No one will see your legs.'

'Maybe you should get someone shorter to do it.' But she dutifully bent her knees. 'That better?'

'Magic. Hold it there. In five, four, three . . .'

Cupidi took a breath and read from the card. 'Kent Police are requesting . . .' She stopped, seeing the dead woman's face again, staring back at her from the mirror. 'Sorry. Can I start again?'

'Is everything OK?'

'Sorry. Fine.'

'Come on.' He clapped. 'Let's go. Try again.'

'Kent Police are . . .' Again she faltered, straightened up.

'Are you all right?' asked the man, looking out from behind his camera. 'Is she going to be OK? We're short on time you know.' Behind him she saw Constable Ferriter and DI McAdam watching her, concern on their faces. McAdam would be wondering if he had made the wrong decision, asking her to do it.

'I'm all right,' she declared. 'Just give me a second.'

'Only I've got a deadline. It's going to go to edit any minute.'

'Go on then.' She crouched down again.

'Go,' said the man.

She ignored the cue card this time, looking straight into the camera. 'We found a body,' she began.

A woman had called in three days ago. Her thirteen-year-old son had woken her in the night, crying. He and his mate had found a body when they were fishing for pike, but they didn't say anything because they were scared they would get into trouble for not having a licence.

'He's a good boy,' his mother had said. 'Normally.' That doubt in her voice that Cupidi recognised. We reassure ourselves that we know our children, that they will turn out fine.

A pair of local PCSOs had gone to take a look. With no tools to hand, they had borrowed a pair of old golf clubs from a nearby house and had spent forty minutes prodding the layer of weed and had almost given up, thinking it was a hoax, when one of the clubs hit something heavy, floating below the surface. Whatever it was sank further down for a few seconds, and then rose briefly to the surface again, pale and white.

The corpse had been lying face-down in the water off Salt Lane; she had remained concealed by a layer of thick green that lay across the top of the water like a blanket.

'How we getting her out?' Sergeant Moon demanded. The ditches round here were deep, the banks steep.

'Call the Marine Unit,' said Cupidi.

'I don't know. Cost a bit.' These days everyone was so nervous about budgets.

They stood looking down at the weed that covered her.

'In you go then,' Cupidi had said, nodding down at the water.

In the end, the men from the Marine Unit had lifted her gently, carefully, with such respect it had almost made Cupidi weep. The dead woman rose from the water, dripping, arms splayed, her corpse pale and shiny, dressed only in a pair of white underpants.

'She would have been in her early forties,' Cupidi was saying, straight to the camera. 'Her eyes are blue and her hair was brown, going grey. There were no identifying marks on her body. We searched the area as thoroughly as we could, but we've found no possessions and no sign of her clothing. If you recognise this woman, call us now. We really, really need to find out who she was.' Behind the camera, the man was making circular motions. Wind it up. 'We think she had been in the water about ten days before we found her. That would make it around the second of July. Think back.' The man's arm movements were becoming more insistent. He was short on time; the longer the news item, the less time he'd have to edit it. 'If you saw her or anyone you think might have been her in the area around Romney Marsh, in the area that's roughly between Fairfield and Lydd, please let us know. There was no abandoned car or bicycle present at the scene. We don't know how she got to the place she was found. Did you see her walking? Did she get a lift? If you think you can help us in any way, call 0800 555 . . .'

'A bit bloody long,' said the cameraman afterwards. 'They'll probably try and cut it.'

'That's why I didn't pause for breath,' answered Cupidi.

'But you don't even know how she died.' He was packing the camera into its case. 'What if it was just a swim that went wrong?'

'What kind of weirdo swims in the ditches round here?' interrupted Ferriter.

The cameraman turned towards the constable, looked her up and down. 'Just saying. Probably just an accident. How do you know she was actually killed?' He stopped. 'Hey. I've met you before, haven't I? You do yoga, don't you? Sundays, up at the Millennium Hall.'

'Yeah. I recognise you.' They smiled at each other.

'You're good.' He zipped the camera case. 'I'm almost done here. Fancy meeting up after, for a drink?'

He'd lost interest in Cupidi. 'Maybe later,' Ferriter was saying. 'I'm working a late in the incident room answering all the millions of calls that are going to come in once you've broadcast this.'

'Billions, probably.'

DI McAdam approached, all smiles. 'That was very good, Alex,' he said. 'Very good indeed. Very . . . passionate. Very real. I liked that.'

'Well, because it was real, obviously,' she said.

'Yes. Indeed. I didn't mean to say it wasn't . . .' He stood awkwardly. 'I just wanted to say well done.'

It was late. She needed to get home. Her shift should have ended twenty minutes ago. Her daughter would be wondering where she was.

'You moved to a house at Dungeness, I hear. Settling in OK?'

'Fine, sir.' She looked down at her watch.

'Extraordinary place. Some people hate it. I love it. Oh. My wife tells me you've joined her book group.'

'Sir?'

'Colette. She said you'd gone to her book thing last week.'

It was true she had joined a book group. It was part of her attempt to make new friends, to fit in around here. It wasn't something she was good at, but here she was trying to make the effort. At the one meeting she had been to so far, she had drunk too much wine and been drawn into a pointless argument about sex offenders. She tried to think which one of the well-spoken women there could be McAdam's wife.

'We must have you around for dinner some time. I'm sure you and my wife would get along.' Cupidi wasn't listening; instead, she was watching Ferriter. The cameraman had taken out a business card, grinning at her while writing his number on the back.

'Sorry, sir?'

'Just a thought,' he said.

Ferriter had given the man a little wave goodbye and was now walking away, back into the station.

'Excuse me, sir,' Cupidi muttered.

'Right. Of course.'

She pushed past her boss, up the ramp towards the doors of the station, catching up with Ferriter in the lobby.

'Are you going to call him?'

'Who?'

'That man. The one who gave you the card.'

'What card?'

'You know what card. I bloody saw you take it.'

Ferriter shrugged, smiled. 'Maybe. He was all right.'

Other officers pushed past them. Cupidi lowered her voice. 'He was trying to get information out of you, you know?'

'No. He was asking me out for a drink actually. He's in my yoga class.'

'He also happened to be asking you to discuss forensic details of the case which we haven't revealed yet.'

'It was just chat.'

Cupidi looked at her; lips neatly glossed, blonde bob carefully combed. 'Look. You're young. All I'm doing is watching your back. If you meet up with him, be careful. That's all.'

Ferriter rolled her eyes. 'Keep your hair on. I wouldn't go out with him anyway. He's old enough to be my dad.'

Cupidi realised he probably was. 'Right. I should go.'

'What? Aren't you staying for the news? Goes out in twenty minutes. Then the phones will start. Hopefully, anyway.'

'I need to be home for my daughter. Call me, won't you?'

Ferriter's smile was small and tight. 'Oh yeah. Right. Forgot.'

Cupidi drove home fast, in a bad mood, cursing the summer insects that splattered on the windscreen.

*

In the light of a summer evening, there was something lunar about Dungeness. It lay on the tip of a vast, flat stony landscape that jutted into the Straits of Dover; banks of shingle built over centuries by the churn of tides. The wooden shacks and chalets that dotted the promontory cast long shadows across the scrubland.

She drove along the pitted track, past the old black lighthouse, towards the huge industrial bulk of the Dungeness nuclear power station, its orange lights already glowing against the red sky. Her mood lifted a little as she approached.

At the security fence, the narrow road turned northwards towards lines of pylons that marched away across the flatland, past the empty Arum Cottage to the row of houses that sat, defiantly suburban, in this wild landscape.

Zoë was sitting on the front door step of their house.

'I don't know why I even bother to pay for your phone,' said Cupidi.

'I forgot it, as it happens.'

'And your keys?'

'Obviously, yes. Else I wouldn't be sitting here.' Spindly-limbed, bleached hair tinted purple, she wore khaki camouflage trousers and a shabby military jacket. Around her neck she hung a pair of binoculars. 'Hi, Mum,' she said, standing. 'Nice to see you too.'

'Sorry.' She folded her arms around the girl.

The summer holidays; a nightmare for any working parent.

The house in the country. Cupidi and her daughter. A fresh start.

Though much of their stuff was still in boxes, she was doing her best to make it home on time, most days at least; cooking meals from scratch instead of heating them in the microwave. And while she had meant to start eating supper at the table, it was easy to slip into the habit of sitting on the sofa with the plates, watching telly with a big glass of white.

'Seriously, though,' said Cupidi. 'I worry.'

'Round here? I'm perfectly safe, Mum. I just forgot it.'

'What if one day you're not?'

'But I am.'

On the television, a chef was tossing a huge salad in a glass bowl. She shouldn't be watching TV. She should be reading her book for the book group.

'See anything good?' she asked.

'Birds? Not really.'

'Trying to make conversation.'

'I just mean, nothing you'd understand.'

'Indulge me,' she said.

'Lesser whitethroat.'

'Not a greater one?'

'You're taking the piss.' Her daughter glared at her.

'Sorry. Is it pretty?'

'It's not about being pretty, Mum,' said Zoë, anger in her voice. Cupidi remembered standing in front of the mirror with the perky young Constable Ferriter. 'It would have been getting ready to go to the Middle East. Sudan. Even further south than that,' her daughter said. 'Three and a half thousand miles. Just think. Travelling all that way.'

'Just to come here, of all places.'

'Amazing, though, isn't it? Titchy little thing.'

This obsession with birds. She wondered about this need to

know every last detail, to record every species. Her daughter was a strange girl, which was almost certainly her fault. She was not the easiest woman to get along with either; on more than one occasion men had told her that. Or maybe Cupidi's own mother's fault; she was no better.

She was topping up her wine in the kitchen when Zoë called from the living room, 'Mum. You're on the telly.'

It was half past ten. They would be showing the segment again.

She arrived back in the living room, glass in hand, to see the artist's drawing of the dead woman on the screen.

'What do you think happened to her?'

'I don't know,' said Cupidi. 'I really don't.'

'Was she raped?'

'No.'

'Strangled?'

'It's not really the kind of thing we should be talking about, you know.'

'But was she?'

'There are no signs of violence at all.'

'Spooky.'

'Yes.'

The phone rang. 'I'll get it,' said Zoë, standing.

'It'll be for me. Probably somebody's called something in.'

The screen cut back to her, standing in front of the station. *Detective Sergeant Cupidi: Serious Crime Directorate.* And then they were talking about the weather. Hot all week, they said, smiling, and getting hotter.

Zoë came back with the phone in her hand. Cupidi held out her hand for it, but Zoë said, 'It wasn't anyone.'

'What do you mean?'

'I just said hello and they rang off. Must have been a wrong number.'

'Right,' she said. Nobody had called; it looked like the TV appeal had not worked, which was frustrating. A woman with no name; no identity. Any murder was disturbing, but this one had spooked Cupidi. No one knew who the dead woman was; nobody had missed her, or come forward to weep over her.

When they'd both finished picking at their meals, Cupidi collected the dirty plates, and, as she straightened, caught a glimpse of herself in the mirror above the fireplace. 'Do you think my hair needs attention?' she asked.

'Thought you didn't care about stuff like that.'

Cupidi frowned at her reflection, offended. 'What makes you think I don't care about that?'

And she would have said more, but for a second time, looking in the mirror, she saw the victim in the mirror looking back at her.

When they had cut her open, they had found no sign that she had drowned; but the pathologist could find no other obvious cause of death. Everything about the dead woman was an enigma.

THREE

'I've made up the bed in the spare room,' Lulu said, standing above the stranger with a towel in her arms and talking as if she was deaf. 'Can I suggest you wash before you get into the bed? I'll show you the bathroom.'

'Sorry if I put you to any trouble,' said the woman quietly. How thin she was, thought Julian.

'You turn up unannounced on a Sunday evening. No trouble at all.'

'Lulu,' protested Julian.

Lulu held out the towel. 'Please use this one.' It was a cheap one they had brought back from a holiday in Ibiza before Teo was born. *Amnesia Espuma: I was there.* 'The other towels are for family.'

The woman sat on the orange chair looking down at the polished wood floor, saying nothing, doing nothing. Lulu dropped the towel into her lap.

'I'll just go and check on Teo.'

When she'd gone, the woman looked up. 'She doesn't like me.'

'She's very protective, that's all.'

'Who's Teo?'

Our son,' said Julian.

The woman's smile showed a few teeth that were mostly brown. 'How old is he?'

'Nineteen months.'

'Can I see him?'

'No,' he said, too abruptly. Teo would be terrified of this strange woman, jaw lopsided, skin wrinkled and dark from spending too much time outside in all weathers, eyes pale with untreated cataracts.

'I understand,' she said.

'Maybe in the morning.' He was normally good in tricky situations. It was why he was so well paid by the design agency. He could analyse a problem and know where to allocate resources in order to solve it. But he felt lost now. 'The thing is, you can't just walk in here . . .'

'Sorry,' she muttered.

It was all she seemed to say. 'I mean. What kind of mother does that?'

'It's difficult to explain.'

'Maybe you should prove it. Yes. Prove it.'

The woman was still holding the mug of tea Julian had made her. It must be cold by now. She said nothing.

'Tell me one thing about myself that only you would know.'

The woman frowned. 'What kind of thing?'

'I don't know. I have a freckle on my left shoulder blade or something.'

'Do you?'

'No. That was just a hypothetical.'

'You cried a lot.'

'Oh for Christ's sake.'

The woman looked up, startled at his sudden anger. Julian was wishing he had never let her in. It was like hard old scar tissue breaking, letting blood seep through.

'If you were my mother, and for all I know you're just some madwoman who's walked in off the street . . .'

The woman seemed to shrink into the round chair as he raised his voice.

'I mean. If you were. And I'm not saying you are . . .'

'I'm sorry.'

'Did you ever even bloody once think about me, wherever you were hiding? Did you?'

And then Lulu was at the door. 'Are you OK, darling?' And when the woman had finally gone upstairs clutching her towel, she opened the window and lit Jo Malone basil-and-mandarin scented candles.

That night, lying beneath white linen, they lay listening for any movement from her room. 'This is ridiculous,' he said.

'You go to sleep. I'll stay awake.'

'She's not going to do anything.'

'How do you know that? You said she was asking about Teo. If she so much as looks at him . . .'

His wife was lying with her back to him. He ran her hand slowly down the line of lumps of her spine. 'What if he's her grandson?'

'Just because you want it to be true doesn't mean that it is. People pretend to be other people. Did she say anything that even slightly proves that she's your mother?'

'No.'

'There.'

'But think about it. What if she actually is?'

The digital clock glowed red in the darkness: *2:07*.

'Did you know,' she said, 'there are teams of people in Israel who go through everything you've ever said on social media, every electronic record they can hack, and build up a file that knows everything about you. They know your date of birth, place of birth, your National Insurance number. They know where you buy your underpants. Anything. They put all this information together, and so anyone who buys it can pretend to be someone you should know, then they sell it on to gangs.'

'Don't be ridiculous,' he said.

'I'm not being ridiculous.' She wriggled away from him. 'You're the one who thinks . . . Your mother is almost certainly dead.'

'Yes. Probably dead.'

'And even if she was your mother, I for one wouldn't want a woman like that to be Teo's grandmother. But she's not anyway.'

They lay apart from each other, in silence and the hours passed with neither of them sleeping, listening for the sound of movement from the spare room.

From somewhere far off came the beep-beep of a reversing lorry making deliveries.

'Do you remember her at all?' she asked.

'I don't know. I was too young.'

'You never talk about her.'

He tried to think. His mother must have held him, nursed him, but there was nothing there. A void. He had been too little. 'Thing was, nobody talked about her. It's not just me.'

But she was asleep next to him now.

He was awake when Radio 4 came on with the seven o'clock pips.

Lulu sat up and exclaimed, 'Jesus.'

'What?'

'Teo. He's usually up by now.' She was out of bed, pulling on her gown. 'Jesus bloody Christ, Julian.'

Julian followed her out of the door and watched her knock at the spare room door. No answer.

She flung it open and gasped: 'She's bloody gone.'

The bed was empty; the crumpled duvet lying on the floor.

'Teo,' Lulu cried, and ran down the corridor. Teo's door had a picture of a giraffe on it, drawn by an artist friend of theirs; it was always open a crack so they could hear if he woke in the night. Lulu flung it wide.

'Julian!' she screamed and turned to him.

He pushed past her. With horror he saw the cot was empty.

'Oh Christ Christ Christ.'

How could it happen? He had heard nothing all night. He hadn't even thought he had fallen asleep, but he must have.

Lulu almost knocked him over shoving past him as she ran back down the corridor. She put her head round the bathroom door; it too was empty.

'Call the police,' she screamed.

As Julian ran back to the bedroom to unplug his iPhone from the charger on the bedside table, Lulu clattered downstairs.

The phone seemed to take for ever to wake up; his whole body shaking, he dialled 999.

'Julian,' came a voice from downstairs.

'Hello? Emergency service operator. Which service do you require? Fire, police or ambulance?'

'Julian!'

'Hold on,' said Julian to the woman on the phone. He followed his wife down the stairs.

She was standing at the living-room door. *Raa Raa the Noisy Lion* was on TV. Sitting on the floor, surrounded by cushions, sat Teo, eyes fixed on the screen. There was no one else in the room.

Julian dropped the phone, picked up the boy, warm and soft, feeling him squirming in his grip.

'She's gone,' said Lulu.

'Hello?' said the phone. 'Caller. Which service do you require?'

As he squeezed his son tight, the child began to cry, upset by the suddenness of his father's arrival, the desperation of his hug.

'I didn't hear her,' said Julian.

'She must have got up . . . gone and taken Teo out of his cot. Then let herself out. She's not anywhere in the house, I've looked everywhere.'

Teo's grizzling turned into a full-voiced cry. The boy would be hungry.

'Caller?' said the phone.

Lulu bent and picked it up. 'Nothing,' she said. 'Just a stupid mistake.' She rang off.

The boy's Pull-Up nappy was heavy and damp. Julian went to

fetch the changing mat, suddenly exhausted. He was supposed to be finishing an urgent job today. The agency designed high-end retail spaces. A major client had been unhappy with his latest work, demanding changes.

His world had been disturbed. The woman had taken the child out of his cot. Lulu had been right. Anything could have happened.

His wife watched him pulling the pyjama top off their son.

'Good riddance,' she said. 'Don't ever, ever, ever let her in here again.'

'I'm sorry,' he said. 'It was just . . .'

She looked at her phone; there was a text message. 'Oh Jesus. The bloody childminder,' she said. 'She's got tonsillitis.'

'Just . . . what if she was? That's all. What if she was?'

'Bloody, bloody hell.'

As her husband dealt with their child, she went into the kitchen to put the kettle on for coffee. An analyst at a Middle Eastern-owned bank, she didn't have time for this kind of nonsense. She would have the locks changed, she thought. Maybe install a security camera outside the door.

It was only when she turned to open the fridge for the milk that she saw the note, written on the whiteboard in green marker.

The handwriting was surprisingly neat and straight, the letters evenly rounded.

I am sorry sorry I shouldn't have come.
It was a mistake.

Goodbye.

PS You asked did I think about you I promise I thought about you every single day.

Staring at it, Lulu jumped when the kettle clicked off.

'Lulu?' he was calling from the other room. 'Have you seen my bike helmet?'

With the sleeve of her dressing gown, she carefully wiped the board clean.

FOUR

Alex Cupidi ran, screaming at the sea and the sea screamed back.

It felt so good.

'*Yaaaaah!*' She kicked stones.

Living here on the edge of the world, she found she rose early. While the teenage girl still slept, she cycled round the flat lanes or walked up the pebble beach beyond the power station. How long had it been since she had felt this wide awake? Out here, by the firing ranges, there was no one to listen. She could scream and shout until her throat turned raw.

She shouted to nobody, for no reason at all. Seagulls drifted over, unconcerned.

She was about to open her lungs again when she felt the phone, tucked into the pocket of her tracksuit, start to vibrate. A number she didn't recognise.

'Damn,' she said to the gulls.

'Bingo,' the voice at her ear said. 'We found out who she was. Thought you would want to know.'

'Ferriter?' Cupidi's voice cracked from shouting.

'Yes, skip. Are you all right? You sound funny. Have I just woke you up? Where are you?'

'Are you at work already?' She checked her watch, panting. It was just gone seven in the morning.

A high, girlish giggle. 'No. Just about to go.'

'What is it you're saying?'

'Local chemist in Lydd phoned us last night. After you'd gone. Victim's name is Hilary Keen.'

Cupidi stopped. 'Last night? And you didn't think to call me?'

The constable went quiet; she had been expecting congratulations. 'That's why I'm calling you now.'

'You didn't think I'd want to know last night? I'm supposed to be running Outside Enquiries.'

'Only you'd left work. Gone home. I stayed on, if you recall.'

New and eager; young, single. And she was right, of course. Cupidi had gone home to look after her daughter. She had no right to expect her to phone.

'I just thought I should leave it till morning.'

Cupidi frowned. 'OK. Go ahead.'

Ferriter took a breath. 'Right,' she said. 'At 18.38 we received a phone call from a woman who said she was a local chemist. Said she thought she knew the woman.' On the phone the chemist had explained that the victim came in regularly to pick up a prescription for ordinary blood pressure drugs. 'Sergeant Moon and me, we jumped in a car and showed her the photo again. She had name, date of birth, everything.'

Cupidi tried to remember which one Sergeant Moon was. The tall, dark-eyed, handsome one who lived with his mother. The one women made lustful jokes about in the locker room. 'And then, after we'd confirmed the name, we went back and checked online records. She has a son, apparently,' said Ferriter. 'Had, rather. Only next-of-kin on record. Nobody else I could find. I have found an address in London for him. And a number. I can phone him if you like.'

'Whoever this man is, the one thing we know is his mother's dead. It would be on the heartless side not to tell him in person.'

'Oh. Right,' said Ferriter, stung.

'Which part of London is he in?'

A gust of wind blew off the sea.

'Sorry. Say again?'

'Something with an E,' said Ferriter. 'London, E something.'

'Because we will need to go there and tell him.' She spelled it out for the young constable. 'Besides, he might have some idea of what she was doing on our patch. And obviously he might even be a suspect.'

Patronising again, and all because of that 'I was working late' thing.

'Obviously, yes,' Ferriter said.

She kicked at the debris at her feet; a cracked red fishing crate with a crab shell in it.

'Want me to pick you up in the car?' said Ferriter. 'I can be there in half an hour.'

'Call DI McAdam first, let him know what we're doing.'

'Hold on. I got it. Postcode's E1.'

Aldgate, Whitechapel, she thought. The old ground she was so familiar with. Cupidi looked at her watch. 'No point leaving till half eight. We'll only be caught up in traffic.'

She ended the call knowing she should have congratulated Ferriter, because it was good solid police work. The mystery woman was no longer a mystery. Cupidi should be feeling that surge of excitement; things were starting to fall into place. Instead she felt angry at herself. She picked up her pace, heading home.

Out at sea, white birds were diving into the grey water. Were they gannets? Zoë would know.

There was an entire medieval town out there somewhere, under the waves. Once, it had been one of the biggest towns in the south of England but the waves had sucked it away some time in the thirteenth century. Another town had grown up inland with the same name; but the old one was dead beneath the water. This was a shifting land, built by the sea and then washed away again. That was something; an entire town destroyed.

In London she had been drowning. She had ended a go-nowhere affair with a married man to come here, to start again. It would be different here.

She was about fifty metres from the nuclear station when she saw a grey shape the length of a man at the top of the bank of shingle about a hundred metres away.

She stopped and stared at it. The longer she looked, the more sure she was about what she was seeing lying along the ridge and silhouetted against the morning sky. There was a herring gull pecking methodically at what looked like the head.

She broke into a trot.

Walking on a beach these mornings had made her wonder if she would come across a body. Police work made you morbid, but it wouldn't be a surprise. This huge triangle of shingle reaching out into the Channel must catch that kind of flotsam from time to time. But why would a body be at the top of the rise, so far away from the waves?

The steepness of the bank forced her to slow. The stones moved under her feet as she climbed, making each step an effort. Panting, she crossed the high line of sea debris – old green netting, old coloured lighters, white bleached yoghurt pots – made it to the top of the slope and stopped. Resentfully, the herring gull flapped away into the air.

It was just a boat; a medium-size inflatable rib. What had looked like a head was just the round end of a buoyancy float. Somebody had taken a knife to the rest of it, ripping the grey rubber. She looked around. This had been happening all along the coast, these last few months. As they tightened controls at the ports and airports, people found other ways across the water. They would have beached the boat here and run off into the marshes.

She would report it, of course, but the occupants would be long gone. They had been organised. The boat alone would have cost a few hundred pounds. The migrants it had contained would have paid the smugglers much more, or would be held somewhere until they had. Both, probably.

When Cupidi let herself in the back door, Zoë was standing at the fridge with a bowl of Cheerios in her hand, dressed in a long T-shirt that had once been white. Her legs were so skinny, thought Cupidi; she got that from her grandmother.

Cupidi put the kettle on. 'I'll be in London today,' she said. 'I may be late back. There's some Brie; you can have it for lunch. You like that, don't you? Fish fingers in the freezer. A bit of pie from last night. Some chicken in the fridge, but cook it properly. Vegetables if you want to make anything. Sorry, love.'

'It's OK, honest.'

'For God's sake if you go out, please remember your phone, love.'

'What are you doing in London?'

'That dead woman. It turns out we may have found a relative of hers.'

Zoë looked at her. 'I've been thinking. What if she was electrocuted? Would that have shown up?'

Cupidi turned down Radio 1. 'Listen. We're not supposed to talk about this kind of stuff. It's not a great idea. You know that.'

'What? In case I tell my friends?' she said sarkily. 'In case you hadn't noticed, I don't have any.'

'That's not true. Twice you've been invited for sleepovers—'

'I'm not seven anymore, Mum.'

'They want to be your friends.'

'I don't like them. Girls round here, they're so immature. So, what if she was electrocuted, Mum?'

'Firstly, it's hard to tell anything after a body has been that long in the water in summer.'

Zoë mimed vomiting into her breakfast bowl.

'You asked. Secondly . . . I'm not talking about this anymore. Will you be OK? On your own.'

'I won't be on my own.'

Other teenagers her age would be hanging out at H&M in County Square in town on these long summer days. Zoë wasn't like other teenagers. She wanted to spend her time with the birds. And birdwatchers. A teenage girl spending all her time like that.

On the plus side, Zoë showed no interest at all in boys yet. At her age, Cupidi had been wild. Also, birds saved Cupidi a fortune on paying for childcare. The birders here all seemed to love her; to look after her. It was as if her daughter had become their mascot.

Strange child. Sometimes she didn't feel like she knew her at all. When had they grown so far apart?

'So how do you actually, really, truly think she was killed, then? The woman. You must have a theory.' Zoë dumped her bowl in the sink, still half full of uneaten cereal. 'If she wasn't drowned, that's pretty weird, isn't it? To be lying in the water. Very Ophelia.'

'Not very Ophelia at all, if you saw her. Rinse it properly and put it in the dishwasher. Repeat. I'm not talking about the dead woman. I just want to know you'll be all right spending the day on your own.'

'I've told you. I'm not on my own.'

'And don't leave your keys behind either. Please, Zoë.'

The teenager took a carton of orange juice out of the fridge and poured a glass. 'Are you going to visit Nan while you're up there?'

'No time. Police business.'

'You never go and see her.'

'I do.'

Zoë made a face. 'When was the last time then? Not since Christmas.'

'I've been busy. Moving house. And a new job.'

'London's only up the road.'

'She and I don't always get on.'

'Understatement,' said Zoë.

'It's not my fault. She's difficult. Always has been.'

Zoë snorted.

Cupidi took the carton which Zoë had left by the sink and opened the fridge to return it. 'What if . . . ?' she said. She closed the door again and turned to look at her daughter. 'What if I asked her to come stay here for a few weeks. It might be nice for her.'

Zoë laughed, spitting orange juice back into her glass. 'You don't like her. You'd hate her being here.'

'No I wouldn't,' said Cupidi, hearing a car pull up at the back of the row of cottages. Through the window she saw Constable Ferriter, stepping out of an unmarked car. 'Besides. She could look after you.'

'I told you, Mum. I don't need looking after.'

Cupidi pulled the back door open. 'Time for a tea . . . If we set out too early, we'll get stuck in traffic.'

'Go on then,' said Ferriter, a waft of floral perfume coming through the doorway with her. Too pretty, too well-turned-out for a copper, thought Cupidi.

'So, what if she was suffocated, then put in the water, to disguise it?' said Zoë. 'You know, like waterboarding.'

'Stop it, Zoë.'

'Why leave her in the water anyway?'

'Quick way to dispose of a body,' said Ferriter, pulling out a chair and grinning at Zoë. 'Plus, the killer might want to hide the time of death.'

'The killer,' said Cupidi. 'We don't know anything for sure yet.'

Ferriter addressed Zoë. 'The post-mortem interval is harder to determine if a body is left in water. It might be to keep the body clean. It's trickier to find the offender's DNA if it's been in the water long. The evidence becomes degraded. In which case it's someone who knows what they're doing.'

'You are aware my daughter isn't actually part of Serious Crime?' said Cupidi, though what the constable had said was perfectly true.

'Sorry, guv.'

Cupidi was aware she was not popular in Serious Crime; she was conscious she wasn't doing much to improve her reputation. It hadn't done her any favours that she had arrived here from the Met. Here in the provinces, nobody had much time for the London police. Nor had it helped that in her very first few weeks she had investigated and arrested a colleague for his part in a killing that had taken place forty years earlier, when he had been just a child. He had been a local neighbourhood policeman; a good man, well regarded around here. Now he was on remand, awaiting trial. Colleagues understood that arresting people for whatever crimes they had committed was the job they did, and she did it well, but it didn't mean that they liked her for it.

'Milk? Sugar?'

'Just black please. No dairy.'

'If someone took her there and dumped her, you'd think someone would have noticed,' said Zoë.

'You sure she's not part of Serious Crime?' The constable smiled at Cupidi's daughter.

'Someone must have seen her.'

'Round there?' said Ferriter. 'Christ, no. Walland Marsh is

dead quiet. The place is deserted these days. Didn't used to be. Walland Marsh is newer than Romney Marsh proper, see, which is the north bit. When I say newer, that's meaning, like, after about 1400, so not that new. My dad's got books on it all. I'll bring 'em round, if you like.'

Cupidi said, 'Well . . .'

'My family's lived here for generations. Dad was in the bloody history society. They have meetings if you're interested. Lots of people your age.'

'My age?'

'I go there,' said Zoë. 'To Walland Marsh.'

'You got friends who live round there?' said Ferriter.

'Go round there sometimes on Mum's bike.'

'Do you?' said Cupidi.

'Yeah. Sometimes. It's quiet.'

'There's nothing bloody there,' said Ferriter. 'Used to drive me nuts there when I was your age.'

'My daughter is an ornithologist. She goes birdwatching.'

'Why?' said Ferriter.

The toaster popped up. Cupidi interrupted Ferriter's quizzing of her daughter. 'Toast?' she asked.

'No, thanks,' said Ferriter.

'What about the dead woman's address? Has someone gone to check it?'

'I went past on my way home last night. Just south of Hamstreet. Place looked derelict to me. Didn't look like there was no one living there.'

'You think she'd given a false address to the chemist?'

'Don't know.'

Cupidi buttered her toast. 'Strange. Worth taking a proper look. Her son, what was the name again?'

'Julian Keen.'

'Have you got his date of birth?'

'Somewhere.'

'Make sure you have. We'll need it. We don't want to go telling the wrong person that their mother is dead.'

'God, no. It's not the wrong person. I checked. Hilary Janice Keen. Gave birth to Julian Shakti Keen. 1982. Stroud Maternity Hospital. There's not going to be two Julian Shakti Keens, are there? That's not a proper name, is it?'

'It's a big thing to tell someone their mother is dead, that's all.' Cupidi bit into her toast; crumbs flew everywhere. 'Let's go,' she said.

'She going to be all right on her own?' asked Ferriter, as Cupidi drove the unmarked car Ferriter had arrived in.

Cupidi held the half-eaten toast in her right hand as she drove. 'Of course she is.'

'Just saying. Didn't mean anything.'

'She's fifteen. Almost sixteen. Why wouldn't she be?'

At the railway crossing, Cupidi took another bite. The toast broke, leaving her with what was already in her mouth, and a tiny triangle between finger and thumb. A car was coming the other way, so she didn't have time to look where the rest had gone.

Beyond the small town of Lydd, she accelerated. At speed, the marshland they passed through looked flat and unremarkable. The thing about a landscape like this, she thought, is that you could pass through it without even noticing the half of it.

FIVE

As Julian walked in the front door, pushing the bike, Lulu was at the top of their stairs, holding Teo on one hip.

'She's probably accused you of molesting her,' hissed Lulu.

The thought shocked Julian.

'My Christ. Is that what they said?'

The two women police officers had arrived at the flat late that morning and asked for him by name. Abandoning his work, he had rushed back home.

'They won't say anything. It's you they want. I told you it was a scam. I bloody warned you. Jesus, Julian. You are such an idiot. This could get ugly.'

He looked at himself in the mirror at the bottom of the stairs. He looked sweaty and out of breath. Cycling home in the midday heat had made him look pink-faced; as if he were already guilty of something. A taxi driver had sworn at him for signalling right in front of him; he had sworn back. He couldn't go upstairs looking like this.

'What did they say about her?' he whispered.

'Well, that's the point. They wouldn't tell me anything. I'm only your bloody wife.'

He walked up the stairs, squeezing past her.

There were two policewomen sitting on the couch in his living room. A strikingly tall woman with straw-coloured hair, dressed in a crumpled pale linen jacket, and a younger one in a neat white blouse and black skirt, who to Julian looked more like the sort of woman he'd expect to see behind a counter at Boots. Despite his anxiety, he found himself staring at the younger woman's crossed legs. And, as he glanced back up at his wife, he saw her looking at him, unsmiling.

'Julian Keen?' said the taller woman, standing.

He looked at her nervously. He was unused to dealing with the police. There had been burglaries of course, and the time someone had run keys down the side of his Saab, but he had never been in trouble himself. He noticed a stain on the older officer's pale trousers; as if she had dropped her breakfast on it. 'What exactly is this all about? I have a lot to do today.'

'Thanks for coming back from your office. We appreciate it. I'm Detective Sergeant Alexandra Cupidi from the Kent Serious Crime Directorate. This is Constable Jill Ferriter.'

The younger woman was standing too, a sympathetic smile on her face. Why? He thought. What had happened?

'So?'

'Before I say anything, I need to just confirm that you are Julian Keen, date of birth . . .'

'Seventeenth of May, 1982,' said Ferriter, reading from her notebook.

Nervously he said, 'That's me. Why?'

There was a flicker in the younger woman's gaze. 'In that case, I'm afraid I have some very bad news,' Cupidi said.

'Has she said something?' interrupted Lulu. 'Has she accused us of something? I think you should know that that woman, who we put up here out of the goodness of our hearts, interfered with our child.'

'She didn't interfere with him, Lulu,' said Julian. 'The worst she did was take him downstairs and stick him in front of CBBC.'

'Don't say anything, Julian.'

The senior officer looked at them, first Julian, then Lulu, and back again, as if trying to figure out what had been happening here.

'I think there must have been some misunderstanding,' the policewoman said. She turned to Lulu. 'A woman interfered with your child?'

'No,' said Julian. 'It's nothing. She didn't interfere with our child. What were you going to say?'

The woman's face softened. 'I'm very sorry, Mr Keen; but your mother is dead.'

The tears came instantly to his eyes, rolling down towards his chin. Lulu looked at her husband, open-mouthed. The constable, too, stood awkwardly, not certain what to do.

Julian himself was as shocked as his wife. He hadn't even known the woman really, had he? It had just been a single night that she was here. And he hadn't cried since he was a boy. So why was he dripping tears now, lip trembling?

Somehow picking up on the disturbance in the room, the child on Lulu's hip began to wail. Only the older of the two policewomen seemed to know what to do; she was standing with a tissue she had found somewhere, holding it out for him.

'Here. Give yourself a minute.'

Julian took it.

'I apologise,' she said as he dropped into a chair, shoulders heaving. 'It must be terrible news. Take your time.'

'Sorry,' he said. 'I don't know what got into me.'

'It's perfectly natural,' she said.

For a few seconds, aside from the sound of crying – man and child – there was quiet, until the sergeant looked up and said to Lulu, 'Well, what about that cup of tea, now?'

Lulu hadn't actually offered to make her one in the first place, but as she moved to the kitchen to put the kettle on, Julian could see the obvious irritation on her face at the way this policewoman had asserted her authority over her in her own home.

'Would you like a hand with that?' suggested Ferriter.

'I can manage perfectly well.' But Julian watched as the younger officer followed her anyway.

'How did she die?' Julian answered, when his wife and child were out of the room.

'I'm afraid it's possible that she may have been the victim of some kind of assault,' said the woman.

'My God. What kind of assault?'

'Her body was recovered recently from a drainage ditch in Kent. We're still waiting for more detail. Obviously if it turns out to be an assault, we want to catch whoever did this to her.'

'Yes.'

'And there is the matter of identifying the body.'

'Kent?' It struck Julian that the woman had said they were Kent police, which was odd. 'What was she doing there?'

'We're hoping you could help us answer that.'

The constable returned with a tray with four black mugs on it.

'Perhaps I can start by asking when you last saw your mother?' said the sergeant.

'Last night,' said Julian. 'She stayed here, actually.'

He wondered why the calm-looking sergeant who had been so in control of the situation up until now was looking so shocked.

'I'm sorry,' she said, flustered. 'Did you say last night?'

'Not possible,' said the constable.

'There must be some kind of mistake.'

And beside the sergeant, the constable was digging in a folder for pieces of paper. 'You did say seventeenth of May 1982, right? Mother's name Hilary Janice Keen?' she said, anxiously.

'Janice?' said Julian, bewildered. 'Is that her middle name?'

The two police officers looked at each other, not understanding what had just happened.

SIX

'So if the woman we've found is Hilary Keen, who was the woman who knocked on their door last night?' The obvious question.

They were driving slowly north along Kingsland Road; the London traffic was as Cupidi remembered, sluggish and bad-tempered.

'It is Hilary Keen. Hundred per cent. Her GP confirmed it,' said Ferriter from the driver's seat, inching the car forward. 'Plus, we've got matching dental records too.'

'You found her dentist?'

'Mm.'

'When were you going to mention that?'

'I only just heard,' she complained. 'Give me a bloody chance.'

'I beg your pardon?' said Cupidi.

Ferriter turned crimson. 'Sorry. I didn't mean to say it like that. It just kind of slipped out. But I found out this guy Julian Keen's name and I tracked him down. I thought I was doing pretty well, but everything I do seems to piss you off.' She paused, then added, 'Sarge.'

Cupidi looked at her. 'You're going to need a thicker skin.'

'I thought I already had one, matter of fact.'

Cupidi smiled to herself. 'Well? What about the dentist?'

'Just got the text a little while back while we were at the flat, as a matter of fact. Honest. The dentist's surgery said it was her too. Definite.'

'Thank you,' said Cupidi.

'You're welcome.' Ferriter glared at the traffic ahead.

Cupidi sighed. 'OK. Good work,' she said. 'Well done. You've been very helpful.'

'Thank you.'

'You're welcome,' said Cupidi.

Cupidi looked around at the people on the streets. London seemed so busy after Kent. Strange being here again. She hadn't been back for months.

'Weird, though, isn't it?'

'Good weird,' said Cupidi.

'What do you mean?'

'We find a dead woman,' said Cupidi. 'The night before we turn up to tell the victim's son, a totally different woman knocks on his door impersonating his mother.'

'Just a bit sad, I thought. I mean, poor guy. He was convinced the woman he'd met yesterday was his mother and now we tell him his real mother's dead. And that wife. God, she was hard work.'

'But what was the woman doing at their house?'

'I'd say she was probably a con woman, like his wife said.

Jesus,' Ferriter said, looking in the rear-view mirror. 'The cyclists here are insane. Are we allowed to hit 'em?'

'You think it's a coincidence?'

'Yep. Got to be.'

'What did you think of her? Lulu. Nervous, wasn't she?'

'I suppose she would have been upset, thinking that a con artist had been at her house.'

Cupidi nodded, opened her handbag and took out a packet of mints, offered one to Ferriter.

Ferriter shook her head. 'Bad for your teeth.'

So Cupidi took two for herself. 'I just don't get it. If this woman who turned up at their doorstep was a con artist, where's the con? She arrives, says she's Julian Keen's mother, spends the night, gets up in the morning and disappears. No harm done.'

'Checking out the place for a burglary, maybe? Maybe she actually nicked something and they haven't spotted it yet.'

Cupidi nodded.

'Maybe she was mentally . . . you know.' She whistled cuckoo notes.

'The terminology is "mentally ill",' said Cupidi.

'Maybe she goes round telling all sorts of people she's their mother, only she just happens on one person who doesn't know who his real mother is.'

Cupidi sucked on her mints. 'Know what, though? His wife seemed almost relieved when it turned out she couldn't have been his mother. We go to tell her husband his mother is dead and she looks – I don't know . . . almost happy about it.'

'She was just happy it wasn't the woman who had stayed in their house last night.'

They drove past Turkish shops and Asian restaurants. She had grown up around here, but the place already seemed strange to her. From the road, you could only get a brief glimpse of Regent's Canal beneath them at the bridge, but you could still tell it was there from the new apartment blocks that clustered on its banks.

'I been thinking,' Ferriter said cautiously. 'What if there's something about the location of where the body was left?'

'Good. Carry on. What are you saying?'

'I don't know. Just . . . The entire place is covered in ditches and waterways. And they all connect up. So what if she was put somewhere else and floated there?'

The hundred square miles of salt marsh north of Dungeness had been drained and reclaimed over many centuries. The water was held back by a precarious network of banks, ditches and dykes, pumps and sluices. Romney Marsh had been won back from the sea, field by field; a landscape as artificial as the urban one they were driving through now.

'I mean. Water moves, doesn't it?'

'Yes,' Cupidi said again.

'So what if the body wasn't dumped there at all? There was heavy rain at the beginning of the month.'

'So you think she might not have been left where we found her? She was in the water, what, ten days? This is very good. We need to look at how the water flows there. OK. Get on to the Environment Agency. See what data they have.'

'Right.' Ferriter nodded. 'There's the Drainage Board. They'll know.'

'The Drainage Board?' said Cupidi.

'Yes. Internal Area Drainage Board. My uncle's a sheep farmer.

Particular breed they have round there. Romneys. Own land on the marsh, you have to pay special taxes to them. They look after most of the drains. It's, like, some medieval law thing from Henry VII or something.'

'I like that. Good idea.'

Ferriter glanced at her from the corner of her eyes. 'Thank you.'

'You're welcome.' Cupidi sucked her two mints thoughtfully. 'It's left here. Sure you don't mind doing this? I'll only be a minute.'

'It's fine,' Ferriter said, though they were on the clock. They should be heading back to Kent now.

These were the streets where Cupidi had played, where she'd bunked off school, where she'd had her first cigarettes, had her first fights.

'Just here,' she said. 'Right, then first left.'

The house they had lived in was tucked away from the high street in a small cul-de-sac.

'Won't stay long.'

'Take as long as you like,' said Ferriter.

Cupidi looked at the house; the big Victorian steps up to the front door. 'I don't really get along that well with my mum, to be honest.'

'DI McAdam's away today, anyway. He's not going to be chasing us. He's at a conference on the future of policing. If there actually is such a thing.'

'I thought I was supposed to be the cynical one.'

Ferriter grinned back. 'I'll just stay in the car.'

Cupidi hesitated. 'No. Come in,' she said in the end. 'She likes coppers.'

'Does she?'

'Yep. She used to be one, as it happens.' Cupidi rang on the doorbell.

Cupidi's mother opened the door dressed in a large man's shirt, untucked above a pair of leggings.

'What rank?' she asked Ferriter, looking her up and down.

'Constable,' said Ferriter.

'CID?'

'I told you, we call it Serious Crime in Kent,' said her daughter.

'It must be pretty bloody serious if they'd have Alex,' her mother said to Ferriter, and laughed with the rattle of a woman who had spent much of her life smoking. 'Joke,' she said.

She led them to the kitchen at the back of the house where music from some retro digital station was playing loudly.

'Mind if I turn it down, Mum?'

Her mum had painted the kitchen lime-green in the 1990s. Where Cupidi had once done her homework on the kitchen table, there was now an ashtray and a copy of *Time Out* open at the Books and Poetry pages. Since her father died, her mother had started going out a lot. She bought tickets to the cinema at least once a week, or sat through free lectures at the Conway Hall. She ventured across to the Union Chapel to see rock bands sometimes. Cupidi couldn't help thinking that her mother was deliberately making a point; that her husband and her child had held her back all these years.

'Weird one,' said Cupidi. 'We just went to tell a man that his mother had been murdered over a week ago. He said he's just seen her last night,' said Cupidi.

'This a ghost story?'

'No. It's real.'

'Who was it, then?' That had caught her interest, at least.

'That's the point,' said Cupidi. 'We don't know. This woman just turned up out of the blue yesterday, claiming she was his mother, and then disappeared again. But the woman we found dead is his mother, so she can't have been.'

'I was saying, I think she was just a con woman,' said Ferriter.

'You'd think he'd know what his own mother looked like,' said Helen, pouring water into the kettle.

'That's the point,' said Ferriter, still standing in the big green kitchen. 'He was adopted when he was two by his aunt and uncle. He never met his mum. He wouldn't have recognised her anyway.'

Helen looked at them. 'I have mint, chamomile or black-currant,' she said.

'Not ordinary tea?' said Cupidi, opening drawers and cup-boards.

'Mint's great,' said Ferriter.

Cupidi found a box of Tetley's at the back of the cupboard.

'What about his aunt and uncle?' asked Helen.

'Dead,' Ferriter answered. 'Car crash when he was seventeen.'

Helen nodded. 'Poor lad. So who was this other woman? The one who turned up out of the blue?'

'We don't know.'

'What if it was a ghost of the dead woman coming to see her son?' Helen said, grinning.

'Except his mother didn't look nothing like the woman he saw,' said Ferriter. 'We showed him the photograph.'

'Can I see?'

'No!' said Cupidi.

But Ferriter was opening her shoulder bag and pulling out the photograph.

She looked at it quietly for a while. All she said was, 'About your age?' and looked at her daughter.

Cupidi nodded.

They sat in silence for a while with the photograph, suddenly solemn, until her mother spoke. 'And what about you?' she asked Cupidi. 'How are you fitting in down in Kent?'

'I'm not sure I fit in anywhere. But I like it there.'

She turned to Ferriter. 'Is she making friends?

'Mum!' said Cupidi.

'Well? Are you?'

Cupidi didn't answer.

'My daughter has a knack of winding people up the wrong way. She did that very successfully with her last job.'

'I can see where she gets it from,' said Ferriter.

Helen laughed loudly.

She shouldn't be annoyed by their instant intimacy, Cupidi thought. She took a sip from her scalding tea and said, 'So I was thinking. What about coming and staying with us for a week?'

'I don't know,' said her mother. 'I've got a lot on.'

'Like what?'

'I'm learning Spanish. I'm having lessons with the University of the Third Age.'

'Why?'

'Why not?'

'It's summer. It's glorious down there.'

'Is that you as a child? You're so absolutely cute,' said Ferriter, pointing at the black-and-white photo in the frame on the wall.

A teenage girl sat in a grassy meadow wearing flared trousers and a John Lennon fisherman's cap on her head.

Ferriter didn't notice the glance Cupidi gave her mother; or the slight pause before Helen said, 'No. That's my sister, Alexandra. She died young. Alex was named after her.'

'She's beautiful.' Ferriter turned. 'Matter of fact, you look a lot like her, Sarge.'

'Yes. She was beautiful,' said Helen. Before Ferriter could ask anything more, she turned to her daughter. 'What you actually mean is, you want someone to babysit Zoë.'

'Obviously, yes. Not that she's a baby anymore.'

Ferriter stood awkwardly between mother and daughter, looking from one to the other.

'I'll think about it. I promise,' her mum said, though Cupidi knew that meant no.

Cupidi took the wheel for the drive back down to Kent. It took longer than it should have; a lorry had shed its load on the M20, scattering timber across three lanes. According to police radio, a woman had been seriously hurt. They sat in the car, not moving, listening to the traffic officers trying desperately to get an ambulance close to the site.

'Your mum seems nice,' said Ferriter.

'Seems,' said Cupidi. 'We never really got along that well. It was my dad that wanted kids, not her.'

'Brothers and sisters?'

'Nope. Just me.'

'That girl. The one you were named after. You look so much like her. She died, your mother said.'

Cupidi looked at the constable, but ignored the implied question.

'Sorry. Nosey,' Ferriter said, when it was clear that Cupidi wasn't going to explain. She pulled down the sunshade on her side of the car and looked at herself in the mirror. 'What was that she was saying about you and the Met? Did you fall out?'

'In case you didn't notice, my mum is a stirrer.'

'Difficult, though. I mean. For your career. Kind of like a step backwards, joining us peasants in the provinces, isn't it?'

'As DI McAdam would doubtless say, I prefer to see it as an opportunity.'

A lorry driver ahead opened his cab door, got out, walked to the verge and began to urinate, in full view of the waiting traffic.

'How disgusting.' Ferriter wrinkled her nose. 'So what was it then? Made you want to make the move?' she asked.

Cupidi turned to her. 'What have you heard?'

'Nothing, really. I was just wondering . . . that's all.'

'Nothing, really? What are people saying about me?'

'Oh it's nothing like that. I was just, you know . . .'

She eyed the constable. 'They have, haven't they?'

'No. No. Nothing. Honest.' Ferriter said, eyes wide.

The police were the worst gossips. Just because Cupidi had changed forces didn't mean stories about what had happened in London wouldn't have followed her.

'I was just trying to make conversation, that's all,' Ferriter said.

The faint noise of a siren; she tilted the rear-view mirror and in it saw the blue lights. Behind them an emergency vehicle was trying to make its way between the vehicles. To make matters worse, the hard shoulder on their section had been blocked by roadworks. Cupidi got out.

'Come on.'

Pulling out a high-viz jacket from the boot, she put it on, handed another one to Ferriter, and started moving the traffic cones back so that she could direct a lane of cars into the vacant tarmac, making space for the ambulance that was edging along the long flat road towards them.

The high-viz had its effect. Sitting in their cars, everyone could already see the problem, but nobody had felt like doing anything about it. Now they scuttled to obey.

There was something about being a copper which made you despise ordinary civilians, Cupidi thought. But they were the ones you were supposed to be doing this for.

She leaned forward and rapped on the window of a Nissan. The driver was asleep, head back, mouth open. He woke, startled, and, once he'd figured out what she was trying to tell him to do, stalled the vehicle in his panic to get it out of the way.

Now fifty metres up the road, she looked back and saw Ferriter, radio receiver in one hand, waving wildly, shouting something, but she couldn't hear her above the noise of the approaching ambulance.

At first she thought she was yelling at the drivers, but then the ambulance's wail paused for a second.

'Body!' Ferriter shouted.

'What?'

'Another body.'

Then the siren started again.

SEVEN

'So he literally drowned in shit?' said the scrawny uniformed PC, trying to peer into the dark hole.

'Keep back,' the farmer said. 'There may be fumes.' He was a sandy-haired young man, skin red from working outdoors, dressed in jeans and a maroon polo shirt.

'How did he even get in there, like?' asked the copper. 'Pissed?'

Cupidi and Ferriter stood outside the barn, a little way off, waiting for the specialist body recovery team to arrive. This time there there was no question of a copper retrieving it. The body was submerged in a slurry tank full of cow excrement.

They had come straight here instead of heading back to the station to write up their report, waved on by the police at the car-crash site; the motorway ahead of them had been deserted. 'Horse Bones Farm,' said Ferriter. 'Charming name.'

The farm lay on the southern end of Walland Marsh, north of Lydd. The old farmhouse had been sold off and a more modern one built close to the road. The cowsheds were well away from the new farmhouse, in the middle of flat fields.

Sergeant Moon had arrived shortly before them and was on the phone attempting to get a CSI on site. Cupidi was trying to remember his first name.

The air was thick with the smell of urine and cow dung, stirred up from the slurry pit below the concrete.

'Ten yards back, please. It's not safe,' said the farmer. Even with his summer tan, he looked pale with the shock of discovering a body on his land, but was still determined to be in charge here; it was his farm.

'It's only shit,' muttered the lanky copper.

'Do as the man says, Constable,' ordered Cupidi. 'It could have been the fumes that killed him.'

'Really?' The constable took a step back, suddenly less cocky.

The farmer looked at her. 'You know about farms, then?'

'Some.'

Enough to know that a farm was a farmer's kingdom and you did as they asked. And, with a body in his slurry tank, this farmer was in a whole lot of trouble and would be defensive. She was going to need his cooperation. She took her phone, squatted down and photographed the slurry-pit lid.

'Stinks,' grumbled the copper.

'It's a farm. It's supposed to. If you don't have something useful to do, go and see if the crime scene manager is here yet.'

The smell of cow dung made her feel like a child again. How long was it since she had spent time on a farm?

'Gentleman here says the cover was always shut. No way could it have been an accident,' said Sergeant Moon, nodding at the farmer.

'On the other hand,' said Cupidi quietly, 'if he admits he left it open, the Health and Safety Executive will have his bollocks and we'll be looking at corporate manslaughter.'

'Oh. You reckon he's lying?'

'It's definitely Option One. Did you notice that sign over there?' She pointed to the end of the barn. There was a red warning sign fixed to the side of it: NOT A PUBLIC RIGHT OF WAY. 'Bloke forgets to close the gate on his slurry pit by accident one night. Someone wanders along. Maybe it's dark. Falls in. Next morning your man over there comes up and notices the thing's open. Oh bugger. Quietly closes it thinking no damage is done. Think about it. You don't fall in and then pull the lid shut after you.' She looked at the farmer across the yard, rubbing his chin anxiously. 'How did he say he found him?'

'He went to agitate the slurry this morning. Slurry's what they call all the—'

'Cow shit,' interrupted Cupidi. 'I know.'

'Right. Machine jammed and he took a look in the tank to see what was wrong. You reckon he was just making that up, then, about when he discovered the body?'

A Massey Ferguson tractor was parked near the sluice with a giant galvanised-metal pole attached, with what looked like a muddy propeller on the bottom still dripping onto the concrete. Cupidi wandered over to look at the small, thick blades and and noticed redness among the brown sludge. She had seen a lot of bad stuff in her line of work, but her stomach heaved at the sight of it.

'I think we can say he wasn't making that up, no. That's how he found a body in there.'

'Oof,' said Moon, looking over her shoulder. 'That's blood, is it? What's that thing?'

'It's like you use for whipping cream. You stick that in the slurry and mix it up. Helps it break down into manure.'

'How do you know all this?'

'I know everything.'

'Right.'

The truth was, as a girl, she had spent summers on her grandparents' farm in Devon while her parents stayed in London. The weather had always been hot and the grass had always been vividly green. She had loved it there.

'So the body must have jammed up that propeller thing, I guess.'

When her grandparents had both died, Cupidi had been in her late teens. The visits to the farm stopped. Her mother sold the house and the land around it, glad to be rid of the place. They had never been back.

'So anyway, the farmer pulled out a mobile, leaned in and took a photo. Guess the rest.'

Cupidi wandered over to the farmer.

'Cross-breeds?' she said, nodding at the herd in the fields beyond.

'That's right. Mostly Holsteins and Swedish Reds.'

Cupidi nodded. 'The sergeant here says you took a photograph.'

The young man pulled a phone from his jeans, swiped the screen then handed it to Cupidi. At first it was hard to make out what she was looking at. The farmer had aimed his camera into the chamber below the barn floor into which urine and cow shit were swept every day. Finally she made out that the pale smudge in the centre was a man's face, crusted brown with manure, and a little to the right, a finger was pointing up above the surface.

She pinched out. The mouth was wide open, gasping for air, teeth a white oval against the darker brown.

'What a horrible death.'

'Awful,' said the farmer.

'How deep is it down there?'

'Deep enough to stand up in, but he wouldn't have lasted long. All sorts of gases come off it. We're not supposed to go anywhere near it if it's not ventilated.'

'So he'd have collapsed into it and drowned?'

'Pretty certain, poor bastard.'

They stood well away from the opening, on clean concrete. The excrement would be sluiced down from the sheds and the yard. There were two big structures on either side of them; the larger was the milking shed; the other stored feed and hay. Lined up on the roof ridges of both, starlings chattered ceaselessly.

'I saw the sign. You get many ramblers coming through here?'

The farmer pointed to a thick hedge beyond the sheds. There was a track running west along the far side of it. 'That's a bridleway. Some of them try to cut through the yard to get back up to the main road. I give them a good bloody shouting-at if I see them. They don't know how dangerous it is round here.'

Cupidi nodded. 'So how do you think he ended up in there? By accident?'

The farmer removed his hands from his trouser pockets and rubbed his chin awkwardly. 'Like I said, the cover on the slurry pit is always closed.'

Cupidi could see it. Three hinged galvanised-metal struts that could be lifted easily; they had been raised now to let the agitator in. The gap between them was wide enough to slip a foot through, but not a body. Someone could have only fallen in if all three were open.

'You a hundred per cent sure about that?'

'Course.'

'There'll be an inquiry now, anyway. You know how it is.'

'Yep.' Farmers didn't like officials coming to tell them how to run their farms at the best of times. A fatal farm accident would mean scrutiny and fines.

She stared at him. 'I'm going to ask you just once more.'

He looked her in the eye. 'I left it shut.'

'And your farmhands?'

'Wasn't them. I only open it when we stick the agitator down there and I don't let them go near it unless I am there. Swear to God. I know what you're thinking. Didn't happen.'

'And someone didn't come by one morning to do the cows and notice the cover had been accidentally left up. So that someone walking along that bridleway and not paying attention could have tripped . . .'

'No,' he said again. 'Definitely not.'

The birds chattered, jostling each other for position on the roof above them. She stared at him. 'The thing is, if it's not negligence, and you're saying that it's not, then that makes this a possible murder investigation. Because as I was just telling the sergeant here, you could hardly slip in there and pull the lid down after you, could you?'

'No,' said the farmer quietly.

She looked around. 'You realise that if it's a murder, you're not going to be able to use this yard till we've searched it from top to bottom. Forensics. Fingertip searches. The whole lot. Which means you're going to have to keep those cows out of here.'

She let that sink in. If he was lying to protect himself, it was still not going to go well for him. She was giving him a last chance to change his mind. 'No, it was down,' he said. 'Swear to God.'

She nodded. 'One more thing. When did you last agitate the slurry?'

'Last month. Four, five weeks ago, max.'

Moon was standing making notes. In his low-slung skinny jeans and slim-fit shirt, she could understand what all the women saw in him.

Cupidi walked over towards her. 'Patrick, is it?'

'Peter. Peter Moon. Bet you didn't get this kind of stuff when you were at the Met.'

'Possibly the worst forensic scene ever,' said Cupidi.

'Bar none.'

'And I have news you are going to absolutely love,' said Cupidi. 'It's possible this might not have been an accident, either.'

'Oh shit,' Moon said. Then, 'Sorry. Wrong word, under the circumstances. You serious?'

'It looks very much like someone may have put him in there.'

Moon looked around. 'Jesus. So where do you think forensics are going have to put the perimeter then?' He was one of those people who spoke languidly, as if everything wasn't as important as other people thought it was.

Cupidi looked around. How could you tell where a crime scene like this began? They didn't even know when he had died. He could have been in there for anything up to five weeks.

'A lot wider than you have it now, that's for sure. Sir?' She called out to the farmer again. About twenty metres from her, he had been heading away from the barns. 'Sorry. One more question.'

The man stopped and turned.

'Has there been any sign of anything being disturbed on the farm around here? Any unusual comings and goings?'

The farmer hesitated, his mouth open.

'What?' prompted Cupidi.

'As it happens, yes. Hadn't thought of it till you asked. This way,' he said, and started walking back towards them.

EIGHT

The farmer led them away from the open slurry tank towards the smaller outbuildings on the other side of the yard from the cowshed. Inside, to the left, it was piled with bales of hay.

Hoisting himself up, he held a hand out for Cupidi. 'Come up,' he said. Then he turned and did the same for Ferriter.

At about two metres above ground the hay formed a flat platform on which the farmer stood, pointing at a higher pile of bales. As Cupidi approached, she saw that they had been laid out so there was a small tunnel, big enough for a man to crawl into.

'About four weeks ago I found this.'

'What am I looking at?'

'Someone built himself a little hidey-hole in the hay. There was a bag with some clothes in it too. You get a lot of rough sleepers, this time of year. It's not just the towns anymore.'

'Did you report it?'

'What's the point?' said the farmer. 'Somebody down on their luck.'

'Where are the clothes?'

The farmer shrugged. 'I chucked them.'

'Did you look at them?'

'Not really. Just a couple of jumpers, pair of trousers. Some underpants. Nothing much. It's not the first time, either. There's more of them about than ever. What am I supposed to do? Wait for them to come back and claim them? Feel sorry, but I don't want to do anything that encourages that stuff. Like I said, it's not safe here.'

Cupidi knelt and peered into the hole in the stack. 'Nothing that would have told you who he was? No wallet? Letters?'

The farmer shook his head. 'There was a book in there, though. I kept that. Didn't seem right to chuck that.'

'What kind of book?'

'Koran.'

'Koran?' said Ferriter. 'Bloody hell.'

Hay prickled Cupidi's hands and knees. The tunnel, made by arranging the bales, was just deep and wide enough for a man to sleep in. 'So you think the victim might have been whoever stayed here?'

'Just a guess. He never came back for his belongings, that's for sure.'

The farmer had used the phrase 'hidey-hole'. He was right, thought Cupidi. The person who had slept here had taken care to remain out of sight.

'I suppose he might have been using the sluice for doing his business into,' said the farmer. 'Those places, you can get pretty dizzy from all the fumes coming up, see? But physically he couldn't have just fallen in, could he?'

'Be pretty convenient, closing the sluice gate behind him. That's assuming it's the same man.'

The farmer nodded.

Getting back down, Ferriter jumped straight off the top, landing like a gymnast. The farmer was already holding out his hand for Cupidi.

She was on the point of saying she could manage on her own, but it was simpler to take his hand again. 'Can I see the book you found?'

Brushing pale stalks from her clothes, she followed the farmer as he led them away from the yard towards a modern farmhouse a couple of hundred metres away. It was a neat red-brick bungalow surrounded by cypress hedges, big picture windows along one side, a pile of wellingtons in the tiled entrance hall.

'I should feel sorry for him, shouldn't I, but I don't. All I'm thinking about is how busy we are this time of year and how much bother all this is causing me.'

His wife was in the living room, on the couch, watching *The Lego Movie* with a child.

'This is the police,' said the farmer.

'Please don't get up,' said Cupidi.

She was in her twenties, plump, red-cheeked and big-eyed. 'Don't say nothing about . . . you know,' she said, toying with a gold heart locket that hung around her neck. 'Gives me the heebie-jeebies.'

'Say nothing about what, Mum?' said the child, a boy who looked about five, who was lying with his head in her lap.

'Nothing, sweetcake.' She stroked her son's hair.

The room was tidy, but for a few toys on the carpet: a helicopter, a Darth Vader mask. On one end of the mantelpiece sat a collection of white ceramic deer, big-eyed and Disneyish; on the other was a small huddle of snow domes.

Bored, the boy stood and walked to the window.

The farmer went to a sideboard, pulled open a drawer and held out the book. Cupidi dug in her handbag for a pair of plastic gloves. He was right. It was a copy of the Koran, well-thumbed.

'Why are those men dressing up, Mum?'

Outside, police officers were donning overalls. The CSI team must have arrived.

'Maybe we should go and stay with my mum for a couple of days,' said the mother.

'I suppose,' said the farmer unhappily.

'Did you see or hear anything unusual over the last four weeks?' Cupidi asked.

The woman curled her lip. 'No.' But the barn was not close to the house. It would have been easy for someone to reach it and stay there unnoticed by anyone here.

'Mum. Why's that lady got washing-up gloves on?' asked the boy, looking at Cupidi.

Cupidi turned to the front of the Koran and looked for a name or any inscription that might say who this man was, then remembered it was in Arabic and turned to the other end of the book, but there was nothing there either.

They walked back out into the sunlight and the buzz of flies.

The specialist unit had arrived too; they would need breathing gear to recover the body.

'Got another one for us then?' said a young man, struggling into neoprene as he sat on the back of the police Land Rover.

'Do you give a discount?' asked Cupidi, looking around.

Ferriter was grinning at Sergeant Moon. 'You here as well, Peter?'

'No peace for the wicked,' answered Moon. 'Looks like we're trying to beat the record for turning up bodies in disgusting places.'

'Yeah.' There was that little flicker of her eyes as she looked at him, too.

Cupidi looked from one to the other.

Moon looked around him. 'I mean. Where to bloody start? How long does he reckon the body's been down there?'

'Could be up to five weeks.'

Sergeant Moon shook his head. 'Needle in a haystack,' he said and looked round with a grin. 'Joke.'

Cupidi didn't laugh.

'Chance of finding much around here that hasn't been trampled on by a herd of cows is zero, I'd say.'

'The man didn't die to inconvenience us,' Cupidi said.

'Succeeded, though.'

'And whatever happened, he would have had a miserable, terrifying death. Before you go to sleep tonight, think about that for a while. What it's like when you find yourself in a place like that and you know you're going to die and there's nobody there to help you. I know I will.'

'OK,' said the younger sergeant quietly.

'So it's our job to find out why it happened.'

'Right.'

As she turned away, she caught a conspiratorial smirk on Ferriter's face – a glance that must have passed between her and Moon.

Cupidi swivelled back to Moon in time to see his own smile vanish.

'Peter? It was you who went to the house that Hilary Keen gave as her address, wasn't it? With Jill here.'

'We went to confirm the address last night, but couldn't. Drove past. It was a bit Scooby-Doo there. Creepy, you know?'

'And?'

'Didn't look like anyone had lived there for a while, ask me.'

'I was thinking, what if it was the crime scene we were looking for for Hilary Keen?'

Moon fanned himself with his clipboard. 'I considered it, obviously, but we weren't authorised to search it.'

'Right,' said Cupidi.

Moon shifted feet uncomfortably.

'And talking of crime scenes, you know we're going to have to include the barn as well?' said Cupidi. 'Looks like the victim may have slept there.'

'Gets better and better,' said Moon.

'A man is dead. We need to make a scene assessment.'

'Yeah. It's just I'm allergic. Hay brings me out in hives. OK. Show me where.'

'I'll take the barn if you like,' Ferriter offered.

'It's Sergeant Moon's job,' said Cupidi.

'Yeah, but I might as well. We're finished up here, aren't we?'

'You don't mind?' said Moon. 'That would be great.'

'No. It's fine.'

Quickly Cupidi checked her watch. Gone five. Zoë would have been expecting her. Ferriter must have seen her doing it. She said, 'It's all right, you go. I can stay if you like.'

Cupidi pulled Ferriter a few metres away from the yard. 'We've pretty much finished here,' said Cupidi. 'You don't have to stay.'

'Honestly, it's fine.'

Cupidi hesitated, looked over at Sergeant Moon. He gave a little wave. 'If you're sure? I'll take the car. Tomorrow morning I'll ride it over and take a proper look into Hilary Keen's address this time. Want to meet me there?'

Ferriter didn't answer.

'Is he more your age then?'

'What?'

'Moon.'

'What? God no,' said Ferriter. 'Bit tall.'

'Bit up himself, if you ask me.'

Ferriter flushed. 'You got him wrong, Sarge. He's all right. It's just his manner.'

Cupidi looked at the constable a second, then said, 'So I'm having the car, then.'

'Right.'

'Can you cadge a lift back to the station? Maybe with Sergeant Moon.'

'Just 'cause I offered to help him, don't mean nothing,' Ferriter said.

But Cupidi was already heading away down the track towards the police car. Inside it, she sat writing up notes for a couple of minutes, then turned the key in the ignition and drove away down the narrow lane, away from the farm, away from the dead man still lying at the bottom of the pit.

NINE

'You could get a summer job if you wanted. There must be something,' said Cupidi. She was speaking to her daughter on the phone. 'I can help you.'

'Don't want to work in a shop. I'd hate that. It's my summer, Mum.'

When she had got up for work that morning, Zoë had still been asleep. Cupidi had left five pounds on the kitchen table: CALL ME WHEN YOU WAKE UP.

Of course she hadn't called; in the end, Cupidi had dialled her mobile when she'd parked the car outside the address she'd been given by Ferriter. Zoë had picked up, half asleep. The conversation wasn't going well.

Cupidi looked around for a sign to check she was at the right place. All she had was a postcode, just off Hamstreet Road.

'If you don't like shops, maybe you should do something outside. The farms round here must want people. There might be fruit-picking or something.' She imagined Zoë sitting in her greying Mickey Mouse pyjamas, wrinkling her nose. 'I just worry that you're bored, that's all.'

'I love being bored,' said the teenager. 'Being bored is the best thing ever. Don't you wish you were bored sometimes?'

'God, no. Are you going to eat anything for breakfast?'

Cupidi switched off the engine. Moon had said the place looked derelict. Maybe she'd been a bit harsh on Moon, questioning why he and Ferriter hadn't entered the building; that said, it didn't look as if it would be difficult to break in. The front door had tendrils of ivy growing up it. It looked as if it hadn't been opened for years. The windows were dark.

She could wait for Ferriter, or she could try to go in herself.

Checking her watch, she got out of the car, phone still in her hand, but just as she did so she noticed a man standing to the side of the house, on a track that led round the back.

Why hadn't she spotted him before? Leaning against the brick wall, he was dressed in clothes that seemed too hot for the summer weather: a jumper and thick woollen trousers. Cupidi had a sudden premonition that maybe she should not have come here alone.

'Have to go,' Cupidi told her daughter, eyeing the man. 'I love you.'

'Mum?'

'I mean it. I love you.'

'What?'

'Call you back,' she said, ending the conversation. She stood, watching the man for a minute; he was staring back at her too. He was in his sixties, Cupidi guessed.

Eventually, she called over the roof of the car, 'Speringbrook House?'

The man said nothing. Moving towards him, she saw he was badly shaven; tufts of white hair sprouted from his chin.

Cupidi pulled her wallet out of her shoulder bag and opened her warrant card to show him. 'Detective Sergeant Cupidi, Kent Police. Did a woman called Hilary Keen live here?'

The man looked at her some more. Finally he said, 'What about her?'

'We're investigating her death. Do you have a minute to talk?'

The man didn't move; he stayed leaning against the wall. 'Can't stop you, can I?'

She looked up at the house. On the first floor, the bedroom curtains were closed; once pink, they were faded and tatty. Was he the dead woman's partner? No. She didn't think so. That would have shown up in her records, wouldn't it? Or he would have reported her missing. Would he?

Why did this feel so wrong?

'Do you live here?'

'Maybe.'

'Did Hilary Keen live here?' She pointed at his house.

The man shook his head slowly. 'Nope.'

'She gave this house as her address. But you're saying she didn't live here?'

'Nope.'

Cupidi squinted at the man, trying to work out what he meant. 'You knew her?'

He chewed his lip. 'Wouldn't say knew.'

'When did you last see her?'

The man shrugged. 'Maybe three weeks.'

Though he had still not yet come up with any cause of death, the pathologist had been pretty confident that her body would have been in the water for over a week. However unhelpful he was being, the man had admitted he was acquainted with her, at least.

Cupidi took in the surroundings. To the right of the driveway there was a white shed, listing to one side; its peeling paint revealed old, dark wood. Foxes had ripped a black rubbish sack that had been left out, tugging bones, plastic and tin over the grass.

'Why did she say this was her address?'

'Was. Kind of. You asked if she lived here.' He pointed to the house. 'She didn't. She lived round back.'

'Right. Can I see where?'

He chewed his lip a bit more. 'Nope.'

Cupidi stood a little straighter. 'This is a murder investigation, sir. Obviously we can obtain a warrant, but it would be much simpler if you could show us.'

Why had she said 'us', when it was only herself? She was on the verge of stepping back into her car and requesting backup when the man spat onto the ground, then turned his head back towards her and said, 'I can't show you where she lived, 'cause it's gone.'

'I don't understand.'

'Come on. I'll show you, for all the good it'll do.'

For the first time he moved, walking towards Cupidi, arms swinging as he did so, until he was only inches away from her, and stopped with his face close to hers. Cupidi smelt cigarettes.

'Boo,' he said, and, despite herself, she flinched, just enough to make him smile. He turned and walked the other way, on down the track between the shed and his house, then turned left and disappeared. After a moment's hesitation, Cupidi followed.

Behind the house sat an ancient black Ford Prefect that looked like it hadn't moved in decades and an orange-painted short-wheelbase Land Rover. A bag full of empty vodka bottles lay by what she guessed was the door to his kitchen.

Between the dead car and an old brick wall at the far side that enclosed the yard, there was a dark rectangle of bare earth, grass growing around its four sides. An electrical cable with an old black mains hook-up plug lay on the ground.

'See? That's where she lived.'

'I don't understand.'

'She had a caravan, didn't she? That's where she lived for the last six, nope, seven years. Nothing to do with me.'

'You were her landlord?'

'She parked her crappy old caravan here, that's all. Pile of rubbish.'

'Somebody came and towed it away?'

'Didn't bloody fly, that's for sure.'

'Who took it?'

A damselfly hovered in the yard, iridescent green. 'Me, course. She hadn't paid any rent for the last three weeks. So I sold it. She's not going to be complaining now neither, exactly, is she?'

'She's dead, Mr . . . I didn't catch your name.'

'She owed me rent. Took it to the breaker's yard last Wednesday.'

The hairs on her back of her neck prickled. Stay calm, she told herself. 'She paid you rent to park a caravan in your yard?'

'Caravan was rubbish. Didn't get me half of what she owed me.'

Cupidi looked around her. Her brain was racing now, trying to take everything in. This was not the kind of place you parked a caravan if you enjoyed views. It was bounded on three sides; old outhouses to the north, the wall to the west and the house to the south. But there was access to electricity, running water and what looked like an outside toilet in one of the sheds. She was also conscious of the fact that the man was now standing between her and the only route back to her car.

'She have friends?'

'Never saw anyone. You done here? Only I'm busy.'

He didn't look busy, just angry. 'Which breaker's yard?'

He hesitated. 'Over Sittingbourne way.'

She looked up. The back kitchen door was open a little. Inside she could see a small patch of greasy lino floor. He must have come out when he heard her car. Had he been here, lurking in the darkness, when Ferriter and Moon had come here two nights earlier? 'What about mail? Did her post come to you?'

They were standing side by side in the yard; him just a foot to her left. 'She didn't get much, really.'

'Did you keep any of it? Do you have any of her post now?'

'Nope. Like I said, weren't that much of it anyway.'

'Bank statements?'

'She didn't have a bank account.'

Cupidi looked at the man. 'How did you know that?'

'She told me. Never paid by cheque. Always cash.'

'What about a mobile phone?'

'Nope,' he said, and shook his head.

Cupidi stared at him. 'So you searched the caravan before you towed it, then?'

'Quick look round, maybe.'

Cupidi nodded slowly. 'You don't mind towing somebody's caravan to the breakers because she owes you a few quid in rent, so don't tell me you're too polite not to go through her drawers to find out if she's left a bit of cash lying around.'

The man said nothing. Turning back to gaze at the empty rectangle which marked where the dead woman had lived, her skin tingled. A meagre space in a dingy yard. A small pile of bricks lay at one end; presumably they had been used to keep the caravan stable. The man she was talking to had admitted to deliberately destroying evidence. In situations like this you had to take everything in; be sure of yourself. She felt a kind of hum; a mixture of fear and certainty.

She raised her eyes to meet his; defiantly, he stared right back at her.

She should go back to the car, call in a team.

Breaking the gaze, she turned to walk back to the car, but the man stepped abruptly sideways, blocking her way. 'She owed me for the rent.'

'How much was there?'

'You're trying to say I did something, aren't you? You're trying to make it look bad for me.'

'How much did you take?'

'I'm not listening to this . . . shit,' said the man.

'Just asking. Hundred? Couple of hundred?' She was pushing it, but at times like this, when people were angry, they didn't have time to think their stories through. Apply a little pressure and you could trip them. If Hilary Keen didn't keep money in a bank account, she would almost certainly have kept it in her caravan. Cupidi wondered how much it would have been. The kind of amount that would be worth killing her for?

'Three hundred? A grand?'

'Fucking hell. What are you trying on?' Spittle fell in her face but this time she didn't blink.

Stay calm. 'What about her phone?'

'Told you, she didn't bloody have one.'

'And you didn't take any money from her caravan, either.' She wondered if she had already gone too far. While her eyes were back fixed on his, she was conscious of him flexing his fists, opening them, closing them. She thought of the pale body in the brown water.

'Do you mind giving me your name, sir?'

'I don't think I will,' he said.

If he was the man who had killed Hilary Keen, he had used violence before. Somewhere amongst the noise in her head, she was calculating the distance to her car. It was true she was fitter than she had been in years, but she'd still have to open the door. She might make it, but then again, she might not.

She closed her eyes and opened them again. 'OK,' she said, and smiled at him.

'What?' He seemed confused.

'I said, OK. You don't have to give me your name. You're right.'

She turned again and walked slowly, as calmly as she could, past him.

'Where are you going?'

She didn't answer.

'I haven't finished with you,' he shouted. 'I didn't say you could go.'

At that, she broke into a trot. When she made it to the car she got in, locked the door behind her, laid her head on the steering wheel and took what felt like the first breath she'd had in minutes.

Discreetly she reached down for the radio. She should call this in. Get a team down here.

His open palm banged on the bonnet. 'You cunt.'

His face was red with anger. He slapped the bonnet again. The car rang with the noise. 'Delta Sierra Four.'

'It was my money. It was my fucking money.'

'I'm going to need urgent backup. Speringbrook House, just south of Hamstreet.'

'You can't fucking pin that on me. There's nothing to prove it.'

'About two hundred metres north of the junction with the A2070.'

'I could shut you up easy.' He mimed taking a gun – a rifle – aiming at her, and pulling the trigger, jerking his arm as he fired the imaginary bullet.

'I need assistance to apprehend a suspect in the Hilary Keen murder case. Suspect is unidentified male, sixty years old. Suspect is acting aggressively.'

The man walked to the driver side of the car, held his face up to her window and bared his teeth. 'Nosey fucking . . .'

Spit flecked her window. She started the car engine, figuring that she needed to keep a distance from him. Her presence was only making him angrier. She should have left the scene earlier; she should never have let it come to this. What was it about her that meant that she always went too far?

'Run away,' he shouted. 'Run a-bloody-way.'

Cautiously she backed out and pulled into a muddy gateway on the far side of the road, watching him.

Looking down at her hands, she realised they were trembling. She wished she had a cigarette.

'Shit,' she said out loud.

He had disappeared to the back of the house. He might be running away across the fields now. Should she leave the safety of her car to look?

There would be no way of contacting her colleagues if she left the car and its radio. And she would just make herself vulnerable. Rationally, she knew the best thing would be to stay where she was until help arrived, but she felt stupid doing nothing.

Or he might be going to fetch a weapon. So she kept the car engine running, eyes glued to the side of the house, waiting for him to return.

But after several minutes she noticed the pale yellow curtains upstairs moving. Then out of the darkness, his face appeared, lit by the summer light. He was glaring down, lips moving.

And when she finally saw the blue lights coming he was there watching her still from behind the filthy glass, mumbling curses at her.

TEN

Her heart sank when she saw the first police car slow, then jerk its steering wheel to the right to park sideways across the road, lights still flashing.

She got out of her car and approached it, peering at the four uniformed men inside. 'I asked for support,' she said. 'Not the entire force.'

'Another two units will be along in a minute. McAdam says nobody's to approach the house until they're here. He in there?'

'Another two? Jesus Christ. Why?'

'Homeowner's name is Stanley Eason,' answered the officer, who stayed sitting behind the driving wheel; a man Sergeant Cupidi didn't recognise. 'He has history of threatening behaviour.'

And this, she thought, is where it will all start to go wrong. The hum returned.

'He threaten you?' the sergeant asked.

'Well . . . yes.'

The man spoke into the radio again. 'Suspect in Hilary Keen murder threatened officer. Confirmed.'

'Know what? It wasn't that bad. He's just a gobby arse.'

'Where is he?'

She looked up at the window. The man was still there, looking down. Somehow, in a few minutes, this had got out of hand. 'First floor. Behind that curtain.' She pointed. 'He's been watching me since I called in.'

A brassy-haired woman in a white Mercedes had arrived and was trying to nose her way round the parked car. The officer got out and shouted across the roof of his car, 'Sorry, madam, road closed.'

'She's just trying to drive up the street,' said Cupidi.

'Orders are we secure the area till he's out.' He turned back to Cupidi and asked, 'Do you know the layout of the house?'

'I didn't get as far as that.'

'Before he was violent towards you?'

'No. Just a bit lairy.' There were more lights now, approaching from the other direction. 'All I wanted was one copper to help me take him in for questioning.'

'Murder suspect?'

'Possible murder suspect.'

'And violent.'

'He didn't actually touch me.'

'Duly noted.' Only doing his job.

The next car to arrive was driven by Ferriter. When she had used her the vehicle to block the road fifty metres north of the house, she jumped out and came trotting towards the rest of the police.

'You're late.'

'Sorry, Sarge. Got held up at the station,' she called. 'DI McAdam's on the blower now. Wants a word.'

'Blower,' thought Cupidi. For Christ's sake. She looked up at the face in the window again, but the room was dark and the glass dirty; Eason had pulled back a few inches. It was impossible to see any expression on his face. Did he have an inkling about what was happening out there? The way things were inexorably leading? She turned, walked slowly north up the lane, got into the car and picked up the radio. 'Cupidi here, sir.'

'What's the situation?'

She explained what had happened. 'At best he's stolen and destroyed evidence,' she said. 'Don't know if that's deliberate or otherwise.'

'At worst it's him we've been looking for?'

'Him being the murderer would certainly be one explanation why he's got rid of evidence, yes.'

'What's going on now?'

'He's gone back inside his house and he's just sitting there, watching us now.'

'Could he be drunk? On drugs?'

'Don't think so, sir. Do we know if he has any record of mental health issues?'

'Not so far. What's your assessment?'

'My assessment? Police make him angry. You know the type. Middle-aged man. Now we've got a lot of coppers here I doubt he's happy, to be honest. My opinion, I'm not altogether sure it's wise, this many officers being on site. I'd advise standing them down, sir.'

DI McAdam said, 'Nope. He's got some history. Couple of years ago, we had a report of a man from round here threatening a local. We talked to Eason about it, but he flat out denied it. It was him, though. Now we have him as a suspect in a murder case threatening an officer.'

'He's not actually violent though.'

McAdam chewed this over for a second. 'From my point of view, I have to assume the threat was real. I don't like this either.'

There were four cars now. Cupidi could see the men inside putting on their vests.

'Right,' said the copper who'd been the first to arrive. 'I'm going to knock on the door.'

There was a crackle of radios. Somewhere, far away, McAdam confirmed: 'Go ahead.'

Cupidi returned to her car and pulled a stab vest out of the boot. It felt absurdly heavy, but then maybe she was tired. She was struggling with the zip as the copper made his way through the small wooden gate, to the front of the house.

'Mr Eason,' he called. 'Can we have a word?'

No answer.

She didn't recognise the policeman. 'Hey! Officer,' she shouted. 'He doesn't use that door.'

The man at the door looked round, annoyed, but didn't pay any attention to what she'd said. With the side of his fist, he banged on the door.

Cupidi saw movement from behind the curtains on the first floor; he was there again, face close to the glass, looking down.

'The wrong door,' she said again. 'Try round the back.'

She looked to her left. In the distance she could see yet another car had arrived to close the lane off completely down by the main road, a couple of hundred metres away. Blue lights, blinking over the green of the marshes. They were keeping the cordon large.

'Mr Eason? Can you come to the door. It'll be easier to speak, that way.'

Again, nothing. The policeman knocked, then tried the door handle. Unsurprisingly, it didn't move.

Stupid.

'Nothing bad is going to happen to you. We just want to talk.'

Seriously? Nothing bad is going to happen to you? She looked around and counted twelve officers now.

The flat countryside was oddly still. All traffic on the road in front of the house had stopped now. Overhead a light plane flew. A huge bumblebee buzzed up the lane, attracted by the shine on a copper's uniform. It fizzed around the man as he tried to wave it away.

The policeman backed down the path, looking up to the window. 'Mr Eason?'

But, looking up, she saw that Eason had retreated into the dark interior of the house. The sergeant turned, pointed towards a constable and then to the back of the house. They would need someone to cover the back door, in case Eason made a run for it.

Nothing else happened. But for the movement of birds and bugs, everything was still. For the moment, anyway.

Ferriter walked over to Cupidi. 'OK?'

She nodded.

'It's him, then?' she asked.

'If I was a betting woman, which obviously I'm not, given my luck, I'd say the odds are high. He's admitted to destroying material that belonged to her. He's acting defensively . . . What's happening now?'

'Negotiator's coming down from Canterbury.'

'Oh for God's sake.'

Cupidi approached the latest car to arrive. Three men were inside, all in vests, waiting.

'All I was asking for was another copper, not the cavalry.'

'Procedure, Sarge.'

'We're doing nothing till a negotiator gets here?'

'That's right.'

'The longer we wait here, the longer he's going to get dug in. Why don't I go and try and talk to him again?'

The sergeant in charge thought about it for a couple of seconds.

'You don't think he's a direct risk?'

'He didn't lay a finger on me. It was a show, I think. You know. Men are like that.'

He shook his head. 'I don't think so. Let's do this by the book. The negotiator'll be here any minute.'

'Half an hour, at least,' reckoned Cupidi.

'Patience is a virtue.'

'And Grace is a little girl who should be taken into care,' muttered one of the team sitting in the car behind him.

The silence of the morning disappeared; the noise of a helicopter. She looked around and saw it, approaching from behind the sun. 'Bloody hell,' she said, looking up. 'Talk about overkill.'

'That's not us. Press probably.'

'Brilliant.'

The helicopter slowed, coming to a standstill a little way off, steady in the summer air. They would be filming the scene. It would make it on to the lunchtime news.

It would be a long wait. Cupidi walked back towards Ferriter who was looking at her phone, laughing at something.

'What is it?'

'Peter Moon. He's just asking what's going on.'

'Do you do yoga with him too?'

'Shut up.'

'Bet he looks nice in Lycra.'

'If you was a bloke, Sarge, that would be sexist.'

'Seriously though, Jill. Word of advice. Dating fellow officers. Never a great idea.'

'Personal experience?' she said, all butter-wouldn't-melt.

Cupidi looked at her for a second, then said, 'Naturally.'

'It's not actually like that at all, anyway.'

'Right.' Cupidi unzipped her stab vest and threw it over to her. 'I need to pee,' she said. 'Look after that, will you? We're going to be here a while.'

A blackbird chuckled as she ambled slowly up the narrow lane towards a garden centre on the far side of the Military Canal. As she crossed the bridge she paused for a minute to peer into the dull brown water, then walked a little further, turning right into a car park, where a man was struggling to put a large shrub into the boot of a Volvo.

'Is the road still closed that way?' he asked. 'What's going on?'

'Don't know,' she lied, leaving the man clutching the heavy plant.

After she'd found the toilets she picked up a handful of energy bars and a bottle of juice.

The till was staffed by an elderly man in an olive jacket, who should have been retired at his age. 'Do you know the man who lives in Speringbrook House?' she asked him.

'That where the police are?'

Cupidi nodded.

'What are they bothering him for? Didn't pay his telly licence, or is it some other capital crime? I was just done for going thirty-eight miles an hour on the road up at Winchelsea. A hundred bloody pounds for going eight miles an hour over the limit. You'd have thought those pointy-headed buggers had something better to do, excuse my language.'

'It would have been over forty if you received a ticket,' she said.

'How do you know?'

'I know everything.'

'I've never had an accident in my life,' he said. 'Not once.'

'What's he like?' she asked.

'Who?'

'Mr Eason?'

'Stan?' he said, passing the scanner over her snacks. 'Keeps himself to himself since his wife died. Always gives me the time of day, mind. Like most round here. Just gets on with it. Not exactly talkative, but that's what we're like. Four pounds ninety-five. What's going on up there?'

'You ever meet the woman who lived on the caravan behind his house?'

'Woman? Didn't know there was one. Stan's a dark horse.'

The man turned frosty. 'Why you asking all this? Are you a journalist?'

'No.' She picked up the carrier bag and smiled. 'One of the pointy-headed buggers.'

She ambled back towards the house, enjoying the sunshine. It was a beautiful day, at least. Above, in the blue sky, the press helicopter was still circling the farm.

She paused at the Military Canal, leaning over the edge of the bridge again as she unwrapped an energy bar. Chewing on it, she thought she saw something large and dark moving in the water below. She shivered, broke off a crumb and dropped it into the water. The fish below paid no attention.

When she looked up, she saw Ferriter ambling towards her. 'Anything happening?'

'Negotiator just arrived. Being briefed.'

'What's this, then?' She pointed at the canal.

'They dug it in 1805 to stop Napoleon invading,' Ferriter answered.

'It worked then.'

Ferriter looked at her, unsmiling. 'Fifteen hundred men, it took,' she said. 'You can walk all the way to Sussex along here. If you want to.'

'And if you dumped a body here, could it end up at . . . what's it called?'

'Salt Lane? I don't know.'

Cupidi nodded. 'I need to speak to those drainage people. Can you sort it out?'

'The Drainage Board,' she said. 'You think she was murdered here?'

She stared down into the water, waiting for one of the fish to take her crumb, but none did. 'I don't know. But I think we may have just found the murderer, don't you? Now we have to get him to admit it.'

'Makes you wish he'd have a go,' said Ferriter. 'Couple of minutes of battering by the lads out there might loosen his tongue.'

Cupidi looked at her, eyebrows raised.

'Sorry. Bit incorrect,' added Ferriter with a small laugh.

'Our job is to get them to trial in one piece.'

'It was just banter.'

Ignoring her, Cupidi looked round. 'You ever worry that everything here is at sea level? All that's holding the water back are a few walls.'

'Never thought about it, really. I mean, it's been like this all my life, round here.'

'Walls are only so high, that's all I'm saying.'

'Very cheery, Sarge.'

Cupidi straightened. 'Let's get back,' she said.

Back at the house, a young man in a blue suit was craning his neck up at the bedroom window. 'Stanley. My name is Kevin.'

There was no response from inside.

'Is it Stanley or Stan?'

Nothing.

'Trained negotiator,' said Ferriter.

'Obviously,' said Cupidi.

Cupidi handed Ferriter an energy bar, unwrapped a second for herself and stood chewing as the negotiator tried to elicit some kind of response from the man inside.

'It's all about minimising risk to us,' Ferriter said. 'Except the longer he's in there and we're out here, the greater the risk to him.'

Cupidi nodded, reached into the car and pulled out her stab vest.

'Studied it a bit,' said Ferriter. 'You know, hostage negotiation.' She hadn't opened the bar. Instead she was reading its list of ingredients.

'I'm here. Just talk to me, whenever you want,' Kevin was saying.

'First step,' explained Ferriter, 'open communication. Second step, build empathy.'

'Is that right?' said Cupidi.

'Like dating, really. Best thing is to make yourself clear right at the start.'

'Only that was when he was threatening me and calling me a cunt.'

'Not a good date, really, then,' said Ferriter. She held out the bar, returning it to Cupidi. 'Trans fats,' she said. 'You shouldn't eat them.'

Cupidi rolled her eyes, but took it back. 'What if us just being here makes it harder for him to back down?'

'Yeah, well,' said Ferriter. 'There is that.'

'Always is hard for that type of man. And it's always the men, isn't it? When was the last time you had a siege with a woman?'

'There you go again. Bit sexist, isn't that, Sarge?'

'Bit true though, isn't it?'

'Bitter divorce, was it?'

Cupidi laughed. 'Actually, no.'

'I could come in and chat. Or stay out here, if you prefer,' Kevin was saying. 'You tell us what you want to do.'

Towards the north, a group of schoolkids on bikes had arrived and were peering over the police tape, chatting to a constable. The helicopter had disappeared. The air around them was still.

She was unzipping her vest again, feeling too hot in the sun, when she heard a regular creaking noise above her, almost like a heartbeat, and looked up. Two swans were flying low above the field opposite the house; magnificent in the summer light. She wished Zoë was here; she would have some ridiculous fact about swan behaviour to tell her. As they approached they banked towards the right, heading straight over the house.

That's when she noticed a snake of pale smoke coming out of the red-brick chimney.

'Oi. He's burning something,' she called out.

Heads turned to look.

'Evidence?' suggested Ferriter.

'Well, in this weather I don't think he's doing it to keep warm,' said Cupidi. 'God. How bloody frustrating. We can't get in there, and meanwhile he can do what he likes in there.'

The sergeant who'd arrived with the team to surround the building had finally got out of his car and was standing next to her.

'See that?' she said. 'That could be the difference between us being able to make a case against him and not.'

'What would he be destroying?'

'I don't know.'

'What do you think?'

'We should go in,' said Cupidi.

'I'll run it past McAdam.'

'Or you could actually make the decision yourself.'

'Fire!' shouted Kevin the negotiator, who was closer, but who had noticed the smoke for the first time.

Cupidi took a couple of steps towards the building and saw that the pale curtains were suddenly silhouetted by a flare of light behind them. In a horizontal column, smoke, darker now, was pouring upwards from the chimney.

'Fuck,' said the policeman. 'He's not just burning something. He's gone and set fire to the whole fucking place.'

Cupidi was running now. A copper pushed Kevin aside and was slamming himself at the front door, uselessly. By the look of it, it was firmly bolted. 'Get the Enforcer,' he was shouting; the door-ram.

'We haven't got one on board. You?'

'Jesus.'

As they stood around, Cupidi sprinted round to the back, where another copper was waiting.

'What's going on?' he demanded.

'He's set the place alight.'

She looked around. Ferriter had followed her to the back door. Cupidi tried the handle. It was locked, of course.

'What you doing?' asked the constable who had been stationed there.

The frame was PVC with toughened glass so they'd never get through it, but the kitchen window was next to it. Cupidi looked around and saw the pile of bricks left where the caravan had been. Picking one up, she chucked it straight into the glass; it broke with little noise.

'But . . .' said Ferriter.

She threw a second to make the opening bigger, then took off her stab vest, laid it over the spiked shards of the kitchen window and pushed the remaining pieces inwards. At the gaping hole, she could feel the air flowing in to feed the flames above.

'Petrol!' she shouted as she tipped, head forward, into a kitchen sink below. The tang of it was all around her.

Pulling herself inside, she twisted her body, bringing her legs round so she could drop onto the floor.

She heard screaming now; from somewhere above her came the sound of a man in pure pain.

She paused for a second, orientating herself. The kitchen was a muddle of pans, plates and empty tins. Moving again, she stumbled through, into a hallway beyond, hitting her ankles on boxes and piles of newspaper. The house was a mess. He was a hoarder.

The screaming from above had risen to become an animal roar of pain and fear.

She yanked at the stiff bolt on the front door to let the other coppers in, but it wouldn't give. In the dim light, she realised that it wasn't just locked. Eason had fastened the entrance shut with wood and screws. She would never get it open. Smoke was drifting down from the ceiling, darkening the hallway.

Outside she heard shouting, men kicking at the door.

Coughing now, blinking, she turned to look up the stairs. Air was rushing higher, sucked by the heat.She could hear the flames now, crackling, consuming the house. A redness flickered on the landing above her.

She would have to go up, she thought. The screaming seemed

to be quieter all of a sudden. Or was it that the fire itself was louder? Where was everyone else? She looked round, praying that someone would be following her, but smoke was curling through the laths where the plaster had cracked and fallen.

Pulling her blouse over her face, she started up the stairs. Another lump of ceiling, bigger this time, crashed down on her and she lost her footing on the loose scraps.

Now she was tumbling backwards toward the front door, one arm flailing for a banister, the other raised to protect her head.

She hit the floor hard and lay dazed for a second, her heart suddenly hammering. Must get up. She knew she had to get out, but she had lost any sense of direction in the fall. As dust and smoke obscured the air around her, she tried to work out which position she had fallen in. Disorientated, she stood slowly, hands out to feel around her. Taking a step forward, she immediately fell again, tripping on something she couldn't see.

Now, as the noise of the fire rose to a roar, panic set in. She had very little time to get out of this building.

And then someone was lifting her, hands under her armpits.

'I'm OK,' she shouted.

She looked up and made out the face of Constable Ferriter as she dragged her backwards out towards the kitchen, just as the front door finally came crashing down.

She sat on the grass, blinking soot from her eyes as she watched flames start to find a way through the tiles of the roof.

A uniformed WPC stood next to her with a cup of water. 'You were lucky,' she said.

'That's me.' She was grateful for the water, though. Her mouth was filled with the rancid taste of burnt plastics and wood. She took a mouthful and swilled it round, then spat it out on the ground beside her. Small flecks of blackness lay on the bright green grass. She noticed her ankles. Blood streaked from her right foot down into her shoe, but the cut was not deep.

'You might want to adjust your clothes,' said the WPC.

'What?'

'Your bra's showing.'

Cupidi looked down. Her blouse was still pulled up from where she'd tried to cover her face with it. At least the bra was a newish one.

Tugging her shirt down, she looked around. 'Where's Constable Ferriter? I should thank her. I think she may have saved my life.'

'Who?' said the WPC.

Cupidi stood, looked around, suddenly worried. There was no sign of her.

'Ferriter!' she shouted above the clamour of the fire. She was running now, towards the burning building, past the startled policemen.

'Oh shit.'

A row of coppers had gathered behind the house, watching flames burst out of the windows, curling round the edge of the roof. Blinking from the smoke, she scanned their faces, but none of them was Ferriter's.

ELEVEN

Everything seemed to slow. Constable Ferriter had entered the burning building and had probably saved her life. Had she gone back inside afterwards to try and save Eason's too?

'Ferriter!' she shouted into the broken window.

Now, though she was racing back to the open front door, it seemed to take an age to reach it. When she did, all she saw was more coppers standing motionless around it, unsure of what they were supposed to be doing. She pushed her way through them to the door. Pulling her blouse back up over her mouth and nose, she stepped forward.

Hands grabbed her shoulders and arms. 'You can't go in there.'

'There's a copper still inside. Jill Ferriter. I'm pretty sure she went back in.'

Mouths open, everyone stared into the house, beyond the splintered door and up the stairs to where Ferriter would have headed.

'Oh Christ.'

The flames had broken through the old roof. Around them black smut and burning embers were falling slowly from the sky.

The fire engine had been called, of course, but it would still be minutes away. Going back into the building to the upstairs floor could be suicide; she knew that. Cupidi shook herself free of the holding hands.

She looked around and saw the sense of shame on the officers' faces.

'I'll go,' a burly man shouted.

But before anyone moved again, she saw something dark moving at the top of the stairs.

'Look.'

The young copper next to her burst through the line of officers into the burning building. Another two followed him in.

A few seconds later they emerged, crashing down the steps. The two uniformed police were supporting Ferriter by her elbows. Over another's shoulders was Stanley Eason.

The policeman collapsed onto his knees, dropping Eason face up on the ground. The unconscious man's head bounced on the grass as he fell.

Someone started clapping, but stopped quickly as soon as he saw Eason.

The front of his shirt had been burned completely away, exposing a mess of reddened flesh. His face, too, was unrecognisable, crinkled and distorted by the heat. Beneath the frizzy stubble that was all that was left of his hair, a single eye stared out, his eyelid peeled back by the flames.

Now a copper was kneeling by the man, head down to his burning chest. 'Get water. He's still alive.'

And then everyone was running around, pulling out first aid kits from the boots of their cars.

At the hospital, still grimy from the fire, she found Jill Ferriter in the reception area at A & E with a box of tissues in her lap. She fetched two cans of Coke from the shop and handed one to her.

'Just minor burns on my hand,' Ferriter said, holding it up, wrapped in gauze. 'I'm fine. It's just a little tender.'

'You were fantastic,' Cupidi said. 'I think you saved my life.'

'Thank you.'

'You're welcome.' Ferriter smiled back at her.

'Why did you do it?'

'Like you said. You can sit around waiting for orders, or you can actually get off your arse and do something good.'

'I should probably be more careful what I say.'

People moved around busily, ignoring them. A man in blue scrubs, running with a white polystyrene box, through swinging doors. A receptionist straining to understand what a mother was telling her about her child.

'Besides, everyone else was standing around until you picked up that brick. I was just copying you,' Ferriter said, coughing into a tissue. 'Bosh. Amazing.' She lowered the handkerchief and grinned.

'But you shouldn't have gone back in.'

She shrugged. 'Had to, didn't I? He would have died, otherwise. Our job is to get 'em to trial. That's what you said.'

'Very funny.'

'He was a bugger to pick up. Wriggling like a bastard. Thought I'd given myself a hernia getting him to the top of the stairs, but then the others came. And? How is he?'

She sat on the chair next to his. 'He's in intensive care.'

'Yeah, but has he said anything? Did you arrest him?'

'He's in a coma. He hasn't said anything at all.'

Ferriter looked shocked. 'But . . . he was conscious when I got him. He swore at me.'

Cupidi nodded. 'Third-degree burns. The body goes into shock.'

On the TV behind him they were showing the news. A clip of a helicopter above the marshes.

'He was pushing me off him and everything. That's why I took so long. He can't be that bad, can he?'

She looked at Ferriter and saw shock on her face. She was young; unused to death. 'Sorry. You did great, Jill. But he's deteriorated. He has kidney failure, apparently. They're not sure if he's going to make it.'

'What? Die, you mean?'

'Maybe,' Cupidi said. The consultant had said the next twenty-four hours would be critical. 'It doesn't alter the fact that you did everything you could. Fucking stupid, but great.'

'Jesus.' Ferriter looked at the bandage on her hand, then started coughing again, louder, unable to dislodge the phlegm in her throat. Cupidi patted her on the back, not sure whether it was doing any good at all. 'Take a drink,' she suggested.

When the fit subsided, Ferriter looked down at the handkerchief. Her spit was flecked with black. She crumpled the tissue.

'That's kind of normal,' Cupidi told her.

'I thought I'd saved his life.'

'Who knows? Maybe you have. Only time's going to tell. You did great. Is there anyone who I should be calling who can come and pick you up?'

She shook her head.

'I can drop you somewhere if you like.'

'No.' Her small smile trembled slightly. 'I'll be fine.'

Cupidi stood. 'Right,' she said. 'I'll go then.'

Ferriter nodded, and Cupidi was relieved to walk away because the constable was going to start crying soon, and she wouldn't want her watching.

DI McAdam was on the other side of the hospital sliding doors, talking on his mobile.

There were worse coppers than McAdam. He was a good policeman, dedicated, efficient, intelligent; one of those men who thought of themselves as forward-looking. While other officers might complain about government cuts destroying the police force, McAdam saw it as his job to get on with it all without moaning. He was the kind of man who always came to birthday and leaving parties, bought rounds for others but drank only sparkling water himself.

When he saw her through the glass, he ended the call and beckoned to her.

'You were right,' he said. 'I arsed it all up, didn't I? Bloody hell. They'll hang me for this.'

'Like you said, it was process.'

As she pushed through the doors, he asked her, 'What about Constable Ferriter in there? She going to be OK?'

'Shocked more than hurt, I think,' she said. 'She took it badly when I told her that Eason might not make it. She thought she'd saved his life.'

'Let's hope for everyone's sake she has.'

'It would make life a lot easier, you mean?' She took a gulp from her can, her throat still dry. There would have to be an investigation into what had gone wrong with the operation at Eason's house; a fatality would make that much more serious.

'Frankly, yes. If we can get him to stand trial and he's guilty, then everything I did looks shiny.' He looked at his neat black shoes. 'But if he dies . . .' He raised his hand to his head in the shape of an imaginary gun.

'Can't be that bad, can it?'

'They'll be asking why I surrounded the building against the advice of one of my own officers.'

'You said it yourself. You had no choice.'

He nodded. 'How is she?'

'Surprising. Tougher than she looks.'

'Right,' said McAdam. 'I should go and thank her personally.'

He looked through the glass at the constable. She was still dabbing her face with tissues.

'I'd give her a minute, sir. She's a bit weepy. I don't think she wants to be seen like that.'

'Ah. Yes.' He looked back at Cupidi. 'And the house?'

'A mess. The fire's out, but it's still too hot to get anywhere near it. You could see the smoke in Rye, apparently.'

They were replaying footage on the news now, too, the helicopter circling round the building as the flames licked through the tiles.

'As soon as it's safe, put the team in to see if we find anything that links Eason to the murder. Do you think the chances are we'll find something, Alex?'

'Honestly, I don't know, sir.'

'Attempting to burn down your own house is not the behaviour one would expect from an innocent man.'

An elderly man in pyjamas emerged from the front door of the hospital in a wheelchair, pushed by a porter.

'Some men find it a little hard to back down.'

The patient in the wheelchair lit a cigarette. 'And some women, obviously,' said McAdam.

'As soon as it's safe to go in there I'll see what I can find, sir. The evidence that links him to Hilary Keen's murder has to exist.'

'Thanks, Alex. Better get to it then. We've two murders on the go in this neighbourhood now.'

It took a second for Cupidi to realise what he said. 'Two?'

'Weren't you told?'

'The man in the slurry pit?'

'I've just heard that the preliminary investigation of the body shows significant bruising that wouldn't be consistent with just falling into the tank.'

'He was assaulted?'

'I don't have the precise details, but it looks very much like it.'

'God. And thrown into the pit?'

'And left to die, yes. That's not the worst of it. The press have got hold of the fact that he's probably an illegal immigrant.'

'Being forced into a hole full of shit is not the worst of it?'

The smoker in the wheelchair stared at them. McAdam took Cupidi by the elbow and led her away. 'There's a story going out on *Meridian News* tonight.'

'Two stories on the same day. Press office must love us.'

'We appear to be very much in the media's eye. And that was the Chief Constable on the phone.'

'I don't suppose he was happy.'

'Not at all.' Her senior officer, normally so positive, so full of energy, looked weary now. 'You may have noticed there's a certain amount of interest in illegal migrants in this area,' he said drily. 'From your report, he appears to have been a Muslim migrant. More petrol on more flames. You understand the sensitivity. There are all sorts of people around here who love to stir that pot. So, hopefully we can wrap up the Keen death as soon as we can. If there's forensic evidence in what's left of Eason's house, let's find it and job done. Write it up. We already have the killer. We need the paperwork. Then we concentrate what resources we have on the case where the murderer is still on the loose. Can you do that?'

Cupidi ran her hand through her hair. It felt greasy from the smoke. 'Right. Course, sir.' Though she wondered how much there was to write – or to find. They didn't know how Hilary Keen had died, so how would they know what to look for?

'There's another possible crime scene in the Keen case. We know that she had lived in a caravan behind his house. Maybe she was killed there.'

McAdam looked encouraged. 'Good,' he said.

Eason had said he had towed the caravan to Sittingbourne. He might have been lying, obviously. Cupidi looked at her watch.

It was three in the afternoon. If she went there now, she'd be late back home. Zoë would be on her own again. But if she was right, she had to find it before it was destroyed.

'Oh, by the way, Alex. Were your ears burning yesterday? I met one of your Metropolitan Police colleagues.'

'Did you?' she asked. 'Who would that be?'

'What was his name?' he frowned as he tried to remember.

She raised her Coke can so he wouldn't be able to see her face.

'Superintendent David Colquhoun . . . That was it.'

'Oh.' She gulped hard, coughed on the fizzy drink. 'David Colquhoun is a superintendent now?'

'Recently promoted I believe, Detective Superintendent, running Whitechapel CID. Did you work closely with him?'

She looked down at her sooty linen trousers. 'No. Not really at all.'

'Oh. He seemed to know you well. He spoke very highly of you, in fact. He said you were a talented officer.'

'Talented?'

'Yes. He said you were very passionate about your work. And I would agree with him there. It's a good quality in a copper. He said I was lucky to have you. Which I am.'

She looked up and examined his face for any sense that his words might mean more than he was saying.

'Was that all he said?' she asked cautiously.

'Should there have been more?'

'No.' There was an awkward silence.

Excused, she locked herself in a disabled bathroom to wash herself as much as she could. Stripped down to her bra and pants, she stood in front of a sink and padded herself clean with green paper handtowels. Then she dabbed at the black smudges on her blouse. She looked in the mirror at herself, standing half naked in a small hospital toilet, urine stains on the floor, and sighed.

Jammy David Colquhoun. Five years younger than her and he makes bloody Superintendent while she's still a sergeant.

TWELVE

Cupidi found the owner of the breaker's yard in the lot behind the office. He was wearing swimming trunks and dark glasses. A man in his fifties, greying hair swept back across his head, sitting on a plastic chair next to a swimming pool with a can of lager in his hand.

The pool was surrounded by piles of old tyres and rusting gas cylinders.

'Hard day at the office?'

His leathery tan suggested he was out here most days during the summer. He fancied himself; worked out a bit. His stomach was flat for a man his age, his arms muscular.

'Work, work, work,' he answered, smiling. 'What about a dip?'

'Detective Sergeant Cupidi,' she responded. 'I called you about an hour ago.'

The man took a gulp from his lager, stood, slid his feet into a pair of slip-on shoes. 'Like I told you, not much left. Hardly worth me buying it.'

'What do you mean?'

He put the can down beside the pool, ran his hand through his hair. 'Nobody wants old caravans. All we do is strip out anything that's worth taking. Fridges. Cookers. Foam fetches a bit these days, you'd be surprised. The rest goes for scrap or straight to the tip. Hardly anything of value in there.'

Cupidi followed him around the edge of the swimming pool. An oil drum, cut in half, made a barbecue. A fridge, presumably from one of the caravans, sat on a pallet, a long orange flex leading off towards the office.

'All mod cons,' said Cupidi, looking round.

'Ain't much, but it's my slice of heaven.' The man led her to a fence at the back of the yard and opened a small gate.

'Here you go,' he said. 'You're pretty flukey. I was planning on taking it to the scrap-metal merchant today, only the sun was out.'

Parked in a narrow lane behind the property was a dropside truck. Stacked upright on the back were sheets of aluminium, strapped together with webbing and rope. A couple of axles, a rusty wood-burning stove and lengths of chimney flue lay alongside them.

'Oh.'

'Yep. That's the caravan, said the man. 'What's left of it, anyway. I cut 'em up, see?'

'What about the contents?'

He jumped up onto the back of the truck's bed, looking down at her and rattling the sheets of aluminium. 'Weren't much else. Couple of books. A few photos. Burned those at the weekend. Lit the barbie with them. Spare ribs with sauce.'

'Brilliant,' said Cupidi.

'It's my job. Why you so interested, anyway?'

Cupidi looked at him. 'Because it's possible that this was a murder scene,' she said, looking at the remains of the caravan.

'You're having a laugh,' he said, standing in his snug black trunks.

'No. The caravan was brought in by Mr Eason. Did he sound keen to get rid of it?'

A shrug. 'Wanted a hundred for it. I offered him twenty. He took thirty in the end.'

'How did he react? Disappointed? Or so eager to get it off his hands he'd have taken anything?'

'Don't know. Man of few words, as I remember.'

'How did he get it here?'

'Towed it.'

'Do you remember the vehicle?'

'Ratty old Land Rover.' The orange one that had been parked in the yard.

'So, from what you saw of it before you smashed it up, what kind of woman lived in it?'

'Bit of a hippie, ask me. Woodburner. Dead giveaway.'

'Who was in the photographs?'

'Didn't really look. When it's a caravan someone's been living in, it's like house clearance. You don't want to get too caught up, do you?'

Sitting in her car on the breaker's forecourt, Cupidi called the incident room at Ashford on her mobile. Moon picked up. 'We'll have to impound it. Get it picked up from here somehow.

Though I'm not sure what we're looking for. There won't be any blood.'

Was there even any point? She dug in her handbag for something to eat and came up with one of the energy bars she had bought that morning; suddenly she didn't feel hungry anymore. She left it in the bag. 'What about the man in the slurry pit? McAdam said it was a murder investigation now?'

'The man had significant bruises on his body, apparently,' said Moon. 'It looks like he was assaulted.'

'What about Ferriter?'

'What do you mean?'

'You're her friend, aren't you?'

A pause.

'Sort of.'

'She likes you.'

'Does she?' Like he didn't know it already.

'So I assume you might have heard from her.'

'Yeah. She messaged me a couple of times. Think she's a bit shook up, to be honest. Says she wants to come back in, else it will do her head in.'

Still dressed in his trunks, the caravan-breaker was watching her from his office window. 'What else? Anything new on Hilary Keen?'

'We've managed to dig up some old arrest records from the eighties and nineties. And the dentist. The woman who treated Hilary Keen has retired, so we haven't been able to speak to her. They're trying to find contact details for her. We got him, though, haven't we? I bet you we'll find something that links him to her within the next twenty-four hours.'

'I'm glad you're sure.' As she turned the key in the ignition, something made her look round. Still dressed only in his swimming trunks, the caravan-breaker was running towards her shouting, 'Wait!'

He caught up with her, panting. She rolled down her window and turned off the engine.

'Just remembered something.'

In his office there was a large desk. While she stood waiting, he sat down on the chair behind it and pulled open a drawer full of papers. 'Hold on,' he said, still breathless. Rifling through it, he picked out a small, slightly faded, colour photograph. 'I kept that one, see? On account of the caravan. It's a classic.'

She took the picture from him and looked.

It was parked in a meadow; two boys, long-haired and grubby, sitting in front of it. It had been taken in late summer, around this time of year. The grass was long and dry, lit by low evening light. The oldest looked about eight; the younger maybe five or six. It was easy to see the similarity in their faces. They must be brothers. Shirts off, chests brown from living outdoors, the younger one sat on the step of the caravan, the other in a camping chair, both grinning at the camera.

On the caravan was written, in green paint: 'WE ARE WATER'.

'Why did you keep this one?'

'It's a classic two-door, built around 1970, I reckon. Look at the lines on that. Beautiful, isn't it. Still got the Royale badge on it.' He pointed to a small winged insignia at the front of the white streamlined mobile home. 'Royale Touranger. Not any of this modern rubbish. She must have liked it, too. It was pinned on the shelf above her bed.'

There was a small mark at the top of the picture, from where the dead woman had fixed it onto the wood. She looked at the picture for a long time, fingering the small indentation Keen had made in it.

THIRTEEN

She was late home, tired, dirty, hungry.

Tourists were sitting outside the Britannia Inn eating chips, basking in the evening light, seagulls padding around looking for leftovers. Artists had put their work out on displays by the road for everyone to see: paintings, sculptures made from plastic found on the beach.

Everybody seemed so happy. It was tempting to join them, to sit down with a large cold glass of wine. Filch a cigarette off someone. Find some swarthy fisherman to talk to. Anyone, really, who could just tell her ordinary stories about their lives. That would be nice.

But only this morning she had stood by a house where a man had tried to kill himself; time would tell if he had succeeded or not. Wine would only make her morose.

Besides, she had promised herself she wouldn't drink during the week. And Zoë would be waiting for her, wondering where she was.

*

Except she wasn't.

The house was locked. She let herself in to see if her daughter had left a note on the kitchen table, but she hadn't. She called her mobile and heard a soft buzzing from upstairs. When she looked in Zoë's bedroom, her phone was lying on the floor, plugged into her charger. The home screen showed only her own missed calls.

Slumped against the doorframe she looked around the tidy room, bed made, clothes folded on the chair, her daughter's careful drawings of birds on every wall. Was it normal for a teenager's bedroom to look like this?

Downstairs, she took a sheet of A4 from the printer and wrote 'CALL ME!!!!' on it, left it on the kitchen table, then locked the front door and set out again across the shingle, shouting her daughter's name.

A woman with a ponytail was jogging with her dog along the footpath. 'Have you seen a teenage girl?'

The jogger took out her ear buds. 'What?'

'Have you seen a teenage girl? Short hair. Purple streaks in it. Thin.'

The jogger shook her head. 'No. Hey. You were on the telly, weren't you?' She put her headphones back in and carried on jogging up the path.

It was eight in the evening. Zoë must be hungry. Did she have money for food?

Cursing, Cupidi got in her car and travelled the short distance to Arum Cottage. She was looking after it for the owner while he was away; nobody knew how long he would be gone. Sometimes Zoë let herself in here when she wanted to be alone. Cupidi banged on the door and peered in through the dark windows, but the house was empty. She got back in the car and drove around, peering between the beach huts and cabins as she drove. A rich smell of smoke and burning meat drifted over the promontory; people were having barbecues. Her stomach lurched. The smell of burning meat brought back this morning's horror; Stanley Eason's charred skin.

A car had its limits here. Many of the shingle banks were inaccessible except in a four-wheel drive. A fenced track leading to the power station cut the place in two. If you were in any vehicle, you had to go out onto the main road and travel halfway out to Lydd before you could head back in towards the bird reserve.

She sighed, stopped the car and checked her phone to see if her daughter was back at the house already, but no, she hadn't called. U-turning, she made her way back out to Dungeness Road, more anxious now.

She thought of the empty rib boat she had found. What if Zoë had come across men like that? No. They would be arriving at night, wouldn't they?

Would they?

The road was straight and clear. She drove fast, missing the turning the first time, then reversing back to it; a sandy track that crackled beneath her tyres.

There were still two dozen cars parked in the car park of the bird reserve. The visitors' centre was brightly lit, full of people gazing at chintzy tea-towels and porcelain mugs.

There was a small table and chairs by the huge window that looked out over the wetlands. The evening light pouring across the flatland from the west had turned the reeds that fringed the water a rich red. The water beyond was almost ridiculously full of bird-life.

Cupidi marched across the room, past the people browsing bird books, and climbed onto one of the chairs, noticing as she looked down at her blouse that there was still a black smudge on it that must have been there all day; one she must have missed when she had tried to clean up.

Close by, a woman wearing a headscarf covered in horseshoes looked at her, startled.

Cupidi was too tired to mind making a fool of herself. Above the quiet chatter of the room, she called out, 'Has anybody here seen a fifteen-year-old girl on the reserve? Bleached hair with purple in it. Possibly with binoculars.'

People turned. The room was silent, baffled by her outburst, until the woman behind the till said, quietly, 'Zoë, you mean?'

'You know her?'

'Little Zoë? Is she your daughter?'

'Have you seen her?'

'Well, no,' said the woman. 'Not today. She doesn't usually come in this way. She's not actually a member. She just sneaks in over Springfield Bridge. We don't mind.'

'You let an unaccompanied teenager just walk about?'

'We encourage it, really,' said the woman, smiling at her. 'Are you OK?'

Cupidi climbed down from the chair. 'Not really.' She looked around. Everyone was looking at her like she was mad. 'So. Where is Springfield Bridge?'

The woman picked up a printed map of the reserve.

'Thin-looking strip of a thing?' said an elderly man in corduroy trousers.

'Yes.'

'Down by Christmas Dell an hour ago. Nice girl. There are spoonbills there today. I expect she's been watching them.'

'You spoke to her?'

'She didn't really talk very much,' said the man. 'Fine by me.'

'Where is it?' asked Cupidi, and by now people were crowding around the till with fingers pointing at the map.

'I saw her down here,' said one woman, gesturing through the glass towards another of the ponds.

'She was definitely at the Dell hide an hour ago.'

'Do you see her here often?'

'Quite a lot, yes. She's no bother.'

'Is she in some kind of trouble?' someone else asked.

'God, yes,' muttered Cupidi.

Clutching the map, Cupidi pushed out of the door beyond the till and walked fast down the tracks, passing streams of birdwatchers who had called it a day and were coming the other way, towards her.

'I'm looking for a teenage girl. Have you seen her?'

Spooked by the way she stomped down the pathway, a huge flock of geese erupted noisily from one of the black patches of water, slapping wings on the water, honking as they rose into the air.

Cupidi paused, amazed by the number of birds suddenly filling the sky. She looked up at them as they wheeled in the dark blueness above her head. The sheer scale of nature here was awesome; disturbing.

Setting off again, sweating in the evening heat, she broke into a trot as she found another sign pointing to Christmas Dell hide.

'Zoë!' she called.

More birds flapped away, startled by her shout. A young man in army fatigues glared at her angrily as she passed.

She burst into the hide, expecting to see her daughter inside. It was like a long wooden railway carriage with a thin window down one side, overlooking a huge marshy lake dotted with birds, but the benches were empty. No one was here.

Running out again she paused to look, and saw a slender figure on the far side of another stretch of water to the east. 'Zoë!' she called.

The person continued tramping away along a track that headed towards the coast.

'Zoë!'

The girl stopped. Turned. Raised binoculars, then after a couple of seconds, waved.

'How many times do I have to tell you?'

'I don't know. You tell me.'

'I was worried. What if something happened?'

'It didn't. It never does.'

She couldn't help it. She tried not to lose her temper with the girl, but sometimes it was hard.

'You're infuriating.'

Zoë just tramped silently alongside her mother as they returned to the visitor centre. Cupidi's feet hurt; she was wearing the wrong shoes for walking over this uneven ground for what felt like bloody miles.

'Look, love. I've had an ultra shitty day, and all I want to do is sit on the sofa. If you'd taken your phone . . .'

The last of the low sun was casting a rich purple light across the reedbeds and stones. That only made it worse.

When they reached the visitors' centre, the woman behind the till smiled. 'You found her, then? Good. See anything much, Zoë?'

'Arctic tern.'

'Are you sure?'

'Yes,' said Zoë. 'I was watching it for an hour.'

'Gosh. How exciting. I'll add it to the record.'

'Yes. Flew off when my mum got there, though, she was making such a racket.'

'Well, I'm sorry,' said Cupidi. They looked at her as if she were the one who had behaved badly, not her daughter.

When the car door was unlocked, Zoë got in silently and pulled her seatbelt across.

They drove in back towards the cottage without saying another word. Cupidi stopped outside the Britannia. 'I haven't had time to cook,' she said.

'I don't like pubs,' said Zoë.

'Well I do,' said Cupidi, getting out. 'Come on.'

The decor was faux nautical – pine walls and brass fittings, a ship's wheel hung from the ceiling with a specials board attached to it. She chose battered cod and chips and a large dry white wine. Zoë said she just wanted tomato soup.

'Aren't you hungry?' She was starving, herself. She was desperate for a shower, but needed to eat even more.

'I thought you weren't going to drink wine during the week,' said Zoë.

'Today is an exception. I have had the crappiest day imaginable.'

Zoë scowled. 'You shouldn't drink so much.'

'I don't.' A gale of laughter came from a group standing at the bar. They were talking about something funny and trivial. Cupidi envied them right now.

'Let's talk about something else, shall we? You said you were watching a bird. For an hour. You have so much patience.'

Her daughter made a face. 'Arctic tern,' she said.

Cupidi pulled her phone from her and googled it. 'Wow,' she said. 'It says here it migrates almost fifty-five thousand miles, from the north of the planet, right down to the south, and then back again. It's the longest migration known in the animal kingdom.'

Zoë said, 'Yes.'

'That's amazing.'

'Yes.'

Cupidi pinched out the picture. 'And it's so tiny.'

Zoë shrugged.

'I mean. Don't you wonder why? It's crazy. Using all that energy.'

'No.'

Cupidi leaned forward and took a large mouthful of wine. 'Surely you've got to wonder. Why it does it?'

'I don't wonder. I know,' said her daughter wearily. 'It's not crazy at all. It's just nature. It's to do with food and daylight length. The Arctic tern needs to feed every hour of light there is. Close to the Arctic Circle, where it would have been coming from, the days are longer in summer.'

Another burst of laughter from the group by the bar.

'About fifteen hours here, this time of year. In the Southern Ocean they're longer in winter. They need to be where the days are longest so they can feed for the longest time. It's simple. So they go up and then down. And up again.'

'OK. That's amazing,' said Cupidi.

'Yes. Amazing. Wow,' said Zoë, unsmiling.

'I'm just trying to be interested in what you're interested in.'

'Now that *is* amazing,' said Zoë.

'That's mean.'

'Yes. I'm sorry.'

They sat together in silence. Cupidi said, 'The food is taking ages. What's wrong, pickle?'

'Nothing.'

'Something has to be,' said Cupidi. 'You're being weird.'

'You're being weird.'

'OK. I'll leave it.'

Cupidi stood and went to the bar to ask about when the food would be there. While she was there she ordered another glass of wine.

'You're the copper, in't you?' said one of the men by the bar.

'Yes.'

'Found out who that woman was yet? The one up Salt Lane?'

'We think so, yes.'

'Found out who killed her yet?'

She gritted her teeth, smiled. 'We are working on several lines of enquiry,' she said.

'What's taking so long?'

The laughter had stopped now. They were all looking at her seriously, as if waiting for her to say something important. What could she say? They would charge the man if he regained consciousness, though there was a good chance he wouldn't.

But when she looked back to her daughter, sitting alone at a round wooden table with a glass of Coca-Cola in front of her, she saw tears pouring down the girl's face. In the middle of the pub, her daughter was crying.

'Excuse me,' she said and strode back across the room, to her daughter. Cupidi pulled her chair round next to her and wrapped her in her arms.

'What's wrong, darling?' Zoë was shaking now, big drops rolling down her face onto her T-shirt.

'I want to go,' said Zoë. 'I don't like it here.'

Cupidi looked up. The group of men and women at the bar were all staring at them. The food she had paid for had not arrived yet, but she stood, taking her daughter's hand and leading her outside.

It was dark now. Far away, waves rippled on the stones. The tide must be low.

'What is it?' They stood on the shingle on the other side of the road from the pub. 'Just talk to me, Zoë. Please.'

Between sobs her daughter said, 'I don't know what it is. It's just that all the time I feel so sad. And it's just so big.'

'Are you lonely?'

'No.'

'Is someone being cruel to you? Someone from school?'

Shaking her head, Zoë said, 'No. It's not like that. It's nothing like that at all.'

'Come on, let's get you home.'

Cupidi holding her girl's arm, they walked past the odd cabin and shack. The beam from the new lighthouse swept over their heads.

'Are you missing London? Your old friends?'

'Maybe. I don't know. I don't think so.'

'Are you missing your dad? You know you can see him whenever you want.' Her father lived in Cornwall with his new girlfriend and their children.

'No. It's not that.'

'I just want to know.' Cupidi tried not to let her frustration show. She had always blamed her mother's brusqueness for finding it so hard to communicate with her; but here she was, floundering just as badly as her mother had. She loosened her grip on the girl. 'Have you done something wrong?'

'Mum. Why on earth would you think that?' Zoë wailed.

'I'm sorry. I'm just trying to help.'

'I don't know what it is. You always think there's got to be an answer. Maybe there's not. I just feel so sad all the time.'

'You're a teenager,' tried Cupidi.

Zoë grasped her arm again; clung on tight.

She had always believed she would be so much better at this than her mother had been. And she had always blamed her mother for everything that had gone wrong between them.

Zoë leaned against her, then recoiled. 'Oh God. You smell,' her daughter said, stepping away. 'Your hair stinks.'

'Long story.'

Ahead, the lights of the power station blared in the darkness. When had she stopped being able to talk to her daughter? Without her noticing, a gulf had grown between them.

That night, after she'd showered to get the stink of the fire off her, she opened the wine. After two more glasses she was ready to call her mother.

'Are you still awake? I need to talk to you,' she said.

'Of course I'm awake.'

Why did she find it so hard to tell her mum that she needed her?

Afterwards, she tried to start the novel that her book group had chosen. It was crime fiction of some kind set in Sweden. The plot was grisly and ridiculous and she found herself picking apart inaccuracies in basic procedure. She had promised herself she would finish it.

But she couldn't concentrate. Zoë was in the next room. Cupidi could feel her unhappiness pulsing through the walls.

After ten pages she found the book dropping from her hands.

FOURTEEN

The incident room was empty when she arrived; it was early. She checked the corridors. No one was in. She wouldn't be disturbed for a while. So, alone at her desk, she dialled Whitechapel CID.

'Oh,' said David Colquhoun, when she was finally put through. 'It's you.' Then, to someone else in the room, 'Excuse me a minute. I just need to take this call.'

'Is it a bad time?'

'Diary meeting with the Commissioner's office.' He lowered his voice and added, 'Couldn't be better.'

'Superintendent now, I hear? Things must be bad there, then?'

'Let me just close the door,' he said, and the noise of the office behind him vanished. 'How great to hear from you. I've been wondering how you are. Pretty much on a daily basis. How are you settling in down there?'

It was good to hear his voice again as well. It was always full of warmth and enthusiasm; she used to mock it, saying he sounded like a vicar. 'It was you calling the other night, wasn't it? Zoë picked up the phone.'

A short pause. 'God, yes. I'm sorry. I'd had a couple of drinks. Normally I resist. Did she know who was calling?'

'I don't think so.'

'Daft. Sorry. Shouldn't have.'

'No,' she said. 'You shouldn't.'

'Neither should you.'

'This,' she said, 'is work.'

'If it was work, you'd have called my assistant.'

'What's the use of friends in high places?' she said.

When she'd split from Zoë's father she'd slept with a few men. None were real relationships. They were just a series of one-night stands, sometimes with the same man; the kind of life it was easy enough to fall into on the force, when the hours were long and the days intense. But David had been different. As with so many affairs between coppers, alcohol had been involved. They had both been at an excruciatingly dull, day-long Home Office seminar on digital crime, and in the bar afterwards they'd waited side by side for ten minutes to be served. All she'd said was, 'Denial of Service Attack,' and nobody had got it but David Colquhoun, who'd laughed so loudly, even though the joke was pretty thin, that she insisted on buying the drink for him when the barman finally arrived.

David had been a rising senior officer in a different department. He had a boyish face she found oddly sexy and claimed to know the words to every Black Grape song. He was kind, understanding and discreet. And because he was happily married to Cathy, who regularly posted photos of them and their three children on Facebook, he'd wanted to keep it that way – which just how Alex had liked it. At first he would say how guilty he felt about the affair. 'End it then,' she had said. But he hadn't. He enjoyed catching her eye in the canteen, or passing in a corridor, sharing a space in a lift, knowing that nobody knew. She had enjoyed it too.

They had been careful. The weekends that Zoë visited her father, he would sometimes come over and they would drink wine and have sex. They would go and see Xavier Dolan films at the Renoir, knowing that there was little risk of colleagues being at an art house movie.

But somebody had found out. Somehow. No surprise, really. They were working in a job where everyone around them was paid to suspect and to see through lies and deceptions.

One day, her boss called her into the office, and there was some woman from the Practice Support Team standing next to him. She asked if Cupidi was having an affair with a married officer. In front of the DCI, she had had to deny it. And that had been the end of it. She never knew how they'd been found out, but because he was married and a senior officer, they had ended up deciding it was too risky. The best thing would be for her to move away. They ended it, and that was that. She was not sorry. It was done.

'I need a favour,' she said.

'What?'

'I'm looking for a homeless woman who's been seen on your patch. Mid-forties. May have given her name as Hilary Keen, but that's not her real name.'

'What is, then?'

'We don't know.'

Cupidi gave him the description of the woman Julian and Lulu Keen had given her.

'I'll see what I can do. If she's still around here it shouldn't be too difficult.' He paused. 'It's actually good to hear your voice.'

'Yours too.'

'Tell me why you need this. It's not just about a homeless woman, is it?'

'It's a case. A dead woman who this woman was impersonating. I think it's going to be mothballed unless I can find something good.'

'Oh. One of those.'

'What do you mean.'

'I know you. The way you become sometimes. It's one of your babies. The ones you don't want to let go.'

'You make it sound like something irrational, David. It's not at all. The woman was murdered. We may have found her killer, but . . .'

'But what?'

'But . . . just but. It doesn't quite make sense to me. I need to know why she died.'

'I like it when you're passionate.'

She laughed.

'I'll see what I can do. I promise.'

'OK.'

They faltered.

'Right,' he said. 'Got to go.'

'Me too,' she said, put down the phone and stood. The office around her was still empty; it felt suddenly very provincial here, and far away from the fast-paced, busy offices she had worked in in London.

Fifteen minutes later, at 8.30 in the morning, she stood on a sodden carpet dressed in her protective suit, addressing officers.

'First, anything that explains who Hilary Keen was and what she was doing living in Eason's backyard.' They were gathered downstairs in Stanley Eason's front room, armchairs piled to one side, damp wallpaper peeling off the walls. 'Any property that might have belonged to her. Any mentions of her name or who she was. Bank statements, a rent book, anything. It's possible that Eason took her mobile phone. Look for cash. It's also possible that he stole money from the victim at some point.'

She had been in enough of them to know the stink of burnt houses, of charred wood and every pungent chemical stench set loose by flame. The windows had been opened, but it made little difference. It clung.

The house was surrounded by tape; its entire ground floor was still wet from the water the firemen had poured onto the house. They had pulled a tarp over the wrecked roof to protect it from the elements.

Two constables stood waiting for her to tell them what to do. A bigger team would have helped.

'Secondly, anything that might relate to or explain her murder. That is going to be harder. We are still not sure how she died. The current theory from the pathologists is some kind of asphyxiation. Any material that hints of a sexual motive for the killing. Hilary Keen was not sexually attacked, but rule nothing out.'

'Jesus. Is that a rat?' One of the policemen pointed at a sodden dark shape in the corner of the room. Evidently Eason wasn't the only victim of the fire.

'Fortunate we're all wearing protective clothing, isn't it?' said Cupidi.

'This paper suit ain't protecting me from nothing.'

'I hate rats.'

'Boys.' She clapped her hands. 'Come on. Pay attention. Finally, use your instincts. This whole case is a weird one. We don't know how she was killed or why. We're looking for anything that might give us an insight into this man and his relationship with the murdered woman.'

'Instincts?' said the older of the constables.

'He didn't have a computer, but is there a diary? Letters, photographs, mementoes. Right?'

'So. Pretty much anything,' said the man.

'I suppose that's a reasonable way of putting it,' said Cupidi. 'Pretty much anything.'

'So we don't know what we're looking for at all?'

'Socrates would say that is an advantage,' said Cupidi.

'Who's that when he's at home?' asked the younger copper.

'He's that new Crime Commissioner,' said the older one. Cupidi wasn't entirely sure he was joking.

As they started their work on the ground floor, she went upstairs to the bedroom where Eason had set fire to himself.

The sunlight filtering through the tarp bathed the place in blue light. Up here the reek of smoke penetrated everything. Everything – sheets, carpets, clothes, furniture – was covered in a black oily film. It was a double bed, spread with a pile of blankets.

On the bedside table, next to a radio, was a photograph, entirely obscured by the blackness. She picked it up and wiped the glass with her blue plastic glove.

A black-and-white picture emerged of a man and a woman at a wedding. In it, a young Stanley Eason stood stiff-backed, unsmiling but proud, next to a black-haired woman, shorter than him, with a plain face, who squinted into the camera. It must have been taken outside one of the local Marsh churches. *Keeps himself to himself since his wife died*, Cupidi remembered the man in the garden centre saying.

She pulled open the bedside drawer; it contained a Bible, a blister pack of indigestion pills and a box of buttons. She left them; one of the constables would later come and record this room methodically.

Underneath the layer of soot, the place looked neglected. There were piles of newspapers and farming magazines lined up along the wall and a collection of old wellington boots in another corner. She wandered to the bathroom and opened the smoke-blackened window, leaning out.

The caravan where Hilary Keen had lived would have been parked beneath it.

One of the coppers emerged from the back door with an armful of coats and dropped them down onto the ground. He then picked one up and started going through the pockets.

'Anything?' she called down.

'Pile of his bank statements, that's all so far. I've bagged them. Reckon we'll find anything?'

'We won't know until we do,' she said, though she wasn't any more certain than he was that there was anything here to find.

Outside, she was grateful for clean air. She lifted up the tape and was walking under it as a car pulled up. 'Is he going to be OK?' the driver called from his window.

Cupidi recognised him as the cashier from the garden centre whom she had spoken to the day before. 'I hope so.'

'They're saying he killed someone, is that right?'

'We were trying to speak to him in relation to a possible murder. That's all we're able to say at present, sir.'

'Same thing, though, isn't it?' The man didn't drive off; just sat there with the engine running as if waiting for something. 'Terrible, isn't it? I mean, you'd never have guessed. Always seemed such a quiet chap. Still waters. There was always something odd about him.'

Only yesterday, according to this man, Eason had been a victim of police harassment.

She paused, wondering if there was something else he wanted to say. You had to be open. People volunteered their part of the story in many ways.

But he just sat there staring at her, and she stood by the car, until it became embarrassing. He was just another rubberneck.

'Oi, Sarge! Something you should see.'

She turned and went back into the house. 'Here, in the kitchen.'

She followed the voice. It was dark in there. Someone had secured the window she'd smashed by screwing a large sheet of chipboard over the frame. Her feet crunched on broken glass.

The man was holding the door to Eason's old freezer. Thick pink blood was oozing out, down the pale door and onto the floor.

'This lot's going to start stinking,' he said.

'Meat?'

'Yeah. But it's not that.' He shone a torch into the compartment. Next to the packets of defrosting meat was a blue plastic bag full of rolled banknotes. There had to be several hundred pounds there. 'Bingo,' he said, grinning.

FIFTEEN

When she arrived back at the incident room, she saw that McAdam had added a photo to the whiteboard. The face of the dead man from the slurry pit, skin washed clean, eyes half closed. The chairs around the table were only half full. It was high summer. With the holiday season they were low on numbers.

Cupidi was digging in her bag, struggling to find a pen that must have fallen to the bottom, pulling out lipstick and mascara, when the constable next to her stood and started clapping. Others joined in. Cupidi looked around, and there at the door was Constable Ferriter, pink T-shirt and skirt, smiling back at them.

Cupidi stood, too, and joined in the applause, and now the whole room was clapping a young copper. 'Proud of you, Constable,' said McAdam, smiling.

'God. Don't. I'm embarrassed,' said Ferriter, though she didn't appear to be. She made her way to the empty seat next to Cupidi.

'Though make sure you don't do anything that reckless again. We're short enough on staff anyway,' said McAdam.

Clapping changed briefly to laughter.

'So. First things first. Anything from Eason's house?'

'Maybe,' said Cupidi. 'We've found a roll of notes. It doesn't prove anything, of course, but it may have been money that Stanley Eason stole from Hilary Keen's caravan. We're sending it to forensics to see if we can trace Hilary Keen's prints on it. It's not exactly a smoking gun because we know she paid him rent, so even if she's all over the notes, it's possible he came by the money through legal means.'

'Good. Good. Any news on how Eason's doing?'

'Not great. He regained consciousness last night for a couple of hours but was incoherent, and this morning he's back in the coma. He appears to have multiple organ failure, including a heart problem of some sort.'

McAdam seemed to shrink a little. If Eason died, it would be difficult for him.

'And the caravan you spoke about? Did you find that?'

'Sort of.'

'Sort of?' McAdam frowned.

Cupidi explained what she'd found at the breaker's yard. 'I had it impounded but to be honest, there wasn't much there.'

'Right,' said McAdam resignedly. 'All we have so far that suggests guilt is the money and Eason's behaviour, then?'

Cupidi frowned and was about to answer, but McAdam continued. 'We're now concentrating our resources on the body at Horse Bones Farm. This is what we know. Victim is aged at around thirty. Probably North African origin. So, Algerian,

Tunisian, Moroccan, Egyptian, Libyan. Possibly Syrian even. No name. No identifying details. He was in good health when he died.'

The photo in the centre of the board was of the man's head and bare shoulders. His eyes were half open and the skin had sunk down towards his skull; the relaxed muscles of the unmistakably dead. 'So who was he?'

'The gentleman had no papers on him. No ID of any kind was found,' said Ferriter. 'The coastguards have been warning about the uptick of boats arriving on the coast. I'd guess he was one of them.'

Cupidi paused from rummaging in her bag.

'An uptick,' repeated Ferriter. 'A rise. Like on a graph.'

'I didn't say anything,' Cupidi protested, and went back to delving.

'So what was he doing on the farm?' asked McAdam.

'The barn was pretty isolated. He was hiding, I presume,' said Ferriter. 'Finding a place where he could conceal himself from the authorities. Sufficiently far from the house to avoid notice from anyone living there.'

'Maybe it was the farmer found him,' suggested a constable. 'Didn't like the idea of someone trespassing. You know what they're like.'

'It was the farmer reported him dead,' said Ferriter. 'And the farmer who showed us where he'd been sleeping.'

'All the same, it's possible,' said McAdam.

'It didn't look to me like he'd slept there for more than one night,' added Cupidi, pulling a packet of Anadin Extra out of the bag and adding it to the pile on the table in front of her. 'If someone homeless has been in a place for a while there would be signs he'd eaten there. The place would have looked more used. I think he was there one night, two at the very most. He was on the move.'

McAdam nodded. 'Good.'

Cupidi continued. 'But he had made a serious attempt to hide himself. He'd built himself a kind of bunker in the hay. So the question is, who was he hiding from? The farmer? Goes without saying. But maybe other people as well. If he was killed, maybe he was running from whoever killed him. What about the signs he had been assaulted?'

'Which brings us to these,' McAdam said, turning his laptop round so the rest of them could see the screen. 'What do you see?'

Cupidi finally found a biro and looked up. He was scrolling slowly through a slideshow of photographs, each showing a different part of the murder victim's torso and limbs. Each showed at least one dark semi-circular mark; some several, clustered together. Some had laid a white ruler on the dead skin.

'They're like . . . moon shapes,' said Ferriter, peering at a photo of the man's thigh on which the maroon C-shape was clearly visible.

'Is that religious? Like a crescent?' somebody chipped in. 'That's a Muslim thing, isn't it? And the dead guy, he's a Muslim isn't he? Some kind of ritual killing?'

They moved on to the next picture. 'It's not a crescent. Some of them are round.'

McAdam read aloud from a printed report: 'The ecchymoses are all the same size, of a diameter of around five centimetres, and would suggest repeated blows with a single weapon. We haven't got any more yet.'

'Ecchymoses?'

'Doctor-speak for bruises,' said Cupidi.

'So he was . . . tortured?'

Those who had laptops with them tapped keys, searching for the folder containing the pictures on their own devices. Others stood and crowded McAdam's end of the table so they could get a closer look. Cupidi leaned in. It was more than just bruising. The force of the assault meant that the victim's skin had been ruptured in a couple of places.

'Is it a weapon of some sort?'

'I know what that is. Scaffolding,' said Cupidi.

'What?'

'The end of a scaffolding pole.'

For a second, nobody spoke.

'Two, maybe three people, holding scaffolding poles,' she continued. She mimed hefting a long heavy pole and jabbing it towards Ferriter, who was standing next to her. 'That would make that mark. They drove him into the pit. Like an animal.'

'No need to look so enthusiastic,' complained Ferriter.

'Just demonstrating.'

'Jesus,' said a constable, looking at his phone. 'You're right. Diameter of a scaffolding pole, 48.3 millimetres, says Google.'

'So *they*? Two people? More?'

'There's no mention of ligature marks on the body?' asked Cupidi.

'No,' said a copper who had the report open in front of him.

'So if he wasn't tied up, we can assume it wasn't one person, going for it.'

Cupidi turned again towards the photographs. 'The bruises are all around his body. The victim was a fit young man. Plus, those poles are heavy. They're, what, two metres long, even the short ones? You couldn't swing them easily and if it was just one person, it would be easy to get away. He was trying to get away from a bunch of them, ask me. You'd need at least three people, or a man like him could just dodge them. I'd guess it was a few of them – four, maybe five.'

'A gang.'

'Know what? I think I remember there were scaffolding poles in the hay barn,' said one of the officers. 'A pile just inside the door.'

'Did you log them, Peter?' McAdam looked at Moon. 'Are there photos on the shared drive?'

It would have been Moon's job. He had been in charge of the scene that day.

'That was where the victim had sheltered, I understand,' said McAdam.

Moon hesitated. He hadn't gone into the barn. 'Yeah . . . but—'

Ferriter butted in. 'My fault, sir. Sergeant Moon tasked me with recording the barn. I didn't notice them, sir. Sorry.'

After yesterday, Ferriter was the golden girl. Nobody minded her not noticing.

McAdam turned to Moon and said, 'That was your responsibility, Moon. Get down there right away after this meeting and collect them. Hopefully they haven't been contaminated further.'

Then he turned to the rest of the team. 'So these injuries may suggest that he was hiding from more than just the farmer.'

'Yeah. Well. If they're the sort of people who do something like that –' Cupidi pointed at the screen – 'you'd hide from them, wouldn't you?'

'What's this about, then? Drugs? People-smuggling?'

Nobody answered.

'Two deaths,' said Cupidi at last. 'Both bodies disposed on farmland, about five miles apart.'

There was a moment of silence.

'Are you suggesting there's a connection between the two?' asked McAdam.

'Doubt it,' volunteered one copper. 'The dead man at Horse Bones Farm was young and fit. I can't see him being killed by a man Eason's age. Just don't see it. Different offenders.'

'That's assuming Eason killed Hilary Keen,' said Ferriter. 'Everything we have on Eason so far is circumstantial.'

Cupidi looked at her curiously. It was a point. What if Keen's killer wasn't Eason at all?

McAdam pressed his fingers together. 'Like the constable says, I believe we should assume this is a separate case,' he said. 'Different methodology.'

'Listen, though,' interrupted Ferriter loudly. 'Up to now, we don't have anything that strong on Eason. Nothing that would stand up.'

As she spoke, Cupidi watched the frown form on McAdam's face. If the killer was Eason, then he could brush off criticism of how he'd handled the siege at the house. But if it wasn't, then he might find himself in trouble.

Ferriter ploughed on. 'If we can't just take it for granted he killed her, we can't assume they're different cases.'

Suddenly everyone was talking. 'So why did he try to top himself when you turned up at his door?'

'I have that effect on people,' said Cupidi, before anyone else could. There was murmuring in the room.

'Well,' said McAdam. 'Obviously it's important to consider that point, Jill. Thank you. Well done.'

Not understanding the implications for their boss, Ferriter looked around the room, pleased with herself.

Digging in her bag again, Cupidi pulled out the envelope and removed the photograph. 'Oh. And there's this.'

She stepped forward to the whiteboard and added it to an empty space on the right of the picture of the face of the dead man.

'What is it?'

'It's a photo that was recovered from Hilary Keen's caravan. She kept it above her bed.'

'Her kids? I thought she only had one,' said Ferriter, peering at the photo.

'Maybe. But neither of them is Julian, I don't think. He was taken away from her when he was two. They're older.'

'They look like brothers.'

'I don't know who it is or where it was taken,' said Cupidi. What if Julian had other brothers, she wondered? He would want to know.

'What does that say? "We are water"? What's that?'

There was a pause until McAdam spoke: 'I'm not entirely sure I see the relevance, frankly.'

'Neither am I,' said Cupidi, staring at the photo. 'Frankly.'

McAdam turned to Ferriter. 'So tell me why you think the two deaths are connected?'

'I didn't say that at all. The point is, we can't assume Stanley Eason killed Hilary Keen, can we?'

'And if that's true,' said Cupidi, 'then we can't rule out that the two deaths are not linked in some way.'

McAdam nodded slowly. 'Will you look into that, then, Alex? If there's something that links Eason to the death of Hilary Keen, find it. If there isn't . . .'

'Right.'

'Given that we have seriously limited feet on the ground, we'll concentrate our other efforts on the murder of the young man, around which there is considerable sensitivity right now. Right. Actions.'

Ordering officers to widen the cordon around Horse Bones Farm and question the locals within a three-kilometre radius of the murder location, he picked out one of the older men to look at the gang angle. 'Get on to the Regional Organised Crime Unit. Cannabis farms, heroin, trafficking. Ask them what they've got. Get it all written up on HOLMES before you make a move. Any questions? Oh. And one more task. Who hasn't got enough on their plate?' McAdam looked around the room, searching for another officer to give the job to. 'We need someone to research the North African angle.'

'North African?'

'Yes. Find local communities. Liaise with them. See if anyone knows the victim and can identify him.'

Cupidi looked around the room. Everyone had already been given tasks. She sighed, raised her hand. 'I'll do it.'

He nodded, snapped his laptop shut and stood.

Afterwards, in the Ladies, standing in front of the mirror, she called to Ferriter, who was sitting in a cubicle behind her. 'What is it about Moon, sticking up for him like that? "My fault, sir."'

'It *was* my fault. I said I'd do it.'

'It was his job. Not yours. He's lazy.'

'You don't know him. He's nice. He's asked me out, Saturday.'

There was the sound of a flushing toilet.

'Did he now?'

'Nothing serious, obviously.'

'Obviously. You were right about one thing, though. We can't be sure it's Eason.'

Ferriter emerged and turned on a tap with her unbandaged hand. 'We'll know when he wakes up, though, won't we?'

'So far, I've not heard anything about any bruises on Hilary Keen,' said Cupidi. 'And no obvious sign of trauma. We still don't know how she died. It's incredibly frustrating. We don't know anything about her.'

'Weird, isn't it?'

'And like you said, whoever put her in the water knew exactly what they were doing.'

'Did I say that?'

'In as many words. To my daughter, the day before yesterday.'

'Yeah. I suppose I did. What is it about this one?'

'What do you mean?'

'It's like . . . you've made this woman your personal thing, haven't you?'

Cupidi didn't respond at first. She put her hands under the tap and cleaned them slowly, feeling cold water over her hands. 'It's always like that, with a murder, isn't it?'

'I suppose,' said Ferriter.

'When we were at my mum's, you asked about that photo. Alexandra, my aunt.'

'Sorry. Yes. None of my beeswax.'

'At the age of sixteen, she disappeared. They didn't find her for days. When they did, they discovered she'd been sexually assaulted, then left, naked in a ditch.'

'Christ.'

'Yes.' Cupidi put her hands under the dryer. 'Big thing for my mother, obviously, growing up with that happening.' She spoke over the roar of hot air. 'It wasn't like she talked about it, but it was always there.'

The penny dropped. 'You were named after a murdered girl.'

'That's right.'

'You grew up with that story?'

Cupidi nodded.

'Jesus. That's a bit fuckin' weird, isn't it? Shit. Sorry. Didn't mean to put it like that.'

'Yes. It is.' Cupidi took her hands away from the dryer and the room was suddenly quiet again. 'A bit fucking weird.'

'Sorry. Didn't know.'

Cupidi paused. 'I don't usually tell people.'

Fumbling with her bandaged hand, Ferriter unzipped her cosmetics bag. 'Eason had a temper on him, didn't he?'

'Exactly. He might have been capable of murder, I just don't see him planning something that carefully. Not so that we're still trying to figure out how she died.'

Ferriter tugged the cap of an eyeliner pencil with her mouth. When she had removed it and put it on the sink, she spoke again. 'When I was assigned to you, I thought you didn't like me,' she said.

'Who says I do?' said Cupidi, unsmiling.

Ferriter laughed, a high, tinkly laugh, and set about touching up her eye make-up, one-handed.

SIXTEEN

Cupidi spent the rest of the morning alone in the incident room, answering other people's phone calls while she worked through a list of council services, agencies and refugee charities. It was slow work. The men and women she spoke to were either evasive or outwardly hostile to her because she was a police officer looking for information about migrants.

'That's not the kind of information we share,' a nice middle-class woman at a charity in Canterbury told her.

'I'm not asking for your bank account details. I'm just trying to talk to a few people.'

'Perhaps if you put the request in writing?'

A man from the Border Agency at Dover was more helpful. 'Yeah. Most weeks. North Africans all claim asylum of course. It's a joke.'

'And where do they end up?'

'All over the place. They're here for a few hours and then we send them on. Some to detention centres, some to hostels. A load get carted straight off to the Removal Centres. We've got a few short-term holding places where we'll keep them while they're being processed. Loads of the ones we release abscond anyway before their asylum hearings. You wouldn't believe the half of it.'

'So he might have been through your hands. Or another centre?'

'Have you checked his fingerprints on the database?'

'There's nothing.'

'Not one of ours, then. We fingerprint all of them.'

'So if this guy's an illegal migrant, he's one of the ones who got through without you knowing?'

'Don't quote me on that, but it's entirely possible. There's only a handful of us. What do you expect? Come on down. Not now – there's a ferry just coming in on the tide. Best time today is around four. Warn you, though, it's pretty basic here.'

Afterwards, a half-eaten cheese sandwich from Greggs in one hand, she spent half an hour improvising a poster, using the photograph of the man and Google Translate to turn the phrase 'Do you know this man?' into Arabic and hoping that what she was pasting made some kind of sense. Then she added Uzbek, Kurdish, Pashto and Persian, just for the hell of it.

On her way to Dover, she stopped in Sandgate. The dental practice had tracked down Hilary Keen's former dentist: the one who had retired. She had just moved into a flat there.

A modern block, five storeys high, on a sweep of coast away from the more run-down bits of Kent's seaside; the kind of place people went to die. The dentist lived on the third floor. She buzzed Cupidi up. The stairs smelt of disinfectant and nylon carpet.

They stood in her small living room staring out at the sea through the large French windows that opened onto a balcony that was just wide enough for a small table and chair.

'Wonderful view,' said Cupidi.

'Isn't it,' said the dentist, as if she needed persuading. 'It's not often quite this blue. They say it's going to rain this afternoon. Tea?'

The flat had been newly painted. Photographs of children and grandchildren had been carefully hung on the wall, alongside a chubby gilded plaster angel.

'You were Hilary Keen's dentist?' she called through the door as the woman boiled the kettle in her kitchen. 'Can I show you a photograph? I should warn you, it's of the victim after she died. And she had been in the water for several days at this point.'

Cupidi waited until the woman had returned with a teapot, cups and saucers, and then lifted up the picture.

'Yes. That's her.'

'You're sure? That's the woman you treated?'

'Absolutely.'

'Do you remember any conversations you may have had with her?'

'She wasn't really the type to have conversations with. She was very quiet.'

It was just what the doctor had told Ferriter. *She kept herself to herself.*

'Anything at all?'

'But I do recall she had awful teeth.'

'Really?'

'I had put crowns on quite a few of them. Veneer too. I don't remember how many.'

'That must have been expensive.'

'God, yes. It was. Hundreds and hundreds, all told. It would have been thousands altogether over the years I worked on her. Doesn't come cheap.'

'So she had money?' Cupidi thought of the caravan parked in a squalid yard. Curious.

'Must have done. Biscuit?'

Cupidi declined. The cheese sandwich she had eaten in the office still sat heavily in her stomach.

'Do you remember how she paid?'

'How she paid? No. That was usually dealt with by the front desk. I remember she always asked how much it was going to cost, though, before I went ahead and wrote it down in her diary. As if she wasn't sure she would have enough.'

'Or as if she needed to know how much cash to bring?'

'I suppose, yes, maybe.'

A pair of yachts moved slowly across the water in front of them, about a quarter of a mile out at sea. Again, it suggested that money might have been the motive. Eason was broke; Keen kept cash. Then again, where was Keen getting that kind of money from? She didn't have a bank account. There was no record of her paying tax on any income. So was she doing something off the books that paid her good amounts of cash?

'How long had she been at your practice?'

'I think about five years. Possibly six. Lord, I remember her turning up and thinking, there's some work to be done here.'

Cupidi said, 'So you would have been passed the records from where she'd come from?'

'Well. Yes and no. I think she must have been phobic. She hadn't been to a dentist for about thirty years. We eventually got her records, which is a miracle in itself, but they were so old and she'd lost so many teeth since that time, they weren't worth having.'

'Really? So she hadn't been to a dentist in that long?'

'It happens. You should have seen the inside of her mouth.'

'Five years, you said?' She had registered with her GP around the same time, Cupidi remembered them telling her. The GP had said the same. She hadn't seen a doctor for years.

'I don't know if it's relevant, but I think she might have been a drug addict,' said the dentist. 'Former drug addict, that is.'

'Really?' Cupidi leaned forward.

'You come across people with teeth like that, occasionally. Heroin users as a rule. Amphetamines, sometimes. They don't look after themselves, I suppose. I've heard that opiates can affect your ability to salivate which means bacteria breed in the mouth more.' She made a face. 'Not sure if that's true or not, but hers were absolutely awful.'

'But she was fixing them? So presumably she was clean by that point?'

'Yes. I assume so. I never saw her . . . intoxicated, if that's what you mean.' The dentist sat with her saucer in her lap, her cup in the air. 'You know, I'm bloody glad I don't ever have to look inside a mouth like hers again. It was foul. Years of it, I've had. I won't miss it.' And she laughed.

Cupidi walked down the stairs. Keen may have lived in a small caravan, but she had money – or so it seemed. So if she wasn't poor, why was she living like that?

She walked to the road and bought herself an ice cream, then sat on the concrete sea defences trying to eat it before it melted, looking at the still sea.

Afterwards she licked her sticky hand and called the London number of the pathologist; she was surprised to be put through straight away.

'Do you know when you're going to submit the final report on Hilary Keen?'

'Actually, I'm glad you called,' the man said, which was unusual in itself. Normally the pathologists hated officers pestering them.

'Why? Have you found something new?'

'No. That's the point. Still nothing at all.'

'I thought you meant—'

'However, I saw on the news you've got the killer. Has he confessed? I don't mind saying, I'd be deeply interested to know how he killed her.'

Cupidi blinked into the glare of light off the sea. 'Conventionally, that's supposed to be the other way round. You're supposed to tell us.'

The man giggled. 'Yes. Rather. However, this is an interesting one.'

'And the problem is, our suspect's not saying anything at all. He's in a coma.'

'Back to the drawing board, then. Fascinating.'

'So you're still not at all sure how she died?' She was used to the fact that initial reports from pathologists had a scientific caution about them. But within a few days they were often at least favouring a hypothesis.

'No. And I'm getting the sense that you're not, either. Let me guess. As the suspect was injured during the arrest, there's a certain amount of pressure to wrap this up?'

'Exactly.'

'Oh dear. Well, I can't help you there, I'm afraid. I can only say what I see.'

'But she didn't drown.'

'One hundred per cent not. She was almost certainly dead when she was put in the water. She wasn't breathing, at least.'

'Wait,' she said. She was thinking. 'The fact that you can't work out how she died . . . Is that significant?'

'That is a much better question. Is it significant? I don't know, yet. But it's certainly interesting, isn't it? We still don't have any idea how she died, you see? Beyond indications of some hypoxia in the fingertips – and even that is difficult to assess because of the post-mortem interval – her body is healthy.'

'Hypoxia. Which is an indication of suffocation?'

'Correct. Or hypothermia. Less likely, given that it's July. But even then, this is not on a typical scale. That might be because of the fact that the body was in relatively warm water for the length of time it was – or that it's not even a significant indicator. We don't know.'

'How often does that happen?'

'I mean, it's common enough for us not to be a hundred per

cent certain. We can only ever suggest. But this one is certainly interesting. As I said, if we could find out how he killed her, we might have a clue what to look for.' And he laughed abruptly.

'One more thing. Were there signs she was a heroin addict?'

'Not "was". Had been, yes. Signs of scarring in veins on her arms and legs. Historic damage to the septum. Some damage to the kidneys.'

She sat in her car for a minute with the windows open, writing notes, thinking. From her bag she pulled out the photograph of the dead woman's face; the one the police artist had used for a sketch. She stared at it for a while.

Hearing a thump, she looked up to see a herring gull standing on the bonnet. It was huge and beautiful, pure white feathers with dashes of colour on its beak, but also somehow primitive. They looked at each other for a few seconds, then she stuck out her tongue at it, switched on her windscreen wipers, and the startled bird flew off up into the air.

It was a room, with a pile of blankets, jugs of water, a bible and a copy of the Koran, a few leaflets and not much more.

'There you go. These ones –' he pointed to four young dark-skinned men lying on the floor – 'were in a parcel truck on this morning's tide. They're from Niger. Those two over there are more what you're looking for.'

Two older men sat on plastic chairs on the other side of the room. They looked red-eyed and exhausted.

The Border Agency man was large, a little overweight, but strong-looking for his age. 'They were hidden under a tarp at the back of a flatbed,' he said. 'Got them with the CO_2 detection gear.

You poke it up into whatever you can't reach. They had plastic bags over their heads to try and stop themselves breathing. Good thing we found 'em. Probably be dead otherwise. It happens.'

The men looked passive. They smiled at Cupidi with slightly bewildered expressions on their faces.

'Just, like, plastic bags from some French supermarket. They say they're both from Tripoli. One had a passport, but it was fake. Only their word for it. Could be from anywhere, really. But they say Tripoli and they're in with a chance, at least.'

Both men were scrawny: one was older than the other, grey-moustached, wearing a pink rugby shirt that looked donated, the other smaller, less worn-looking.

'You really from Tripoli?'

'Refugees,' the younger man said.

'Speak English?'

He smiled and shook his head.

'Don't believe it,' said the Border Agency man quietly. 'They probably understand every word you're saying. They just don't want to answer any awkward questions.'

Cupidi sat in a chair next to them. 'Where were you planning to go, if you'd have got through without being found?'

The men smiled pleasantly, but said nothing.

'I used to imagine they think it's all a joke, them smiling like that,' said the Border man. 'They all do it. It's just the way they are. Something about a situation where nothing makes sense anymore.'

Cupidi reached down into her bag and pulled out a plain envelope. 'I'm going to show you a photograph of a man. He's dead. He was killed. OK?'

She was talking loudly, she realised, as if to children. As the Border Agency man said, they probably understood everything.

The younger man took the poster she had made and frowned at it.

'Do you recognise him?'

'No,' said the man.

'Would you know where he was from, by looking at him?'

'He's just a man,' said the migrant. 'Like me. Like him,' he pointed to the customs officer. 'Like them,' he said, pointing at the men from Niger. 'We are all men.'

'Fair point,' said Cupidi, standing.

'Except, mate, you're a man without a British passport,' said the Border man. 'Or any passport, for that matter, worse luck.'

'I have passport,' said the young North African. He pointed at the agent. 'This man took it.'

'Because the photograph on it looked more like your ruddy granny,' said the Border man. 'We're getting so many forgeries these days. Some are pretty good. Yours was an insult to my profession.'

'It was a good passport.'

'You should ask for your money back. It was crap. Just 'cause you've a bit of paper doesn't mean nothing. Half these people aren't what they say they are. Are we done here?'

As she followed him out of the room, she asked, 'What'll happen to them?'

'They'll be kept in a detention centre and they'll get an asylum hearing. Fifty-fifty they'll be sent home again. If not, then they're on your street corner on handouts. The whole thing is a giant farce.'

'Tragedy, more like.'

'Same difference.'

Cupidi showed a couple of her posters to the man. 'Can I pin these up, in case anybody recognises him?'

'Good luck with that,' he said in the kind of voice that suggested she would need it.

On a noticeboard by the toilet, she spent a minute rearranging all the leaflets to make space.

She took out her phone to take a picture of the number of a refugee support agency, when she saw she had a text message. It was from her mother: 'Where are you?'

She looked at her watch. It was twenty past five. 'Oh shit,' she said.

'What's wrong?' said the Border agent.

'Shit, shit, shit. I forgot my mother,' she said. 'She's at the station. I'm supposed to be picking her up.'

'*Running late*,' she texted, as she made her way back across the huge empty car park to her car. The sun had gone. Cumulus clouds were swelling above the Channel, blocking the light.

SEVENTEEN

'No,' said her mother, standing outside the metal and glass of Ashford International with her small suitcase. 'I completely understand. You're busy.'

'I texted you to say I was running late.'

'You did. Is this a police car?' her mother said, peering inside.

'I know. I didn't have time to go back to the station and pick up my own.'

It was a short distance back to the station. Cupidi pulled into a loading bay outside the TSB, far enough from the nick. In the old days, nobody would have minded bending the rules a bit, but you weren't allowed to give anyone lifts in a police vehicle. 'I have to go and swap. You mind waiting here? Only for a minute, I promise.'

Her mother got out and stood by the front of the bank. Helen drove the fifty metres to the police station and turned right into the car parking area. She had just returned the keys and was walking to her own car when she saw McAdam striding towards her.

Hoping to avoid getting caught up in a conversation, she pretended she hadn't seen him, but he called out, 'Alex. Anything on the Eason situation?'

'Nothing new from the scene of crime.'

McAdam looked gutted. 'We've been bounced into a press call on the murder of the unidentified man. Politics.'

The local MP was under pressure on illegal immigrants and had started talking tough about anything he felt he might lose votes on.

In spite of wanting to get away to pick up her mother, Cupidi found herself saying, 'Thing is, the dead woman. I've been thinking. How do we even know she's Hilary Keen?'

'What?'

The darkening sky above them dropped spots of rain. Cupidi held her handbag over her head to keep her hair dry.

'The dead woman. Our confirmations of her identity are a doctor and a dentist. We've found nobody who knew her in her ordinary life. No friends. No work colleagues. Apart from Stanley Eason.'

Suddenly a gust of rain swept across the yard. She had to raise her voice at the sudden noise.

Something the Border Agency man had said had swung unexpectedly into her head. *Half these people aren't what they say they are.*

'There were two Hilary Keens. Remember? What if our one is the imposter, not the other one?'

He pulled up his jacket over his head. 'Jesus. Tell me about it tomorrow.'

'And that photograph. Who are those children? If she was

Julian Keen's mother, wouldn't she have had a photograph of him, not the other children? It doesn't fit.'

The rain was hammering now.

'Tomorrow,' he shouted back, above the din of drops hitting the cars around them.

Inside her own Micra, she switched on the windscreen wipers double-speed and realised that her mother would be waiting for her again; there was no shelter on Tufton Street.

'Oh fuckity hell!'

And the police station was on a one-way street. In her hurry to drop her mother out of sight of the station, so that no one saw her using the car, she had left her waiting in a place where it wouldn't be easy to pick her up. Cupidi would have to drive round the whole block.

And, typically, at the end of Vicarage Lane the lights weren't working properly. There was a temporary traffic control which seemed to be stuck on red as the rain drove down. When she finally got through, a van courier delivering a package had parked in the filter lane on the next right-hand turn. Cupidi leaned on her horn, for all the good it would do. Other drivers joined in.

She found her mother standing next to a young man who was holding his small umbrella over her while the rain soaked him. 'Thank you so much,' said Cupidi to the man, putting her mother's sodden suitcase into the back of the car. 'You're a godsend.'

'You got caught up again, I expect,' said her mother.

'God, I'm so sorry, Mum. I've messed this all up, haven't I?'

'I'm going to need to change,' said her mother. 'I'm quite wet.'

Cupidi put the heater on, but that just made the windscreen steam up, and she had to open the window a crack, letting the spitting rain in on her side of the car.

As soon as she turned onto the road to Dungeness it stopped, sun suddenly golden, shining on the wet tarmac.

'Is this it?' said her mother as they approached the the end of the shingle promontory.

'I love it here,' said Cupidi. 'We both do.'

Her mother said nothing more until they were inside the house.

Zoë flung her arms around her grandmother. 'Nan. You're soaking.'

'Your mother abandoned me on a street corner while the heavens opened.'

'Mum,' scolded Zoë.

'I'll show you to your room,' said Cupidi. 'So you can change.'

Hers was to be the third bedroom, an oblong room with a single bed, a bookshelf and a desk. 'I'll move the computer downstairs in a minute. And the books. Then you can have some space.'

The bedroom looked out at the front of the house, towards the power station. Her mother looked in the small wardrobe. 'There are no clothes hangers,' she said.

'I'll get you some from my room. Will you be all right in here?' she asked, suddenly conscious of how small the room was.

'I'll be fine,' said her mother. 'What about you?'

'I'm OK,' she said, going to her bedroom and opening the wardrobe.

‘And Zoë?’ asked her mother, following her.

‘I don’t know. Maybe it’s just teenage mood swings,’ said Cupidi.

‘I don’t mean that. I meant . . . God sake. Is she ill? She’s got so thin. There are bones everywhere.’

Cupidi drew her head back a little. Had she? ‘I suppose she has. I feed her and she eats. She’s just active all the time. She’s changed.’

In her room, she took a dozen work blouses off hangers and laid them on the bed. She looked at them and decided they were all horrible anyway. She should throw them all out and start again.

While Cupidi made supper, Helen disappeared into Zoë’s bedroom. When the pie was cooked, she had to shout up the stairs for Zoë to come down and lay the table.

‘What were you two talking about?’ she asked.

‘Nothing, really,’ said Zoë.

‘You’ve been in there an hour.’

‘All sorts,’ said her mother vaguely.

They ate together round the dining-room table; after weeks of sitting in front of the television it seemed oddly formal.

‘Wine, Nan? I don’t normally drink during the week, but . . .’ said Cupidi.

‘I do,’ said Helen.

‘Yes you do, Mum,’ said Zoë. ‘All the time.’

‘Not every day.’

‘Most. Can I have a glass?’ asked Zoë.

‘Of course she can, can’t she, Alex? What’s for supper?’

'Fish pie.'

'How very coastal,' said Helen, and Zoë burst out laughing in a way Cupidi hadn't heard her laugh for so long, and for the first time Cupidi was glad to have her mother here. Three generations. Her mother, her daughter and her. However much they rubbed each other up the wrong way sometimes, it felt good. Maybe everything would be all right, here on the edge of the world.

And then the house phone started ringing again. Cupidi looked at the handset, its keys lit up, lying on the table in front of her.

EIGHTEEN

Before she could reach it, Zoë snatched the handset up from the table. 'Hello? Who is it?'

Cupidi watched her.

'I think it's a pervert. I can hear him breathing.'

'Don't,' mouthed Cupidi.

'I can actually hear you breathing,' said Zoë.

'Someone's there?' asked Helen.

'Oh God,' said Zoë. 'Do I actually know you?'

'What did he say?'

'He put the phone down when I said that,' said Zoë, holding the dead device.

'*He*, you said?'

'Yeah. He. He didn't say anything, but I could hear him there.'

'Who?' asked Cupidi.

'I get those all the time,' said Helen. 'People from India mostly.'

'Do they breathe like this?' said Zoë, panting.

'It's not funny,' said Cupidi.

'Do you know who it was, Mum?' asked Zoë, a hint of accusation in her voice.

Cupidi didn't answer.

'You should call the police,' said her mother, only half as a joke.

Cupidi woke, thick-headed, long before the alarm went off. Pulling open the curtains, she looked across the land. To the left stood the lighthouses, to the right the power station. She squinted; the sunlight outside seemed too bright.

Her mother was already in the kitchen, making tea. 'I don't sleep so well,' she said.

'Nor me. What are you going to do today?'

'I'll see what Zoë wants to do. She can show me around. Is she still crazy about birds?'

'Insane.'

'God help us,' said her mother, looking out of the kitchen window.

'Thanks for coming down, Mum. It means a lot. I know you and me don't always get along.'

Her mother wrinkled her nose. 'What are you working on?'

Cupidi, putting on her boots for her early morning walk, hesitated. 'That woman I told you about. And a man was murdered on a farm just north of here. We don't know who he was, but we think he was probably an illegal immigrant. It makes it twice as hard to solve if we don't know who he was.'

Still looking out of the window, her mother said, 'These days, there are so many of them, everywhere. They should have done something about it ages ago.'

'What?' Cupidi was looking for her phone.

'I don't know. Nobody does. That's the point, isn't it?'

Afterwards Cupidi drove to work. Traffic on the Dymchurch Road was slow. As she passed the Warren Inn, she noticed half a dozen people waiting in the car park. They were white, young, ordinary but unmistakably foreign, out of place. Four men and two women, both with brightly dyed red hair. She realised that she drove past them most mornings on this road. Stationary for a minute, she gazed at them. They were staring down a line of traffic, as if waiting for someone. One of the women turned, looked Cupidi in the eye for just a second, then looked away.

She wondered if she should try talking to them. There seemed no other sensible place to start, looking for a man with no identity. But the traffic ahead of her started to move, so instead she put the car back in gear and drove on.

The offices of the Romney Marshes Internal Area Drainage Board were on the top floor of a low converted barn in the middle of flatland just outside the town of Rye. The windows looked east out over the Folkestone Road, and beyond onto the land it was responsible for.

Cupidi was standing, looking at a large map pinned to the wall, which showed a blue spidery pattern of watercourses that had been had dug from the mud and silt over centuries.

'Where exactly was it found?' The engineer corrected himself. 'I mean, *she* found?'

The man's elderly dog stood by Cupidi's side, watching her as she orientated herself on the map. The higher ground, the older coast, formed a huge C-shape that curved for about twenty miles inland. It ran from Rye in the west, all the way up to Hythe in the east. Below that were the huge flat acres of marsh, stretching out in a giant triangle into the Channel, uninterrupted by a single contour. The land lay at sea level, or lower. How precarious it looked. She traced her finger down to the house she shared with Zoë, sitting on the most exposed extremity, the headland at the end of the marsh that pointed into the Dover Straits.

She moved her finger northwards, following the black line that indicated the railway track that carried nuclear waste away from the power station. The body had been a few metres from the track, close to the culvert that allowed the water to flow under it.

'There,' she said. 'Salt Lane.'

The man peered at where her finger was pointing. A small kink in the road, just by the unmanned crossing, with the thin blue line that represented the drain running through it.

'Not one of ours, though, that sewer. One of the smaller ones running off Jury's Gut.'

'I thought you did all of this.'

'We couldn't do all of this on our own. A lot are maintained by the riparian owners – it's an obligation that comes with the land. Know the spot, though.'

She gazed at the map, mesmerised. *Riparian.* A lovely word; the land by a river.

'Sewer?' she said. 'That what you call them?'

'Old English. When you dug a ditch to drain a field, you were sewing,' he said, pronouncing it as if he were talking about needle and thread, not mud and water. 'Sewing in the land.'

A vast, natural patchwork, hand-sewn, entirely created and maintained by riparian owers, people with shovels, people operating pumps, sluices and diggers, drawing the land from the water. A purposeful landscape, she thought.

Every year, the man explained, the whole network, hundreds of miles of drains, had to be dug out and cleared of weeds, over and over again. It was an amazing structure; a hidden wonder, a massive complex system of arteries that had been working precariously for centuries. If they stopped their activity for just a few years, it would go back to marsh, or to the sea itself.

She thought of the town beneath the waves.

'All this. It's amazing.'

'Yes,' he said sombrely. 'It is.'

Water attempts to find its own level. On her morning walks she had seen the leaking sluices, dribbling water that had escaped their barriers. To look at all this was also to imagine it overwhelmed. Man could attempt to hold back its force, but one day it would fail.

'The body had been there at least a couple of weeks. What I need to know is, could it have moved, or did we find it where the killer put it? Does the water flow much?'

The dog gnawed at something in its paw. 'In winter, our job is to stop the water from coming in, prevent the land from flooding. In summer, the farmers like us to keep the levels high for wet fencing. Stops the sheep from straying. It's been a dry month, up until yesterday's storm. Risk is, the water levels get too low. Two weeks back we had to top up the levels from the canal. Might have caused a little movement where she was, but not much. A few yards at the most. Not for a body in a ditch that shallow.'

Cupidi looked for Speringbrook House, then traced her finger up the Hamstreet Road until she found the point at which it crossed the Military Canal; it was on the far side of the Rhee Wall, the thirteenth-century earthwork that had once marked the western edge of the marsh.

'So there's no way it could have been put in here –' she pointed to the spot close to Eason's house – 'and ended up where we found it?'

'Simply not possible,' said the man. 'Couldn't have crossed the Rhee Wall.'

So that ruled out any idea that the body had been put into the water around Speringbrook House. Of course, if Eason had killed her, that didn't mean he would have dumped the body near his house. He could have driven to Salt Lane, but why would he have come all that way to dump a body? Wouldn't anybody have noticed the ancient orange Land Rover she had seen parked in his yard? It was an unusual vehicle. People noticed it.

She looked at the map. 'Why would someone leave a body there?'

'Sure she didn't just fall in? Happens every few years. The banks can be treacherous.'

'No. She was definitely dead when she went in.'

He looked back to the map. 'See, it's not guaranteed anyone would find her at all there, this time of year. Few years ago, we had a lad went missing down here –' he pointed to the south-east corner of the marsh, closer to where they were now – 'where the sewers are similar. He'd fallen in. Took us two weeks to find his body. She could have been there in the reeds until the weed cutters came.'

'Really?'

'That's a quiet spot. Gets quite overgrown up there. Some landowners are better than others, see. I know that stretch.'

She looked at the map again. 'So you think whoever put her there knew what he was doing? Or *she* was doing?'

He held a mug of tea in one hand and patted the dog with the other. 'Think about it. How are you going to get a body there?'

'Drive it, we reckon,' she said.

'Exactly. Look at all these roads. He'd have driven past a hundred ditches on his way there, all in the middle of nowhere. Why not dump her in one of them?'

'Tell me.'

'Because that place is where she's least likely to be found. And I'd say whoever dropped her there knew that.'

'Someone who lives round here?'

'Only a guess.'

She nodded. 'Good.'

If it hadn't been for the boy bunking off school, she would have been undiscovered for a few more weeks. Leaving her there had almost certainly been a calculated move.

It suggested that whoever had dumped her there had been local. Which didn't rule out Stanley Eason. But was he that kind of calculating man? And would he live long enough for them to be able to question him?

NINETEEN

When she got back to the office, Ferriter was carefully slipping her injured hand into a jacket sleeve.

'Where are you going?'

'Moon asked me to go and see if I could find a large-scale map of the area.'

'Did he? You're supposed to be working with me.'

'There's no "I" in *Team*,' said Ferriter.

'But there's a "U" in *Fuck him*,' said Cupidi. 'Leave him alone, for God's sake.'

Ferriter laughed. 'Aw. He's cute. He still lives with his mum,' she said. 'She made him peanut butter and jam sandwiches to bring to work. I think it's sweet.'

'It's pathetic. Where's he taking you on Saturday?'

'Nowhere special. Pub with his mates.'

'That's not a date, you know,' said Cupidi.

'It's whatever I say it is.'

'Go,' said Cupidi. She had three calls to make.

The first was to Julian Keen; she got through to him straight away. There was the sound of an electric drill in the background. 'Sorry. I'm on site. Speak up.'

'How are things with you?' she asked.

'Weird, really.' He stepped out to somewhere quieter. 'I've been finding it hard to concentrate at work. I can't get her out of my head, whoever she was. Have you made any progress discovering who killed that woman?' He spoke quietly, more hesitantly than he had before.

'You still don't believe it was your mother?'

'I don't know what to believe,' he said dejectedly.

'I want to ask you a few questions. Was there ever any talk of you having brothers?'

'What?' He sounded stunned by the question.

'Among her belongings I found an old photograph of two boys. Neither of them were you.'

'And you think they were her children?'

'I don't know.'

'No. God. No. Nobody ever told me anything. But then they told me my mother was dead.' He sounded bitter. 'What if she went on to have other kids? Do you think I do have brothers?'

'I'm not sure. Please don't go assuming—'

'I don't know how I feel about that,' he said. 'It's like, everything I knew has gone up in the air.'

'It was just a photograph,' she said. 'It doesn't prove anything at all.'

'No, but . . .'

'I have to ask something else. Do you know why your mother gave you up to your aunt for adoption?'

'Yes I do, as it happens. First time I ever got drunk my aunt told me. My mother was a heroin addict. She was unable to care for me. My aunt was terrified I'd go the same way.'

'Ah.'

'Why "Ah"?' he asked.

'Well, the woman whose death we are investigating – the one we think may have been your mother . . . she may have been a heroin addict.'

There was a long pause. 'So you really think the dead woman is my mother, then?'

'The woman whose body we have appears to have been a heavy drug-user for a significant period of her life, yes.' So maybe the dead woman was Hilary Keen, after all.

It was not what he wanted to hear. She could tell he wanted so much for his mother to be the one who was alive. In a way, she realised, she did, too. 'That doesn't prove anything,' he said. 'The woman who visited me looked like she was a druggie too.'

'I'd like to arrange for you to have a blood test. That way we'll know for sure.'

'I don't know,' he said. 'I don't know if I'm happy about that.'

'We could rule it out either way, then. That way, you'd know for certain.'

'I'm not sure.'

'Think about it,' said Cupidi. 'Please. It would be confidential.'

'Wait,' he said. 'I wanted to ask you something.' He hesitated.

'What is it?'

'Thing is, me and Lulu, we've been having a rocky time. She would rather we don't discuss my mother at all. These last few days, at night, after Teo's gone to bed, I've been going out on my bike, round all the streets here, looking for her. The woman. The one who said she was . . . Last night, Lulu caught me coming back in . . . It was around five in the morning . . . and we had a big row about it. We've never argued much until now. Now we're arguing all the time.'

'I'm not so good on marriage advice—'

'But I don't want to upset her.' He lowered his voice. 'I was thinking of hiring a private detective to look for her. Are they any good?'

'It depends what you want to hire one for.'

'Did you know your parents?'

'Yes.' Her father, a wise and quiet-spoken man who drew and painted; her mother, wayward and spiky, a woman who danced in the kitchen.

'See, I didn't. I wouldn't have thought twice about it until I had my own kid. It was starting to go around in my head already. And then this woman turns up.'

'It sounds harsh, I know, but you have to accept that she probably wasn't—'

'I know. I know. But she was in my house. She slept in our bed. She played with Teo. And for a while, just a little while, I thought she was actually my mother. And you know what? I know she was a tramp . . . sorry, a homeless person. And she stank. And she was probably an alkie or a druggie . . . but it didn't feel that bad, thinking that she was there after all this time.'

A voice said, 'Hey, Jules. You coming for coffee?'

'Can't you see I'm on the phone?' Then, 'I'd like to know she's OK, whoever she is. I have to, for my own sanity now. And I'd like to find out what happened to my real mother. Whoever she is. I have to go now. Sorry.' Then, before he ended the call, he said, 'You will let me know, won't you? Whatever happens.'

The second call was to David Colquhoun. She lowered her voice to a whisper. 'Were you drunk again?'

She heard Superintendent Colquhoun talking to someone in his office. 'I'm sorry. I have to take this. It's an important call.'

'You were, weren't you?'

He was alone now. 'I may have been.'

'Don't. OK? It's creepy. Zoë is getting suspicious.' Like her mother, her daughter had never approved of her relationship with him. 'Any news on my homeless woman?'

'Sorry. No. I'll chase it, I promise.'

'And don't call me at home anymore. Not like that. OK?'

'Wait,' said David. 'I have something to say. I was excited about it. It's why I called.'

Cupidi looked up. Other officers in the incident room had stopped work and were looking at her. 'What?'

'I said I missed you. I know you missed me. So I've booked a cabin at Dungeness. A week's holiday.'

'What?'

'I miss you,' he said again.

She blinked. 'You didn't think to ask me if I thought that was a good idea?'

'I thought you'd be pleased. We can see each other.'

'We're not seeing each other, David. It's over.' She looked around. Without realising, she had raised her voice.

'It doesn't have to be. When you lived in London it was complicated. But you're not there anymore. It can be like it was. It was good, wasn't it?'

It had been good, yes, she thought, but it had been a mistake to call him. 'Cancel it, David.'

When she finished the call, everybody in the room was silent. They seemed to be concentrating very hard on their screens.

She put her head in her hands for a minute.

The third call was going to be to the hospital to check on how Stanley Eason was doing. In the end, it wasn't one she needed to make. Before she had a chance, her phone rang.

She assumed it was going to be David, apologising for his behaviour, but when she picked it up a nurse said, 'We have a note on Mr Eason's file to call this number if there was any change in the patient's condition.' Cupidi already knew what she was going to say. 'I'm sorry to say that Mr Eason passed away about twenty minutes ago. Multiple organ failure. I'm afraid that's often the case with burns victims.'

'Bugger,' Cupidi said, shaking her head. Then, 'Apologies. Didn't mean to say that.'

'We say it all the time round here, believe me.'

'And it would be too much to expect that he'd said anything in the last day?'

'He's been unconscious the whole time, I'm afraid.'

She had hoped they would find something beyond the circumstantial suggestions that Eason had killed her for money, but there had been nothing. And now he was dead.

She stood and went to McAdam's office to tell him the news. She could see through the glass door he was on the phone, nodding as he talked.

She knocked.

*

'Well. That's probably that, then,' he said.

'Probably.'

'Obviously, we'd have liked it to be more clear-cut.'

'Obviously.'

'I'll contact the IPCC,' he said heavily. He suddenly looked much older. The Independent Police Complaints Commission were not coppers, but they had the power to end careers. They would come in mob-handed now there had been a death following police contact, demanding to see the reports, questioning why McAdam had surrounded the house. It would be him they would be blaming. A single event like this could hang over an officer for years.

'Sorry, sir,' she said.

'Can't be helped,' he said flatly, as if he knew how meaningless that sounded. They would be asking Cupidi why she had called for backup in the first place.

'You have my full support,' she said. 'I promise.'

'You advised me to stand down the officers. I ignored you,' he said.

'You didn't ignore me, sir. You were the one who had to make the call, not me.'

He rubbed his forehead with his fingertips. 'They'll ask for your account of the day, obviously.'

'Yes.'

She waited for him to offer his interpretation of events, the hint of what he hoped she should say, and was grateful when he didn't.

'It's possible that I'll be suspended, or at least be so tied up with all this that I'm not going to be able to give you much support,' he said. 'You should carry on as best you can. You'll do that, won't you?'

She nodded. All of the team would be under scrutiny, but McAdam most of all. He could lose his job, his pension, his reputation, everything.

He sighed. 'So. What were you trying to tell me in the car park yesterday?'

'I was thinking, what if it's not Hilary Keen?'

He blinked. 'I'm sorry?'

'We don't know for sure that that's who's dead.'

'But she was identified from dental records.'

'A woman turns up five years ago at a dentist and a GP's surgery with an NHS number and says she's Hilary Keen,' she said. 'But before that, she hasn't had anything done to her teeth in thirty years. I called the pharmacist who first got in touch when we did the TV appeal. Know what she said? Hilary Keen signed on there in 2012. Five years ago. Before that, no records since 1985. Again, that's thirty years, near enough.'

She pulled the chair out from next to his desk and sat in it.

'Don't you think that's just a teensy little bit weird? A woman disappears off the radar and appears thirty years later. How do we know it's the same one?'

McAdam tilted his head a couple of degrees to the side. 'Does it actually matter now?'

'I don't know. From the body, it looks like the victim was a former intravenous user, and we know that Hilary Keen had a history of heroin abuse, so most likely it's her. But what gets me is that the only fact we really know is that the same woman registered at the GP and her dentist under that name about five years ago. That's as far back as she goes. Anyone can register at a GP and claim to be someone else. The weird thing is that Hilary has no other current records we can find. There's no credit record. No bank account or anything. She appears to have paid for everything in cash, including her new teeth, and we have no details of any employer. You have to admit, that's pretty suspicious.'

McAdam picked up a pen and started flicking it round in a circle. 'Go on.'

'And we have someone else claiming to be Hilary Keen, who we assumed wasn't her because we thought we had her in the morgue. But what if that woman in London was the real one?'

He flicked the pen once more and then stopped, leaning back in his chair.

'All our victim would have needed is an NHS number, and who's going to know? That's the only real piece of evidence that our dead woman is genuinely Hilary Keen.'

McAdam chewed thoughtfully on the inside of his cheek.

She carried on. 'Either she wasn't Hilary Keen at all –' she paused – 'or she was, and had some reason for keeping an extremely low profile for the last thirty years.'

He nodded.

'I realise this is an inconvenient line of enquiry.'

McAdam gave a small, sad laugh. 'It is, rather, isn't it? If Stanley Eason had nothing to do with her death, I'm going to be completely hung out to dry, aren't I?'

If she proved that Stanley Eason didn't commit the murder, then his escalating the siege at Speringbrook House looked more and more like a bad call. 'Of course, it doesn't mean that Stanley Eason *didn't* kill her,' she said.

'But you don't think he did?'

'Honestly? I don't know now. Whoever killed her was methodical. They knew what they were doing with the body to make it as hard for us as possible. Does that sound like Stanley Eason to you? But like I said, the point is, you did what you thought was right. That's all we can do, isn't it?'

He looked up at her. 'I somehow doubt our friends in the IPCC will be as charitable.'

His phone started ringing again. Yesterday Eason had been a murder suspect; today he might be a martyr.

By the time she emerged from McAdam's office, Ferriter had returned from her errand. 'Are you OK, guv?' she asked. 'You look a bit ticked-off.'

Cupidi sat down at a spare desk and turned on the computer in front of her.

'Oh, I'm fine,' she said. She paused. 'No, actually,' she added, looking back at her screen as it started up. 'I'm not. Stanley Eason died this morning. Bloody stupid self-centred bloody idiot.'

Cupidi was waiting for her email to load when she looked up. The bandaged hand Ferriter held up in front of her face didn't quite hide the wetness on her chin, or the judder of her chest.

'Bollocks,' Cupidi said quietly to herself and stood. 'I'm the idiot.'

She went to the constable and put her arm around her awkwardly, feeling the shaking in her body as she wept.

'Sorry,' Ferriter mumbled. 'It's stupid.' She wiped her eyes with the back of her shirtsleeve.

'No. I'm the one who should be saying sorry. I was really thoughtless. That must have been a shock.'

'I'm not normally like this. Fuck sake. He was a murderer, wasn't he? I shouldn't feel like this.'

'You risked your life to try to rescue a man.'

Cupidi sat there quietly for a minute or so while Ferriter wiped the tears away. She looked vulnerable and small, her skin blotchy and red from crying. 'Just a bit bloody shocked,' she said. This petite little constable had dragged the bulk of a man's body towards the stairs. She had thought she had saved his life.

'You sure?' Cupidi released her from the hug.

Ferriter nodded. 'So he never regained consciousness again?'

'No.'

She made an effort to get on with her work, looking at her screen, but after a minute she turned to Cupidi. 'Do you think that was what he wanted? To kill himself? Because he was ashamed of what he'd done?'

'I don't know. Some men just blow up when they're threatened. They don't know what they're doing.'

'So we still don't know why he killed her?' she asked.

'That's the point. I don't even know *if* he killed her.'

'Really?'

'Something's off about the whole thing.'

'I dreamed about him last night,' said Ferriter. 'It was like he was on fire, and if I touched him I would catch light too. But I did. And I died. I was in my dream and I actually died. It was scary.'

'Maybe you shouldn't be back at work yet. Maybe you need a couple more days off.'

The office door opened. Moon came in, chewing on a Twix. 'You got that map?' He smiled.

'Here.' She smiled back, and handed it to him.

'Thanks. You're a star.' He paused. 'Are you all right?'

'Fine,' she said.

When he'd gone, Ferriter said, 'It was just a dream. Give me something to do. Please, Sarge. I don't want to think about it all, right now.'

Cupidi looked at her, then said, 'Hostels. Shared houses. Get a list of Home Office temporary accommodation. Anywhere where recent North African migrants might be. Can you do that?'

'I think so.'

When she had started, Cupidi called her mother. 'I'll probably be home late,' she said. 'I have to go and visit some hostels and places. We're looking for some information about the murdered man.'

Her mother said nothing.

'There's no other time to do it,' said Cupidi. 'That's the way it is these days. We don't have an endless supply of officers any more. The people in these hostels are out at work all day. Only chance of catching them in is to get them in the evenings. Sorry, Mum. It's something we need to do.'

'I'm babysitting then,' said her mother finally.

'I'll make it up to you.'

'What does she eat, even? I'm worried about that girl.'

Behind glass, in his office, the normally calm Inspector McAdam was chewing his nails. The dark weight of Eason's death hung over them all now.

TWENTY

By five they had enough of a list to get started on.

'You don't have to come,' said Cupidi. 'I can always get someone else.'

'Be honest, I'd rather be doing this,' said Ferriter, buttoning her jacket with one hand.

Cupidi moved a pile of papers and files so that the constable could get into the passenger seat of the police car.

The quality of information on the list they had put together was mixed. There were bona fide hostels, hotels and boarding houses, but there were also ordinary addresses where suspected illegal migrants could be living, picked up from council officers, agencies and fellow coppers. Migrant workers were mostly young men. However discreet they tried to be, they created their own kind of noise. Curtain-twitching neighours of a rented house might make complaints about vans coming and going late at night; a dozen men cramped together in a house would never be inconspicuous.

Cupidi had gathered printouts of maps, addresses and emails and had tried to compile them into a route that roughly circled the farm where the body had been found. Ferriter held them on her lap, fumbling the pages with her bandaged hand.

The first place they visited was a small terraced house on a new estate, just to the west of the town. The homes here were all shapes and sizes, some clad in fake plastic planks, attempting to look like some architect's idea of a village, but there was no hiding how cheaply they had been put together. Already green slime dripped down the wall below a broken gutter. Cars were parked haphazardly on pavements.

'Remind me. Why this one?' asked Cupidi.

'About three weeks ago, neighbours here reported a street fight between two gangs of young men. Community officer said one of the groups were Tunisians.'

The curtains were drawn, but all the lights were on, upstairs and down.

'I'll knock,' said Cupidi. 'And maybe you should head around the back, just in case.'

'Oh. Right.'

Cupidi rang a bell. Almost simultaneously, curtains pulled back and a man's face peered out from behind them. She could hear voices inside; scuffling feet. She pushed the button a second time.

A voice from behind the door said, 'Yes?'

'Can you open the door? I'm a police officer. I would like to talk to you.'

There was talking, whispering. Across the street, a light came on. A man was standing on his porch with a smartphone, filming her. Cupidi turned and gave the neighbour what she hoped looked like a reassuring smile, then rang the doorbell again.

The door opened a crack and a man's face appeared. He looked to be Asian, Cupidi guessed, rather than North African. 'I'm Detective Sergeant Cupidi. I'm investigating the murder of a man . . .'

The man interrupted. 'It's all legal here. We all have visas. We have papers.'

'I'm sure, sir. I'm not here to ask about your status. I want to know if you know this man.' She held up the photograph of the victim to the crack in the door. The man shook his head, though he had barely looked at it.

'What about anyone else in the house, though?'

The man hesitated. 'Give me the picture.'

'Maybe if we just opened the door a little wider, sir. Nothing bad is going to happen to you. I promise. I'm only interested in finding out what happened to the person in the photo.'

The man turned to speak to someone behind him. There was another muted conversation. These were people who had grown up in other countries, who always distrusted police, who would not be sure what was happening right now.

All the same, the man opened the door a little further. Behind him, a shirtless youngster muttered something angrily in a language Cupidi didn't recognise. This time, the one behind the door turned round and replied, equally tersely, then spoke to Cupidi. 'Welcome,' he said, holding the door for her.

The small hallway into which she stepped was now crowded with people. Faces craned from the living-room door. Two women stood on the staircase, looking down.

Cupidi held up the picture of the dead man and talked slowly, unsure how many would understand what she was saying. 'This man has been murdered. We want to find his killers, but we don't know his name. Do any of you recognise him?'

The man who had opened the door took the photo and translated.

Under a bare light bulb in the hallway, the men and women handed the photograph around, pausing to look at it.

A woman mumbled something.

'What did she say?'

'She said he was handsome,' said the man. There was a muted laugh. She in turn gave it to the woman on her left, who shook her head and handed it on again.

Just because these workers said they had papers didn't mean they were telling the truth. They would have their own reasons for not wanting to talk to police. Cupidi scrutinised the faces looking for any hesitation, any sign of recognition.

'Who was he?' asked the man who had opened the door.

'I don't know,' she said, pulling out handful of flyers and handing one to him.

'Anything?' asked Ferriter, when they were both back in the car.

'I counted ten people in there. How many bedrooms do you reckon that house had?'

'Two. Three maybe.'

Cupidi nodded.

Ferriter looked at the house. 'No wonder my little brother can't get a job round here. Living like animals they are. They can work for bloody nothing. I thought we were putting a stop to all that. I thought that was the whole idea.'

'Jill,' she said. 'I'm not in the mood.' Cupidi put on her seatbelt and checked her phone. Nothing from her mother, or from Zoë. She started the engine.

It was a long night. The second place had been empty, its tenants evicted weeks ago. The third, a hostel, turned out to have been closed down after a campaign by local residents.

They drove from one address to another. 'Waste of time. We're getting nowhere,' said Ferriter, frustrated.

'This is what it's like. You don't know what you're looking for, so you have to look everywhere. Ruling things out can be progress too.'

'So there's nothing at all to go on as far as Hilary Keen is concerned, either, is there?'

'No,' said Cupidi cautiously. She had steered clear of raising the topic of Hilary Keen in case Ferriter was still raw about the death of Stanley Eason. 'There's nothing on her. We've found a birth certificate and school records. But then nothing until she turns up five years ago to have her teeth fixed at the cost of thousands. Can you get the Anadin out of my bag?'

'Something wrong?' she asked, dipping into it.

'Headache,' she said.

'Surely there are previous NHS records?'

'Nothing. I've requested they dig around, but nothing was sent on to her GP.'

'So she just appeared out of nowhere?'

'Looks like it.'

Ferriter handed her the packet of pills. 'Don't you need water?'

They were stationary, at lights. Cupidi shook her head and popped a pill from the pack.

'Left here,' Ferriter said. The fifth address they visited was in a new apartment block just west of the town centre. A couple of dozen squeezed onto a former petrol station site.

'Why here?'

'North African asylum seeker. Name of Abdussalam Hasan. Address from the Home Office register. Not sure how current it is.'

'Your turn,' said Cupidi.

She watched from the car for a minute as Ferriter stood pressing buttons at the entrance to the flats. She could see her leaning forward, talking into the speakerphone. Eventually she gave up and wandered back towards the car.

'He's in. I can bloody hear him. When I told him why I wanted to talk he said, "No English." Lying bastard.'

'Let's give it a minute. We'll try again,' Cupidi said.

'What if we ring another bell? Or just wait till someone comes out.'

'We can't force people to open the door to us,' she said. 'They've done nothing wrong.'

'Not that we know about.'

They sat waiting in the car. A drunk man moved unsteadily towards them, first on one side of the pavement, then the other.

'I could wait till someone comes out and go in. His flat's just up there on the first floor, I reckon.'

'It's a private building. He's not a suspect,' Cupidi said. 'We're trying to win these people's trust.'

'Right.'

The drunk man passed on. At the corner he leaned over and vomited into the gutter, then walked on again.

'Nice round here.'

'Thing is, I'm that starving, not even that has put me off,' said Ferriter.

'I didn't think you ever ate anything.'

'He's watching us. Look.'

Above the ground floor each flat had what estate agents like to call a Juliet balcony, which meant it wasn't a balcony at all, just railings across the lower half of a window. Behind a first-floor window, there was a man peering down at them from behind the curtain.

'Might not be him.'

'Bet you it is. Shall I try again?'

Cupidi opened the car door a crack, but just as she did so, a small, slight, olive-skinned figure in a green military jacket appeared on the pavement. Over her head she wore a black scarf.

'She could let us in,' said Ferriter, 'couldn't she?'

'Stay there. Let me,' said Cupidi.

Startled by the opening car door, the woman looked round. She was pressing the entry bell, but no one was opening the door. Cupidi looked up. The man at the window had disappeared.

'Excuse me,' called Cupidi. 'I just want to ask you something. Do you know a man called Abdussalam Hasan?'

The woman was speaking urgently into the small grille, pressing the button with her left hand. Cupidi noticed she held her right one close to her chest, as if protecting it.

Cupidi raised her palms. 'I only want to talk.'

'*Iftah albab*,' the woman pleaded.

The door stayed closed. The woman removed her hand from the buzzer.

'Do you live here?'

The woman didn't answer, just looked blankly at Cupidi.

'It's all right. I'm not going to do anything. I just need to talk to you. Do you speak English?'

'Of course,' said the woman quietly.

'You live here?' Cupidi asked again.

The woman gave a small nod.

'But you don't have a key?'

'No.'

'Listen. My name's Alex. I'm just trying to find information about a man who may have gone missing.'

'I don't know any man who is missing,' the woman said. Her English was perfect.

'What's your name?'

The woman squinted at her for a second, but said nothing.

'The man upstairs.' Cupidi pointed upwards. 'He won't let you in because we're here?' said Cupidi.

'He has his reasons.'

Ferriter approached. 'And what would they be?'

'We're not interested in him,' said Cupidi, as much to Ferriter as to the woman. 'And we're not interested in you. We're asking questions about a dead man.'

The woman shrugged. 'We just want to be left alone.'

'This is Detective Constable Ferriter,' she said. 'I didn't catch your name.'

'I didn't tell you it,' she said.

'He's not going to let you in, is he?'

'Not until you go away. If he doesn't know who is at the door, he doesn't open it.'

'Wait here with my colleague. Just for a second. I want to show you something. OK? Don't go anywhere.'

The woman shrugged again. Back at the car, Cupidi dug into her bag for a copy of the poster; as she looked up she saw the young woman talking to Ferriter.

When Cupidi returned from the car, she had pulled off her woollen hat and lowered her scarf. Her hair was thick, black and straight. She had fine cheekbones and high, rounded eyebrows. It was hard to tell how old she was; maybe in her early twenties.

'What have you two been talking about?'

'She was asking what I'd done to my hand. I told her I burned it, trying to save someone from a fire.'

'It's true. She did,' said Cupidi.

The girl lifted her hand. She had a small bandage on the same side.

'Twins,' said Ferriter.

'But the man died, she says.'

'That's right,' said Cupidi, looking cautiously at Ferriter.

'I am sorry,' she said. 'That is terrible.'

'What did you do to yours?' asked Cupidi.

The dressing was fresh, wrapped around her wrist and palm. 'She said she fell from a ladder.'

'It's nothing,' she said.

Cupidi smiled as reassuringly as she could. 'Here. Do you recognise this man?'

The woman took the paper with her good hand and held it up to the light coming through the entrance hall's glass door, chewing on her lip. 'Do you know who he is?'

'No, that's the point. He's dead, and we want to find who is responsible, but it would be easier if we knew who he was.'

'You are just the ordinary police?' Her English was clear, despite an accent Cupidi couldn't place.

'That's right. We're part of a murder investigation, looking for whoever killed this man. We're nothing to do with immigration.'

'I'm sorry. I don't know him,' she said with another small smile. Her eyes were red-rimmed and weary.

Cupidi tried again. 'Looking at him, could you guess who he might have been?'

'Why would I know?'

'I think he might be a migrant worker of some kind.'

Again the woman shrugged, looked at her feet. 'Maybe. There are many, many workers.'

'What nationality would you say he was?'

The woman seemed puzzled by the question, but looked at the paper again. 'Syrian, maybe. Or Libyan. I don't know. Romanian. There are Romanians here.'

'We found a Koran with him. Apparently he was a Sunni.'

She nodded. 'Maybe.'

Cupidi hesitated. Ferriter had been right. They hadn't learned anything useful this evening.

Constable Ferriter stepped forward. 'Look, what if we bought you a coffee? My boss isn't as bad as she looks. She just wants to talk. To be honest, she's floundering around here. Just talking to you for a bit would help her out.'

Cupidi raised an eyebrow. The woman looked up at the window above again. 'I'm tired and hungry. I just want to go to bed and sleep now, but my friend is not answering the door.'

Ferriter said. 'Tell you what. I'm bloody starving too. It's been an ultra shitty day all round. I could do with a bite. What if we get something to eat?'

'I don't know,' the woman said. She looked around her, as if wishing she could disappear.

Cupidi said, 'I promise everything is just between you and me.'

'You and us,' said Ferriter.

The woman hesitated. She asked, 'What happened to the man in the photograph?'

'Do you really want to know?'

A small nod.

'He was beaten and left to drown in cow shit,' said Ferriter. 'We don't know why, but we're pretty sure that several people were involved in killing him. It was very brutal. I want to find out who did it.'

The woman looked at the flyer for a long time. 'You'll buy me something to eat?' she asked Ferriter, putting her scarf back up onto her head.

TWENTY-ONE

'Where are we going?' asked Cupidi, striding after them.

'Do you like Nepalese?' Ferriter said. 'There's one on the high street.'

All the way there, the woman remained silent. She walked with small paces but was surprisingly fast.

'You're paying, you realise,' called Cupidi after them.

It was only a short walk from the flats to the high street. 'Do you know who the man was who died in the fire?' the woman asked Ferriter as she strode ahead.

'A suspect,' she said. 'We think he may have killed a woman.'

'He killed a woman? So why did you save him?'

The restaurant was next to a Kentucky Fried Chicken. Cupidi held open the glass door. 'It's what you're supposed to do, isn't it?' Ferriter said.

On a weekday evening like this, the place was completely empty and overlit. They could hear tinny pop music playing on a radio somewhere in the kitchen.

While Ferriter was asking for a table, the young woman pursed her lips, then said to Cupidi, 'I think she is a good woman.'

'So-so,' said Cupidi.

'She is very sad about the man dying. The man she tried to save.'

'Yes. She is.'

The woman nodded.

'You're hungry?'

'How much can I order?'

'Pick what you like. The good woman is paying.'

'I don't eat much.'

'I do,' said Cupidi. 'Go on.'

The waiter tried to seat them near the window, as any restaurant would on a quiet day to show they had customers.

'No,' said Cupidi. 'That one.' She pointed to the table closest to the small bar at the back of the room. She imagined their guest might appreciate a little discretion.

They sat, Cupidi and Ferriter facing the front of the restaurant, the woman opposite them. Cupidi took out her photograph again. 'So we're attempting to find out the identity of this man. He had no papers on him, but we think he may have been working somewhere in the area. All I want to do is try and figure out a little about where a man like him would have lived or worked, that's all.'

'Why do you ask me? I don't know him.' The woman gave a small shrug, looking past Cupidi at the bar behind them. 'I don't know many people.'

'Tell me about where you work.'

'I don't work.' The young woman tugged her scarf back down

around her shoulders. Her black hair was held back in a band. She shook her head slightly. 'I'm not allowed. I don't know anything about people who do.'

'So you are a refugee? An asylum seeker?'

The woman laughed out loud for the first time. It was a surprisingly big laugh, from someone so petite. 'Yes. I seek asylum.'

Cupidi nodded. 'But you've been refused asylum?'

'I thought you wanted information about the dead man,' the young woman said, narrowing her eyes, quiet again.

'OK. I'm not asking about you. I apologise.'

A cheery-faced waiter in a buttoned-up jacket came and arranged cutlery on the table.

'Has the vegetable chilli got cashews in it?' asked Ferriter. 'I can't eat them.'

Cupidi watched their guest; she seemed to have no problem reading English. 'This man,' she said. 'The one who was killed. He had no documents on him. I'm trying to learn how people who don't have the right paperwork live. How they get by.'

The young woman chose a lamb curry and a Fanta, but carried on scanning the columns. 'I am not like him. I have documents. Can I have pickle also?' The woman looked up from the menu. 'I have plenty of documents.' There was darkness in her voice. 'You want to see them?'

'But not the right ones?' guessed Cupidi.

'Of course not.'

'But you're a registered asylum seeker. So you're not allowed to work.'

'That's right.' The can of drink arrived. 'Unlike this man,' she nodded at the waiter. 'I am not allowed.'

'But you do.'

'No. I am not allowed. Instead I have to beg. I have handouts from kind people. It is all I can do.'

'I promise this is confidential. As I said, I'm just trying to understand.'

'I cannot help you. I am not allowed to work,' the woman repeated cautiously, taking a sip straight from the can, then laying her hand flat on the table. 'It is illegal.'

Cupidi reached her hand over the table and laid it on the young woman's bandaged hand. She flinched at the contact. 'Trust me. Please,' said Cupidi. 'The dead man worked,' Cupidi said. 'I could tell from his hands. You fell off a ladder, you said?'

The woman tugged her hand away from Cupidi and stood, angrily, scraping the legs of her chair along the floor. The waiter looked round anxiously, startled by the noise.

Cupidi said, 'I'm not saying you work. I totally accept that. But if you did, what would you do?'

The woman said nothing. She turned and strode to the bathroom at the back of the small restaurant.

After a couple of seconds, Ferriter leaned forward and whispered, 'Nice one. She's probably just skipped out of the back now.'

'Whatever she says, she's working illegally. We need to find out what the local network of illegal workers is around here. If she comes back and talks to us, she comes back. If she doesn't, and doesn't want to talk to us, we can't do anything about it. She can only help us if she wants to help us.'

'No need to be so nasty, that's all I'm saying.'

'What happened to "They work for bloody nothing, these immigrants"?'

Ferriter made a face. Cupidi took a sip from her coffee. It was horrible.

'Think I should go to the ladies and see if she's still in there?' Ferriter asked.

After a minute, a young couple appeared to pick up a takeaway, standing at the door arm in arm. They were drunk and loud.

The waiter smiled at them benignly while they waited. Their refugee still hadn't reappeared by the time the two had gone, laughing into the night with a plastic bag full of food.

'I'll have hers if she's not coming back,' said Cupidi.

But just then the door to the bathroom opened and the young woman came back, sat down and looked Cupidi in the eye. 'I want to tell you something.'

'OK.'

'Just listen, please.'

'Fine.'

'My family are from the Western Sahara. Have you heard of it?'

Cupidi said, 'Maybe. I think so.'

Ferriter said, 'The capital city is Laayoune.'

'Yes. How did you know?'

'Pub quiz,' she said.

'I have never been there,' the young woman said. 'I have never been to my country. They say the Moroccans stole it from us,' she said, still looking Cupidi in the eye. 'I grew up in a refugee camp in Algeria.'

She took a toothpick from a plastic container in the middle of the table and rolled it slowly backwards and forwards. 'There was no life for us there. So I came here eight years ago. Two years travelling with my cousin.'

The woman's sentences were short and flat, one following the other automatically, as if she had had to explain herself like this many times.

'I applied for asylum, but I was refused. When I was nineteen I had some trouble with the police. I was arrested.' She broke the toothpick in two. 'They said I was stealing. I took some clothes, that's all. From someone. Not from a shop. It was a misunderstanding. It's not important. But now the police know who I am. Sometimes they detain me and try to send me home. It's the same with my friend in the apartment. That's why he is nervous. They wanted to remove me, but I have no home. There are many of us like this. Sometimes I am detained. Sometimes they let me go. The immigration judge ruled that because I am a Sahrawi, I have nowhere to go home to. So now they cannot deport me. I have no country. I have no state. But they will not let me live in this state. I have no passport. I am not allowed to live. I am nothing. That is my story. That is all.'

'You have no status?'

'Yes. Limboland. That's what the lawyers call it.' She turned to Ferriter. 'Have you heard of that place too?'

Ferriter shook her head.

'I live in the capital city of Limboland,' she said with a small smile. 'There are many people like me. No right to remain, but nowhere to go.'

'That's awful. I'm sorry,' said Ferriter.

'What for?' the woman asked, unsmiling.

'Your situation.'

The woman looked away.

The food arrived. When the waiter put down the plates, the young woman looked at him, then said, 'Why is it fair that this man can work? He can have a life, but I cannot?'

'It's not,' said Ferriter.

Cupidi had ordered a prawn starter. It was disappointingly small. She picked up her fork. 'I can't make things fairer for you.'

'Everyone says the same thing,' the woman said.

Cupidi looked at her. 'I just want to find out who killed a man. That's what I can do.'

The young woman tasted her food. 'It's good,' she said.

'Now. About this man,' Cupidi said.

'You think he was a man with no papers?'

'It's one line of enquiry,' said Ferriter, toying with the food on her plate.

'As I said, from the roughness of his hands, it looks like he worked.' Cupidi glanced again at the young woman's hands.

The woman chewed for a while, picked up the can of drink and washed the food down. She looked at them both. 'So . . . there are places where people who don't have documents live. There are always agencies who take workers who don't have good papers. They are not supposed to, but they do. The more your laws insist on this document and that one, the worse the money gets for the people who haven't any. But there are always, always jobs. They pay less, but what can people do? They take the job or they have to steal. Or starve.'

'Where are these places?'

She lifted a napkin and touched her lips with it. 'I cannot help you. I do not know them.'

'Do they have offices? How will people find them?'

She ate quickly, pausing to talk. 'No offices. They work with real companies who have offices, but they are just people. Somebody tells someone else. You know how it works.'

'Illegal gangmasters,' said Ferriter.

'Call them what you like,' said the woman. 'Some of them are legal but they don't obey the law. Some of them . . . Just because you make them illegal doesn't mean they don't exist.'

'Like failed asylum seekers,' said Cupidi.

The woman nodded and wiped her mouth again. Her plate was already half empty. Cupidi realised Ferriter had hardly touched hers. 'You call them illegal gangmasters. So what? They are illegal. They just hide better.'

'So where would we find these people? Especially North Africans.'

'I can't tell you.'

'Why not?' asked Cupidi.

'I don't know them. Now I have to go. I am tired.'

'From all that not working,' said Cupidi.

'Do not judge me, please,' said the woman.

'I'm sorry. I just say stuff. Bad habit of mine. Pay no attention.'

'But you haven't finished,' said Ferriter. 'You could have some pudding if you like.'

'I must sleep.'

'We'll walk you back' said Cupidi.

'No, please.' The woman shook her head. Taking her scarf, she laid it across the top of her head.

'Will you be able to get into the flat?' asked Ferriter.

'If you are not with me, of course.'

Cupidi stood, too. Reaching into her handbag she pulled out her wallet. 'Will you ask your friends? If you think of anything, or hear any one . . .' She produced a card and held it out towards the young woman.

'If I find something, can you help me? Maybe you can ask them to let me be a citizen?'

Cupidi looked at her. 'It doesn't work like that, I'm afraid.'

The woman smiled, leaving Cupidi holding the card. 'No. You cannot help me. I cannot help you. This is what happens. Nobody can help anyone else. Thank you for the food.'

She held out her hand to shake. Ferriter took it.

When the door closed behind her, Cupidi put the card back in her handbag. 'Poor girl,' she said.

'We can't just let her go like that.'

'What are we supposed to do?'

'Go after her. Say we'll help her. Jesus. What a shit fucking life.'

'An hour ago, wasn't I listening to you saying that migrants were taking all the jobs?'

'She can't help it, can she? Didn't you hear? There must be something we can bloody do.'

'Do you know what it even entails, trying to help someone in her situation?'

Ferriter looked stung.

'You really think they're going to treat her differently from every other failed asylum seeker just because we ask them to?'

Ferriter said, 'Yeah. But we didn't even try.' And then she was pushing past and out of the door. Cupidi went to the window to see where she had gone.

'Wait,' Ferriter shouted. Cupidi could see Ferriter running, catching up with the woman just outside the estate agent, several doors down. Ferriter was in darkness, but the woman was lit from the shop window. Something Ferriter said made the woman smile at her.

She watched as Ferriter pulled out a card. This time the young woman took it, then turned and walked away.

'What did you say?' asked Cupidi, when Ferriter was back in the restaurant.

'I just told her I'd try to help her. That's all.'

They walked back down the deserted shopping street. By the time they reached the police car, the woman was nowhere to be seen and the curtains to the flat above were closed.

TWENTY-TWO

She got in late.

'There's sausages in the oven.'

'It's OK. I've eaten.'

Her mother had never been much of a cook; Dad had always done most of it. Helen was sitting in front of the telly with a glass of wine and a paperback beside her.

Cupidi sniffed the air. 'Have you been smoking?' She wouldn't mind one herself, but she was determined not to start again just because her mother was here. 'Where's Zoë?'

'Asleep I think. She went up an hour ago.'

Cupidi went to look and saw no light showing from under her daughter's door. Back downstairs she opened the fridge, looking for wine for herself, but there was only a dribble left in the bottle. She could open a warm one, but it didn't appeal, so she closed the door again.

'What was your day like?' she called.

'Exhausting,' answered her mother, from the living room. 'She took me for a walk around the bird reserve. She seems to know everyone there. And every bird. Is that normal?'

'Not remotely.'

Cupidi joined her in the living room. 'She didn't touch her dinner. I was starving after all that tramping around.'

'I'm glad you could be company for her, though.'

With the telly chattering away, Cupidi sat down next to her mother on the sofa and picked up the paperback that was lying next to her. It was the one she should have been reading for her book group. The meeting was tomorrow and she had barely started. Turning the pages, she searched for her bookmark; it was gone.

'Not bad, that,' her mother said. 'I read it this afternoon after our walk.'

'You finished it?'

A nod.

'So. What was good about it? The book?'

'The main character; she was good. And the way it dealt with genetics was very interesting.'

Cupidi struggled to remember anything about genetics in the few chapters she'd read.

'Zoë took me down to the beach, too. Said she could see porpoises, but they could have been anything for all I could tell. She loves it here.'

'We both do.' Cupidi flicked through the novel trying to find the page she'd been reading. 'But it's not even remotely believable. The crime scene work is all wrong,' said Cupidi.

'You're too serious,' said her mother. 'Like your father. He would have hated it.'

'Yes,' said Cupidi, smiling. 'It's true. He would have. Are you getting on OK with her?'

'Fine. Why shouldn't I? She's strange, but she's lovely.'

'Just that her and me . . . I just feel there's a distance growing between us. If I'm honest, it frightens me a little.'

'Natural I suppose. Mother and daughter.'

'Is it? It happened to us, didn't it?' Her mother's eyes were glued to the TV. Cupidi wasn't even sure she was listening properly. 'You and me, Mum. We kind of drifted apart at the same age as Zoë is.'

Her mother nodded. 'We did.'

'I suppose the difference is, you went away. It was just me and Dad.'

'I didn't go away. I just had things to do.'

'Sometimes you were away for months.'

Her mother turned the TV up a little, saying nothing. The conversation was over.

She remembered her mother being absent; turning up after months away, often late at night with women friends who smelt of woodsmoke and patchouli oil. They talked politics all the time. She and her father would sit upstairs in her bedroom listening to the chatter of their voices for a couple of days, then she would be gone again.

Cupidi tried to concentrate on her book. She'd struggled through a couple of pages when her mother spoke again. 'That house down the lane. The little wooden one. Zoë showed me it.'

'It belongs to a friend. We look after it for him. What about it?'

'Do you think your friend would mind if I stayed in it?'

Cupidi looked up from the pages. 'Why?'

'Would he mind?'

'What's wrong with staying here?'

'I was just asking,' said her mother.

'At the weekend I was thinking of going out and getting some new curtains for your room. You can choose them. We could put some photographs up. Make it how you'd like it. I'll clear all of my stuff out.'

'It seems a waste to leave that place empty,' her mother said, staring at the TV again.

'Don't you like it here with me and Zoë? The three of us.'

'I just like to have my own space, that's all.'

Cupidi said nothing; tried to read the book.

'It's up to you, really.'

'Fine,' said Cupidi, looking up again. 'I'll sort out some sheets in the morning.'

'Don't sound like that.'

'I was just hoping we'd get along better down here. You and me.'

'We are getting along,' said her mother and went back to watching the TV.

She tried reading the book again in bed, but only managed half a dozen pages before her eyes closed.

She was back at her desk on Friday morning looking through Hilary Keen's arrest records that Moon had left for her: CONVICTIONS (8). DATE FIRST CONVICTED. 14/1/1983.

Her first two convictions had been for criminal damage. The subsequent six had been for possession of controlled substances. She thought of what the dentist had said about the dead woman's teeth. Maybe she was Hilary Keen. She was making too much of her hunch.

Two people in plain clothes pushed open the door to the office; Cupidi didn't recognise them, but straight off she knew who they would be. Each held a folder. The man wore a light grey suit, his hair tightly cropped; the woman short, thin, with a diplomatic smile fixed to her face. 'We're looking for Inspector McAdam,' she said.

'You're IPCC, aren't you?' Cupidi led them back out of the incident room door, towards McAdam's office.

'That's right.' It was the smile of a vicar visiting a mosque.

Cupidi walked to the back of the office, knocked on the door and opened it. 'To see you, sir.'

'Ah.' McAdam stood, did his best to return the smile.

'That will be all, thank you so much,' the woman said to Cupidi and turned towards her, waiting for her to close the door.

Back in the office, people chattered obliviously. Ferriter was sitting on Moon's desk; Cupidi could smell her perfume across the room. As she watched her she pulled her buzzing phone from her jacket pocket and looked at the screen. 'Shit!' she said.

Moon looked up.

'Can't make tomorrow night,' she said.

'Why not?'

'Something better to do.' She smiled. Ferriter walked across the room holding the phone out to her. 'Look.'

Moon just shrugged.

Cupidi stood, took the device and read the text message: *Meet at the tank tomorrow 10 pm. Have info. Najiba.*

'It's her, isn't it?' said Ferriter. 'The woman from last night.'

Cupidi nodded. 'I think so. What's the tank?'

'You know, that socking great one in St George's Square. There goes my Saturday night.' She looked back at Moon.

Cupidi remembered now. The ugly rhomboidal First World War machine plonked in the middle of a small urban square, oddly out of place.

'You think she's got something for us?'

'If it is her, you can't go alone,' Cupidi said.

'Why? Don't you trust me?'

'No. Of course I don't.' And Cupidi started to tidy her desk, dividing the piles into those she'd leave and those she'd take home to work on at the weekend. Before she left she glanced back at McAdam's door; it was still closed.

TWENTY-THREE

Friday night was the book group. She cooked a casserole for her mother and Zoë and then took a taxi to Lydd.

The meeting was held in the large house of a woman who used to be a TV producer and had a habit of dropping the names of famous people she knew into the conversation, but she was the only one of them with a big enough living room to host a gathering like this. Peering at the label of the bottle of wine Cupidi had bought, she said, 'I'm sure it's lovely.'

They were all women, mostly Cupidi's age or older. Two younger members sat apart, discussing their children and schools. Somebody was complaining about the council.

'How are you, Alex?' Cupidi turned. She recognised the well-dressed woman in her thirties who had moved to make space for her on the sofa from the last meeting, but had no idea who she was.

'Fine.' She sat down. 'And you?'

'Pretty awful,' the woman said quietly. 'As you might expect.'

'Sorry?'

Cupidi tried to place her. The woman was very beautiful. Her dress was plain but in a classy way. She stared at her with dark eyes. 'You don't know who I am, do you?'

'I'm so sorry,' Cupidi said again, helplessly.

'I'm Colette. Colette McAdam. I'm married to your boss.'

'God. I'm mortified. New round here.' She accepted a large glass of wine from the host. 'So many faces.'

'It's OK,' said Colette.

'The IPCC inquiry?' she asked.

Colette nodded. 'It's not bloody fair,' she whispered. 'He's a good man.'

'These things can be extremely stressful.' It was true. The whole team were feeling it. It was hard enough to do this job without the sense of someone waiting for you to make a mistake.

Colette bit the side of her nail. 'He likes you. When you applied for the job he said he wanted people like you.'

'I like him too, a lot. He's a good boss.'

'He said you told him not to bring in the all the extra police.'

'He was just doing his job. He'll be fine, I promise.'

Colette leaned in close, took her hand. 'What if you don't actually tell them that, though? He wouldn't have done it if he wasn't trying to protect you.'

'Enough chatter,' interrupted the host. 'We should probably talk about the book for at least ten minutes. Otherwise, what's the point?' People laughed. Then she looked straight at Cupidi. 'As we've got a real-life policewoman here, maybe we should find out what she thought of it first.' Colette let her hand drop.

And everyone was gazing at her now. Cupidi glanced around the room. All those expectant faces looking at her to say something clever about a book she hadn't even read; Colette next to her, still frowning.

'Well, I didn't think it was bad,' she said quietly, taking a sip from her wine.

'In what way?'

'The main character was good. Excellent in fact. And the way it dealt with genetics was very interesting,' Cupidi said.

The host looked fascinated.

'And did you find the policing details plausible?'

'Not in the least. But that's not the point is it?' she sidestepped. 'You wouldn't be interested in half of what I do. This was entertainment.'

And suddenly everyone was pitching in, agreeing with her that it was a very good book and saying how much they had enjoyed it. All except for one of the younger women who said she found it too violent for her taste, but nobody agreed with her.

As they chattered, a woman with expensive-looking tattoos down the length of one arm leaned in. 'I never actually got around to reading it,' she confessed. 'Do you think I should?'

'Can you keep a secret?' Cupidi lowered her voice. 'Neither did I.'

'Oh.' Tattoo Woman laughed. 'You're very good.'

'Of course, there's been an awful murder close to here,' the host said. The room suddenly quietened. Again, everyone was looking at Cupidi. 'Are you involved in that?'

'Yes,' said Cupidi. 'I am.'

On the sofa next to her, Colette was still looking at her pleadingly.

'The *Messenger* says it's criminal gangs of illegal immigrants. Absolutely terrifying.'

'We don't know that,' said Cupidi.

'Well, it's what it says in the papers,' said the host. 'Who was he? The dead man.'

'We have no idea. That's part of the problem. We're still working on trying to discover his identity.'

Tattoo Woman said, 'Didn't I see you on telly the other week talking about a dead woman too? What about her? You caught the man, didn't you?'

'Was our Alex on the television?' said the host, perking up.

'It was just an appeal for anyone who could identify her,' said Cupidi. 'We think we may know who killed the woman, yes.' She felt uncomfortable discussing this here. There was little she could share, and besides, this was supposed to be her escape from work. 'Should we be choosing our next book?'

'It was about money, wasn't it, I heard. Some guy strangled her for her cash.'

'That's terrifying.'

'I can't say. We're not allowed to talk about the detail of investigations,' Cupidi said.

'Oh come on. Just a bit,' one of the younger mothers said mischievously, already tipsy.

Another said, 'I think we should have a right to know, just for our own peace of mind. After all, we're the community, aren't we?'

Tattoo Woman came to her rescue. 'What about something

a bit racier next time?' she asked loudly. 'Anyone fancy reading something a little naughty, maybe?'

The room went quiet.

'I really don't think so,' said the host. And suddenly everyone was laughing again. Cupidi gave Tattoo Woman a grateful glance.

Moths flapped at the glass behind them, attracted by the light through the French windows.

On balance, she was enjoying herself, she realised. It was nice to drink wine and swap inconsequential talk in the company of other women. At the end of the evening, she was just about to call for a taxi when Colette McAdam appeared beside her again. 'I can give you a lift if you like. I don't really drink.'

'I wouldn't dream of it. It's out of your way.'

'I don't mind,' said Colette.

Cupidi didn't want to accept the lift with her, but didn't see how she could refuse.

She drove fast, braking hard at junctions. The air was full of flying bugs, caught in her full-beam lights.

Colette was silent until they reached the single-track road on the beach, when she blurted, 'Toby says you're trying to prove Stanley Eason didn't kill anyone.'

'Well. It's not really like that. I just want to be absolutely sure we are accusing the right person.'

She stopped the car. 'I mean, you can see how that looks, can't you, questioning his judgement like that?'

'Is that what he thinks I'm doing?'

She laughed abruptly just as the lighthouse ahead of them flashed brightly. 'No. He thinks the sun shines out of your bloody arse. He doesn't even see how you're undermining him.'

'I'm not.'

'God. I'm sorry. I didn't mean to say it like that.'

Cupidi wondered if she should just get out of the car.

'Just . . . Can't you try and help him? How do you even know Stanley Eason didn't kill that woman? You can't prove it, can you?'

'He's a good boss, Colette. I'm sure the IPCC recognise that.'

Colette grabbed her arm. 'Please don't tell him I said this. I'm only trying to help him.'

'I won't.'

The two women sat in the car while the engine purred. Every ten seconds the lighthouse ahead of them flashed; each time it lit Colette's face, the tears had trickled a little further down.

Saturday was windless. Cupidi left the front and back doors of Arum Cottage open, in the hope of a breeze. She stood in the living room, looking at the dust that lay on the empty bookshelves. Her mother was in one of the two small bedrooms, unpacking her bag.

'It's a bit of a mess, I'm afraid,' she called.

'It's fine.'

'I meant to give it all a clean.' She turned to look through the open back door, at the empty land dotted with pale curls of sea kale that rooted among the stones. Most of the other chalets were clustered together. This one was on its own, fifty metres from its nearest neighbour.

Carrying fresh sheets she had taken from Cupidi's airing cupboard, her mother walked from one bedroom, into the other.

'You're making up both beds?'

'Didn't I tell you? Zoë wants to sleep here tonight. To keep me company.'

Through the bedroom door she could see her mother, putting clean linen onto the second double bed. 'No, you didn't.'

With the flat of her palm, Helen was smoothing the sheet. 'Is that OK?' She paused, straightened, looked up. 'Just for tonight? You're out, anyway, aren't you?'

'Yes, of course,' said Cupidi. She left her mother to it and walked back up the track that ran alongside the power station's perimeter fence towards her house.

'I can't help it,' said Ferriter.

Cupidi had just come back from the bar with half a lager for Ferriter and an orange juice for herself, to find Ferriter being chatted up by two young men.

'Get lost,' said Cupidi, and the men retreated, laughing. That evening, they sat at a table outside the Old Prince of Wales in Ashford. It was on the west side of the tiny square, at the centre of which sat the First World War tank, just a few metres away.

'Used to be an electricity substation,' Ferriter said. 'No. I'm serious. Army gave it to the town as a thank-you for their effort in the war. What are you supposed to do with a bloody tank? So they gutted it and turned it into an electricity substation.'

On a hot Saturday evening, the small square was full of drinkers spilling out of the pub. Cupidi was watching out for the woman they had seen on Thursday night. A couple of men were throwing beer mats, trying to make them land in a boot that seemed to belong to no one. 'Move the boot closer,' a woman said.

It was ten o'clock now and there was no sign of the woman who had signed herself Najiba.

'No,' said one of the men. 'I can do it.' He threw another and missed by a metre. Everybody laughed.

'Round here, folks make their own entertainment,' said Ferriter drily. 'Not used to drinking halves.' Cupidi looked at Ferriter's glass. It was empty already. 'Mind if I get another?'

'Go ahead. But you're on duty, remember.'

'A pint's OK, though, isn't it?'

The woman arrived in the square while Ferriter was back at the bar. Cupidi watched her for a few seconds, scanning the crowd, scarf draped over the top of her head.

A cheer went up, startling her. The man had finally succeeded in getting a beer mat into the boot. As she looked towards the noise, the woman spotted Cupidi raising her hand in greeting.

Najiba frowned. 'I was expecting the younger one,' she said when she had pushed through the crowd to the table where Cupidi was.

'The nicer one,' said Cupidi.

Najiba smiled. 'Yes,' she said.

'Would you like a drink?'

'Yes. I am tired. I would like a beer.'

Ferriter arrived with her half and smiled. 'You made it.' Like it was a girls' Saturday night out. 'A beer? I thought . . .' She pointed to the headscarf.

Najiba shrugged. So Ferriter returned to the crush of the bar to fetch Najiba her drink.

She sat quietly while Cupidi looked at her.

'What do you want from us?' said Cupidi eventually.

'Why do you assume I want something from you?'

'Don't you?'

'Yes. I want you to help me,' Najiba said. A man carrying four pints of lager spilled some onto the ground; Najiba moved her feet away from the pool of beer.

'I am assuming you've been refused Indefinite Leave to Remain by the court?'

'Yes. Of course.'

'And you appealed?'

'All appeal rights exhausted,' she said.

'There's no way back from that, is there? You have no legal right to be in this country.'

She didn't answer.

'Do you ever want to go home?'

'They would like me to. It is so inconvenient of me to exist. But I cannot go home. There is no life for me there. And so I would like you to help me, but you cannot.'

'No.' In the small square people drank and laughed. 'If it was up to me, you could stay. But it's not.'

'No.'

'Don't you have friends from there . . . other refugees?'

'I used to. When I first arrived. But they are all politics, politics, politics. I hate politics. Politics is why we have no country.'

'You fell out with them?'

She looked down at her lap. 'Yes. They want our country back from the Moroccans. They would fight for it if they had to. That is what I grew up with in the refugee camp. I don't care anymore. All it has brought us is pain.'

Ferriter arrived finally, with a bottle and three packets of crisps.

Najiba looked up, smiled, took her drink and sipped from it. 'That man . . .' she said, 'the one who died. Do you know why he died?'

Ferriter pulled open a packet of crisps and laid them out on the iron table. 'No. Do you?'

'No.' Najiba's answer was curt; she picked up a handful of crisps and put them into her mouth.

'I have been talking to your friend,' Najiba said to Ferriter when she'd finished chewing.

'My boss,' said Ferriter.

'You said you could help me,' Najiba continued. 'She says she cannot.'

'I'm going to do everything I can,' Ferriter answered. 'I promise.'

Najiba smiled at her. 'What will you do?'

'I can tell people you helped us.'

'You see?' said Najiba, turning to Cupidi. 'She said she will help.'

'I will. Really,' said Ferriter.

Najiba looked at her, still smiling. 'One day I would like to have a farm here. In Africa my mother kept goats and chickens. I would like that too. A small house and a little piece of land. I think there might be economic value in raising goats here. There are immigrants who like to eat the meat. It is difficult to find here.'

'Well,' said Ferriter, slightly anxiously. 'I can't promise any of that.'

'But I would very much want a farm.'

'Well . . .' Ferriter looked at Cupidi uncomfortably. 'That's not really down to us.'

'She's teasing you, Jill,' said Cupidi.

Najiba laughed loudly and took another gulp of her beer.

'Very funny,' said Ferriter.

'Do you have a husband?' Najiba asked Ferriter.

'She's in love with a sergeant at work. He's not interested in her,' said Cupidi.

'Shut up! I was supposed to be going out with him tonight.'

But Najiba clapped her hands, as if delighted to be doing something as simple as gossiping for a change. 'Is that true?'

'He is interested. Maybe he just doesn't know it yet,' said Ferriter.

Najiba laughed.

'What about you? Do you have a boyfriend?'

'I have too many to choose from,' said Najiba.

It was Ferriter's turn to laugh now. 'Get you.'

'Refugees are nearly all boys,' said Najiba, suddenly serious. 'It is hard for a woman. You have to keep them at a distance. Some are nice. Some not so.'

'What about the man you share an apartment with?'

'He is very nice, but he is married. His wife is in Libya. He is simply being kind to me because he knows it is hard for a woman on her own. What about you?' she asked Cupidi.

'I'm divorced.'

'You have a boyfriend though?'

'You bet she does,' blurted Ferriter.

Cupidi looked at her. 'What do you mean?'

'Sorry. Just guessing,' the constable said awkwardly. 'I need to go to the loo. Save my seat.' And she stood quickly.

When she was gone, the smile left Najiba's face. 'She is nice,' she said. 'A good person.'

'She's a pain in the arse,' said Cupidi.

Najiba smiled. 'But she is young. She does not know the world.'

'No. Not yet.'

A drunk woman with a single rose in one hand and a glass of something purple in her right was singing 'Galway Girl' with more enthusiasm than familiarity with the words.

'She says she wants to help me, but she does not know that she can't.'

Cupidi said, 'Ah. You mustn't blame her for not knowing how it works.'

'You, unfortunately, are honest,' said Najiba. 'But what you said is true. You cannot help me.'

'I'm truly sorry,' said Cupidi. 'It's ridiculous.'

The young Sahrawi woman nodded. 'So I think it would be wiser to give this to you.' Najiba reached inside her jacket pocket and brought out a small piece of folded paper.

'What is it?'

'Some addresses where people stay.' She looked around her, then handed it to Cupidi. 'Please be careful with it.'

'Why are you helping us if we can't help you?'

'Because a man is dead.'

The woman with the rose had started the same song again.

'Tell me. Did you know him?'

The woman didn't answer; she put down her half-finished bottle and stood just as Ferriter returned.

'I have to go,' she said. 'I am very tired.'

'But we haven't even started yet,' complained Ferriter.

The woman put her arms around the constable and the two

hugged for a minute. 'We can meet another time, I hope,' she said.

'Thank you,' said Cupidi.

Najiba turned and walked around the corner, up New Street towards her flat, away from the noise of a Saturday night.

'Why did you let her go?' said Ferriter. 'What were you thanking her for? She only just got here.'

Cupidi raised her glass and drained it. 'She gave us some addresses,' she said. 'Places where migrant workers stay.'

Ferriter sat down hard. 'Why didn't she give it to me? I'm the one who got her here.'

'Come on,' said Cupidi. 'You're off duty now. I'll get you another drink.'

As she returned from the bar, a drink in each hand, she caught the scent of dope in the air. Someone was smoking a spliff. She looked around and saw a young mod smoking a rolled-up cigarette. But it was much simpler to pretend she hadn't smelt it. The boys were flocking round Ferriter again, and this time she seemed to be enjoying the attention, so she handed her her drink and stood a little way off.

She reached inside her bag and pulled out the note Najiba had given her. There were four addresses on the list; three she already had. The fourth she didn't recognise.

That night she found it hard to sleep. The house felt hot, airless and empty. Zoë was with Helen in the wooden cottage.

Pulling off the sheet that covered her, she stood naked at the open window, listening to the pulse of a single cricket which sang against the low rumble of the power station.

TWENTY-FOUR

Nobody was looking forward to Monday. The IPCC had taken an office on the first floor and were calling people in, one by one.

They interviewed Cupidi for over an hour. 'He did the right thing,' she insisted. 'I had requested backup. The man had threatened me.'

'It wouldn't be the first time you've been threatened by a suspect, presumably?'

'No.'

'So what was special about this time?'

'What do you mean, special?'

'There were sixteen officers present. DI McAdam must have thought Stanley Eason represented a very significant threat. Why do you think he came to that conclusion?'

'Because he was a murder suspect, threatening an officer with violence.'

'Did you tell Inspector McAdam that?'

She hesitated. 'Yes. I did.'

There were three of them in the room: Cupidi, the small woman with the smile, and the man who never seemed to say anything. The woman looked down, read through her notes for a second, then looked up again: 'So why, on the day, did you criticise him for ordering so many officers onto the scene then?'

'Listen. If anyone should take the blame for Stanley Eason's death it should be me.'

The woman nodded. 'Go on. Explain.'

'I was the one who wound him up in the first place. I went too far. He was a suspect in a murder case and I thought I could get him to incriminate himself by pushing his buttons. It was a mistake. I'm the reason why he lost his temper, not DI McAdam.'

The woman made a small note. 'I'll ask again. Why did you criticise your senior officer during the operation?'

'It wasn't criticism. I was just suggesting other ways we could have gone forward. In retrospect, I still think he made the right call.'

The woman raised her eyebrows. 'It sounded like a criticism to other officers who were present. Do you accept their account of what you said? That it was a mistake sending in a team of that size.'

'They don't normally work with me. People who do know I just sound like that.'

'I asked, do you accept their account?'

'Yes,' she said quietly. 'I do.'

The woman stared at her. 'Right.' The man handed her a piece of paper. She looked at it for a second and then asked, 'Inspector McAdam refers to a report that a man answering Eason's description in the vicinity of Speringbrook House threatened to assault a member of the public approximately two years ago. Were you aware of that report?'

'I'm new on this unit. It would have been before my time here.'

'I know you are new. But have you ever seen any record of it?'

'No. What are you suggesting?'

'Did Inspector McAdam make any mention of the previous incident during the operation?'

'Yes. He did. He said he'd remembered that there had been an earlier situation involving Mr Eason in which he'd been aggressive to a member of the public.'

The woman raised her eyebrows. 'Yet he made no mention of this in his contemporary notes. And we are unable to find any record of any previous threats made by Mr Eason.'

Cupidi blinked. Damn. There should have been a record; the woman was right. But just because there wasn't didn't mean it hadn't happened.

'On the days following the siege, what discussions have you had with Inspector McAdam about your account of events that day?'

'Are you suggesting in some way we've colluded . . . to create a story?'

The woman leaned forward a millimetre. 'Have you?'

'Of course not.'

'So what discussions have you had?'

'He mentioned he was concerned about how people might interpret his decision to send the officers to back me up. I told him I would support his decision. Because I do.'

The woman twisted a ring on her finger. 'Naturally we are used to officers closing ranks at times like this. It's never particularly helpful.' She looked at Cupidi, who was grinning back at her. 'Why do you think that's amusing?'

'It's the first time anyone here's accused me of being a team player.'

'You're an experienced officer, Sergeant Cupidi. Do you really think he's a capable team leader who's fully in control?'

'Somebody has to make the call. If nobody feels they can make decisions anymore then we might as well give up.'

'The wrong decision, though, in your opinion. As you made perfectly clear on the day, whatever you are choosing to say today.'

'My judgement call was different from his on the day. But I was an ordinary officer on the ground. If it was my responsibility to protect the necks of other officers, I'd have probably ordered tanks.'

The woman made a face; made another tiny annotation in the margin of the piece of paper she was looking at.

Back in the incident room, the mood was subdued. There was too much routine work to get through for such a small team without the distraction of the IPCC inquiry soaking up time and souring their mood.

Tongue protruding slightly from her mouth, Ferriter plotted the addresses they would visit onto Moon's big map.

'Know somewhere named Saddlers Wall?' Ferriter called out to the office.

'Never heard of it.'

That had been the fourth address on Najiba's list. Cupidi had typed out everything she had and handed them all over to Ferriter that morning.

‘I can’t bloody find it anywhere.’

Even without the extra address to visit, it was going to be a long night. Cupidi phoned home to tell her mother not to save dinner for her, but she was out. Zoë’s number went to voicemail too.

‘I looked at Google Maps. I can’t find it.’

Moon stood and started squinting at the map too. ‘Here,’ he said eventually. ‘Saddlers Wall Lane.’

The ancient banks that had originally been built to defend the fields from floodwater had become a network of small single-track roads. He was pointing to a place about six inches to the right of the red pin that marked where the dead man’s body had been found. Cupidi joined the two of them at the map.

She traced a finger from there, south, to Salt Lane and the ditch in which the woman’s body had been floating. Saddlers Wall Lane was about three miles miles north as the crow flew. Of all the addresses they had, it was the only one that was on the marsh.

Working west into sunset they drove towards Brissenden Green. A social worker had told Cupidi about two Roma families living in a small flat there.

The Roma men had been playing cards in a tiny kitchen; they looked at the photograph silently, serious expressions on their faces, and shook their heads.

The hostel in Kingsnorth had been full of bored men, young and old, mostly Lithuanian apparently. In a communal TV room that stank of sweat, a Chinese-looking man with weepy-looking eyes muttered angrily when he looked at the photograph.

'What's he saying? Do you recognise him?' asked Cupidi.

One of the Lithuanians, a stocky youngster with a hare lip, took the Chinese man by the shoulder, pulled him away. When he came back, he said, unsmiling, 'It's nothing. He's a racist. He hates all the black men.'

'You sure?'

'Of course I'm sure. I apologise for him.' The Lithuanian stood, arms folded, in the living room while the photo was passed around. Nobody else said anything.

Some people talked to the police; others didn't. Sometimes that was because they had nothing to say; sometimes it was because they didn't like the police.

Cupidi pulled out her card and handed it to the Lithuanian. 'If anyone hears anything . . .'

'Of course,' said the man with as much earnestness as he could muster. As they drove away, she could see him in the rear-view mirror, standing in the building's brightly lit porch to watch them go.

Saddlers Wall ran north–south. Cupidi travelled up the lane but found only a couple of expensive-looking private houses, set back from the road; one an old farmhouse, the other a barn conversion, each with two or three upmarket cars parked outside on gravel.

'We must have gone past it,' said Ferriter, examining the map by the light of her phone.

Cupidi turned at the next crossroads and drove back the way they'd come. Again, there was no sign of anything other than well-off houses.

'Must be the wrong address.'

The first stars lit the blue sky.

Cupidi edged the car cautiously up the dark lane. A rabbit sat in the middle of the road transfixed. It didn't move until Cupidi was just a couple of metres away, then bounded off into the grass.

'Stop,' yelled Ferriter suddenly. 'Go back.'

Cupidi reversed back to the gap in the hedge. Through it, about twenty metres away, she could make out illuminated patches in the middle of the field.

Ferriter got out. 'Reckon this is it?'

'Are they caravans?'

The gate to the field was locked, but in the distance were two grey shapes, lights burning in the windows. Hammered into the ground next to the gate was a small sign: NO HUNTING.

'The entrance must be on the other side,' said Cupidi. 'Did you notice a turning?'

'Think we must have gone past it.'

They got back in the car and and found a narrow track. They came to another gate.

'Pikeys, you reckon?' asked Ferriter.

Cupidi didn't respond. Now wasn't the time. 'Come on,' she said.

The gate opened inwards, scraping across the uneven ground.

Twenty metres away, the caravan nearest to them had its door open. Lit from the back by the glare from inside, a bare-chested man was sitting on the step, smoking a cigarette.

The man's head twitched round at the sound of the gate. A dog barked; a deep, throaty noise that made Cupidi jump. She looked around to see if it was tied up, but couldn't make it out in the fading light.

The smoker spotted them, shouted something.

'My name is Detective Sergeant Cupidi,' she called out to him.

The man stood, peering at them.

She walked through the gate into the field. Seeing them coming towards him, the man called out again. Was he saying something to them, or was it a warning to the rest of the people in the two caravans that strangers were approaching?

'We just want to talk to you,' said Cupidi.

He stood, watching them approach. Another figure, an older man, appeared out of the caravan behind him.

The man shouted again. It was clearer this time. 'Go away.'

She stopped. 'We are police,' she said again.

Abruptly, from the other caravan, a man sprinted out across the long meadow grass, running away, tripping, getting up again. There was something almost comical about it.

'Stop!' shouted Ferriter, calling after him.

And then the whole place burst into life. Half a dozen men and women came flying out of the two caravans and set off at a sprint.

'It's OK,' called Cupidi, trying to reassure them. 'It's not a raid. We just want to talk.'

But it was pointless. Panicked people were running in every direction. A young woman, probably a teenager, barefoot in just a pair of knickers and a shirt, dashed out, ran four or five paces towards them, then stopped and turned.

'Right,' Cupidi shouted at Ferriter. 'Just grab someone. Anyone.' She looked at the car. The right procedure would be to call for backup, but that would give the teenager time to get away. She set off after her. 'Stop. Police.'

A man had got into an old Subaru and had switched the lights on full beam.

'Bloody hell.'

Car doors were slamming. Other engines started up. The Subaru lurched straight at Cupidi, bumping across the uneven ground. The sump scraped against earth, but it didn't slow, heading towards her. She jumped out of the way in time, looking round to see where Ferriter had gone, just as the car mashed into the half-open gate, buckling it back. The constable, she was grateful to see, was safe too. She was already chasing the first man, far to the right. The car ground for a second against the metal of the gate, then seemed to lurch free, away into the small lane they had just walked down.

Cupidi looked around to see where the young woman was; she was already well on the way towards the other gateway, the one they had been looking through just a couple of minutes earlier. Snapping back into action, she began to chase her again.

It was a simple choice; the teenage girl was someone Cupidi felt she could catch and handle. OK, she was younger and ran fast, but the locked gate ahead would slow her, hopefully for long enough for Cupidi to make up some ground.

Sure enough, at the gate the girl paused, then looked round. By now, Cupidi was close enough to see her eyes widen.

Deftly, the girl placed both hands on the top of the gate and vaulted straight over. By the time Cupidi reached the gate she was sprinting barefoot down the tarmac lane.

Cupidi's negotiation of the gate was less elegant but equally fast, and she hit the ground running, having the advantage now on the harder surface. In a few paces she was matching the girl's pace, shouting, 'Stop!'

The pale soles of the youngster's feet flew up as she ran into the gathering darkness ahead of her.

Another twenty metres and Cupidi was starting to tire. The girl had a younger woman's stamina. In the dark lane Cupidi stumbled in a pothole full of water, sending her falling face down, scraping her palms on the rough tarmac.

She bounced up, but by now the girl was already metres ahead, a dim shape disappearing into the gathering darkness. There was no way that Cupidi could catch her now.

She stood in the middle of the lane panting for a second. Then looked around. 'Jill,' she shouted.

After a minute of chaos and shouting, everything was suddenly quiet.

'Jill?'

No answer.

She should make the call, get back to the field and see if there was anyone left there.

A dog started barking again, loudly.

When she reached the caravans, still out of breath, the lights were all on and there was no one in any of them. Empty plates had been piled in a sink. Blankets lay discarded on the floor. A cigarette still burned in an ashtray.

'Jill?' Again, louder.

And then, suddenly, the screaming started; inchoate, wordless, terrified. It was Ferriter's voice.

TWENTY-FIVE

She ran to the sound of screaming.

It seemed to be coming from the far side of the field, from the direction she had seen Ferriter running towards minutes earlier.

Her progress across the meadow seemed impossibly slow; she stumbled across the hummocky land, lungs already aching from her sprint to try and catch the girl.

Ahead, a pair of mallards rose, startled, quacking, flapping into the air. Something had disturbed them.

As she reached what she thought was the edge of the field, she saw it curved away further to the right. At the far side, the land was hedgeless. Against the broad horizon the figures of two men were silhouetted against the dark blue evening, one plump, the other thin. They were shouting at each other, or at someone down below.

She ran faster; though marshy, the ground was more even underfoot.

When the yelling stopped, briefly, she heard the dog barking and snarling. It was down in the ditch where the men were looking. 'Christ.'

There was the sound of frantic splashing. And then the screaming started again.

The noise covered Cupidi's approach. About twenty metres away she began to be able to make out that this field ended in a ditch, much like the one they had found Hilary Keen's body in. Panting hard now, a stitch starting to burn in her left side, she could see that the two men looking down into the water were on opposite sides of it, one closer to Cupidi, the other in the next field.

And now, from the left, she caught sight of someone else running towards the men.

A woman. A sensibly dressed, Hunter wellies and olive-green gilet kind of countrywoman. Absurdly English.

She was speeding alongside the far side of the water towards the commotion. Cupidi didn't have time to wonder what she was doing.

Out of sight, Ferriter's voice came again, 'Help me!' But Cupidi was still frustratingly far away from the slope to see down into it.

'Jill,' she shouted back. 'I'm coming.'

The fatter man on the far side looked up, saw her approaching, shouted urgently down into the ditch.

Cupidi tripped, fell.

When she got up, the man who had seen her was scampering away. The second man, now covered from head to foot in dark mud, was desperately trying to scramble up the side of the slope, finding it impossible to get a hold on the wet bank.

He must have tried to jump the ditch to get away, she realised.

She was up again now, running towards where she had heard Ferriter's pleading coming from.

The other woman reached the place first. She paused at the top. Cupidi could see shock in her eyes. 'Call it off,' the woman shouted. 'Call the bloody thing off.'

And then the woman plunged downwards, feet first, out of sight, slithering down the steep slope and knocking the escaping man backwards, into the water.

The dog had its jaws clamped on Ferriter's calf. It was shaking its head methodically from side to side as the police officer tried in vain to kick it off.

Ferriter's head thrashed sideways. She was trapped halfway up the opposite bank, trying to escape the dog, which was also scrambling for a foothold.

It looked like some kind of mastiff. Large, floppy-jawed, it seemed unbothered by Ferriter's attempts to struggle free, or by the mud it was caked in. Ferriter's other foot was below the water; but each time she bent her leg to try and kick the dog away, she slithered downwards to the surface of the water, losing what little purchase she had. Instead she began desperately to try to push the dog's head off with her hands, still yelling in pain as she did so.

'I'm coming,' Cupidi shouted.

Next to them the other man was struggling to get back up the steep bank. Cupidi leaped feet first into the dank water below her.

It was a mistake; she was too far from Ferriter. The bottom of the ditch was soft, giving way under her. She realised why attempting to cross here had been such a poor move for the escaping men – and for Ferriter, who had presumably been chasing them. It was a natural trap. As she tried to move in Ferriter's direction, her feet stuck in the sludge, ooze sucking at her shoes.

Ferriter caught her eye as she flailed towards her. She was desperate, in pain and exhausted from struggling with the animal. The dog's spittle flew from its gums as it shook its head.

Next to her, gasping for breath, was the other man, face black with silt.

The other woman had known what to expect. Instead of jumping like Cupidi had, she had slithered down the bank on her backside.

Now, with the kind of decisiveness you rarely saw from members of the public, she launched herself in a tackle onto the dog's body, her arms around the mastiff's chest.

As Cupidi was edging closer, one slow step after another, she heard the woman order, 'Bend your leg.'

With her free arm she slapped Ferriter's thigh. 'Bend it,' she hollered.

Shocked, Ferriter bent her right leg – the one the dog was not latched on to.

The woman barely had time to take a breath before she and the dog disappeared under the water's dark surface.

'Hold on!' Cupidi shouted to Ferriter, who now understood what the woman was trying to do.

Ferriter nodded, grimacing. Meanwhile the man she had been chasing was halfway back up the slope.

Cupidi lunged out, caught the runaway's ankle and tugged.

With nothing to grab on to, the man came tumbling back down easily.

'Christ,' screamed Ferriter. The dog had finally released her. She straightened again.

Using her good leg and her arms, she tugged herself along the bank, away from where the dog had been holding her.

The woman's face emerged from the water.

Took a breath.

Submerged again. From below the water came a desperate kicking, frothing the dark surface.

Came up again for a second time.

Then suddenly everything was calm.

Under the water, out of sight, the woman let go of the dog and it floated slowly to the surface, pale coat matted wet, lifeless now.

The woman stood dripping, dark hair across her face.

Ferriter began shivering.

The runaway stared, shocked, turned. Realising he was still free, he started trying to wade along the silted watercourse, one slow step after another.

'Oh for God's sake, stop,' said Cupidi.

The man took another heavy foot forward. And another.

Cupidi reached inside her jacket pocket and pulled out her mobile phone. The screen was dead, the device ruined. 'Oh, bloody hell,' she said.

Cupidi wanted to ask the woman who had saved Ferriter what she was doing here, to thank her for what she had done, but the man was still splashing away down the trench so she set off painfully slowly after him.

It was comical, this slow-motion chase through the sludge. He was only three or four paces away, and with each absurd step, she was gaining on him. He was heavier, she realised. His feet sank deeper than hers, and took more energy to dislodge. She had the edge over him.

'Please,' she called. 'For God's sake stop. You're going nowhere. This is exhausting.'

He hesitated, but then took another slow step. But what would happen when she got closer? Would the advantage be back with him when they were next to each other? He looked stronger. There was no time to think. She had to catch him.

As they reached what first looked like a bend in the watercourse, she realised they were at a T-junction. Another wider ditch lay ahead of them. The water seemed to have suddenly deepened. It was above her belly. The banks were steeper and it would be even harder for either of them to climb out, but the deeper water would make it lighter for him.

But it meant she could swim. Kicking off her shoes, she started to move towards him.

He looked round and then, just as abruptly, disappeared below the water, a look of panic on his face.

A hand surfaced, splashed, then sank again.

He couldn't swim, she realised. The clothes he wore had pulled him under.

'Christ,' she said.

She paused to pull off her sodden jacket, but it caught on her watch. She tugged again, heard a ripping sound. It would be ruined anyway. Her watch as well, she guessed.

His hand emerged again from below the surface, then his head, then he sank again.

She counted to ten slowly, threw the shredded jacket onto the bank, took a deep breath and dived into the black cold water.

TWENTY-SIX

Eyes shut, her fingers found the fugitive low down in the brown water and she grabbed him, at arm's length, taking hold of some material. His trousers she guessed.

Panicking, he struggled and kicked, hitting her hard on the shin. He was strong, she had to give him that.

She was being pulled down in the water with him, but she had deliberately filled her lungs; he had already been half a minute underwater. He was frightened; she was not. He would tire, she knew that.

He did eventually; his limbs loosened. With a heave, she dragged his head to the surface. He gasped for oxygen, sucking in water as he did so, bursting into a fit of coughs.

The bank was close, but it took an age to get to it, manoeuvring his reluctant weight. When she did, she paused for breath, one arm grabbing a handful of reeds.

'Jill,' she called.

'Sarge,' she shouted back. She was just out of sight around the corner of the ditch.

'You OK?'

'Sort of. Fuckin' dog.'

'Got a phone?'

She had one arm around the suspect's neck, the other held his wrist in an armlock. The man turned to try to look at her; the side of his face was streaked with dark mud. Cupidi raised the arm at his back just an inch; enough to cause him a pain.

'Shit. It got a bit wet, Sarge.'

'I'll bet it did. Can you move?'

'Sort of,' she said again.

'That woman there?' she asked.

'She's just helping me up the bank now.' Cupidi could hear the sound of scrambling. At least Ferriter was safe.

'Let's hope she's got a phone, otherwise we're up shit creek,' she said.

'Ha very ha.'

It was getting dark now; the sky above them was a deep blue. She turned to the man, rasping in her headlock.

'What's your name, sir?'

The man gasped something; she realised she was probably holding him a little too tightly, but right then she didn't feel like loosening her grip.

'Can she get to a phone?' Cupidi called. 'We're going to need backup.'

There was a noise above her head and the woman appeared on the bank. Cupidi had to twist her neck to see her. The woman was short, had straw-coloured hair and wore a man's checked shirt. 'I'm very sorry to say your colleague has been hurt by that bloody dog,' she said in a rosy-cheeked English accent.

'Thank you,' said Cupidi.

'Had to kill the dog, I'm afraid,' she said, as if a little shocked by what she'd done.

'You did the right thing,' Cupidi said. 'Do you have a phone?'

'In the house, yes.'

Cupidi wondered how long she could physically hold the suspect for. His strength would be coming back to him soon.

'How far is the house?

'Ten minutes. Five if I run.'

'We need police. And ambulance. My name is Sergeant Cupidi.'

'Will you be OK? With him?'

Cupidi was propped at the side of the ditch, shivering a little, covered in mud, pondweed in her hair, with her arm around a muscular man half her age who had tried to injure or even kill her colleague. 'Fine,' she said.

'Righto.' The woman disappeared from view again.

'What happened?' called Ferriter.

'I think we are on to something.'

'No kidding,' said Ferriter. 'My bloody leg. You got him?'

'Yes. I'm holding on to him by his neck.'

'Give it a squeeze from me.'

Something rustled in the reeds on the far bank. Cupidi hoped it was a vole, not a rat. 'Bleeding much?'

'Not too much. I fuckin' hate dogs, that's all. Always have done. I can move my foot a little. That's good, isn't it? I think it's OK. Ow.'

'What?'

'Tried to stand up.'

'Don't then.'

The man was wriggling slowly, pushing away from her. She pulled the arm up his back a little more; it would hurt. He wheezed in pain.

'What's your name?'

He stopped moving. Grunted again.

'If I loosen my grip on your neck, don't try anything,' she said.

'Yes.'

She slacked off her grip a fraction. 'Name?'

He said, 'Can't breathe.'

Reluctantly she relaxed her left arm a little more.

'OK. Now,' she said.

'My hand,' he said. 'You're breaking my hand.' He spoke with an accent.

'Tell me your name,' she said.

It was quiet now. There were crickets singing in the grass around them. Vapour trails turned pink against the darkening sky above.

'OK,' he said. 'My name . . .'

'I didn't hear,' she said.

And then, maybe because she was tired, maybe because he was much stronger than her, he shifted suddenly and she found she could do nothing to halt his momentum. Jerking his right arm from her grasp wasn't as hard as it should have been; her skin was still slippery from the water.

To compensate, she tightened her left arm on his throat, but she couldn't hold him. Spinning round, he lifted his right arm and went straight for her face with his fingertips.

It all happened in a second. She raised a knee, to try and

connect with his groin, but it was already too late. He was in motion. She was cold and tired now. Her kneecap connected with his hip instead.

And he was clawing at her face now, fingers closing on her eye.

Her head was back against the muddy bank with nowhere to go. To protect herself, she had no choice but to let go, hoping she could get a better grip on him once her hands were free.

With a splash, he fell back into the water.

She raised her other leg, attempting to kick him into the deep again. This time she would let him bloody drown.

But a second time he dodged her, twisting his body back the way they had come, towards where she had left Ferriter.

He found what had eluded him earlier – something to grip on the opposite bank, a loose root – and by the time she reached him he was already hauling himself up the slope.

She grabbed the same root herself and, limbs aching, pulled herself up after him.

By the time she made it to the top he was close to the bend in the field, flailing arms as he ran back towards the caravans.

'I saved your bloody life,' she muttered to herself.

She stood unsteadily, limbs aching, and considered running after him, but he would already be a long way off. There was no point. Instead she walked up the ditch to Ferriter.

She was on the other side of the bank from her now, sitting up in the grass in the disappearing light. Her legs were smeared with mud and blood. 'Was that him, running away?' she asked.

'Yes.'

'You let him go?'

'Well, not on purpose, obviously.'

'Bloody hell,' Ferriter said, exhausted. 'What a joke.'

Soon the unlikely woman in wellingtons came trotting back along the opposite bank. She had a bottle of water and bandages with her.

She stopped and looked at her across the sewer. 'What happened to the other . . . ?'

'He got away,' said Cupidi.

'Oh dear,' said the woman. 'And you're bleeding.'

'Am I?'

Cupidi looked down. Her sodden blouse had blotches of red on it. She put her filthy hand up to her face, where the man had clawed at her skin, and when she brought it down again it had blood on it.

The woman threw a small orange package across the stream. 'Here,' she said. 'It's a dressing. It's meant for horses, but it'll be fine. It'll stop the bleeding, anyway.'

'Horses?' said Cupidi.

'They bleed just the same,' said the woman. 'Just hold it on the wound.'

'Is that what you're using on her?'

'It's sterile, that's the main thing,' she said. She was kneeling now, washing Ferriter's cuts with the bottle of water. 'How's the leg? Not broken or anything, is it?'

'She won't have to shoot you then,' said Cupidi.

'What?' said the woman.

'Sorry. Not funny. What were you doing here, anyway?' asked Cupidi.

'Here? This is my land.'

'And the men in the caravans?'

'They were renting off me,' she said. 'Unfortunately. Just for a few weeks. They come and go, this time of year. Nothing but bloody bother.'

'Cash in hand?'

The woman tore open one of the packets with her teeth. 'Am I in trouble?' she asked, looking anxiously from one to the other.

The first car arrived, blue lights flashing, then two more.

The third had a man in custody in the back. 'Recognise this one?' called the copper in the back seat with him. She had seen his hand as it had clawed towards her eye.

'Yes,' said Cupidi. 'I bloody do.'

'Almost ran over him.'

'Shame you missed.' She pointed to the white bandage on her face. 'Exhibit A. Assaulting a police officer.'

The man's head twitched away, nervously. He was frightened, she realised. That was something, at least, she thought.

TWENTY-SEVEN

'Horses,' said the woman, looking out of the window at the searchlight beam of the police helicopter that was scouring the fields for the runaways. 'Bought the place after my divorce,' the woman said, 'Fifteen years ago. Still trying to make a go of it. Tough here in the country.'

She had given her name as Miss Connie Reed. 'I've gone back to my maiden name. My husband's name was Conway. Connie Conway always sounded ridiculous,' she said, pouring water in a kettle.

'I kept mine,' said Cupidi.

'What?'

'Sorry. My ex's name, I meant. I tend to just say whatever's on the top of my head. My name: Cupidi. I liked the name better than I did him.'

The woman nodded, as if it were a perfectly normal conversation to be having on a night like this after everything that had happened.

Connie Reed and Alex Cupidi sat in the kitchen, next to an Aga. The other police had left, trying to find the people who had run away.

The paramedic had replaced Reed's dressing with a small bandage, covering the cut on Cupidi's face. His colleagues had injected Ferriter with painkillers and taken her to hospital to have stitches put into her leg.

'Twice, now,' Ferriter had said as they helped her up. 'What next, eh?'

Connie Reed's house was small but neat. The fabrics were floral. Amateurish paintings of horses hung on the walls. There was a bookshelf stacked alphabetically from Isabel Allende to Joanna Trollope.

At the house, she had washed herself in the woman's bathroom. Reed had given her a clean blouse and found a wraparound skirt. 'You're a bit bigger than me,' she'd said. 'See how that fits.'

'Seriously,' said Cupidi, emerging from the bathroom. 'You were great. You saved a police officer from much worse injury. I expect the papers will want to make a fuss of you.'

'Oh God no,' said Connie Reed, horrified. 'I abhor that kind of thing. Less said the better.'

'How long have the caravans been parking on your farm?'

'Few years, I would guess. Lot of summer work round here on the farms, see? They come along every now and again asking for places to stay.'

'And they pay you rent, these people?'

'I honestly didn't think it would make much of a difference. It's only a little money here and there. Mostly it was useful to have a couple of men around. They helped me out a bit with the hay, things like that. And now I'm probably going to be in a lot of trouble, aren't I?'

'It depends. Did you know that they were probably working illegally?'

The woman looked away at the kettle, waiting for it to boil.

'You see, I suppose I didn't really ask,' she said. The woman who had looked so in charge when it came to tackling a vicious dog now looked helpless.

Cupidi tried to remember her law. Under the Immigration Act landlords had been tasked with policing immigration; it was their job to make sure that tenants had a legal right to be in this country, but would renting land be different? Presumably it would. Technically, if she had rented a field to illegal immigrants without knowing, had she broken any law at all, beyond not declaring the income?

'If you get in touch with the tax people and tell them you've been receiving some kind of rent, they'll come to some kind of arrangement. I'm sure it wasn't very much. Did you know anything about who they were?'

Connie Reed shook her head. 'Their English wasn't very good. And they came and went. They kept themselves to themselves. That's why I didn't mind having them, really.'

'There was a young woman. Apparently they found an identity card in one of the caravans. She may have been Lithuanian.'

'I don't really know, I'm afraid. As I said, they came and went. I'm quite a private person, really. I prefer the company of animals, I'll be honest. It's why I like it. Some people say it's lonely around here. I don't mind that at all.'

'What about the man who did this to me? The man they arrested? He didn't give a name.'

The kettle boiled. She poured water into a pot. 'Sorry. I think he was new. I didn't really recognise him.' She looked around. 'I think your colleague is OK. Flesh and muscle, the dog got, by the look of it. She'll be limping a bit, I'll bet. And it'll probably scar. Hate killing an animal like that, though. I'll have nightmares now.'

'You live here on your own?'

The woman nodded. 'Apart from the horses, obviously.'

They drank tea. It all seemed ridiculously calm and domestic now. All very English.

'Are you going to be OK? You're not afraid of them coming back?'

'Why? Should I be?' said Connie Reed, surprised by the question. She looked completely unafraid, just as she had been when Cupidi had watched her jump down into the sewer to save Ferriter. She had acted decisively and bravely. An eccentric, perhaps, but a woman who seemed entirely content to exist on her own terms.

Cupidi smiled at her and reached her hand across the table, laying it on top of the other woman's. 'No. I don't suppose you should.'

'You could have called,' said her mother.

'Not really. My phone got wet. It's ruined. When the man was trying to kill me,' said Cupidi. She had put the device into a pot of rice to try and dry it out.

Her mother peered at the bandage. 'It doesn't look like he tried that hard,' she said.

'Nan!' said Zoë.

'Sorry,' said Cupidi's mother. 'I'm not very good at sympathy.'

'You can say that again,' said Zoë.

The two of them laughed. Cupidi looked from one to the other.

'I need a bath,' she said.

'Yes,' said Zoë. 'You do.'

She sat in the water with a glass of white wine, trying to get the stink of mud out of her nostrils and her hair.

Dropping her head back into the bath, she lay, listening to the noises of the house, amplified by the water. Najiba's tip-off had meant they had stumbled into something; she was sure of it now.

One thing had convinced her: the look on the man's face in the back of the police car. The way he had fought with her to get away when they were both stuck in the watercourse had been more than vicious. It had been desperate. But the world was full of desperation.

It was when she had looked into his eyes as he sat there, hands bound by the cuffs; it was real fear she had seen there.

She had made a serious mistake going there unprepared, she realised.

It was on the TV news in the morning. The tickertape under the newsreader read: ILLEGAL MIGRANTS ATTACK POLICE.

Her mother was watching it, a mug of tea in her hand.

'That was you?'

'The TV are making a meal of it,' Cupidi said.

'I suppose it must have been frightening,' her mother said.

'Yes. It was.'

She took a sip from the cup, then said, 'I am proud of you, you know.'

'Are you?'

'Don't sound so surprised. Of course I am. Always have been, doing what you do.'

The local MP was on the TV saying this showed why they had to take a tougher line on people coming into the country. Zoë appeared at the door, yawning.

Cupidi looked at her face in the mirror in the hallway. Behind the scab of where his nails had cut her, the man had bruised the skin between her temple and her eye. It had turned an unpleasant greyish-yellow. 'What are you two doing today?'

'Going for a walk.'

'Again?'

'I'm ashamed to say I'm enjoying it, really,' her mother said. 'I haven't spent this much time outdoors since I was a kid, on the farm. Is that all you're having for breakfast?'

Cupidi had wrapped a jam sandwich in foil.

'That's not even healthy.'

She was missing her regular morning walk, but there seemed to be no time for it on days like this. 'I need to be at the station for eight. Don't forget your phones.'

'Don't drop yours in the water,' Zoë called after her as she closed the back door and walked to her car, digging in her handbag for the keys.

She tried switching on her phone. The rice hadn't worked. The phone was still dead.

TWENTY-EIGHT

'Turn it up,' said Cupidi.

The video feed from the interrogation room was showing on a computer screen in the incident room. Sergeant Moon pressed the volume key until they could hear the hum of the quiet room.

The camera was focused on the young man whom they had arrested last night and the duty solicitor sitting next to him.

Leaning back in the chair, the immigrant tried to appear relaxed, but he wasn't. His fists were clenched, nails digging into his palms. He was dressed in a tracksuit and a New York T-shirt somebody in the custody unit must have given him. The top was too small for him; it strained at his chest. The solicitor was a young woman who sat scratching her scalp with the blunt end of her biro.

'Please tell us your name and date of birth.' It was one of the other sergeants speaking. You could see her on the second camera.

'We believe your name to be Hamid Fakroun. Can you confirm that for us?'

'How do they know his name?' asked Cupidi.

'Fingerprints. He came through Dover last year. Failed asylum seeker. Was due for removal, but he disappeared.'

'What were you doing on the farm, Hamid?'

The man's lips twitched, but he said nothing. He looked small and uncomfortable on the plastic chair.

'You were seen coming out of one of the caravans. Were you living there?'

Again no answer.

The sergeant's voice was quiet, slightly distorted. 'We have reason to believe you were working illegally in the neighbourhood. Where were you working?'

Cupidi unwrapped her sandwich.

'Do you recognise this man?' The sergeant's hand appeared in shot holding a photo. 'For the record, I am showing the man known to us as Hamid Fakroun a photograph of the unidentified deceased man whose body was found at Horse Bones Farm.'

The man didn't even look at the picture. Instead he stared at the edge of table in front of him.

'He's actually bloody avoiding even looking at it,' said Moon. Cupidi pulled up a chair and sat next to him, taking the first bite into her breakfast. Did that mean he did recognise the man and didn't want to look at him? The man's eyes were small, hard to read on the screen.

'What were the names of your other companions?'

Again, nothing. He remained still, his lawyer silent at his side.

Frustratingly, they had recovered little in the way of documents from the two caravans. A few worn photographs of children in some faraway country. There was a single blue Permanent Residence Certificate; that of a Lithuanian. It had been the young woman Cupidi had chased and lost.

'Do you recognise this woman?' The sergeant was saying now. 'For the record, I am holding up the identity card of Rasa Petrauska.'

This time there was the smallest of smiles on the man's face; then he shook his head.

'Why are you smiling?'

The man's expression turned to sneer.

'Was she in a relationship with any of the men in your group?'

The face returned to expressionlessness.

The sergeant was saying, 'If you're able to shed any light on the killing it would be helpful. I'm sure your lawyer has already informed you of the trouble you are in.'

Silence.

'He's not going to say nothing, is he?' said Moon. 'Straight to jail for him.'

'What's in it for him to talk?' said Cupidi. 'Even if he's not prosecuted, he's still on the next plane home. Besides. I think he's scared of something. Look at him.'

She pushed back her chair. On the screen he looked so much smaller than the man who had tried to gouge her eyes.

Moon looked round. 'Anything from Ferriter?'

'She'll be off for a couple of days. She needed stitches in the leg.'

'She won't be liking that.'

'You should visit her. She's back home. Take her flowers.'

Moon nodded, chewed on his tongue. 'Maybe.'

She went to Najiba's flat, but as before, no one answered. This time no one peered down from the window above either. She waited a while and watched, but there was nothing to see.

Ferriter's address was a flat in the Panorama building. The Panorama had been built in the 1970s as a grey concrete office block, a huge V-sign of concrete spread out in two angled wings, but it had recently been refurbished as what were now called luxury apartments.

Ferriter buzzed her up. 'Seventh floor,' she said.

She opened the door on metal crutches, her wounded leg wrapped in bandage. She was wearing a pink towelling dressing gown.

'Look at you,' said Cupidi.

'Sorry. Not dressed.'

'You look pretty good for someone who was mauled by a dog last night.'

'Little fucker,' she said, hobbling back down the corridor to a living room whose window looked out over the flat town. 'If it scars I'm going to have a fit. Your face looks worse though.'

'Thanks,' said Cupidi.

'Yeah. Well.'

The room was white, dominated by a large mirror framed in artificial red and pink flowers. A purple beaded lamp hung from the ceiling, while a white teddy bear with a red bow tie sat on a plain grey sofa. Above it, a poster of swirly writing encouraged the reader to 'Live well, laugh often, love always'.

'You live here on your own?'

'Bought it when my mum died. Do you like it?'

'When did she die?'

'Couple of years back. Brain cancer.'

'I'm sorry. It's lovely,' said Cupidi, looking around. On the table sat a purple glass bowl full of gold-painted pine cones. No bookshelves, just a large TV on, beneath the big mirror, volume turned down. And all neat and spotless.

Ferriter dropped down onto the couch, resting the crutches beside her, pulling her pink dressing gown around herself. 'Did they catch any of them? Have any of them said anything?'

'They're still looking for the rest. It's just the one man who tried to poke my eye out who we've got, for now, anyway.'

'Bastard.'

Cupidi nodded. 'Everybody at work says hello.'

'God. I never thought I'd want to be back at work so soon. One morning at home and I'm bored just sitting around, being honest. Tea? Coffee?'

Cupidi told her to stay where she was and walked to the small kitchen next door. It was just as tidy.

'I'll have rooibos,' Ferriter called.

Cupidi opened cupboards until she found one with tea in it. There were several herb infusions, and a 'wellness' tea, but she couldn't find either ordinary tea or coffee.

'I came to say sorry,' she called from the kitchen.

'Don't fret. Wasn't your fault.'

The kettle was starting to murmur. 'Yes. I think it was.'

'What you talking about, Sarge?'

'That address,' she said, when she returned with two cups of rooibos. 'You understand where I got it from, don't you?'

'I think so. Najiba. She gave you it, didn't she?'

'Yes. And she was clearly worried about passing it over.'

'Was she?'

'Think about it. It's not surprising. First off, she's working illegally.'

'Yeah, but it's that or begging.'

'The point is, she knows if she is found out it'll be another reason to deport her, so her first instinct is to say nothing to us. Which happened when we first met. But she thinks about it and a day later she changes her mind. Even though she's risking everything to talk to us. So it was obviously something that was important for her to do.'

'Because I said I'd help her,' said Ferriter.

'She wasn't naive, Jill. She's been around. But she gave the list to us anyway. And I think she knew what she was going to tell us was dangerous in itself. She knew already what she was dealing with.'

They sat side by side on her sofa, looking out at the blue sky.

'I should have figured that out,' said Cupidi. 'I should have been more cautious.'

'Oh my God,' said Ferriter. 'You think she knew them? The people who attacked us?'

'That's the point. She knows something, at least. I'm pretty sure.'

Ferriter's eyes shone. Cupidi recognised the look. It was something she felt herself; the excitement of getting close. And then Ferriter's mouth dropped as she realised what that would mean for Najiba: the risk of removal. She had not wanted to be involved; now she was, and as a significant witness.

TWENTY-NINE

'It means,' said Cupidi, 'that we're going to have to question her.'

Ferriter glared. 'But I promised her. When I ran after her. That's what I promised her. We'd keep her out of this.'

'You shouldn't have.'

'That's why she talked to me in the first place. She wouldn't have talked to us at all if I hadn't chased after her last week.'

Cupidi nodded. 'I suppose we can still try and keep her identity quiet if she talks to us off the record. But we'll need to speak to her.'

'Have you been to her place?' Ferriter said.

'She's not there. She'll be at work. But she gave you her phone number, didn't she?'

Ferriter grabbed a crutch and was about to stand, then dropped it. 'Crap. Her number's in my phone. It got trashed.'

'Mine too. Have you still got it?'

'Yeah. But it's totally screwed. Won't turn on. There must

be someone who can get the data off it, mustn't there? Besides, you got one of the people from the caravans, didn't you? Can't we just interview him? Then she won't have to say anything.'

'He's not talking. And he has no reason to because he understands perfectly well he's going to be deported whatever he says. If we catch any of the others, my guess is they'll be exactly the same.'

'I think she wants to help us,' said Ferriter. 'I know she does. Shall I go there now? It's only up the road. I wouldn't mind. I could wait for her to come back.'

'Don't be mad,' said Cupidi. 'Did Peter Moon call?'

'No. Why?'

'Nothing.'

She left the constable sitting on the sofa, crutch at her side, watching her silent television.

She was back at her desk, trying to tidy it. Hilary Keen's list of offences had been sitting in her in tray. She picked it up and read through it again: CONVICTIONS (8). DATE FIRST CONVICTED, 14/1/1983.

It was strange. Sometimes you could look at the same document and notice completely different things.

When she had first seen it, she had been drawn to the six convictions for possession of controlled substances, probably because it had chimed with what she knew of her dental record. This time she looked at the first two and realised there was something unusual there. They were both for criminal damage, one in 1983 and the next in 1985. Both had been heard at Newbury Magistrates' Court. She noted the dates. Hilary Keen would have been eighteen when she had been arrested for the first. But both convictions had resulted in thirty-day prison sentences. That in itself was extraordinary.

She looked up and said aloud. 'Why would an eighteen-year-old woman be given a custodial sentence for her first offence of criminal damage?'

'What did she damage?'

'Very good point. I don't know.' She peered at the printout again. As always, the details were so vague. Just a conviction and a sentence.

Moon said, 'You went to see Jill, did you?'

'Yes?'

'How is she?'

'Why don't you give her a call and ask?'

'Has Jill got a boyfriend?'

'What's it to you?'

'Nothing,' said Moon, then looked back at his computer screen and said, 'Refused to pay the fine.'

'What?'

'You asked why an eighteen-year-old would have been given a custodial for criminal damage. Maybe refused to pay the fine. Judge wouldn't have much choice then.'

'Yeah. But then the fine would show up on her sentencing. There's no record at all of her being fined.'

'Suppose.'

Moon didn't seem to be interested in pursuing it any further. Cupidi looked at the date of the conviction again: 14 January 1983. The scab beneath her eye was prickling again, but so was her entire skin. There was something here, something important, but she didn't know what.

On a hunch she put 'News UK January 1983' into her browser. It came up with a Wikipedia list of events that month.

There was nothing special there. So she clicked back to the previous month.

There it was in the middle.

12 December 1982. Greenham Common Women's Peace Camp: 30,000 women hold hands and form a chain around the 9-mile perimeter fence.

She followed another link. And yes, Greenham Common was in Berkshire. Anyone committing an offence there would have been tried at Newbury Magistrates' Court.

She checked the news for that day.

On New Year's Eve 1982, forty-four women had broken into RAF Greenham Common in Berkshire. They had been protesting about the British Government's decision to allow American cruise missiles to be based there. Tens of thousands of women had camped around the base for years. That night, the protesters danced on top of the silos before they were all arrested. Of the forty-four, thirty-six of them were imprisoned; all had refused to pay a fine.

Now it made sense. The protesters must have told the court they would refuse to pay any fine. So the judge would have had no option but to give them a prison sentence.

Hilary Keen had been one of the protesters at Greenham Common.

*

The winter of 1982 had been when her mother disappeared.

Growing up, Alexandra Cupidi had lived in a large house in Stoke Newington with her parents, an only child.

That December, a few weeks before Christmas, her mother had left home. She had been thirteen. As she remembered it, there had been no explanation, no particular build-up to her leaving. It hadn't been the result of an argument with her father, or a breakdown. One day she had been there, the next she was gone. When she had asked Dad when her mother was coming back, he had been tight-lipped.

To say 'disappeared' sounded dramatic, but it was the way she had thought of it at the time. There were no phone calls or postcards.

From then on, that winter and into next summer, her father looked after her alone. Just her and Dad. She had even started cooking for him when he came back from work.

It wasn't that her mother had been entirely absent; Cupidi remembered again how she had come back for a night or two at a time, always with other women, some short-haired, dressed in baggy trousers and monkey boots.

The visits had been unannounced and random. Alexandra had wanted her mother's attention when she was back, to talk to her privately about her periods and about her A+ in maths. Instead, her mother had huddled in the kitchen with her new women friends, talking late into the night, smoking cigarettes and drinking, surrounded by leaflets and documents.

And then she had disappeared into the bedroom with Dad, ignoring her completely.

She remembered that 'Ghosts' by Japan had been in the charts. She had sat in her bedroom listening to it on the record player.

Cupidi had thought it was the best song ever.

At 7 p.m., she drove from the station to Najiba's building and parked outside again and rang the same bell. There was a slow trickle of people arriving back from work, entering through the main front door.

Nothing.

She held her finger on the buzzer, but still no one answered.

Stepping back, she looked up, expecting to see a face peering out of the curtains as it had last week, but the room was dark, even though the curtains were open now.

She heard a voice calling on the car radio. 'They were trying to reach you on your mobile,' a voice said.

'It's in a pot of rice at home. What's wrong?'

'Nothing. Incident room duty officer was just calling to say they found that woman from the caravans yesterday. Rasa Petrauska. She's at the William Harvey.' The local hospital.

Cupidi remembered chasing her; barefoot, the white soles of her feet. 'Why is she in hospital?'

'They didn't say. She's in the antenatal unit, apparently.' She got back in the car and was about to start it when she saw the woman sitting on the wall by the bins, crutches propped against her leg.

Cupidi sighed, got out of the car and walked over.

'How long have you been here?'

''Bout two hours. Set off after you'd gone.' On the wall next to Jill Ferriter sat one of those bottles of water with a charcoal filter in it and a packet of Japanese rice crackers.

Cupidi looked at her supplies. 'Proper stake-out.'

'I'm so bored at home,' she said.

'You shouldn't be here. You're not on duty.'

She looked away, sucked at her cheek for a second. 'That's why I'm here. Because I'm not on duty. Not a copper.'

Cupidi looked at her: summer dress, bandaged leg and crutches. 'So you thought you can just chat with her, off the record and she'll tell you what's going on?'

'Kind of.'

'It doesn't work like that,' said Cupidi. 'But you may not need to speak to her. We've found someone else. They just picked up the woman from the caravans, the one I tried to catch. She's at the hospital, in the antenatal unit.'

'What's she doing there?'

'At a guess, I'd say she's pregnant, wouldn't you? I'm just going to see her.'

'Can I come?'

'No. I'll drop you home.'

'I'll wait in the car. I promise. You can drop me off after. Then you can tell me what she says.'

Cupidi said, 'I thought you'd have seen quite enough of hospitals by now.'

It was ten minutes' drive to the William Harvey. Cupidi parked in front and spent another ten trying to find the antenatal ward. 'Tell me,' she asked. 'Have you ever heard of Greenham Common?'

'Is that in London?'

'No. Berkshire. It was a big demonstration in the early 1980s.'

'Way before I was born.' Ferriter shook her head.

Cupidi showed her warrant card to a nurse on the desk, a smiley, middle-aged woman wearing a blue uniform. 'I'm looking for a Rasa Petrauska,' she said.

'I'll take you down there,' said the nurse, standing.

'How did she end up here?' asked Cupidi as they walked down the corridor, avoiding a man coming the other way pushing a trolley loaded with monitors.

'She appeared at A & E about two hours ago asking for a doctor . . . Well, asking for something. The receptionist couldn't understand a word. Luckily there was this cleaner; anyway he was passing by and understood what she was saying, and he's been interpreting for her. He's in there with her now. She was quite distressed, you see. I don't think she'd eaten for a while and she was pretty dirty.'

'How pregnant is she?'

'We think about five months.'

'Christ.' Cupidi remembered chasing her across the field, seeing her vault the fence. She felt bad about how hard she'd run now.

The nurse stopped outside a plain door with a small window in it; the blind behind the glass was down. 'Has she committed some kind of offence? Because I'm not having her going into custody. She needs to be properly examined. She doesn't appear to have seen a doctor at all since she was pregnant.'

'Nothing like that. Not as far as I know,' said Cupidi. 'We just need to question her.'

'OK,' said the nurse, knocking on the door, then opening it. Rasa Petrauska lay on a bed in a small side room. Cupidi hadn't had a good look at her before; she had been chasing her. Her chubby face had a large strawberry birthmark on one cheek. As she realised who had just walked into the room, her eyes opened wide. Like the man in the interview room, she was terrified.

THIRTY

A young broad-shouldered man in a blue NHS shirt sat on a chair by Rasa's side, his name on a badge: Kriss Jansons. 'Hello,' he said, standing. He grinned. 'I think Rasa is feeling a little better.'

If she had been, seeing Cupidi had not helped. Petrauska sobbed out loud; said something in her own language. Looking back at the patient, the porter registered the expression of panic on her face, and asked her a question. The answer came back in a whisper.

Jansons looked at Cupidi, frowning. 'She thinks you have come to arrest her.'

Cupidi held up her hands. 'I just want to talk.'

The cleaner translated again. 'It's OK. It's OK,' he said, trying to calm her.

'Are you Lithuanian too?' Cupidi asked.

'I am Latvian,' he said. 'The language is a little the same, but different.' His accent was strong, but his English was clear.

'Rasa said you were chasing her and her boyfriend. She is very, very frightened of you.'

'Tell her she has no need to be. We weren't chasing them. They just ran when they saw us. I just want to know what she was doing there.'

Jansons nodded and translated for Petrauska. She frowned at them, as if not believing what Cupidi was saying. 'She was very upset, I think. Her boyfriend told her to run. Since then she has been looking for him, but she can't find him anywhere. Last night she slept in a car park.'

'What is the name of your boyfriend, Rasa?'

Kriss translated.

'She says his name is Hamid.'

'Hamid Fakroun?'

Rasa Petrauska nodded.

'And he is the father of your child?' she pointed at the woman's belly. The swelling was not large for five months.

Again, the woman nodded. Her movements were swift and bird-like, her big eyes blinking nervously.

'Well, that explains why she hasn't seen him then. He's in custody. He's an illegal immigrant.'

When Jansons told her this, she began to weep.

'What is she saying?'

'She says they are going to be married. Before the baby.'

The nurse clucked her disapproval. 'Mother of God,' she said.

'Can she tell us where she met him?' asked Cupidi.

'In a meat-packing plant,' came back the answer. 'She was working there in the spring.'

'Which one?'

Jansons asked her. 'She doesn't know. She has been labouring in factories and on farms here. I think, from what she says, she has been paying this man money. It is hard to understand what she says. She is confused.'

'Have you asked her why she didn't come to hospital before now to check on her baby?'

'Because Hamid was afraid they would find out he was an illegal immigrant. I don't think he would permit her.'

'Hamid would not allow her to come to hospital?'

'Yes. That is what she said.'

Cupidi looked at her: young and scared. 'Can she give me a list of all the farms she's been working on?'

Jansons and Petrauska spoke for a little while, then he shook his head. 'She does not know. They are just driven to the places. They work, then they are driven away again.'

'She must know some names.'

Jansons looked at the woman sympathetically for a second, then turned and said, 'I don't think she is a very clever woman. She has speaking difficulties.'

'Learning difficulties?'

'Exactly.'

The nurse shook her head and said, 'Oh Christ. What a story.'

'Which agency does she work for?'

'When she came here she worked with one agency, but after she met Hamid she worked for another one. She does not know the name. Hamid arranged it.'

'What about the names of the people she worked for?'

After Jansons had translated, the pregnant woman shrugged. She had no idea.

'What does she think is going to happen to her after the baby?' asked Cupidi.

'She will live with Hamid, she says. I told her she should go home. To her mother or father. But she is worried now, because she is pregnant. And by a black man too. She is like a child.' Jansons smiled at Petrauska sadly and ran his hand over her hair. Petrauska looked back at him through damp eyes, grateful for his kindness.

'I have heard of this,' said Jansons, still looking at her. 'They get a girl pregnant here because it means they can stay.'

'That's right,' said Cupidi. 'A father of a child born here could apply for leave to remain.'

'Yep. We've had a few like this already this year,' said the nurse quietly. 'The fathers come in. All they want to see is the baby is out and then they bugger off. The mothers can be crying their heads off, they don't care. They've got what they want. At least, we assume that's what's going on. Nothing we can do about it, 'cept look after the mums.'

'Do you think it's that cynical?'

'Absolutely,' said the Latvian. 'Completely, absolutely. These people like Rasa come here. They are country girls, they are not well educated, they don't speak English, they don't understand this country. They are easy to control.'

'What a horror,' said Cupidi.

Rasa Petrauska was looking from one to the other as they spoke, a concerned look on her big moon face, understanding none of it.

She found Ferriter sitting on an orange plastic chair in another corridor.

'Did she say anything?'

'Not in as many words,' said Cupidi. 'But quite a lot in other ways, yes.'

Cupidi explained; it was possible that she had been made pregnant by the man simply so that he could stay in the country.

'That's horrible,' Ferriter said. 'What vile rock have we just turned over?'

'I know.'

She got into the car slowly, wincing as she swung her bad leg in. They drove back to Najiba's flat and tried the bell again, but no one answered; no lights were on.

'I'll stay here,' Ferriter said, a crutch under one arm.

'No. I'm taking you home.'

'You'd only be making a cripple walk twice as far as they need to. I'm coming straight back here.'

Cupidi stood a second, then nodded, and got into the car alone.

Afterwards, she drove back to the station, swapped cars and then drove back towards Dungeness. But instead of turning off towards Lydd, she carried on south, taking the turning towards Saddlers Wall.

She found the small house again easily, set back from the road, a NO HUNTING sign fixed into the ground by the gate, just as there had been in the field with the caravans. There was a single light on in the kitchen when she drove past it, but another appeared at the porch before she'd switched off the engine. Connie Reed was already at the front door, peering into the gloom.

'Oh,' she said. 'You again.'

'I brought back the clothes you lent me,' she said, holding up a plastic shopping bag.

Reed peered into the bag and grunted. 'How's your friend?'

'Angry,' Cupidi said.

'Not surprised.' Reed stood in the doorway, lit from behind.

'Can I come in?' said Cupidi. 'Just for a minute.'

The woman paused; frowned. 'I suppose. Don't normally have visitors, this time of day. Or at all, really.' She gave a small laugh and stood back to let Cupidi enter the house. 'Can I offer you a cup of tea?'

Cupidi shook her head. 'Don't worry. I won't stop long. We found the girl who had been staying in one of the caravans – the one whose ID we picked up. I just wanted to ask if you knew anything about her.'

The woman took the skirt out of the bag and looked at it. 'I'm afraid not. I make a point of staying out of other people's business. Unless they've set a dangerous dog on someone, obviously.' She sat on a wooden kitchen chair in front of the range and pointed to another with a crocheted cushion on it.

Cupidi sat down too. 'She was Lithuanian. Her name was Rasa Petrauska.'

'Not really surprising. There're an awful lot of Lithuanians around here. They do nearly all the farm work, you know.'

'But you don't recognise the name?'

Connie Reed shook her head.

'She had a birthmark on her face.'

'Possibly I saw her, yes, but I didn't know her. Is that bad?'

'No. But she was twenty-one and pregnant. It appears that

the father was Hamid Fakroun, the gentleman who did this to my face.' Cupidi pointed to the scab below her eye.

Reed looked down at the floor. 'I apologise,' she said. 'If I hadn't let them stay on my field, this would never have happened. I'm not having them anywhere around here ever again, I promise.'

'I don't need an apology from you,' said Cupidi. 'They did this. Not you. You stepped in and saved my colleague from much worse. All I wanted to know is if you'd seen the woman here much.'

'If it's the one I think you're talking about, I did, yes. She was around. Never really spoke to her. She seemed shy. I understand that. Same way myself.' There was a saddle sitting on the kitchen table, with a cloth and and old toothbrush lying next to it. 'You have to understand, I'm not the kind of person who goes out of my way for company.'

'Did you at any point feel she was frightened?'

'No. I mean, maybe. Not really. All I noticed was she seemed out of place, certainly. But so many people do, don't they?' She picked up a buckle and examined it. 'Was she being mistreated?'

'I'm not sure. She is five months pregnant, but hadn't been for any hospital visits until yesterday. I'm trying to work out if there was something coercive about the relationship.'

She looked up. 'Was there? Is that what she's saying?'

'I don't know,' said Cupidi. 'It's a possibility.'

'How awful would that be,' said the woman. 'If that kind of thing was going on in the field next to my house. I don't really take sufficient interest in people, I suppose. I just find it so hard.'

'You like living on your own, don't you?' She thought of her own mother, wanting independence.

'It's more that I don't like living with people,' said Connie Reed. 'Why are you so interested in this girl?'

'Because I think she's in trouble.'

'With girls like that, I tend to assume it's their own silly fault. But that's probably why you're a better person than me,' she said plainly, with no hint of either irony or self-deprecation.

'Do you have any idea where any of the men worked? Were they on farms? Or building sites?'

'If it was farms it wasn't round here. It's mainly arable and sheep on the marsh. A few cows, but not many. It's not the farms around here that need labourers.'

'What about Horse Bones Farm?'

'Dairy,' she said. 'Oh. That's where the body was found, wasn't it?'

'You heard about that.'

'Cows. None of them would have worked there, I doubt. Nasty man, that farmer.'

'Why?'

'Always trying to block off his bridleways. Not legal, you know. Doesn't like me riding through there. Silly really. Know why it's called that?'

'Sorry?'

'Horse Bones Farm. The army retired their horses there after the Napoleonic Wars. Used to be hundreds of horses on that farm once, now he can't bear a single horse crossing his land, silly arse.'

'You know him?'

'Only by reputation.'

'Which is?'

She looked away. 'I'm sure he's perfectly nice. He's just trying to run a farm, which is tough enough in this day and age.'

Cupidi stood.

'I'm sorry. I haven't been much use, have I?'

'Maybe,' said Cupidi. 'You don't like hunting, I see. Is there a lot of it around here?'

'Some. Don't like them coming on my land. Don't like the cruelty to animals.' The woman who had killed a dog with her bare hands.

Reed walked her to the door again, as if she needed to know that her visitor had gone before she could relax.

She reached Dungeness as the last of the day's light disappeared. Once she reached the place where the sea road crossed over the small railway, she pulled over by one of the big new millionaire's beach chalets, watching the red sky darken, trying to fix the day's events in her head before she arrived home. The discovery that Hilary Keen had once been young and idealistic, going to prison for her beliefs. But more importantly, visible even in the pixellated video link, the fear in Hamid Fakroun's eyes. The father of Rasa Petrauska's child was a man so callous that he had almost certainly coerced a vulnerable woman into having his baby, but even he had looked afraid.

She was finally getting a sense of the malevolence that lay beneath the surface, but it remained obscure, hard to grasp. In neither case, the dead man's nor Hilary Keen's, did the evidence form any pattern she understood.

In the millionaire's black house, a light came on. Someone was in. It looked like someone had hired it for a house party.

There was an expensive-looking German SUV parked on the pebbles next to it, a red sports car of some kind and a classic 1960s Citroën.

People who lived here all year round here resented these new arrivals with their high-tech, architect-designed houses. The older shacks were ramshackle, bent and weathered. These new buildings were all clean lines and flat planes. Their unyielding neatness seemed like an affront to the wildness of the place.

She shivered. The days were already getting shorter. Soon she and Zoë would be starting their second winter here; in this place she liked that season even more than the summer. The tourists left. People ordered in firewood and hunkered down, waiting for the cold to come and for the birds to begin arriving.

Above the black silhouette of the Old Lighthouse, the sky was streaked pink and magenta.

She was about to move off again when someone raised the blind in the black house. A big square window was suddenly illuminated by clear orange light.

A woman was in the bedroom, looking out of the glass towards Cupidi's car.

Cupidi froze for a second, then sank slowly down in her seat until her eyes could only just see over the dashboard.

She knew her.

The woman was Cathy Colquhoun; David's wife. She was standing in a sparse white room, looking out over the shingle, straight towards her car.

Fumbling with the switch, Cupidi switched the lights onto full beam, making it impossible for Cathy to see into the car. The woman stood in the window, lit up. She was wearing a pale grey sweater and squinting out into the evening. Then she turned on her heels and walked to the door, switching off the light as she left the room.

'Shit,' said Cupidi. 'Shit, shit, shit.'

She was angry. This was her own special place; the place she had run away to. How dare he?

THIRTY-ONE

'Your boyfriend called round,' said her mother. She was sitting on a deckchair outside Arum cottage, cigarette in one hand, glass of rosé in the other. She had put candles in jam jars in a circle around her.

'Jesus. David?'

'What's he doing here?' asked her mother.

'He's not my boyfriend. It's over. It was finished ages ago in London.'

'Doesn't look like he thinks that.' Helen took a pull on her cigarette and blew out smoke.

'He came here?'

'Knocked on the door up at the house looking for you. Zoë was in.'

'Oh hell,' said Cupidi.

'Exactly.'

'I bet she loved that.'

'Not much. She thinks you've been lying to her about the

relationship being over. I told her you'd never lie. Would you?'

Cupidi reached out and took the cigarette from her mother's hand. 'Unbelievable. He's gone and rented one of the big beach houses. With his wife.' She took a puff from the cigarette and regretted it right away. It tasted disgusting.

'Oh,' said her mother.

'What did he say?'

'He just wanted to know when you were back. I don't think I've ever seen Zoë that angry since she was small.'

Cupidi looked around. Moths circled the candles. 'Where is she?'

'She went off in a huff. Took your bike.'

'It's got no lights. What did you let her do that for?'

'I don't know if you noticed, but it's not a question of letting her do anything,' Helen said. 'I can make you some cheese on toast if you like. There's nothing much in the fridge.'

'Not hungry. Is she all right?'

'Of course she's all right. She's just angry. I suppose you'd like some wine then?'

Cupidi nodded. Her mother pushed herself out of the deckchair and went to the kitchen, returning with another glass. Cupidi unfolded a second deckchair and set it up within the circle of candles.

She looked up. The stars were disappearing from the western sky; cloud was coming over. The air was thick and muggy.

'Tell me about Greenham Common,' Cupidi said to her mother as she poured the wine.

Her mother looked surprised. 'Why?'

'The murder victim – the woman. I'm pretty sure she was arrested there.'

Her mother filled her own glass. 'It was such a long time ago. What was her name?' asked her mother.

'Hilary Keen.'

Her mother wrinkled her nose. 'There were thousands and thousands of us there. I wouldn't remember one person. I probably never even met her. You have to understand, it was huge. Do you know what gate she was at?'

'Gates?'

'We formed camps around the gates of the base. I was at Turquoise Gate. There were nine of them. Green Gate was women-only. I think it was Violet Gate where all the Quakers were. I can't remember the rest. Oh yes, Red Gate used to have great parties.'

'It looks as if Hilary Keen, the woman whose body we found on Romney Marsh, was arrested for criminal damage during a mass trespass on New Year's Eve in 1982. She refused to pay the fine and had to serve thirty days.'

'I remember that night.'

'You do?'

'I was there, but I usually made sure I wasn't arrested. I always knew your dad would hate it if I was. It wouldn't have been fair.'

'He didn't like it much that you were there in the first place,' said Cupidi.

'That's not true,' her mother said, stung. 'He always let me do what I wanted. He said he was proud of me, in fact.'

'Really?' said Cupidi, disbelieving.

'Absolutely. He backed me going. He was very ahead of his

time in some ways. I mean it was awkward for both of us. All the women knew I was an ex-copper. Some of them didn't trust me. And it wasn't easy for him, on the force. But he wanted me to go.'

'I don't remember it like that at all.'

'You did, too,' said her mother. 'You wanted me to go.'

'I never did. I didn't understand why you'd just left us. I was upset.'

'No you weren't,' her mother said. 'You were happy as anything that I'd gone, I think.'

In the darkness, Cupidi looked her mother. The remark had not been spiteful. It had been delivered as simple report on what had happened back then. 'Was I?'

'You loved it, just you and Dad. You resented it when I came back, in fact. It was hard.'

'But . . . you left us.'

'And you liked it that way. You had Dad all to yourself.'

It was a shock to Cupidi to realise that this was true. She had always complained to friends that her mother had left her and her father when she was a child. But she hadn't minded at all. In fact, when she thought back, she had loved it when it was just Dad and her. A thirteen-year-old girl trying to be so grown-up, looking after her father, setting the table for him for when he came back from work. The smile on his face as he pretended that whatever she had cooked was delicious.

She realised that the anger she had felt when her mother had come back from the camp on her infrequent visits hadn't been about her going away; it had been about her coming back, interrupting the rare closeness Cupidi had enjoyed with her father.

'Wow,' she said.

'It was something I had to do at the time, though,' said her mother.

A gust of warm air blew across the promontory, rustling tufts of dry grass. 'I'm sorry,' said Cupidi.

Her mother looked surprised. 'What for?'

'God. I must have been a bitch. I didn't realise.'

Her mother laughed a rich, phlegmy smoker's laugh. 'Funny how we recall things so differently,' she said. 'We never really got along after that, did we?'

'No.'

'Tell me about this, then. The one you wanted to know about.'

'I hadn't expected you to know her, really. I just wanted to know what it was like. To know what she was like, I suppose. It's frustrating.' Cupidi took a sip of wine.

Her mother settled back into her deckchair, looked up and said, 'It was . . . It felt like everything was changing, do you know what I mean? Margaret Thatcher was Prime Minister. The Americans were coming to put these terrible, pointless weapons in our country. We felt we had to do something. I only went for a day. My friend Elfie suggested we go. Do you remember Elfie?'

Of course she remembered Elfie. A loud, flamboyantly dressed woman who had almost been like part of the family in those days. A chaotic hippie, she had a son the same age as Alex.

'We went and we stayed,' her mother said.

Cupidi tried to see down the road, hoping to see the silhouette of a girl on a bicycle, but there was no one there.

'Don't worry,' her mother said. 'She'll be back.' But she knitted her hands together with an anxiety Cupidi recognised.

'You said the protesters didn't trust you because you'd been a copper.'

'Some of them. But I was useful. Because I knew the law and how the police thought.'

'Double agent.'

'Sort of, I suppose. But it was great to be part of something like that. Something really important.'

'But what did you really achieve? The missiles came anyway. There was nothing you could do about them.'

'We became more confident. More sure of ourselves, as women . . . as a whole generation.'

'Zoë calls you a hippie,' said Cupidi.

'I was never,' said her mother. 'Not a hippie. Not really.'

'So why were all those women imprisoned after that night?'

'Because they refused to be bound over. If you accepted the fine, you also had to be bound over to keep the peace. That meant you couldn't go back to Greenham. It was one of their conditions. They were trying to break us that way. So the women all refused to pay the fine and went to prison instead. They were very brave.'

'You were arrested?'

'Once or twice.'

'You went to prison?' Her mother had never talked about this.

'God, no. They only charged me properly once and it would never stick. The stupid police there didn't know what they were doing.'

'Dad was an inspector in the Met whose wife was being arrested with a bunch of crusties.'

'He understood. He was a good man. It was never that bad, between me and your dad. Honestly.'

Cupidi didn't respond. For a second, Helen's face was lit briefly by the lights of a car turning at the end of the lane; she was smiling. Alex changed the subject. 'Do you reckon you know anyone who might have known her?'

'I could ask around. Elfie is probably more in touch with that crowd. Would that be useful?'

'Very. Yes, thanks.' She smiled at her mother in the darkness. A gust of wind blew out one of the candles.

But though they waited until it got too cold and windy to sit outside, Zoë didn't come home.

'She didn't say where she was going?'

'No,' Cupidi's mother said. 'She didn't say anything. She was just upset. I'm sure she'll be back any minute.'

Together they walked back to Cupidi's house, where she could use the house phone to call Zoë's mobile, but the moment she finished dialling she heard it ringing upstairs.

So they sat down next to each other in the living room, switched on the TV and watched *Newsnight* reports about a famine somewhere and elections somewhere else. Cupidi was tired, but on edge. 'I should go and look for her.'

'She knows her way around. She'll be back soon, you'll see.'

But she didn't come back. Her mother stood and started to pace around the room. It unnerved Cupidi to know that her mother was thinking of her sister, Alexandra, the dead woman Cupidi had been named after; a teenager who had disappeared.

'Are you OK, Mum?'

'Of course I am,' she muttered. But her mother's dark mood was infectious.

Both of them were thinking the same thing: how Alexandra had been abducted, assaulted, and her body left in a ditch.

A little after eleven, Cupidi took the large torch from the cupboard under the stairs, put on her walking jacket and went out looking for her.

Low cloud blackened the stars.

Cupidi climbed to the top of the shingle bank and shouted 'Zoë!' into the darkness.

She turned to see her mother silhouetted at the back door. 'You go and look for her,' her mother said quietly. Her mother was normally thick-skinned. There was a brittleness to her voice now. 'I'll stay here in case she calls or comes back.'

Cupidi nodded; it was better to have something to do. She got back into the car and started the engine.

THIRTY-TWO

In the car Cupidi bounced down the pitted road past the lighthouses. Just beyond the lifeboat station at the bend, she paused, headlights picking out the dark black shape of the cottage David was staying in with his wife.

What had he imagined? That he could sneak off and rekindle their affair while he was here?

From where she was parked, she couldn't see the front of the house, facing the sea, but the ground and shrubs that lay on that side caught the light that flooded from its big glass doors. It was as if the black wooden cabin were sucking in the brightness from her headlights and spilling it onto the shingle beyond.

This was all his fault. If he hadn't turned up at her door, Zoë wouldn't have run off like that.

Putting the car back into gear, she drove off down the single-lane track, dodging the rabbits that sat on the narrow tarmac lane, eyes shining back at her headlights.

After half a mile, she reached the bird reserve's main entrance, pulled up outside and parked. The way in through the visitor centre would be locked up now, but wouldn't there be other ways round? She looked left and right. Sure enough, she found a marked path to the right of the building and began trotting down it, mud pale at her feet in the dull moonlight as she ran.

When it divided she veered left, southwards, towards the beach and the reserve, the way she had come before. Ahead of her on the track a fox turned, stared for a second, then ambled off into the long grass.

Though she was tired, it felt good, running through the night like this; it eased her anxiety. The land opened out; she must be moving alongside the first huge open expanse of water now.

It was surprisingly loud here. Waterfowl quacked and squawked around her in the darkness. She heard birds abandoning their perches at the waterside, launching themselves into the safety of the water.

At another fork she stopped, panting, to examine a wayside map. 'Zoë!' she shouted.

A bird flapped loudly out of the undergrowth, startling her. Nobody answered.

When she reached the first hide, it was half past midnight. It was empty.

The second, too. At the third, Christmas Dell hide, she sat on the cold bench and fumbled in her pocket for her phone, then remembered she didn't have it. What if Zoë were safe at home already? Maybe she was. She'd be laughing, now. Silly Mum, going all the way to the bird reserve to look for me. Serve her right.

She stepped out of the hide into the night. In this flat land, there was so much sky. Even from here, the glow of the nuclear power station lit the southern sweep of horizon. Above her, stars started to prickle through the haze. A three-quarter moon shone on the water. This place they had moved to; it was so different from the city. It wasn't small at all. It was gigantic.

She heard a rustling to the right. Swinging her torch round to shine it into the air, she caught a huge heron in the beam. It took wing above the black water, curving away northwards.

She drove back to the headland more slowly. Zoë had probably gone to bed already.

The road was empty; there were no other cars driving at this time of night.

At the bend, she paused again before the big black cabin. The lights were still on.

Parking the car, she got out. On the far side of the lane was a single postbox, and behind it a telephone box, lit by the orange street lamp.

It took credit cards. She dialled home, still looking at the black shack. The speed with which her mother picked up the phone and said 'Zoë?' betrayed her nerves.

'Sorry. No, it's me. Nothing?'

'I'm afraid not,' her mother said. 'Annoying child.'

Damn. 'OK. I'll keep looking.'

'Right.'

'Are you all right, Mum?'

'Not really.'

She thought of the bodies; the woman in the water. The empty boat on the beach. Alexandra.

She left the telephone box and crossed the tarmac, walking over the wide beach, looking at the large black beach house. Stupid David.

Had her daughter come here? To confront David? With Zoë, anything was possible.

She made her way to the far side, to where the house's entrance faced the sea. Out of sight, behind the slope of the beach, the tide was low. Waves lapped slowly. In the quiet night, her footsteps seemed ridiculously loud on the loose stones.

And then she was standing in front of a large rectangle of glass looking into the folding doors that were ajar at one end, opening onto the beach. In a gentle light, half a dozen people sat around a table full of wine glasses, bottles and candles.

They had guests.

It was like watching a cinema screen, one of those nice middle-class dramas, people smiling at each other, raising drinks. They all looked well-off, happy, beautifully dressed, almost as if they had been posed by some European film director. In a pale blue shirt, David was sitting next to Cathy, who was still in that grey sweater. There was no sign of Zoë among them, but that didn't mean that they wouldn't know something.

Cathy was laughing at something clever somebody had just said, her mouth wide, her teeth perfect.

And then a man she didn't recognise, bearded, hair shoulder-length, stopped talking and stared at Cupidi, stationary on the shingle.

He must have said something, because now everybody turned towards her and gawped. The film paused.

She stepped forward into the light. 'Hello, David,' she said. 'What a surprise, finding you here.'

With the job, and being a mum, she had never been that interested in long-term relationships. Flings had suited her perfectly. There hadn't even been that many of them.

David was only supposed to be a fling; the whole stupid thing had just carried on longer than it should.

But all through it, she had been convinced that Cathy, David's wife, had never known about the affair. David was a man who wanted it both ways. He had no wish to lose his nice home and family. He kept photos of them on his desk.

But from the way Cathy looked at her now, she knew that wasn't true at all. And Cupidi had been stupid to think that she had harmed no one but herself.

Cathy's mouth was open; she looked wounded.

After a second's hesitation, Cupidi took another step towards them. David was up, almost running to the door in his haste to block her way into the room. 'What are you doing here?' he said, lowering his voice so the others couldn't hear.

'Actually, I live here,' she said loudly, still striding forward.

'David. Who is it?' said someone.

He turned, flustered. 'Cathy. Remember Alex? DS Cupidi? She used to be a colleague at the Met.'

'Oh yes,' Cathy said quietly. 'I remember her very well.'

Cupidi stepped inside the room; it was neat, geometric, its walls and eaves lined with perfectly painted tongue-and-groove boards. A lavender-scented candle was burning somewhere. With everyone looking at her, she felt she had to say something. 'I'm so sorry to barge in. But my daughter's gone missing.'

There was suddenly silence in the room.

'I mean, it's probably nothing. But I was wondering if she was . . .'

'Oh,' said Cathy.

It had been a mistake to blurt it out like that. A child is missing: it sounded so dramatic. As her mother had said, she was probably sulking somewhere.

'Obviously she's not here. I realise that now. But I thought—'

'How did you know we were . . . ?' said Cathy, and she slowly turned her head to look at her husband.

'When did you last see her?' interrupted David. 'Your child.'

'This is quite awkward, isn't it?' Cupidi said. 'She's not here. I should go.'

'Yes,' said David.

'What's going on, David?'

The other guests sat silently, uncomfortable, embarrassed. Of course, she should try to pretend it was just a coincidence, her being here; that she had just stumbled here by accident, but right now she couldn't be bothered.

'I don't understand,' said Cathy. 'What are you doing here in Dungeness?'

'I live here,' said Cupidi. 'With my daughter. About a quarter of a mile away, past the lighthouses.'

'You knew that?' Cathy turned back to David.

'We should probably go to bed,' said the bearded man, standing. 'It's late. It was a long drive.'

'Obviously not when we booked . . .' said David, reaching for a bottle of wine. He poured a glass for himself, then held it up, as if offering it to guests.

'I need to speak to you in private,' said Cathy to David.

'I'll go,' said Cupidi.

Cathy looked at her. 'Yes. Maybe you should.'

'I'm very sorry,' said Cupidi.

The others were scuttling out of the room. David was looking apprehensive. Cupidi moved backwards to the open door.

Back in the car, Cupidi sat with her head on the steering wheel for a minute. 'Shit, shit, shit,' she said.

Her mother was at her back door as she drove up. 'Nothing?'

Her unflappable mother looked frightened now. Cupidi put her arms around her, and they held each other for a minute. It felt strange. They hadn't done anything like that for years.

THIRTY-THREE

By one in the morning, Cupidi had called in the news of her missing daughter to the officer on duty, in case anybody heard anything. The woman on the phone was sympathetic, but said there were so few officers on roster on a night like this, and there wouldn't be much she could do except keep an ear out for any information.

'I know how it is,' said Cupidi.

'We'll do what we can.'

She and Helen sat up in the living room as her mother dealt out patience cards on a coffee table. She watched her picking up columns and shifting them, but she wasn't really concentrating at all.

Be methodical, she thought. What is the best thing to do? 'I should go out again and look.'

'Look where?' her mother said.

They both jumped up when the doorbell rang.

David and Cathy stood at the door; beside them was Zoë, her hands and face covered in dark oil.

'Oh, Zoë.' Helen rushed forward and grabbed the girl, throwing her arms around her. Cupidi watched them: granddaughter and grandmother hugging each other tight.

'You have to help me,' said Zoë, pushing herself free of Helen's grasp. Her face was black, her eyes red. Cupidi noticed blood on her knee.

'What happened?'

'We found her walking on the road outside our house,' said David.

'She said she had an accident on her bike,' said Cathy. 'She abandoned it somewhere a couple of miles away.'

'Help me,' said Zoë. She was crying. 'Please.'

'She was really distressed.'

'Come in,' said Cupidi. It was her turn to put her arms around her shivering daughter.

'I'll stick a kettle on,' said her mother. Cupidi noticed her wiping her eyes with the back of her hand and realised she had never seen her mother cry before; never once.

'You have to believe me,' Zoë was wailing.

'Believe what?'

There were streaks in the dirt on her face. 'I promised I'd go back for her. But then your bike broke and I didn't have a phone and I waved at cars and nobody would stop and I had to walk all the way back on my own. I promised her I'd come back for her and now I've left her alone. We have to go.'

'Back for who?'

'The girl!' Zoë shouted. 'I told them but they wouldn't go with me.'

'She kept talking about this girl,' said David.

She was sobbing hard now, juddering in Cupidi's embrace.

Cathy said, 'Obviously we told her she had to come back here first.'

'Thank you,' said Cupidi. 'I'm very grateful.'

'It's OK. We were awake anyway. We had a few things to discuss,' said Cathy, unsmiling.

Arms still around her daughter, Cupidi looked at her and said, 'I want to say sorry . . .'

Cathy nodded curtly as Zoë unwound herself from her mother, tugging at her hand. 'We have to go and get the girl.'

'I don't understand.'

'I was cycling out Walland Marsh way and met a girl. She was just running along the road. On her own. I promised to go back.' Zoë was practically screaming now.

'Shh, darling,' said Cupidi. 'Take a breath. How old was the girl?'

'My age. I think. Bit older.'

'Sixteen? Seventeen? What was she doing out at night?'

'I don't know. That's what I'm saying. Except she was scared.'

'Do you think she had been sexually assaulted?'

'No. I don't know. I don't think so.'

'Where is she now?'

'I'll show you,' she tugged. 'She's waiting for me. I promised to be back ages ago. She was so frightened, Mum. You have to come.'

'She was like this with us too. Wanted us to go with her,' said David.

'I'm going to call the police and tell them what you saw,' Cupidi said to her daughter. 'Then I'll drive there, OK? We'll go and look for her now.'

'And you should go with them,' Cathy said to her husband.

'It's all right,' replied Cupidi. 'I can manage.'

'It's not that. I don't really want him around right now,' said Cathy.

Cupidi said, 'I didn't ask your husband to come here. I don't want anything to do with him, I promise.'

'That's not what I heard.'

Cupidi and Cathy looked at David, then turned to meet each other's eyes.

'So you lied to both of us?' said Cupidi.

'It wasn't like that,' David answered.

'Really?'

'Mum. Not now. Please,' said Zoë.

'Maybe you'll need some help,' suggested David.

'I'll be fine.'

'She'll be fine,' said Helen.

'She may be. But I may kill him if I spend another hour in his company,' said Cathy.

There was an awkward second in which nobody spoke. 'OK. Come with us,' said Cupidi. 'You're a policeman, after all.'

'Come on!' Zoë was screaming. 'Now.'

'What do you think, Zoë? Is it OK if David comes with us?'

'I don't care. Let's go. Please. She's waiting.'

'My car's round the back,' said Cupidi. 'Wait for me there.' Before she left, she called up the officer on duty again, repeated what her daughter said, then followed David and Zoë out of the back door to where the car was parked.

David folded himself into the back seat while Zoë fumbled with her belt.

'Go,' said Zoë. 'Hurry.'

They passed the black house, lights still on.

The roads were empty at this time of night. Zoë led them through Lydd and past the church.

'Right here, right here.' Zoë pointed. 'Now left.'

They turned off Midley Wall, heading into the middle of the marsh.

'You cycled all the way out here?'

'It's easy. It's flat.'

'And then walked all the way back?'

'I had to. Your bike was broken. I hit a ditch in the dark and it bust the wheel.'

In the headlights, the small trees leaned to the right across the road, shaped by the winds that blew across the flatland. The lane curved one way and the other, following the ancient pattern of dykes.

'Left . . . left.'

Caught in the full-beam headlamps, a black telephone cable looped rhythmically from pole to pole. They drove through a small hamlet; a children's swing in a bare garden; then passed the narrow bridge that led over White Kemp Sewer and veered off to the right, passing under the huge electricity pylons.

'Look. There's the bike.'

Cupidi's bicycle, front wheel bent, was abandoned in the grass at the side of the road.

'Leave it. We'll pick it up later. Why did you come all this way?'

'I don't know. To get away.'

'Because David turned up?'

'You promised you weren't getting back together with him.'

'We're not. Swear to God.'

David said nothing, just huddled in the back of the car as they swung round corners. These roads could be treacherous at night.

They crossed the railway line, then Zoë shouted, 'Here! Stop.'

By the side of the narrow hedgeless road, Cupidi pulled the car over, switched off the lights. The night was still. Zoë got out and looked around.

'It's me,' she said to the blackness beyond them. 'I'm back. Sorry it took so long.'

Nobody answered. Nothing moved.

'Don't worry. This is my mum.'

'Who are you talking to?' asked David.

'The girl.'

There was silence. 'I can't see anyone,' he said.

'Quiet,' said Cupidi. Further up the road, the street lights of Snargate shone orange, but as far as she could see in this darkness the flat fields around were empty.

Zoë stood there twitching her head from one direction to the next, looking.

Then her daughter started up the road, first walking, then breaking into a trot.

'Where are you going?'

'She came from over there,' said Zoë. 'She was running over the fields when I saw her. Maybe she's gone back there.'

'I'll come with you,' Cupidi said.

Zoë stopped. 'What if she's scared, still? It was me she talked to.'

'I thought you said she didn't speak English?' said David.

'She didn't. I mean, she was trying. Something had happened and she was frightened. That's why she was running away.'

The teenager looked anxiously out over the marshes.

'Where exactly was it you saw her?'

'Right here,' she said, agitated. 'I think. She was coming from that direction –' she pointed into the field – 'and I almost cycled straight into her. Let me go. I'll find her on my own.'

Cupidi walked up to her and handed her the torch. 'Don't go too far.'

The girl had found a small plank footbridge across the dyke and was walking northwards, into the stubbled field, into the darkness. 'Tell me, David. What were you trying to do, coming back here?'

'I miss you, that's all. I wanted to be with you.'

'Hello?' Zoë's voice came from the field. 'I'm here. Where are you?'

'Cathy knows about us, doesn't she?'

'Well, she does now,' he said.

'She knew before. The first time she looked at me in the beach house tonight, I could tell she knew.'

'I swear. She never knew. I had kept it from her, I promise.'

But she did know, thought Cupidi. From the look on her face, she had known for some time. It had been her keeping that knowledge from him, not the other way around. 'You shouldn't have come here,' she said.

They watched the torch beam flickering in the distance.

'But you made the first move. You got back in touch,' he said. 'It was you who called me.'

'I was asking for your help with a case, that's all.'

'That's not what it sounded like to me.'

'You're vain, David. You think it's all about you. That's all it was. A case I wanted you to help me with.'

'Jesus. Where are we, anyway?'

'Near a place called Fairfield,' said Cupidi. Somewhere to the south-west was the church of St Thomas à Becket, marooned in the middle of marshland. Which meant that they were close to Salt Lane.

The torch was getting further and further away.

'It didn't really end, did it? You just went away.'

She looked at him unbelievingly. 'Yes, it did. I went away. I protected you, David. I moved out of London for your reputation. It finished.'

'But I still have feelings for you,' said David.

Cupidi cupped her hands round her mouth: 'Zoë? Are you OK?'

No answer, but they could still see the torch moving.

'Do you think this girl – the one Zoë says she saw – is even real?' David asked.

A brief hesitation before she answered, 'Of course she is.'

'Mum?' came a shout.

'Wait here,' said Cupidi. She made her way across the plank bridge into the empty field, towards the torchlight.

'She's gone,' said Zoë miserably. 'She was there by the road, and then . . . she was pulling me over here. I said I'd get help, but I took too long and now she's gone.'

Cupidi looked back at the silhouette of David. 'What nationality do you think she was?'

'I don't know. I couldn't understand what she was saying.'

'What colour was her skin?'

'I don't know. It's dark.'

'Darker than yours?'

'No. Yes. A bit.'

'Asian.'

'Maybe. She had black hair.'

It was three in the morning. She would have to be up early. The night was turning cold.

'Do you think that's where she came from?'

'That direction . . . there. I think something awful had happened to her. You should have seen her, Mum. She was so frightened.'

She put her arms around her daughter. 'What do you think was going on?'

'I think someone had attacked her. She was doing this.' Zoë pulled away from her and mimed a fist descending, like someone being beaten. Cupidi peered at it. Zoë brought her hand down again onto her shoulder.

The clenched fingers could have been wrapped around something. 'Was that a knife she was miming?'

'I suppose it could have been.'

'Was she hurt?'

'I didn't see. It was dark. I didn't have a phone or anything, neither did she.'

'Did you see any blood? Or bruising?'

Zoë hesitated. 'No. I don't think so.'

'You asked her where she was from?'

'She was pointing over there.' Zoë gestured to the north. 'Oh. And I remember now. She was miming this kind of biting action.' Zoë lifted her hand to her mouth and bit into air.

'You think she was trying to tell you something?'

'You never listen!' Zoë screamed. 'That's what I've been telling you. She was trying to tell me something really important. Only I couldn't understand.' And fresh tears shone down her face in the torchlight.

Cupidi put her arms around the girl. 'Come on. We'll drive around a bit more then.'

Zoë nodded glumly. She took a breath from between her crying and asked, 'Are you sleeping with David again?'

'Jesus, no. I'm not. I promise. He just turned up. It's over between us.'

They walked back across the uneven ground, hand in hand. 'He was calling you on the phone. Only, if I picked up he wouldn't talk. It was him, wasn't it? He's a creep.'

'No. He's not. He's just . . .'

'Stupid,' said Zoë, snot bubbling at her nose. She wiped it on her sleeve.

When they got to the car David asked Zoë, 'Are you OK?'

She didn't answer.

Cupidi said, 'We're going to drive around a little more . . . take a look. Zoë said there was a girl out here in trouble. We're going to see if we can find her anywhere.'

'Right.'

She set off towards the small hamlet of Snargate, but Zoë said, 'She wasn't pointing over here. She was pointing over there.'

'How can you tell with these roads?' said David.

Cupidi turned around, drove back down the lane until she found a right turn, heading more directly east. She was aware of the significance of the land she was driving through. Just to the south lay Salt Lane, and the ditch where they had found Hilary Keen.

'She could be anywhere,' said Cupidi.

'Come on. That way. That's the way she pointed.'

'How can you tell? It's dark.'

'She pointed this way.'

Cupidi tried to picture the area in her head and realised they must be heading north-east. Pretty much the direction Zoë had indicated earlier. It was so easy to get lost around here, but Zoë seemed to understand the landscape better than any of them. Whatever turns they took, she was consistently leading them in the same direction, northwards. Cupidi put the car into a low gear and drove up the small lane. All this area was new to her. The land was changing; there was a slight slope to the road now; they were at the edge of the marsh.

In half a mile, they came to a T-junction. 'Where now?'

'I don't know,' Zoë said. 'I don't know. I don't know.' She was rocking backwards and forwards in the seat, distressed.

They sat there for a minute, engine running.

'Call it in again,' said David. It'll be light soon. The logical thing would be to organise a proper search in the morning.'

Cupidi wanted very much to believe the girl existed; but he was right. There was nothing useful they could do now. Most of all, Zoë needed a bath and to sleep.

A faint light was filling the horizon to the east.

'I was thinking,' Cupidi said. 'Do you want me to call a doctor in the morning?'

'Cross my heart, I saw her. I promise.' She was about to start crying again.

'I believe you. I do. Just . . . I don't think you're happy, that's all.'

'So what? Everybody doesn't have to be happy, do they?'

'No. It's true, they don't.'

She swung into the junction and began a U-turn. That's when the headlights caught the sign: *Sheepfold Orchard. Cherries. Apples. Plums.*

Her daughter holding something to her mouth and taking a bite.

The girl had been miming eating fruit. She was real. She existed.

THIRTY-FOUR

It was light by the time she put her daughter to bed, hanging a blanket over the window to try to darken the room.

David was still in the kitchen, making himself coffee. 'A spare bed?'

'My mother's asleep in it.' She hadn't gone back to Arum Cottage last night; she was upstairs in the small bedroom.

'What about the couch?'

'No,' she said.

'Right. Bad idea. I'll go. Are there any hotels? Sorry. Seaside. Of course there are.'

Checking the clock, Cupidi realised there was barely any point going to bed now anyway. She would have to be at work in three hours.

'What a gigantic cock-up,' said David.

'Use my laptop. Book yourself into a hotel. Call Cathy in the morning. I'm going to go up and change.'

'I don't suppose there are any jobs going here, are there?'

'Fuck off, David,' she said. 'Go on. Or I'll call the police on you.'

'You're joking, obviously.'

'Try me.'

And by the time she had come back downstairs, dressed in her walking gear, he had gone. She took her mobile out of the rice for a second time. This time when she pressed the button the screen lit up.

That morning she tramped up to the firing ranges, trying to add together the pieces of what she knew in a way that made some sense. In so much of this job, you could never make things better, but you could stop them getting worse. You could, at least, make things right. That was what had always been important. For the first time since she had seen the dead woman emerging from the black water, she felt sure she was on the right path. There was still so much she didn't understand, though.

Ahead, the swallows were already dipping in the warming air, but it would be autumn soon.

She walked fast, longing for vicious storms to come sweeping up the channel, for waves crunching into the stones, for the dangerous high tides that could sweep everything away.

By the time she arrived back she was covered in sweat. Her mother was sitting at the kitchen table, tapping at her laptop.

'That man, he's gone then?'

'Don't start, Mum.'

'He's an arse, that's all I'm saying.'

Cupidi put her arms around her mother's shoulders. 'No one's good enough for your daughter.'

'At your age you should take what you can get, obviously,' her mother said. 'As long as it's not him.'

Cupidi leaned forward and kissed her on the top of her head.

'What was that for?'

'You were thinking about your sister last night, weren't you?'

Her mother nodded. She kissed her a second time.

'I don't think I ever realised what that had done to you,' Cupidi said. 'I always thought you were so hard.'

Her mother just sat, saying nothing.

The phone in Cupidi's pocket started to buzz. She looked at the screen; a number she didn't recognise. 'Hello?' she said, cautiously.

'She didn't come home last night,' said a voice.

'Jill?'

'Yeah. Sorry. New phone.'

'You were there all night?'

'Pretty much,' said the constable. 'Do you think she's scarpered? I'm worried about her.'

'What are you doing? You're supposed to be resting.'

'I can't,' said Jill. 'I'm going to come into work today. It'll drive me nuts staying at home. Want me to pick you up?'

'Can you drive?'

'With a bit of swearing,' she said.

Cupidi was going through her jackets, looking for her locker key, when her mother said, 'Oh. Breaking news. You asked me about Greenham Common.'

Cupidi looked around.

'Look.' She was pointing to her laptop. 'I just had an email from Elfie. She remembers Hilary Keen. She says she had a boyfriend called Daniel.'

'Elfie?' Her mum's best friend; the hippie woman who lived in a huge, dark attic flat full of fake Tiffany lamps draped with scarves. 'You're kidding me.'

'No. I have a number for him. Elfie was one of his old flames too, it turns out. This Daniel, he lives in Hertfordshire apparently. She says he's a healer.'

'For God's sake.'

'I know. But you know Elfie. All ear candles and St John's wort. Give me your notebook.' Cupidi pulled out her police book from her handbag and her mother wrote the number in it. 'Elfie says he's expecting your call,' she said.

In the farmyard, Ferriter got out of the car, opening the back door to pull out a crutch.

'Finest plums in the world, round here,' she said. 'Ripen slowly, see, on account of the Kent climate? Not like Spanish plums. They don't get a chance for the acidity to come out.'

'That so?'

'So,' she said, hobbling as she closed the door, 'You say Zoë saw a girl who was upset about something, and that's why we're here?'

The farm, which had seemed so quiet last night, was alive. A group of young men sat on the grass, drinking coffee from a flask.

'Yes. I think her mother may have been a worker on one of the farms around here.'

'That all?'

Cupidi was tired, couldn't face the idea of explaining everything she had been through last night to her younger colleague.

A tractor drove into the yard pulling a trailer full of empty plastic boxes. Cupidi left the car and called over to the driver, 'You in charge?'

The man stuck his head out of the cab and pointed to a low brick building with a wooden sign outside: *Office*.

Cupidi knocked on the door. A man in his forties in a light-blue shirt looked up. His blue eyes matched his shirt, and the pale eyebrows above them made them look bluer still.

'Kent Police,' she said.

He frowned, holding out his hand. 'Anything I can help you with?'

'I had a report of a teenage girl out on the marsh last night. She was distressed, apparently.' Standing, the man looked suitably concerned, though puzzled. So she added, 'She wasn't an English speaker, either.'

'And?'

'Everyone on your farm speak English, do they?'

'So you think she might have been from one of the families of our temporary workers?'

'This is your farm?'

'I'm just the manager. So you'll want to ask them, I suppose?'

'Is that possible?'

'Of course. We'll do it right away.' He strode back out into the morning sunlight. 'That your car? Jump in. We can drive up to the top fields. That's where they're working today.' He opened a steel gate at the far end of the yard, waited for them to drive through, then closed it again behind them as Cupidi sat, engine idling.

'Did you ever employ a woman called Rasa Petrauska?' she asked, when he had got into the back of the car.

'May have done, but I never know the names. The agencies take care of that. We subcontract to them. What nationality?'

'Lithuanian.'

'Yep. We have plenty of them.'

'Are there many orchards around here?'

'Not round here. We're the only one. Most of the big orchards are further north, the far side of the Weald. Around here it's arable and sheep, mostly. We're pretty new. Still getting a hold. Tough business.'

So if the girl had signalled that she was a fruit-picker, she must have meant this farm, thought Cupidi.

'What's the youngest age of your workers?'

'Eighteen, I suppose. You'd have to ask the gangmasters. Everything's legit. We have all the paperwork from them.'

Could the girl Zoë had seen have been that old?

The car bumped up a concrete track, past neat rows of young apple trees, limbs weighted with fruit.

Leaning back, Ferriter asked, 'Any North Africans ever work here?'

'No, wouldn't say so. A few Poles sometimes. Never any English. Can't get them. Would love to employ local people, but nobody turns up. Getting seasonal labour is a nightmare. Harder every year with all the new legislation. It's killing us.'

'Where do they all live when they're here?' asked Cupidi.

He waved his hand. 'All around and about here. The agencies pick them up, bring them here. They rent houses.'

'Which agencies?'

'We use a few, obviously. It's a struggle to get the numbers, this time of year. Fruit needs to get picked. Head between that row of trees there.'

Cupidi left the track and drove a little way up between the plum trees. Workers were tucked into the foliage. Some wore hats, some wore scarves or handkerchiefs tied loosely around their heads. They all had large buckets strapped to their chests supported by shoulder straps, into which they were placing the picked plums. Working steadily, they paid no attention to the approaching car.

'Stop here.'

Further up the row, a tractor was parked with a line of trailers behind it, each loaded with plastic crates that were being slowly filled by the pickers.

'Can I talk to them?'

'You speak Lithuanian, Latvian and Polish?'

Cupidi was tired. She didn't have any energy for humour. Instead she gave the man a glare.

'Right. I'll get one of the gangmasters to have a word.'

She sat on the hot car bonnet as butterflies and wasps circled the trees. The gangmaster was a muscular, fair-haired man in his thirties wearing a checked shirt, who smiled at Cupidi in a way that irritated her. When Cupidi explained what she wanted to know, he leaned inside the police car and blew the horn twice.

The work stopped. People turned.

He spoke briefly. When he had finished talking, the workers all just stared at him. A few shrugged, shook their heads. Then turned back to work.

'Wait,' said Cupidi. 'Ask them again. She was a young girl or woman.'

The man smiled, spoke for a second time. This time, a couple of people answered out loud. Cupidi couldn't see all their faces. Some were hidden by the heavy branches of the trees.

'Ask them if anyone didn't make it to work this morning.'

More people answered this time.

'Several people, naturally,' he said. 'They are free to work or not work if they choose. Some people like to take a rest day.'

'Was any of them a young woman with black hair?'

'No.'

'How do you know? You haven't asked them.'

The man simply said, 'They told me the names of everyone who didn't make it. I know them all.'

Is that what they had really told him? Cupidi had no way of telling. 'What about you? Do you know of a young woman who might be in distress?'

'Of course not. I would have said if I had.'

The workers were already returning to their tasks. Without an interpreter she couldn't even be sure that the questions had been asked properly. Nobody seemed particularly concerned about the idea of a missing girl, anyway.

'Wait. Ask them if they knew a woman called Rasa Petrauska.'

'Petrauska? I know her. She used to work with me last winter. Then she disappeared. She still owed me money for rent.'

'When was that?'

'March, maybe.' He shouted over to a man up a ladder. Cupidi heard the name Petrauska. Without stopping picking, the man answered.

'Yes. March he says too. Maybe February.'

'Why do you think she stopped working?'

'These workers move on if they find something else. Or find a boyfriend.' Again he called out to the man up the ladder. The man said something back. They laughed.

'What did he say?'

'He said she probably found a better agency. One that didn't work them like slaves. He was joking, of course,' smiled the man. 'I told him he was fired. I was joking too, of course.'

'You're registered? With the Gangmasters Licensing Authority?'

'Of course. I can show you the paperwork if you want.'

She turned away to Martin, the farm manager, and said, 'OK if I look around for a bit?'

'Aren't you done here?'

'Would you rather I didn't?'

'No. Of course. Be our guest.'

'Try a plum,' said the gangmaster, tossing her one.

She sat on the bonnet of the car, eating it, watching the people work, aware that her continued presence was making Martin uncomfortable.

'Don't I get a plum?' Ferriter called from the back of the car.

The motion in front of Cupidi was constant. As soon as the fruit from one branch was exhausted, a worker moved up the line of trees. Occasionally someone would stop, to swat away a bug, but they were focused, almost machine-like. Nobody spoke.

When she'd finished the plum, she spat out the stone and said to the farmer, 'No other workers on the farm?'

'One or two back at the yard.'

'Come on then.'

He looked at his watch, impatience more obvious with every minute that passed.

She didn't care. She was sure she was on to something. It was good to stir the pot a little and see what came to the surface.

Back below, Cupidi saw a unmarked police car pulling up. 'Who's that?' she asked.

'Looks like the boss,' said Ferriter.

It was. As McAdam got out of his car, Cupidi was conscious that she'd been up all night; she felt old and crumpled. As always, McAdam looked well-pressed.

'How's he even know we're here?'

Ferriter said, 'I told them at the station.'

'So what's he want?'

But he was already striding towards them. 'Back on duty already, Constable Ferriter?'

'Yes, sir.'

He frowned, then turned to Cupidi. 'What's going on here?'

'My daughter said she saw someone out round here last night in distress,' said Cupidi.

'Look, is something going on that I need to know about?' said the farmer, irritated.

'This inquiry wasn't logged as an action,' said McAdam.

'Is this not an official inquiry?' demanded the farmer.

Cupidi ignored him. 'I didn't have time to log it, sir. Listen. Hilary Keen's body was found about two miles in that direction.'

Cupidi pointed to the east. 'The unidentified man was about one and a half miles that way,' this time moving her hand towards the south-east.

'You didn't say anything about a body,' said the farmer irritatedly.

'The girl my daughter saw was just south of where Hilary Keen's body was found.'

'So what are we doing here?' asked McAdam.

'Apparently the woman didn't speak English. I reckon she may have been a migrant worker, or the daughter of one. I thought I should come straight here.'

McAdam looked around.

'Most of the farms round here are sheep,' Cupidi continued. 'There's a few arable, but not many. They don't need migrant workers this time of year. But fruit farms do, and I think the girl Zoë saw may have worked on a fruit farm.'

'She told you that?'

'No. I never met her.'

'Right. You said. Your daughter talked to her. When was that?'

'Around midnight, I'm guessing.'

'Your daughter was out here in the middle of the night?'

'Yes, sir.'

McAdam frowned.

'And you think she's here?'

'There's no one of that description on this farm,' insisted the farmer.

Cupidi pointed towards a blue metal barn at one end of the yard. 'Ever get any rough sleepers in there?' she asked.

'Rough sleepers? What's all this really about, Sergeant? Is this some kind of murder investigation?'

'Do rough sleepers stay here?'

'Not as far as I'm aware,' said the farmer.

'Mind if I look?'

'Will you be long? This is our busiest time of the year. You haven't properly explained why you're on our land or why you're looking around here.'

'We appreciate the assistance you're giving us, sir,' said McAdam.

Cupidi thought of the man in the slurry; of the places he had chosen to stay. They were hidden, out of the way. Sometimes the farmers didn't even know they were there.

'There is nothing there,' the farmer insisted.

'In that case it'll take even less time.'

He shrugged. 'OK. Go ahead.'

'Are you sure about this, Sergeant Cupidi?' asked McAdam.

'Yes, sir.' She lowered her voice. 'I think something's been going on here. I just don't know what. But that girl, I swear she would have come from here.'

The barn they entered seemed to be full of equipment: fruit sprayers, trimmers, mowing attachments, all laid out on the concrete, but there was no sign that anyone had stayed here.

'Maybe we should take this back to the office?' said McAdam.

'What about through there?' She nodded towards a doorway at the far end, where she could see a second building.

'We store apples there. We can keep them for a year or more, so we sell them when the price is right.'

'Can I look?'

'Why?' said the farmer.

'Why not?'

The farmer sighed and led them through to the far side of the barn. There was a black and yellow sign on the door: DANGER. DO NOT ENTER.

'It's a controlled environment. That's what keeps the apples fresh,' said the farmer.

'Can I see inside?' she asked again.

The farmer's civility was wearing thin. 'Believe me, there's no one in there. And if they were, they'd be long dead. It's a specially created atmosphere. We deliberately lower the temperature and pump nitrogen in to replace the oxygen. It stops the fruit ripening.'

'I don't mind the cold,' she said.

Crossing his hands in front of his chest, the farmer said, 'If I opened the door, we'd have to vent it, then fill it with nitrogen again. At a cost. You going to pay for that?'

Cupidi banged on the door, testing it.

'That won't be necessary,' McAdam said. 'What exactly are we looking for here, anyway?'

Cupidi said, 'I'll know when I see it.'

'Jesus,' said the farmer. He walked to the far end of the shed, where there was a second door with the same warning. 'If you want to see, this shed's identical. OK?'

Opening it, he stepped inside. Cupidi followed. Beyond the first door, there was a second, smaller one, set in a metal wall.

'Go on. Look. This one's empty right now. We'll fill it up over the next few weeks when the apples come in.'

Cupidi looked into a bare, dark room, walls padded with insulation. Empty shelves stood ready to receive trays of fruit. Along one wall there were vents. Again, there was no sign of anyone having been in there at all. She was disappointed. She had been sure she would find something here that would make sense of what was going on, but there was nothing.

Back outside, the sunshine seemed brighter.

'Satisfied?' said the farmer.

'Thank you for your cooperation, sir,' said McAdam. 'It's very much appreciated.' Cupidi was still looking at the locked apple store, wondering if she should demand he open it, when McAdam took her elbow and marched her away from the farmer. 'In my car,' he said. 'Now.'

Opening the rear door, he gestured for Cupidi to get in. Instead of getting in the driver's seat, McAdam walked around the car and got in next to her.

'What, sir?' said Cupidi.

He leaned back and stared at the ceiling of the car. 'The IPCC are going to re-interview you about the Hilary Keen case. I think there's going to be a misconduct hearing. They'll recommend suspension, I think.'

'They don't have enough for that.'

'Don't they? The reason I called so much support for you was because of an incident two years ago that appears not to have been logged properly so it left no record. I know it happened, but they don't believe me. They think I invented it all to justify what happened at Speringbrook House. Now they ask me where you are, and I don't even know, and there's nothing logged either.'

'Sorry, sir.' Instead of making things better for him, she was making it worse.

'This fellow here . . .' He pointed at the farmer. 'He'll be making a complaint about you, I'm guessing.'

'I wouldn't be surprised, sir.'

'At least this was something I didn't give orders for,' said McAdam with a wry smile.

Cupidi squinted into the sunlight. 'Why do they want to ask me about Hilary Keen?'

'Because I told them I knew you weren't convinced that Stanley Eason was the killer.'

'Why? It only gives them the ammunition they want.'

Ferriter was standing in the middle of the farmyard, leaning on her single crutch, looking into the car, as if trying to figure out what McAdam was ticking her off about.

'Because it's true, isn't it? And that's what we're supposed to be about. Finding out the truth.' Suddenly he looked tired. 'They asked if they could interview you again this afternoon.'

'Could I do it another time?'

'No.'

'Just . . . I found someone who knew Hilary Keen. I had planned on going to see him this afternoon.'

'Really? A significant lead?'

'I won't know till I speak to him.'

Through the window, Cupidi could see Ferriter mouthing, 'What's going on?'

'Well, I'm sure the IPCC wouldn't want to interfere with the normal working of a murder investigation,' said McAdam.

'I'll let them know you're busy and can't speak to them until later.'

'Might take me a while, sir.'

He turned to her and smiled. 'Longer the better, Alex, far as I'm concerned.' And he opened the door.

'OK if Ferriter catches a ride back with you?' asked Cupidi.

'Of course.'

Ferriter hobbled across to Cupidi. 'What's going on?'

'He thinks they're going to throw Gross Misconduct at him.'

'Bloody hell.'

'Anything we can do?'

'Get a result for him. That's the best thing. It's a lot harder to argue with results. Go back with McAdam. If you can, try and track down Najiba. It's crucial we find her now.'

As she waited to drive out into the lane she looked back in her rear-view mirror. The farmer was still there, waiting to see if she'd gone.

She gunned the car down the lane, taking a left to head for the main road.

Rounding a corner, she saw the horse too late. Panicked by the car, it reared. Cupidi watched in horror as it raised its front legs in fright.

The rider was a woman; knees tight on the horse, leaning into the horse's mane, she was struggling to stay on, as hooves clattered back down on the tarmac.

Cupidi pulled the car into the opposite verge. She cut the engine. The horse settled.

'You stupid idiot!' shouted the woman.

Cupidi sighed. She would have to apologise. She had been careless.

Where had the horse come from, anyway? It had just appeared, as if from nowhere.

'Oh. It's you,' the rider said. Against the sunlight, perched on the back of a grey mare, Cupidi made out the silhouette of Connie Reed.

'I was going too fast, I'm sorry.'

'You weren't looking properly.' Reed seemed to be scrutinising her. 'No matter. No harm done. Did you find any more of those people?'

'No. They've disappeared.'

'Your friend all right? The one with the leg?'

'Fine. No serious damage done. Like you said.'

Connie Reed nodded.

'What are you doing all the way out here?' asked Cupidi.

'It's pretty close, as the crow flies at least. I take the horses along the Royal Military Road. Give them a good run.' A bridleway that ran alongside the canal.

Something occurred to Cupidi. 'The Royal Military Road, you said? You go as far as where it crosses the Hamstreet Road?'

'Of course. Only two or three miles. Why?'

'Just thinking aloud.'

'I'll be off then. Be more careful in future,' Connie Reed said curtly, and flicked her reins. The horse trotted on. In the mirror Cupidi watched it clopping down the lane for a minute, dark tail swishing slowly from side to side. She noticed the bridleway then, on the far side of the road, almost completely shaded by leaves. The rider must have emerged from there.

Traveller's joy, they called it, the lush creeper that covered old hedges and trees, its pale flowers turning to fluffy white balls of seeds by this time of year. It had hidden the exit into the small lane.

It hadn't been her fault at all, she realised. It was Reed who must have emerged onto the road without looking. She restarted the car and moved off again, though more cautiously this time.

THIRTY-FIVE

The drive around the M25 to the far side of London was exhausting. Lorries filled the left lanes, nose to tail; men in Audis and BMWs weaved round the traffic at ninety and more.

The satnav took her off the motorway at Junction 21A, off down dual carriageways and B-roads until she arrived at a large, white-painted country house. The sign on the gate read: *Anahata Wellness Spa.*

She turned into a short driveway, lined with lime trees that looked tired after a long summer. To the right, a wide empty lawn was being cut by a large man on a small ride-on mower. Cabbage whites fluttered in the air.

A notice said: *If you drive slowly, you notice more.*

If Dungeness were on the edge, this seemed like somewhere in the very middle. Secure, stately and self-confident.

At the front of the house, a couple of cars were parked; she pulled in next to some expensive-looking hybrid. She sat in the car for a minute, sucking a mint, recovering from the journey.

*

'Daniel Kay?' repeated a smiling young woman in a white coat on reception. Her teeth, Cupidi noticed, were perfect. 'Could you sign in, please. Is Daniel expecting you?'

'He is,' said a man's voice. 'I heard you pulling up. You must be Alexandra Cupidi.'

The first thing she noticed was that Daniel Kay had a side parting; slightly ginger, greying hair divided in a neat line above his left temple. No men parted their hair anymore these days, did they? Yet it seemed to suit his square, tanned face.

The second thing she noticed was that the skin on the side of his face was different, somehow. He was close-shaven, too, but now she saw it, there was no stubble on that side of his face either. Whoever had worked on it had done a good job, but the left side of his face had the kind of stiffness that scar tissue has. So much so that when he smiled, as he was doing now, his face became slightly lopsided. That skin moved less. Instead of disfiguring him, it lent him a certain character; his smile seemed quizzical because of it. A car accident, she wondered?

He asked the receptionist to bring tea. 'We have everything,' he said. 'Cardamom-and-ginger is good for energy.'

'You can tell, then.'

'A guess. It's my profession to judge people's wellness. I am a healer.'

'Is my aura a funny colour?'

He laughed. 'No. I'm guessing you've just had a long drive, so you're tired.'

He led her into a sitting room at the end of the building. It was grand and luxurious; a large Georgian space, full of ostentatiously gilded furniture, and French windows that flooded the room with sunlight. She sniffed frankincense, that most pungently devout of aromas.

The paintings that had probably come with the stately home still hung on the walls – landscapes with grazing cattle, portraits of stiff old women – but there were also newer artworks in brighter, lusher colours. A horse surrounded by pulses of bright colour. A hazy, pastel-hued picture of a naked woman, eyes closed, cross-legged, mind apparently on higher things.

'Of course, you know Elfie, don't you? How is she? Beautiful woman. She has a very generous soul. She comes here regularly, you know. One of the clients we look forward to so much. Is she well?'

'You probably know better than me, then,' said Cupidi.

'You don't see her so much?'

'I've come to discuss Hilary Keen.'

'Right,' Daniel said, nodding. 'Of course. How awful.'

'Sorry. I'm not brilliant at small talk. Or whatever that was.'

'No problem.' He spread his hands. 'Directness is a virtue, and I'm here to help,' he said, checking his watch.

'I'll just start, then,' she said. 'If you don't mind. What do you remember about her?'

'Look, Alex . . . May I call you Alex? That's what Elfie calls you.'

She smiled back, looking him in the eye. '"Sergeant" is customary. But it makes no difference.'

'Right. Of course. Fair enough.'

'You knew Hilary?'

'I just want to be clear before we start. I'm really eager to help you. Nothing about my past is a closed book.'

'Thank you,' she replied, though anyone who ever said that always meant the opposite.

'When I knew Hilary Keen . . . it was a very different time in my life, you understand. I still had a lot to learn.'

'What are you trying to say?'

'I was young. We were doing . . . you know, things . . .' He smiled that charming smile again.

Cupidi decided to help him out. 'I know Hilary Keen abused drugs. If you knew her, you probably took drugs too. In so far as I want to know as much as I can about her, that's relevant but, frankly, I don't care about that, and none of that has to leave this room. It's certainly of no interest to the police after all this time. I just want to know as much as I can about her. You were close?'

His eyes flickered to the French windows. 'Sort of close. She was quiet. Quite passionate, I suppose. We all were. I still am, I like to think. This place is all about passion.'

Cupidi looked around. 'What do you do here?'

'*Anhata* is the heart chakra. It means "unhurt" in Sanskrit, but it also means "pure", or "stainless". Rather than just heal or restore, we find people's pure centre here. We help people find their undamaged heart.'

'There was me thinking it was a spa.'

He laughed. 'If that's what you want it to be, it's a spa. We think of it as something a little more fundamental. But it's entirely possible some of our clients just come here for deep pore cleansing or a colonic.'

'Is it expensive?'

'Very.' He smiled. 'But worth every penny, obviously. And we offer generous discounts to people who we think would benefit.'

'Hilary Keen,' she said, nudging him back to the subject. 'Where did you know her from?'

'My God. The Peace Convoy. Do you even remember that?'

Cupidi shook her head. 'The Peace Convoy?' The receptionist emerged with a tray, on which were balanced two tall porcelain cups of tea.

'Oh, Lord. It was something else. We were nomads. By the mid-eighties we had formed a kind of tribe. In those days we moved around the country in buses and caravans and converted trucks. We went to all the festivals and the CND camps. In the papers they called us New Age Travellers!' He laughed. 'Some newspaper dubbed us "The Peace Convoy". I know . . . hard to imagine, with all this . . .' He opened his arms to indicate the solid, bourgeois surroundings in which he found himself.

'You've done well.'

'I have.' He smiled. 'Back then, all I had was a bus. Seriously. A Bristol LH410,' he said, enunciating each letter and number as if it were holy. 'You should have seen it. A complete tank to drive, but it was beautiful. Built some time in the seventies. Bought it off the local football team who wanted something classier.' He laughed again. 'I had a bedroom, fitted kitchen units, bathroom, everything in there. The bed was massive. It was the whole of the back of the bus. It was glorious. This was the eighties, you remember. That was my mansion, back then. I had everything I needed. Just like now, really.'

'Apart from the hot tubs and the swimming pool.'

'Apart from those, yes.' A giggle. 'What were we supposed to do? Stay at home and sign on the dole? There were no jobs for us in the eighties. So we did the best we could. Our biggest sin was that we were so obviously enjoying ourselves. Look. I've got some photographs.'

He stood. She was expecting a photo album. Instead he went to a coffee table in front of the large fireplace, picked up a big white book and started flicking through it.

'Here.' He grinned and passed it to her. It was heavy and solid. She half closed it, to look at the plain white cover.

Embossed on it were the words, *Love Everything That Happens To You*, and the author's name, Deva Kay. 'Deva Kay is you?'

'Daniel, Deva . . . call me what you like,' he replied, adding as an afterthought, 'Sergeant.' Another grin. 'It's a book about what I've learned. I give it away to guests.'

She turned back to the page he opened it at. There was a large, grainy black-and-white photograph of a bare-chested young man, standing in front of an old-fashioned, flat-fronted bus.

His hair had been long in those days, but the parting was on the same side. The man, who must have been in his early twenties when the picture was taken, grinned at the photographer. She peered at his face. The scarring was not there. In front of him, leaping into the air, a grey lurcher snapped at the camera. On each side of Daniel were long-haired women, one with dreadlocks. Both were thin and young, and both wore T-shirts that had been cut short at the shoulder and cropped to show their stomachs.

Together, they looked reckless, beautiful and cool.

The bus's destination indicator read: 'HEAVEN'. The photo was captioned: '*On the road to enlightenment. A journey starts with a single step. For ten years in the '80s and '90s, this was my home!*'

She looked up. Daniel was grinning down at her. 'Crazy days,' he said.

'Who were the women?'

'Actually, to my shame, I don't remember their names. I tend to live in the present. Find eternity in each moment. And we moved around a lot, of course.'

'And you took a lot of drugs.'

'Some of us. That might have contributed.' Another giggle.

She looked at the photograph. He had his arm around one of the women.

'Did you sleep with this one?' She pointed at her.

'I think I probably did.' He smiled. 'I don't want to sound boastful, because it's nothing to boast about. But this was before we knew much about HIV. We thought it was a gay thing. Awful thing to say, I realise, but it's true. Everybody slept around a lot.'

'But you remember Hilary?'

'Oh yes. Hilary was sweet. Quite shy. Stunningly pretty. I mean, really, really beautiful.'

'You don't have a photograph of her?'

'Afraid not. I lost nearly everything I had from those days, you see. A friend gave me this one, years later.'

'Did you sleep with Hilary?'

'Maybe.' A small smile.

'Meaning yes.'

He laughed. 'Yes. We did sleep together. Who wouldn't? She was gorgeous, and so generous. Like diving into warm water. First time I saw her was at Elephant Fayre down in Cornwall. She was singing with some band, I think. Had an amazing voice. She was on the road with us for a while. I wasn't the only one. I remember her getting pregnant, too. I don't think she was at all ready for that.'

'Julian. That would have been the boy's name.'

'I don't know,' he said. 'Probably.' He turned his back, moved to the French windows and opened them. 'She got into drugs, though, I seem to remember.'

'Yes, she did.'

'That was a shame. We were all so naive about that sort of thing then. We thought the world would come around to our way of thinking. Every month it seemed like more people had joined us.'

'What do you mean, your way of thinking?'

'We had real values. We were connected to the earth. You lot were living through this boom–bust, boom–bust. There was an economic crash in 1987. People were having their homes repossessed and even after they'd lost the roof over their heads, they still owed the bank thousands. You'd be amazed how many people came to join us after that. We owned our homes, even if they were just teepees or benders. People would make their houses out of anything. Hazel sticks, tarpaulins, old gas cylinders for stoves. We were living in things that people thought had no value, but to us it was wonderful.'

Cupidi picked up her tea. 'I can see that.' Her own mother, then in her late thirties, had lived in a bender at Greenham Common. When Helen had described it to Cupidi's father, he had been horrified. 'But why?' he'd asked. 'I'll pay for a hotel if you like.'

'We shared everything we could,' said Daniel. 'Back then, farmers used to actually invite us onto their land. We'd do a bit of work for them and then move on. But then it all began to change. All the millionaires who made their money screwing everyone else started buying up houses in the country. And suddenly it was the 1990s and the countryside was just for rich people.'

'You don't look like you've done so badly yourself,' she said, looking out at the lush lawns.

'Oh, this is my company's property, not mine,' he said. 'But yes, you're right. I have been blessed. People like what I offer. They reward me. All this is done in the spirit of openness and generosity. That's why it succeeds.'

A blackbird was digging at the lawn just outside the doors. 'You were talking about the 1990s. You said it had turned nasty. Why did you stay on?'

'It's not so easy to just quit,' he said.

'You mean drugs, or the lifestyle?'

'The lifestyle,' he said. 'And all the ideals we had. At the start we all believed we were changing the world. I still do, actually. But it took a while for us to understand that we needed to move on from it all.'

'From heroin?'

He frowned. 'I suppose it got pretty dark, yes.' The blackbird had a juicy, wriggling worm now; it darted away with it. 'It had all been so optimistic at first. But then in came the Criminal Justice Act. They started treating us as criminals. Do you know labelling theory? People behave how they are treated, if you ask me.'

'So you were little angels until the nasty policeman came along?'

He laughed. 'Obviously not. I won't pretend. There were drugs. Sometimes we stole a bit of wood here and there. There were bad people, just like in the straight world. And there were some people who were mentally ill, too. This was the time when they were closing down mental hospitals. Care in the community . . . remember? Some of these people had nowhere else to go. We tried looking after them . . .'

'Was Hilary one of those?'

'No. Not really, but she was vulnerable, I suppose. She was so pure. I think that's what made her such an easy target.'

'For who?'

'Do you believe in the concept of evil?'

'I'm a police officer. It comes with the territory.'

'As a Buddhist, I believe that there is good and evil in us all, inseparably. Evil is the inner darkness. Someone who allows their darkness to become unbalanced can corrupt the people around them.'

'Hilary came into contact with somebody who was evil?'

'Yes.'

'Who?'

He took a breath. Exhaled evenly. 'Her name was Freya. She was one of those people who is ruled by self. Whether she had been like that all along, before she discovered drugs, I don't know. I suspect so. She was a full-on user. As the authorities were cracking down on druggies in the cities, they came and tagged on to us. Freya was one of them.' Another breath. 'The problem with evil is that it disguises itself so well.'

'A heroin addict?'

'Big time. And a dealer. I remember her arriving. She was driving a beat-up old fifties Mercedes. She had that kind of Nico cool, you know? A detachment that can be really sexy, but it's evil. Evil creates illusion. It is a literal separation from the light, but it can look very alluring sometimes. And all the men were crazy about her, of course.'

'Including you?'

For the first time he had the grace to look embarrassed. 'I suppose.'

'Did she spend time in your massive bed?'

'I thought we were talking about Hilary,' he said, offended. The smile had gone.

'So did I.' There was a moment of awkward silence. 'So it was Freya who got Hilary addicted?'

'Yes,' he said curtly. 'Absolutely.'

'Tell me about Freya, then.'

'Not much to say. She was on drugs. She turned our convoy into a kind of druggie hell, if you ask me.'

A man who talked of evil and hell, she noted. 'When was the last time you saw her?'

'I don't really remember. It sort of just fell apart. I don't usually talk about it.' He looked at his watch again. Outside on the lawn, three women appeared and laid out yoga mats. Dressed in Lycra shorts and tops, they were lean, beautiful, and looked rich. In unison, they began doing stretches, pulling their legs back, thrusting out their chests. It reminded Cupidi of a 1980s pop video.

'You say it fell apart. When was that?'

'We carried on for a few years more, but it didn't mean anything anymore. I think I sold my bus in 1995, went back to the city shortly after that. Licked my wounds for a while, then started teaching Japanese Buddhism.'

'When did you last see Hilary Keen?'

'God. Hilary had already quit the scene by then. She went off to live in Spain. A lot of people left the country around that time. Things were just getting too difficult here by then. The whole trip was starting to die.'

He took a sip from his tea.

'Why did Hilary leave?'

'She was trying to clean up, she said. Get away from negative influences.'

'Freya?'

'Exactly.'

'And you never heard from Hilary again?'

'Nothing. I wasn't surprised. In the nineties the whole heroin scene was just as bad in Spain, it turned out, if not worse. Frying pan into the fire. Not a day went past when I didn't wonder how things had turned out for her, poor girl. I failed her. We all did. And you say she's dead now?'

The women were on their backs nows, legs in the air, opening them them into 'V's. She wondered if Daniel slept with any of them. He probably did, she reckoned. His guru-shtick, plus that hint of a bad-boy past, would be quite appealing to the bored, rich, middle-aged woman. If he hadn't been so self-satisfied, she could have seen the attraction herself.

'I want to show you something,' she said, lifting her handbag from the side of the armchair.

Digging out a brown envelope, she pulled out a picture. 'Who's this?' she asked.

And the widening of his eyes as he took it from her told her she had been right about one thing, at least.

THIRTY-SIX

'Freya,' he said, holding the photograph. 'It's Freya.'

His voice shook a little as he spoke. A piece of the puzzle fitted into place. She had been right when she had suggested the dead woman wasn't Hilary at all.

Daniel peered a little more closely at the picture. 'My God. Is she dead?'

'Very.'

He looked up. 'So both of them are dead?'

Cupidi didn't answer, but watched him lower his eyes again to the photo. 'How awful,' he said.

They were exactly the same words he had used when she had first mentioned the name Hilary Keen. That time he had clearly meant it. This time, though, they sounded as if they were what he thought she expected him to say.

How awful.

If eyes could really sparkle, though, his would have been doing that.

Looking at him, Cupidi could see nerves; excitement, even. They suggested he was glad Freya was dead. Which, if true, would be very interesting indeed.

'What was Freya's last name?'

'I don't remember.'

'Really?' She smiled at him. 'You don't remember?'

'No. I mean . . . it was an informal kind of life we lived then. We didn't go round saying, "How are you, Miss Cupidi?"'

'I don't think I believe you, Mr Kay' she said.

He hesitated just a fraction too long before he said, 'Well, I don't. Simple as that.'

'Were you a heroin-user too?' she said.

'I don't have to answer that.'

'No. Of course you don't.'

'I'm not proud it.'

She let the thought linger for a while. She wasn't threatening him; just letting him know that she knew the man he had really been. He could talk of the seeker's journey, pose like an eco-warrior in front of his humble bus, ooze New Age charisma at middle-aged women, but there were more sides to any story. She knew that; he knew that she knew.

'How much do people here know about your past?' she said. 'Just what's in this book? Or the rest of it?'

'Is that some kind of threat?'

'I just want to know her name. What was it?' she asked again.

'I think she may have been called Brindley,' he said.

'Thank you.' Outside, the women were standing now, stretching down to clutch their calves.

She held up the photograph again. 'Freya Brindley?'

'Yes. How awful,' he said again.

But when he showed her to the door, offering her an expensive-looking washbag full of essential oils and massage lotions as a parting gift – which she declined, obviously, because she was a policewoman – there seemed to be an extra spring in his step.

She took notes for a minute in car. And when she drove back down the driveway, he was there with the three women. They were all sitting in front of him; straight-backed in the lotus position. He was kneeling, lecturing them and smiling beatifically.

London was dying; she did not miss it at all. It was full of small flats, piled in boxes on top of each other, all pretending they were different. Some were rendered, others clad in tiles, wood or glass, but they all had the same pinched size, the same small balconies crammed with bicycles, plastic furniture, dead plants and exercise equipment.

The city was exhausted, burning itself out. She was glad she was out of it.

She crawled though Poplar, drivers inching into the narrow spaces between vehicles, cursing each other all around her. Her phone buzzed. It was a text from Ferriter. She had called the constable from South Mimms services, over a double espresso that she had gulped down to keep her awake, washing down some sweet millionaire's shortbread for the added sugar boost.

Now she had replied. 'Freya Brindley. 1995. Sought for arson and murder.'

Ah, she thought. Ah.

That nerviness on Daniel Kay's face as he had told her the

name. Those parts of the past he was not so keen to share with the adoring, pliable ladies.

At the duplex, Julian buzzed her in. 'And?' he said, at the door.

'Please don't get your hopes up,' she said, 'but I now know for sure that the woman who died in Kent was not your mother.'

'Oh. It's you again,' said a voice from the top of the stairs. Lulu peered over the child gate, pale and tired.

'Really?' Julian grinned.

'I believe she was a woman called Freya Brindley. Does the name mean anything to you?'

'The dead woman's definitely not my mother?'

'Yes.'

His face lit up. 'I knew it. I bloody knew it.'

'What about the name Freya Brindley?'

'No, I've never heard of her.' He led her up the stairs and opened the small gate.

'Brindley appears to have been living under your mother's identity for several years. I need to know why.'

'You come back here stirring this stuff up,' said Lulu. 'Do you know what you're doing to my husband?'

Cupidi blinked. 'I am not doing anything to him. He is helping me find a murderer.' Last night she had been tramping over Romney Marsh searching for her daughter. He had been doing the same, in a way: looking for his mother.

'He barely sleeps now. He's getting into trouble at work. It's affecting Teo too.'

'Is he?'

'I've taken a couple of days off, that's all,' explained Julian.

'It's not necessarily convenient. There's a lot going on just now at work. They'll understand, though.'

His wife snorted. 'You're on a warning. He's spending his time with alcoholics and drug addicts. He comes home smelling like a sewer. He's leaving work most days to meet people who claim they've seen her.'

'I'm sure she's living somewhere near. There's a woman who could be her who's been seen a little north of here.'

'I don't actually want this policewoman in my house, Julian,' Lulu said.

'I invited her in.'

'Well, I didn't.'

Lulu reached down and picked up a pile of printed sheets. 'Look at this,' she said. 'Look at it. His mental health is being affected.' She held them in front of Cupidi's face: *Missing: Woman who may answere to the name Hilary Keen. Age: 50+. Reward paid for information.* 'He's paying people to come to our house with stories they've made up.'

'I'm just asking for help.'

'They're conning you. All of them.'

'The one who saw her in Brick Lane wouldn't take money. He was sure it was her.'

'He's as stupid as you are, then. She's a mentally ill homeless woman,' said Lulu. 'If she's his mother . . . he needs protecting from himself.'

'She's ill. Which is why I should help her,' said her husband.

'He's disappeared off looking for her. Every day, he's going out in the evenings after work, tramping around. He has a son to look after. He has a wife.'

'I have a mother,' he said. 'She's really my mother. I knew she was.'

'You have a family of your own.' Lulu looked close to tears.

'I just came to tell you. I thought you ought to know,' said Cupidi. 'I'll leave you two. I should go.'

'Good,' said Lulu, hands on hips.

And, though she was tired, Cupidi herself drove around the streets for half an hour looking for elderly white homeless women.

She saw none. Too many young homeless men; a few women. She could not be hard to find, surely?

Her own mother was standing on a stepladder, painting wood preservative on the planks of the small cottage.

'It's not yours, you know. He'll be coming back some time.'

'Should be done every year,' she said.

At the bottom of the ladder there was a jar lid full of stubbed-out cigarettes.

'How's Zoë?'

'Still upset. She's inside, sleeping.'

'I should wake her. Take her back to the house.'

'I'll look after her. It's OK.' And she turned back to her painting. 'Do you think last night was some kind of psychodrama about David coming here?' She drew the brush back and forwards over the wood, pushing the hairs into the dry crevices. 'She doesn't trust you about him, you know.'

'She really saw someone in trouble.'

'But you didn't find anybody. Who would have been walking around in the middle of the night?'

'I think the girl she saw was real. It's not like when you were my age. The country is full of people we don't know about any more. They live in the cracks. We don't even know how many of them there are.'

'Maybe she did see someone. But she was upset, too. And behaving strangely. That's real, too.'

Cupidi lay in bed alone in her house that night and waited for sleep to come. Instead of narrowing, the distance between herself and her daughter was getting bigger.

She thought about the woman who might be Hilary Keen. She would be sleeping in some shelter, or squat, somewhere hidden. The weather would be colder soon.

THIRTY-SEVEN

When she opened her email first thing the next morning there was another request from the IPCC team for a follow-up interview.

Ferriter came in backwards through the door. She was down to a single crutch now; in her free hand she held a cup of coffee from Starbucks. 'I thought you didn't drink that,' said Cupidi.

'Decaf.'

'Anything from Najiba?'

Ferriter shook her head. 'She's not at the flat either. Nothing.'

'Damn.' Cupidi closed the email from the IPCC without answering it. 'Show me what you found on Freya Brindley.'

Ferriter sat at her computer and entered her password. 'The case was never closed. It's pretty grim, I warn you. Come and see.'

She double-clicked on a folder, then on a JPEG. The file must have been digitised some time ago. The grainy picture of Freya Brindley was an arrest shot from one of her drug convictions in the early 1990s. 'I printed one out, too.' She pulled one from a pile of paper on her desk.

Cupidi took it, walked across the room and held it up next to the picture of the dead woman that was on the board. Though there were twenty-five years between the photographs, they were unmistakably the same woman. There was no doubt about it this time.

'Listen to this, Sarge,' Ferriter said. 'In 1995 there was a fire at a traveller camp just outside of Evesham. It was in a small clearing in woodland. Six vehicles were destroyed. Two young boys, aged five and seven, were in one of them. Both dead. And another man was seriously injured, though he survived.'

'Daniel Kay,' she said.

Ferriter peered at the screen. 'How did you know?'

That would explain the scarred face. It had been burns. 'He's the one who gave me Freya's name.'

'Bloody hell. I just spoke to someone at West Mercia Police about it, someone who worked on the case twenty-something years ago. It was arson. Someone deliberately poured petrol around a bus and set light to it, possibly intending to murder the owner.'

'The owner was Daniel Kay.'

'Yes.'

'However, it went wrong. It was a windy night apparently. There were other accelerants present on the site and the flames spread through the place. The two boys were in a nearby caravan which caught fire before anyone could rescue them. They both died. From interviews with the surviving mother, and other people from the community, it became clear that the fire was a result of an ongoing dispute on the site.'

'Between Freya Brindley and Daniel Kay.'

'How do you know all this?'

'Because I'm very clever. Carry on.'

'They believe it was an argument—'

'Over drugs and money.'

'Give me a chance,' she said, frowning. 'That's what they said. Two boys, aged five and seven. Jacob and Finn Olsson.'

'And that's them,' Cupidi said, pointing to the photograph she had recovered from the remains of the caravan. Two smiling urchins in a sunlit field. They had names now: Jacob and Finn.

The awful meaning of the photograph and why it had been kept sunk in. 'Freya Brindley killed them by mistake when she was trying to get revenge on Daniel Kay.'

'Oh God,' said Ferriter, looking at the picture.

'If it's them, and I bet you it is, then Freya Brindley kept the photo of the two boys with her for the rest of her life. She had it above her bed.'

Ferriter shook her head. 'Why would you do that? To wake up every morning and see them. And to know what happened. That's gruesome.'

Cupidi looked at the photograph and imagined Freya Brindley. 'Maybe. Maybe not. She had done a terrible thing. I think she wanted to remind herself. Punish herself, maybe.'

Officers were starting to stream into the incident room for the morning's meeting, clutching mugs of tea and sheets of paper.

'So they are convinced it was her that set the fire?'

'Yep. Definitely her. The mother of the dead boys gave a full statement to the police. She knew who had killed her children, for sure.'

'What about Daniel Kay? Was he arrested?'

'They charged him with possession of a controlled substance but the case was dropped because of his injuries. He was pretty badly burned, apparently. He refused to say that Freya Brindley was trying to kill him, but there was enough evidence from the others. But the thing was, nobody's ever found Ms Brindley. She seems to have vanished completely from sight.'

'Until she turned up in our ditch. Because she was living under the assumed identity of Hilary Keen. The real Hilary Keen had left the country and was living in Spain off her head on drugs.'

'Jesus. What a miserable story,' said Ferriter. She picked up her coffee, took a sip and made a face. It had gone cold.

Cupidi let Constable Ferriter tell the whole story again when the room was full.

The young woman stood at the front of the room, explaining the whole thing in detail, pointing to the photographs, one by one.

'Bloody hell,' said Sergeant Moon. 'What about the children?'

'Apparently they were just innocent bystanders. Their mother had pulled onto the site a couple of days before. As far as the West Mercia Police could figure, their mother knew nothing about the conflict, poor woman.'

'Poor kids,' said a detective constable. 'At least Freya Brindley got what she bloody deserved.'

'Good job,' said McAdam. 'Very good job.'

'Only we still don't know who killed her,' said Cupidi, finally.

'Stanley Eason,' somebody said.

'No. We still don't know that. Don't you see? We have to consider whether Freya Brindley was murdered because of her involvement in the incident in Evesham in 1995. Or whether she was still involved in dealing drugs.'

'We've tried that avenue,' someone said. 'There's nothing to suggest that she was dealing.'

'But we do know that she was guilty of identity theft, manslaughter and/or attempted murder,' said Cupidi 'She was not a nice woman. I'd say it's odds on she wasn't simply the victim of a robbery and murder by an unscrupulous landlord – a man with no previous record. She was involved in something, but we just don't know what yet. And obviously, it's a good thing Inspector McAdam here took the decision to keep the case open, otherwise we'd never have known any of this.'

McAdam nodded his head. Out of the corner of her eye, Cupidi saw Ferriter rolling her eyes. When she turned to look, she was mouthing, 'Creep.'

Cupidi smiled back at her and winked.

Cupidi's phone rang. Sergeant Moon was sitting next to her, taking notes about Brindley's record. Ferriter was next to him, tapping on an open laptop.

'Can you get it?' Cupidi asked Moon. 'If it's Dolores Umbridge from the IPCC, tell her I'm busy.'

'Who?'

'Didn't you read Harry Potter?' said Ferriter. She leaned across Moon and picked up the handset.

'I'll ask,' she said, cupping her hand over the receiver. 'It's a Superintendent David Colquhoun.'

'Tell him I'm not available.'

'She's not available, sorry.' She put down the phone. 'Oooh.'

'What?'

'Is that who I think it was?'

'What do you mean?' said Cupidi.

She leaned past Moon. 'Your ex. From London.'

'How did you know about him?'

'Just goss,' she said.

'Gossip? So everyone knows.' Cupidi looked around the office angrily. People concentrated on their screens or phones.

Ferriter looked down at her laptop. 'Not everyone.' The phone rang again. They both looked at Moon, who picked up the handset a second time.

Moon listened for a second, then said, 'It's him again.'

'Christ's sake.'

'He says it's important.' And handed the handset to Cupidi.

And David's voice was saying, 'Don't cut me off, please. I have something important to say.'

'This is my work number,' said Cupidi.

'No, listen. Please. You think this is all about you,' he mimicked. 'We've found her.'

'What?'

The office around her was silent, and she was conscious of everyone in the room straining to hear the conversation.

THIRTY-EIGHT

'We've found Hilary Keen. She is in the Royal London Hospital right now. She was pulled off the street half an hour ago by one of the officers from Whitechapel. She had been sleeping in Victoria Park, apparently.'

'And where are you?'

'Don't worry. I'm nowhere near Dungeness. I'm back at our house in London clearing out my belongings. Cathy said I have to be out by the time she's back from Dungeness.'

She took a slow breath. 'I'm sorry to hear that, David.'

There was a long silence. 'Right. I'd better let you get on with it.'

'Thank you.'

'OK,' he said.

'What?' said Ferriter, eyes wide as she ended the call.

'He's found the real Hilary Keen. She's in London.'

'Bloody hell.'

Cupidi was used to having to tell members of the public that a relation was dead. This time it would be different. She lifted the phone again, to tell Julian Keen that his mother was alive.

As Cupidi walked in, they were sitting together on the grey metal benches at the entrance to the A & E unit of the Royal London on Whitechapel Road.

Julian, with his arm around Hilary, his eyes red from crying.

'I want you to meet my mother,' he said, as if they were at a garden party. 'She's been a little unwell.'

She was bird-like, thin and wizened from the sun. Her grey hair was matted and greasy, and her trousers were filthy. She reeked of the thick acid smell of people who have slept in their own clothes for days on end. Yet Julian held his arm around her and smiled.

'Hello, Hilary,' said Cupidi. 'Your son has been looking for you. So have I.'

The woman nodded.

'They found her in the park. A local copper noticed her. She was unconscious. She had been sleeping under the bandstand. I think they got to you just in time, didn't they?' He ran his hand over her head.

He stood and walked a few yards away, leaving the woman blinking in the brightly lit atrium. She looked worn out, ready to fall asleep at any second.

'Are you trying to find her accommodation?' asked Cupidi. 'I don't suppose you can take her home.'

'I've been trying to get her a bed here. They say they don't have room. I was thinking of renting her a place in a hotel. I'd have to get her cleaned up first, though.'

Cupidi looked at her. 'She doesn't look well.'

'They think she's been using heroin again. Or taking something. I will take her home. But not yet. Lulu is not ready.'

'Does she know where you are?'

'I think she's going to divorce me.'

The second one today, Cupidi thought. 'I'm sorry,' she said.

Julian nodded. 'I can't choose between them. It's not fair to ask.'

In A & E, rows of people sat, waiting to be attended to. A nurse was speaking loudly on the phone.

'Give me a minute,' said Cupidi. 'I need to make a call.'

She stepped out of the doors, pulled out her phone and called her mother. 'I need you to move back to the house, back with us. Only for a few days.'

Her mother sounded annoyed. 'I suppose so,' she said.

When she ended the call, she turned back to Julian. 'I have a place she can stay. It's near me, in Kent. I know it's not very convenient for you, but she'll be safe there. Come down, get her settled, then go back to your wife and child until they're ready.'

They led her out of the hospital towards the police car, one at each elbow. There was not much to her at all.

'Do you know anywhere we can get a good coffee?' Cupidi asked. 'I'm going to need it.'

She drove until she reached the A2, then travelled down it until the city started to thin out. When she looked in the rear-view mirror, they were both awake, saying nothing.

'So, Hilary,' she said eventually. 'Tell me about Freya.'

Hilary Keen's pale eyes looked directly back at her. Cupidi

suddenly saw her as the young woman she had been over twenty years earlier. Stunningly pretty, Daniel Kay had said. *I mean, really, really beautiful.*

She didn't speak for a while; she just stared out of the window.

Drugs and outdoor living had not been kind to her. Her skin was leathery and wrinkled, her hair thin. Freya Brindley had replaced her missing teeth; Hilary Keen had not. Those she had were brown or black. Her jawline had shrunk, altering the shape of her face.

And yet, despite her decrepitude and the sharp smell she gave off, Julian still sat with one arm around her.

'You told my son I was dead,' she said eventually.

'It was a mistake. I apologise. He was always convinced you were alive, you know? He kept looking for you.'

Hilary Keen nodded. 'It was Freya, wasn't it?'

'Yes.'

She sniffled into her sleeve. 'I always thought she'd come to a bad end, I suppose. Who did it?'

'I still don't know. It's one of the things I'm trying to find out,' said Cupidi.

Hilary lapsed into silence again for a while. They had passed through Kidbrooke, and the traffic was moving faster. The A2 was an ugly road, dirty houses on either side here, cheap places that had been bodged and altered, reclad and refashioned over time by people trying to make something of them. Speeding up to sixty, the wind blew hair into her face so she wound the window up. Hilary's stink reasserted itself in the car.

'I used to think she was amazing,' Hilary said eventually. 'I wanted to be like her. She turned up one day in a beautiful old car . . . I don't remember what it was.' Her voice was deep for a small woman; a smoker's voice.

'A Mercedes,' Cupidi told her.

'Yes. How did you know that?'

'I spoke to Daniel Kay.'

'My God. Daniel. He's still alive then?'

'Yes.'

Hilary lapsed into silence again. They passed the junction with the M25, heading into Kent. The bland road was always full of lorries, pouring into the county.

'You're going too fast,' said Hilary.

Cupidi checked the speedometer. She was at exactly seventy now.

'Everyone's going too fast,' she said again.

She had not been in a car for so long, Cupidi realised. It must seem like a ridiculous speed to be travelling if you'd spent much of the last two decades sitting on street corners. She slowed to sixty. Other cars roared past her.

'Is Daniel OK?' Hilary asked eventually.

'Yes. He's doing pretty well. Very well, I'd say.'

Hilary nodded. 'He's clean, then? I'm glad.'

'Who's Daniel?' asked Julian.

'A man I used to know,' she said cautiously.

Cupidi's eyes flicked up to the mirror again. Hilary was looking directly at her, as if trying to work out how much Cupidi knew.

Unwilling to hold the gaze, Hilary turned her head away towards her son. 'It's not like heroin wasn't around before Freya arrived, but we all thought it was a dirty drug.' She laughed. 'We were into weed and pills. But she was so good at it. She made it seem beautiful. For a while. It all became a bit of a blur after that.'

'It was the drugs,' said Julian. He was looking for a reason why his mother had abandoned him, Cupidi supposed.

'Yes. Well. I don't know. I used to wonder about that. It was money, too. For years we'd been travelling around existing on almost nothing. We were so proud of that. We didn't need anything. What we got we earned from farm work. There was always something to do. In Cornwall we picked cabbages. In Essex and Kent we did fruit. I spent days pulling leeks or parsnips. There were organic farms that needed everything doing by hand. The pay wasn't much, but I liked it. Daniel did, too. And that was the whole thing. We didn't have to earn much, which is why the farmers didn't mind having us around. They actually wanted people like us who come by when they need us to and work cheaply. And in return we'd get some food from them. They'd pay us in eggs, or meat sometimes. That was even cheaper for them. We didn't have much money ever, and we were proud of that. Money was a straight-world thing.'

A lorry indicated it was about to join their lane. Cupidi braked to let it out. The car behind her pressed its horn.

'And then the city people started coming in, and the drugs came along and everything changed. Heroin meant money. You needed to earn to buy it. Or steal. You got money if you sold it. Suddenly there was money in our lives and everything was different.'

'There's nothing wrong with money,' said Julian. 'It was drugs.'

'I'm not sure. All sorts of things went wrong. We were all in love with Freya. I was. Daniel certainly was. I remember I caught him smoking heroin one day in his bus. It was her that started it.'

'Love, drugs and money,' said Cupidi. 'If we didn't have them, there wouldn't be any crime at all.'

'If she shot up, then it was OK. She made it all right. I swore I would never do that. The idea of putting a needle into yourself revolted me. But then Daniel was, then I was too, and everything went haywire. I couldn't stop myself. If you've never been into it, you wouldn't understand.'

'No,' said Cupidi. 'I wouldn't.'

'Everything changes when hard drugs come on site. People get paranoid. The police start taking an interest. Freya was savvy. She never used to get caught. I used to wonder why that was. I figured it out in the end.'

'Because she was the dealer, and you were the users.'

'Exactly.' Hilary laughed. 'You understand. It was because she was making her living dealing to the rest of us. I was still going out and earning money on the farms so I could . . . you know, afford to buy her gear. That made me more vulnerable. I'd be shooting up in the mobile toilets they'd bring onto the farm.' She shook her head. 'She never had to leave the site. And then, because I had a kid, they targeted me. Social workers started coming around. I swear to God, however bad I got, I always looked after you, Jules.'

'Is that what you used to call me?'

'Ju-Ju. That's the way you used to say your name.'

'What was I like?'

'A pest,' she said. 'Into everything. Too smart for your own good. Show me your ankle. Roll up your trousers.'

'Why?'

'No, the other one, your right leg.'

He lifted it onto the car seat, pulling down his sock.

'There. You can just see it still. It's faint, though.'

'What is it?'

'You had one of those bouncy balls. It rolled under Daniel's big bus one day. I'd told you not go after it, that it wasn't safe under there, but you crawled all the way under to get it out. Cut yourself on a bit of glass. I was horrified.' She laughed. 'Bandaged it up, though. Look.'

'I wondered what it was.'

'There was I saying I always looked after you. You must think I'm terrible.'

'How old was I?'

'You must have been about to turn three. It was just before I left you.'

'I don't remember.'

'Thing is, I knew I was getting bad. I knew it wouldn't be long before they locked me up. I was a rotten addict. Always have been. I had to do something, else they'd take you away. They kept saying they would. You would be coming up to school age, and what would I do then? And Daniel hated them turning up to the site all the time, the police and the social workers. People blamed me.'

'So you gave me to your sister.'

'I'm sorry. I'm so, so, so, so sorry.'

He nodded, but said nothing.

'Did she ever talk about me?'

'No.'

Tears rolled down Hilary's cheek.

'Never. There were no photos of you or anything. It was like you didn't exist.'

'Can't say I blame her.'

'I do. I suppose the problem was, she never really wanted to bring up a child.'

'I'm sorry, Ju-Ju. It was the best I could do at the time.'

It was as if she had forgotten she was there, thought Cupidi. They have so much to say to each other. She was eavesdropping on their lifetimes'-worth of hurt.

'I had always meant to come back for you. I knew I had to get myself away from other users like Daniel and Freya. There was a truck going down to Spain to meet up with some circus people down there, and I took you to my sister's house and just left you there. I thought it would be a month or two. But I couldn't kick it. I tried. I really tried, I promise you. I tried so bloody hard. But I'm an addict. Like I said in that note I wrote for you. I thought about you every day.'

'What note?'

'In the kitchen. On your board.'

'You didn't write a note,' he said.

'Oh,' she said, and looked away. 'Didn't I?'

'I never saw anything . . .' Then he frowned. Cupidi could see the thought growing.

'No, no. I must have got that wrong,' Hilary intervened. 'I get confused. I probably just wished I'd written something like that.'

Cupidi caught her eye again, for a second when she turned again to look at her son. There was a momentary flicker of darkness in her gaze, but it had gone in a second. Julian never noticed. She was good, thought Cupidi. Years of conniving to get drugs, or a place to sleep, had made her canny.

'Every day,' she said.

'But not enough to stop and be my mother.'

'I'm sorry,' she said.

They stopped talking. Cupidi drove.

At sixty miles an hour, the journey seemed to take an age, both of them silent in the back of the car. Whenever she sped up, Hilary started to look agitated. Only in the early evening light, when they were driving over the marsh towards Dungeness, did Hilary's face change. She pressed her face against the window.

At Lydd, when they turned onto the Dungeness Road, she opened her mouth again. 'You live here?'

'Yes, with my daughter.'

Hilary's eyes lit up. She looked young again.

'We camped here once. Daniel and the rest of us. Before it all went wrong. In the summer. Out on the end by the lighthouses. It was just after you were born.'

'That's where we're heading now,' said Cupidi.

'You're kidding me?' Hilary laughed. 'Oh, wow! It was beautiful here. They moved us on after a while. It took them a while because of you, Ju-Ju. They weren't allowed to evict us straight away because I had a little baby.'

'I had my uses.'

'Be as bitter as you want. I don't mind. It's fine. I understand.'

'I'm sorry. I'm spoiling it.'

They turned onto the single-track road.

'It looks exactly the same. We had all our buses and trailers lined up along there. There are old railway carriages, aren't there?'

'Yes. You remember it?'

'I used to fantasise about living in one of them.'

They passed the Britannia Inn and the lighthouses, turned right in front of the power station, then headed up the track towards Cupidi's house.

'You actually live here?'

'First time I saw it, I thought it was the strangest place in the world,' said Cupidi.

'It's like a weird dream,' said Hilary. 'Like everything is rewinding.'

At the back of the house, they got out, stretching after the long journey. It was muggy and hot. There was going to be a storm soon.

Helen was in a deckchair, a novel in one hand and a paper fan in the other. 'Who's this?'

Cupidi introduced them all. 'I have somewhere for you to stay,' she said to Hilary, 'but I'll need to give you a bath first in my house. Get you into some clean clothes.'

'It's amazing,' said Hilary, slowly looking around.

Cupidi took her mother aside. 'Sorry. You can move back into the cabin when they're gone if you like.'

'I'll cope, I suppose.'

'Where's Zoë?'

'Not back yet. I spoke to her on the phone. She says she'll be back by eight. I made her promise. She doesn't ever come back until it's almost dark.'

'It's going to rain. If she's not back soon, she'll be soaked.'

Behind the power station, thick clouds were building, huge, black and rolling. A hot wind was picking up, scattering dead petals from the scraggy rosebushes at the back of the house.

THIRTY-NINE

With an empty black plastic bag in one hand, Cupidi led the woman up to the bathroom and gradually stripped the clothes from her body while the bath ran.

The woman stood there, acquiescent, unembarrassed by her nakedness and the state of her body. The skin on her neck and hands was thick with grime. Blackness sat under fingernails, in the whorls of her fingertips, in the wrinkles and cracks. It would take more than one bath for her to get completely clean, but at least she wouldn't smell as badly as she did now.

'Arms,' she said, lifting Hilary's vest off, as she had her own daughter's when she was a child. It was stained with sweat. She dropped it into the rubbish bag. 'You can have some of mine to wear. They might be a bit big.'

Hilary didn't react. Years of homelessness and addiction left her passive. Cupidi tested the bathwater, adding shampoo to make bubbles.

Hilary was naked now from the waist up. Cupidi paused.

'What happened at the campsite, the night of the fire? Did you find out about that?'

'I was in Spain by then.'

'But you heard?'

Hilary sat down on the toilet and started rolling her tights down her thin legs. 'Through the grapevine. There was this alternative circus I hung out with. You know, fire-eating, chainsaws . . .'

'Very nineties.'

She laughed. 'Yes. They had an old *finca* outside Lleida in Catalonia. I used to sing in bands, so I told them I was working up some kind of act with my singing. Maybe I was, I don't know. I was a mess. I used to have a good voice once. But they put me up for a couple of years, and during that time other travellers would come through the town. So I learned bits and pieces of what had gone on at the site. People said there had been this fire. That children had been killed. I heard that Daniel was badly disfigured.'

She trod on one half of her woollen tights and lifted the other to pull them off. On her calf, hidden till now, there was a single tattoo, not particularly well done: *Ju-Ju.*

'The poor children. I kept thinking, that would have been Jules, if I was still there.'

Freya was completely naked now: bony, scabbed on her knees and on her shoulder. Abscesses had left red scars on her arms and legs. The paleness of the skin on her body contrasted with the burnt brown of her head and limbs.

Gingerly she lowered herself into the water.

'It's hot,' she complained.

Cupidi added more cold.

'Did you know the children who died?'

'No. They were innocent bystanders, I think. The poor mother.'

'These travellers who came through, did they ever tell you who set the fire?'

'Oh yes. Everyone knew. It was just one of those stories that went around. But it was Daniel's fault at the start of it. Apparently he was clucking.'

Cupidi had been around addicts enough to know their language. 'Clucking' was that skin-scratching, nervy-eyed behaviour of someone who needed the next fix. 'Daniel set the fire? I thought—'

'No. Not Daniel. He wanted some heroin, but I can't judge. I've done bad things, too. I've robbed people because I needed the stuff more than they did. So people say he stole Freya's stash. But, like, all of it. Not just enough for himself. All of it. When she found out, she went ape.'

The obscured glass window darkened. The rain cloud was over them now.

'So you think she tried to kill him?'

'Definitely. Everyone knew it. Or scare him. I don't know. Some people think she was psycho all along. Whatever it was, it just got out of hand. There was a lot of substance abuse. People were nuts. And then Daniel was in hospital and she was never heard of again.'

She picked up a handful of the bubbles that the shampoo had made.

'Are you OK?' asked Cupidi.

'I've been using. I'm not feeling great,' she said.

'You need sleep. I've a bed made up, ready for you when you're clean. I'll give you some food and then you can rest.'

'Is Julian going back to London?'

'He's staying tonight. He's called his wife and told her.'

'He's lovely, isn't he, my son?'

'He's going to need a lot of help working it all out with you,' Cupidi said. 'And with his wife.'

She snorted. 'Don't look at me. I'm no good at any of that.'

'Well, you're going to bloody have to be,' Cupidi said.

'I can't.'

'If you can't, then there was no point tracking him down, was there?'

Rain spattered suddenly onto the window. Cupidi could hear a door somewhere downstairs banging in the wind. She wondered if Zoë was back yet.

'So as far as you know, Freya just disappeared?'

'She used to be my friend. She was in the ward with me, when I had Julian. Nicking the gas and air, mind. Then, after the fire, I never heard anything of her ever again. I asked, but nobody knew anything. I thought she would have died after all this time. Every few years I'd come back to England. I had this dream of finding my son again, of making it up to Julian. I came back last year, and thought I'd try and make a go of it, try and find my feet. I was looking for Julian, and I started asking after her again too, but I didn't really know anybody. Everyone I knew was dead, or they'd moved on. But when I tried signing on, I was accused of having false papers. "That's not you," they said. "It can't be. That's somebody else's identity you've stolen," they said. It was like a nightmare. I couldn't even get straight again because of her. She ruined my life.'

'I think she was living around here for years,' said Cupidi. 'She had cleaned up, but she was hiding. She knew the moment she used her own name she'd be arrested for what she did to those kids. She knew you were gone. And so she pretended to be you.'

'What a hell of a life. All that on our shoulders, all three of us. Me, Freya, Daniel. I suppose she thought I was genuinely dead, too. I was, really.'

'Want me to wash your back?'

'I died a few times, for real. Heart stopped, everything. Overdosed. They brought me back with adrenalin. I didn't care. I just went and did it all again. Wouldn't bloody die.'

Cupidi took a sponge and started rubbing Hilary's shoulders. Hilary was only a little older than Cupidi, but her skin was an old woman's, puckered and wrinkled.

'She was using my name?'

'Yes.'

'And clean? I can't imagine her clean,' said Hilary. 'She was always on drugs. What was she living off?'

'I'm not sure. It's one thing I can't work out. She had money, I know that, but I don't know where she was getting it from. If I did, I might be able to figure out why she died. I was wondering. Did she ever work on farms, like you?'

'Freya? No. She was too good for that. And she had no need. She made plenty of cash. Why? Do you think that's what she was doing?'

Cupidi didn't answer. She thought of the simple caravan, hidden away behind Eason's house.

'In spite of everything she did, I would have liked to have seen her again. Just once.'

'I didn't get the impression that Daniel was so keen. If I read his reaction right, I think he was glad she was dead. He didn't say as much, in as many words.'

'Daniel was always a hypocrite,' she said. 'He loved her once. I think he still feels bad that it was him who set the ball rolling. If he hadn't nicked the stuff, the boys would still be alive.'

'I think it was you he really loved.'

She laughed. 'No. That's not right at all.'

'My impression was, he felt guilty about not looking after you when you needed it.'

'We could barely look after ourselves, back then, any of us.'

The white bubbles had faded; the water around her was dark already. Cupidi took down the shower head, turned the tap back on and tested the temperature.

'Is he married, Daniel?'

'I don't think so.'

'Is he well?'

'He runs a kind of posh New Age health farm north of London. He's quite well known in those circles. He looks very well.'

'I heard he had been badly disfigured.'

'Not really. You can see the burns, but they're not bad.'

'That's good.' She leaned forward and let Cupidi spray water through her filthy hair. The grease was so thick it would take three or four washes to get it clean.

'Is he Julian's father?'

She took her time answering. 'Yes,' she said eventually.

'Are you going to tell him?'

'In time. Why are you laughing?'

It was true: an inescapable giggle rising up. 'You know what? I think his wife, Lulu, might find it easier to accept you as a mother-in-law if she knew her husband's dad was a wealthy spa owner with his own mansion.'

'He's rich?'

'Richer than you or me, that's for sure. You should get in touch with him. I think he'd like to see you.'

'I doubt it.'

'Give it time. Your sister never asked for child support from him?'

'Because I never told her who the father was. She asked. I refused to say. As far as I knew, he was just another smack addict. I didn't want Julian to know anything about it.'

'Now you're laughing too. What's so funny?'

Hilary was shaking, sending ripples through the water. Even with her head down, eyes closed to keep the soap out, Cupidi could see her face was all wrinkles now, showing grey teeth; the biggest smile Cupidi had seen her make so far. 'He always liked money more than he pretended. As I said, he was always a hypocrite.'

Cupidi rinsed her hair until the water ran clean.

When Hilary leaned back and opened her eyes again, she said, 'I shouldn't be so hard on him. I have nothing else to lose. Nothing at all. He has a reputation. He would be afraid of losing it.'

'You have your son back.'

'Maybe,' she said, and slid back underwater. 'I don't know yet.'

Sorting through her wardrobe, Cupidi found some old clothes that might fit a thinner woman and left them outside the door. Downstairs Helen was cooking pasta, something she could be relied on not to cook too badly. 'Is she OK?'

'She's coming off heroin.'

Her mother blew out air. She had given Julian a glass of wine and was drinking one herself.

'I spoke to Lulu,' he said. 'She's worried, of course.'

'Your choice. You can stay, or I'll drive you to the station.'

'I'll stay with her. Tonight, at least.'

'Good. That cottage. It belongs to a man I know. He's away. I'm going to put your mother up in it for a few days. I know he'd approve of it being used like this. There's a second bedroom for you, if you like. And then you need to work out what you're doing. She'll be down in a minute.' She peered out of the kitchen window. 'No sign of Zoë yet?'

'It's pouring down,' her mother said. 'She'll be soaked.' The storm clouds were directly over them now; it was as if night had fallen. Rain was sweeping in waves across the wet stones.

'My daughter,' explained Cupidi.

'What an amazing place for her to grow up,' said Julian.

That was when the landline rang.

'Where were you? I've been calling your mobile and radioing the police car.'

DI McAdam. Shit.

'I should explain. Something really big came up. I was fetching a witness from London. The real Hilary Keen.'

'You found her?'

'Whitechapel Police did.'

‘Where is she?’

‘Right now, at my house. She’s in a bit of a mess. I’ll explain. I was just . . . interviewing her.’ She didn’t say: naked, in the bath.

‘Don’t worry about that now. It’s not relevant. This is more important. We’ve had reports of another body. In the water. By Jury’s Gut. Apparently about a quarter of a mile away from Salt Lane, where the last woman was found. And naked too. I’ve been trying to track you down for the last thirty bloody minutes.’

‘Right. Sorry.’

‘Get there now. Constable Ferriter is on the way out there now. I want you to get a good assessment of the site.’

‘Who’s the victim?’

‘Unidentified. All I know is it’s a young one. Female.’

In that second the panic started. Chest-constricting, limb-chilling horror. Zoë had not come home yet.

‘What’s wrong?’ said her mother, wooden spoon at her lips.

Cupidi looked at her mother, at Julian and, behind them, at Hilary Keen, standing in the doorway, transformed.

‘I have to go. Look after them, Mum.’

‘Alex? What’s wrong?’

But she was sprinting out of the back door through the rain to the police car, fumbling for the keys.

FORTY

The rain was biblical. It sprayed down onto the dark tarmac. She drove with her headlights on, windscreen wipers on double speed, blue lights flashing above the dashboard of the unmarked car.

'Is Moon there?' she asked, calling control to try to find the exact location. Yes, he was. 'Anybody know who the victim is?'

'Naked again. No ID. They're just waiting for the Marine Unit to take her out.'

She tried not to think about her daughter.

Slow down. Stay calm. As a cop, she had told relatives of victims this so often. At times like this, your judgement became clouded. It would be easy to have an accident. The road was treacherous, too. After so many dry days, the tarmac would be slippery.

At Lydd a drain had backed up, flooding the tarmac. She drove cautiously through the water, speeding up again only when she was clear of the village.

Ahead, a slow tractor with a trailer full of sheep blocked the lane on the way to Fairfield. She leaned on the horn, but it was almost a quarter of a mile down the road before the farmer found somewhere he could pull over. She raced past it, water arcing out from under her tyres.

Then she couldn't find the turning.

Jesus.

She had to call control back a second time to check the location, and it turned out to be back the way she had come. The new lane was narrower again, twisting left and right. Then, in the distance, she saw flashes of blue light through the rain.

The cordon had already been set up on the single-track road. She braked in front of the yellow tape. A punctuation mark in the landscape; it signified something awful beyond.

On the other side, in the downpour, figures were moving around on the edge of what must have been a drain running somewhere between the lane and the field. It was difficult to see who any of them were or what they were doing.

She knew she must get out of the car and walk towards it, but for some time she couldn't move. She sat, shivering. The wipers moved frenetically, pushing water off the glass.

She killed the switch. Engine off, the windscreen fogged.

She had to move. The radio buzzed and crackled.

Finally she forced open the car door. Water splashed on her leg.

Getting out, she walked first to the back of the car, to the boot. Within seconds her linen summer suit was soaked. The only remotely waterproof item she had with her was a police high-viz jacket. By the time she put it on, she was already dripping. Tugging the forensic suit over the top was not easy.

Looking back towards the crime scene, she saw the wind blowing curtains of water across the flatland, ripping leaves off the pollard willows that grew around the ditch ahead. She stepped over the stuttering yellow tape and set off on a run through puddles, towards the blue lights.

Ferriter stood in a white suit, hood up, drawstring tight around her pretty face, facemask over her mouth. Raindrops trickled down her nose and chin as she added Cupidi's name to the water-sodden log of people who were on site.

'Who is it?' Cupidi shouted.

'We don't know,' Ferriter called back. 'The body is stuck in the culvert that runs under the railway line. We can't get a good look at it. Trouble is, the water's rising and the stupid body is wedged in there.'

Stupid body.

'My daughter's not back home,' Cupidi said, simply.

'Oh, Alex.' Ferriter's eyes widened.

'I think she may have been out somewhere around here. She was worried about that girl she thought she saw out here the night before last. Remember?'

Saying nothing, Jill Ferriter dropped her clipboard, stepped forward and threw her arms around Cupidi. Other coppers, not knowing what was happening, looked on, confused.

Ferriter, petite and inches shorter than her, hugged Cupidi as she stood, unsure of how to react. The rain fell on them both.

'Whatever you need,' said Ferriter.

'How long is it going to take the team to get here?' she asked.

'Any minute.'

'How do they know she's a girl? If she's under there?'

'The farmer was trying to clear the culvert before the rain came. There were weeds and debris clogging it. He saw her in there. But by the time we got here, the water had already risen. The level's going up fast.'

Cupidi remembered what they'd said at the Drainage Board: this time of year they keep the drains full. The water was running straight off the dry fields. 'Did he describe her at all?'

'Young, he said. That's all. She was naked.'

'Same as the last – Freya Brindley?'

'Looks like it.'

'Rules out Stanley Eason then.'

Ferriter released her. 'You shouldn't be here. Go home.'

Cupidi shook her head.

They could insist she leave; it was their job to keep the area as secure and clean as it could be. Having the mother of the potential victim here was a complication.

'You should sit in your car. Outside the cordon.'

'Don't make me do that, Jill. Please. Don't make me.' Cupidi turned to look at the dark, muddy water.

Puddles were growing larger in the field; black shapes in the darkening green. In a flatland, there was nowhere for the rain to go. The marsh seemed to be returning to water in front of Cupidi's eyes.

'Of course, love,' said Ferriter.

She called home, sheltering her phone from the wet, trying not to sound anxious.

'Why did you run off like that?' her mother asked.

'Police emergency,' she said. 'I'll explain later. Has Zoë come home?'

'Not yet. She's probably in one of the hides on the reserve, waiting for the rain to stop.' Her mother lowered her voice. 'What do I do with these people?'

'I'll be back as soon as I can,' she said. She ended the call, handing the phone back to Ferriter, who said nothing but looked at her with the kind of sympathetic face that would normally have set Cupidi's teeth on edge. She was trying to be nice.

Headlights lit the falling rain.

'That should be them,' Ferriter said.

They lowered the tape to let the Land Rover through, blue light still flashing. Two men; Cupidi recognised them as the same ones that had recovered Freya Brindley's body.

Ferriter stepped forward and intercepted them before they reached the other officers who were waiting for them to do their work. She would be telling them about the position of the body, taking their details, but she was obviously saying more than that, too, Cupidi realised.

Simultaneously both men shot a glance towards her. Ferriter must have told them that it was possible that the victim was her daughter.

To be in the police is to be part of something different. Your job, as a copper, is to deal with the worst in life: the worst events and the worst people. You are apart from the rest of the world and because of that, an injury to one is an injury to all. They looked nervously towards her, anxious now. This was not just another job.

Last time, they had the usual banter about wearing rubber, about not being able to swim. About getting a discount. There were always jokes when there was a dead body. It's what got you through days like this. Today they wouldn't even crack a smile.

Cupidi didn't want any sympathy. It only made things worse. She just wanted them to get on with their work. To find out that the body was someone else's, not her daughter's.

The trouble with calling in a specialist unit is that everything takes so long. If she had stripped off her own clothes and dived into the water, it would have only taken her a few minutes to locate the body.

But that moment had passed.

Instead she had to stand and wait as the two of them opened the back door of the Land Rover and started to don their gear.

They seemed to be taking longer than they had last time. Maybe it was because the rain didn't help. Putting on a neoprene suit is hard enough at the best of times. When it's wet, the rubber sticks to skin.

The two men tugged and pulled at each other's dive suits. She sensed a reluctance to get into the water; they did not want to be the bearers of bad news.

She thought of Julian Keen; he had got his mother back. Was this some kind of nightmarish exchange? The dead for the living?

Finally they were ready. They switched on waterproof head torches and moved towards the bank. The figures standing around the steep slope parted to let them past.

The two men, clad in black, slipped into the dark water. When they were submerged up to their chests, they looked around, illuminating the darkness under the railway line.

'You OK? No. Shit. Of course you're not. I can't imagine . . .'

Ferriter was going to put her arm around her again, thought Cupidi. She wasn't sure she could cope if she did.

It seemed to be taking so long. What was the problem?

'Cupidi?' said a voice. 'Got here as soon as I could.' Sergeant Moon was dressed in a pink waterproof, too small for him. 'What's going on?'

'Alex's daughter is missing,' said Ferriter.

Shut up. Shut your beautiful face up, thought Cupidi.

'Fuck,' said Moon with a look of horror. 'Is it . . . ?'

Ferriter was shaking her head.

'God. Shit.'

'She's probably sitting under a tree somewhere, sheltering from this rain.'

'Right. Yes. I'm sure she is.'

Who was she to judge Hilary when she had made such a hash of being a parent herself?

'Got her,' called one of the recovery team.

Lights focused on the black water, dotted by rain.

Oh Christ.

She was crying now. She couldn't help it.

But even this took time; the cautious disentangling of a woman's body from the concrete culvert. They would want to be careful; a cadaver is a recording. Its contusions and abrasions tell the story of how that person died. These men were professionals. They would want to do as much as they could to preserve that record. Time was not important; she was already dead.

'Young female. Confirmed.'

'What colour's her hair?' called Ferriter. She turned. 'Your daughter's got blonde hair, right?'

'Can't see,' came a voice.

She panicked. She could not be here. 'I'll be in the car,' Cupidi blurted to Moon.

'I thought . . .'

'I can't see this. I can't cope with this.'

In the car, she switched off the police radio. She could not bear to listen to that, either.

She sat, soaking wet inside the vehicle waiting, shivering uncontrollably.

FORTY-ONE

As they lifted the pale shape from the water, she switched on the engine; the windscreen wipers lurched into double-speed.

The scene was revealed. Police crowded at the top of the slippery bank; a civilian from coroner's office stood, miserably trying to keep dry under an umbrella that kept blowing itself inside out. Everyone in white; like ghosts.

The problem now would be how to get the corpse out of the water. Cupidi knew, from her own experience, how challenging it was to climb out of these drainage channels. Hard enough to move yourself, let alone a dead weight.

And then Ferriter was hobbling towards the car.

Shit, shit, shit.

She was shaking her head as she ducked under the tape. What did that mean?

Yanking open the car door: 'It's not her! It's not her. She's got dark hair.'

Oh God.

'You sure?'

'They just said. Black hair. Long.'

You could see the relief among the other coppers; it was visible in the way they stood now, bodies less stiff.

'Jesus.'

They all looked at Cupidi, some grinning. As she emerged back onto the site, a copper clapped her on the shoulder. It was bizarre; as if she had won a prize. *Not one of ours.* But the guilty smiles vanished just as quickly. It was still a body. Somebody else's daughter.

'Let me see,' she said.

The victim was being held in the water by the recovery crew. She was naked, dressed only in fronds of weed that stuck to her skin. The same as Freya Brindley, thought Cupidi; strip the clothes and leave the body in the water to make identification hard and to degrade the DNA. They stood, waist high in water, one on each side of the woman whose head was tilted towards Cupidi. Her dark hair hung down into the water.

From the bank, the people shone torches. Her eyes were wide, whites catching the light. Rain fell into her open mouth.

The men edged forwards, feet unsteady in the mud, and as they did so, the victim's head lolled sideways.

Coppers gasped. Cupidi could see why. There were large wounds where her neck met her shoulder; washed by the water, they were clean, and gaped open as the skin stretched.

She had been stabbed several times close to the nape, the weapon penetrating downwards towards her body cavity. The gashes were so deep, at least one would have passed through the carotid artery.

The woman had the pallor of the bloodless.

A stench of decay rose up from the trench; old mud disturbed by the men released its ancient stink.

'Get a tarp,' shouted one of the frogmen. 'In the back of the van. And rope.'

They threw it to them and the man wrapped the blue sheet under her, tying the line to the tarpaulin's eyes.

Above, coppers hauled on the ropes as the men below lifted the body. Slowly the victim was dragged up the bank, bumping hips on hummocks of grass.

It's not my daughter, Cupidi thought. But where was she, then? She was supposed to be concentrating on the dead woman, on the crime scene, making notes of what was happening.

A copper was kneeling, pulling the rope out of the tarpaulin's eyelets so he could open it.

'God. I'm so relieved it's not Zoë, boss.' Ferriter was standing beside her.

She turned to her. 'Did you see the wounds?'

'No. Bad?'

Cupidi nodded. 'She was stabbed several times.'

The officer had finally managed to loosen the knot and had pulled back the tarp, exposing the body inside.

And as he did so, Ferriter's eyes widened.

Bodies do not look like the people they were. The muscles relax. The face changes shape. Cupidi had not recognised her at first either.

Ferriter did. Cupidi dragged her eyes away from the body and turned to look at the constable. She was standing, shocked, open-mouthed.

There was a reason Najiba had not been home.

Ferriter's chest rose and fell. In the rain streaming down her face, it was impossible to make out tears.

It was Cupidi's turn to put her hand around the constable's shoulders, feeling their judder.

'A shock,' she whispered. 'I didn't really even know her, I suppose.'

The weather was relentless. The bank they were standing on was already a mess of mud.

With a torch, Cupidi knelt at the body's side and looked close.

Normally she would not touch a body herself, but it had been disturbed already. With gloves on, she leaned across the body and picked up Najiba's left hand. There was a slash across the palm. Lifting her right arm, she saw another cut, bone-deep, at her elbow.

'Defensive wounds,' someone said.

She nodded. She imagined Najiba standing, holding her arms up in front of her to protect herself from whoever had the knife.

It had been swift and brutal. Four times the weapon had made it past her raised hands. It was someone who knew how to kill. They were going for the weak spot between the shoulder blade and the spine. Once the knife found the artery, it would have all been over.

'It's our fault, isn't it?' said Ferriter miserably.

'Why?'

'We were so keen to persuade her to give us the addresses. That's why they killed her.'

Maybe it was true. They hadn't known what they were doing when they turned up at the caravans. People had escaped. That's what had put her life in danger.

'It's not your fault,' Cupidi said, but she felt unsettled. She was still too many steps behind.

They had met this woman. She had tried to help them. Now she was dead.

'Why is there bruising around the wound?' she asked.

There were dark marks on the skin where she had been stabbed.

'Jesus. He must have hit her hard with that knife.' Standing at her feet, a copper whom Cupidi didn't recognise was miming downward jabbing actions.

'Do that again,' she said.

'What?'

'That movement.' She watched him stabbing into air, a puzzled look on his face, then looked back down at the open wounds.

The same shape her daughter had made when copying the girl she had seen in the night. The downward motion of the fist.

'Oh,' she said.

'What?'

Taking Najiba's head in her gloved hands she tilted it slightly to one side. Rigor had gone completely. The autopsy would confirm it, but she had been dead at least two days, Cupidi guessed. 'A bit more light, please.'

Somebody shone the torch from their phone onto the woman's other shoulder. And there, on the opposite side, were more bruises; but no wounds this time.

A hand was tugging at her shoulder. 'Your phone's ringing, Sarge.'

Was it? She looked down. The screen was lit up, shining through the wet material of her trousers. She dug it out, stood and held it to her ear.

'Mum?'

'Where were you?' Stupid to let the anger into her voice. 'Sorry. I was worried.'

'At Christmas Dell hide. The rain came. I would have got soaked so I stayed. Are you all right, Mum?'

'Yes. I am.'

'I'm home now. Got soaked anyway. Those people in Arum Cottage. Who are they?'

The body recovery team had arrived. They would be lifting Najiba into the back of a van soon. Ferriter was looking white; Cupidi wondered if she was going to faint. She was young; not used to the dead.

'Mum? Who are they?'

'I'll explain in the morning. It's a long story. I love you, darling.'

'What's wrong, Mum?'

'Nothing. Nothing at all. I just wanted to say I love you, very, very much.'

'You're being weird. When are you coming home?'

'Don't be angry. I have to work late. It's what I do. Go to bed.' Her daughter didn't answer. She looked at the body. *This is what I do.*

She got back into the police car, started the engine and put the fan on, doing her best to dry herself out.

There was not much to do at a crime scene like this. In the morning, after a forensic team had done their work, they would search the wider area, trawl the drain for any clothes or artefacts, looking for the weapon. Even if they all knew that there was almost certainly no chance of finding any evidence here. There had been none when Hilary Keen's body had been dumped; this would be the same. If there had been any tracks or footprints they would have been long gone.

Ferriter opened the door.

'Get in,' Cupidi said. She looked at the young woman. 'Are you OK?'

'No,' she said.

She reached out and took her hand. The interior light faded and they were left in the darkness, watching them struggling over the slippery mud with Najiba's body.

The frogmen were stripping down again; they had done their job.

Nobody was speaking any more; the excitement of a fresh crime scene had gone. In its place was the struggle to carry out these dismal tasks in horrible conditions.

First the coroner's officer left, followed by the Marine Unit. Ferriter had booked them to return in the morning for a fingertip search of the ditch. Finally the pathologist's team closed the doors of their vehicle.

When they tried to leave, they discovered they had driven the van too far into the mud. Wheels spun, uselessly, until a group of the remaining coppers helped push it out onto the tarmac.

When Moon had put the cordon tape back in place, he got into the back of Cupidi's car.

'Jesus,' he said, lowering his hood. 'What a foul night. Not much else we can do here until the morning. Let's hope the weather's better then. Back here at seven? That right?'

'Yes,' said Cupidi.

'Jill? You OK? You're looking a bit peaky.'

'Fine,' she said.

His head appeared between the two headrests. 'Is there a Support Officer on the way to look after the site overnight?'

'Yes, poor bastard,' said Ferriter. 'Don't fancy that much. He's forty minutes away. It's OK. I'll wait. I don't mind.'

'How's your leg?'

'Not so bad,' she said.

'I don't think you should even be out here,' said Moon.

'I won't be able to sleep now anyway. Not after that.'

'You knew her?'

'Yes. She helped us.'

The land around them was black; there was no sign of habitation anywhere.

'Which car are you going to use?'

'Shit,' she said. The car she'd come in had left already.

'You'll have to take this one,' said Cupidi. 'Will you give me a ride home, Peter?'

'Not on your own, Jill,' said Moon, looking round. 'You shouldn't be here on your own.'

Cupidi said, 'I should get a decent look around outside the perimeter, just in case there's anything that's not going to last till forensics get here.'

'In this weather?'

'It needs doing.' A team would search the wider area methodically tomorrow, in the light, but the rain might be washing away evidence. She should take a look round to make sure there was nothing that would be washed away in the next few hours.

'Rather you than me,' said Ferriter.

'Is that your car there, Peter?'

An elderly Subaru; a boy-racer car, metallic blue, with spoilers and alloy wheels.

'Yeah. I was just clocking off when the call came through.'

'It's a good idea of yours to stay with her, Peter, till the relief arrives. Why don't you do that?'

'What?'

'You said she shouldn't be on her own. You're right. She shouldn't. I'll square it with McAdam.'

'I'll be OK,' Ferriter said again.

'Can I drive home in yours, Peter?'

'My car?' said Moon.

'Don't fret. I won't scratch the paint job.'

'You never know, even you could probably pull, driving that one,' said Ferriter.

'That's what I was hoping.' Always the stupid banter. Even on a night like this.

'Right,' said Moon. 'Yeah. Of course.'

'I better get this done, then,' Cupidi said, looking out at the rain.

'You want a hand?'

She shook her head. 'You two are going to be out here a while. Stay in the dry.'

The rain was finally easing. Torch in hand, she walked the length of the road, back and forth, taking photos of an old cigarette packet that, from the state of it, had been discarded here long before the body had been dumped, an empty bottle of Sprite and the insole from a shoe that looked much too large to have been Najiba's.

There was nothing else; none of the victim's clothes, no obvious car tracks apart from their own. She was not surprised.

She returned to the car and sat next to Ferriter. Digging inside her handbag, she brought out tissues. 'Here,' she said, giving her the packet.

'Thanks.'

'If you're using my car, I'll just get my phone charger,' said Moon, getting out.

Ferriter rubbed her eyes with a tissue. 'I barely knew her,' she said. 'I mean. Not really. What was she doing around here anyway?'

'We don't know she was. She could have been killed anywhere.' Cupidi thought for a little while. 'Whoever dumped Freya Brindley knew the land around here. They knew no one was likely to find her for a few days. By which time much of the forensics would be lost.'

The light came on in Moon's car. He was in the passenger seat, checking his hair in the mirror.

'That's right. Whoever did this . . . One thing they're not is stupid,' said Cupidi. 'And I think they're local. And the other one. The man in the slurry pit. He's connected too. Like you thought. Left where the evidence disappears.'

'I just thought we were wrong to assume it was a separate case.'

The rain had stopped now, and the night was oddly quiet. Cupidi wound down the window. 'Something else,' she said.

'What?'

'Najiba's wounds. The girl my daughter met the night before last. She was trying to tell Zoë something but she didn't speak any English. All she could do was mime.'

Cupidi copied Zoë bringing down her fist, just as the copper had done. She was miming someone stabbing downwards; just as Najiba had been stabbed.

'Oh Christ. She'd seen it?'

'That's what she was trying to say. She was trying to tell Zoë she'd witnessed a murder. That's why she was so scared.'

'And she was around here?'

'About a half a mile away. Over there.' She pointed into the nothingness.

Moon got back in the car. 'All right?'

Cupidi switched on the police radio. Flooding in New Romney had closed the road off completely now. She thought of the town below the sea.

'You should go home,' said Ferriter. 'We'll be all right here.'

Cupidi looked at her watch and was surprised to see how late it was. 'I don't know if I can sleep,' she said. 'It'll be light soon.'

It'll be light soon. She thought of the Arctic tern; the migrant who travelled for thousands of miles for the length of the days; for the extra food that provided.

The length of the days; fifteen hours at this time of day. The long daylight of the temperate zone in summer.

'Hundreds of people used to live around here,' Cupidi said, 'labouring in the fields.'

'Are you OK?'

'What if they still are?'

In the back of the car Moon laughed nervously. 'You're spooking us out now, Alex. No people round here now.'

'What if there *are* people out there, only you can't see them?'

'Fuck off.' He giggled. 'You're trying to freak us out. I'm not afraid of the dark.'

'I am, Peter,' she said.

She thought of the buses she had seen picking people up to take them to the fields. Of the girl, biting the imaginary apple.

'Seriously,' she said.

'I don't know what you're getting at.'

'No. Nor me,' she said. She looked at her watch again. It was hardly worth going to bed.

'Just imagine. Coming through all that, living in the bloody Sahara desert, to end up dead in four foot of cold English water. It's not fucking fair,' Ferriter said.

'It's not fucking fair,' Cupidi answered. She turned to Moon in the back of the car. 'I want your keys,' she said.

He pulled them out of his jacket pocket. The key ring was a small white skull.

'I'm going to drive around for a bit,' she said. 'I'll go home, change, be back by seven. Meet back here?'

'OK,' Moon said.

She was halfway out when Ferriter asked, 'You're not going to do something daft, are you?'

'What makes you think that?'

She sat in the bucket seat of his car, adjusting the mirror. The gear stick had been customised; there was a large red dice instead of the knob. When she switched on the ignition, the stereo suddenly played Iron Maiden's 'Run to the Hills', loud.

She thought about lowering the volume, then decided against it. She looked behind her and reversed the car back down the lane. Before she turned she glanced through the windscreen again, towards the railway line and the ditch.

Across the road, the yellow tape. Two people in a police car, interior light on.

FORTY-TWO

She drove along the lanes aimlessly for forty minutes, following the patterns of the old ditches, riding on the centuries of labour that had made this place. Killing time, hoping to chance on something.

Finally she headed the car north of the crime site, to where the land started to rise, and parked on the track that Connie Reed's horse had emerged from, cautiously backing the car behind the curtain of green. She turned off the lights and waited.

If she was so sure of herself, she wondered, why hadn't she called it in when she could? She could have asked for some backup.

Maybe she wasn't sure of herself at all. It was a hunch, not too much more.

She would give herself until five in the morning. No one would have to know she had been here. That would give her time to get home, wash, change, have breakfast and be out at the crime scene at seven, to be there when they began the futile business of searching.

When she had lived in the city, the ghosts had worked in restaurants and brothels, cleaning offices or making beds. She had known they were there. Here in the countryside, they laboured in the fields, or in warehouses, processing the food.

The farmer had said all his workers were documented. The ones who worked in the daylight probably were. But what if there were others who toiled in the semi-darkness of summer mornings, or deep into the night? The migrant hours.

Najiba had arrived back at the flat late in the last light. They had witnessed it. Almost certainly she had left early too. She worked different shifts.

There had been marks on her shoulders. Cupidi had seen them on her body. They weren't bruises from the assault; they were older. They were from carrying fruit buckets like the pickers on the ladders.

What if there were two shifts, she had wondered? The documented one that would provide the paperwork and the undocumented one for those who would work more cheaply, taking advantage of the whole of the day.

And then there was Freya Brindley. After all, she had been undocumented too. Or rather, her documents were entirely fictitious.

Shortly after 4 a.m. a grey minibus arrived in darkness. It drove past and she heard it turn right, up into the fruit farm.

It had been full. Darkly silhouetted, she had made out the shapes of heads, men and women.

Were these the workers she had talked to in the orchard two days ago? It seemed unlikely. It wasn't even light yet. Labour laws meant that it was almost impossible to employ the same people to work from dawn to dusk; the fifteen, sixteen hours a day that the tilt of the earth allowed at this time of year were too long a working day for a single shift.

This was the early shift.

She waited five minutes, grabbed her shoulder bag and then got out of the car. Her suit was still damp. It would be cold, but she couldn't risk the high-viz.

This was stupid. She knew that.

She would get onto the farm, confirm her suspicions, drive back home and call it in. That's all. Nothing more than that.

She got out, quietly closing the door.

The entrance to the farm was silent. The van would have gone straight up to the plum orchard, she guessed.

When she was twenty metres up the lane she saw lights ahead; the farmyard was brightly lit. Tractors were at work already in the darkness.

Not wanting to be seen, she left the tarmac and walked to her right, into a dark grove of apple trees, heavy with ripening fruit.

The plum orchard had been about about half a mile beyond the yard, she remembered.

She made her way up the slope, away from the farm entrance, ducking branches. The first light filled the horizon there already, turning the trees to silhouettes. The grass was long and damp with dew. In no time, her trousers were sticking to her legs, soaked again.

A few metres further and she realised she was crossing a wider gap; a space for larger vehicles to pass through. It was heading in the right direction, up the hill towards the plum trees.

She turned left and set off up it, her trainers squelching now on the wet ground. Ahead she could make out a metal gate and another orchard beyond.

Climbing over, she carried on, as silently as she could. The land here sloped gently up from the marsh, rising towards the Downs.

And then, to the west, through the trees, she heard voices. She walked towards them, but there was a hedge in the way, so she followed it.

Startled, something large scuttled into the undergrowth in front of of her. A fox? A badger? It was too dark to see.

Another gap appeared ahead. This gate was older, and, as she discovered when she was halfway over it, more rickety.

As she wobbled, it clanged back against the gatepost.

Shit. She stood, a foot on each side of the ringing metal. She was close enough for them to hear her.

But they were making their own noise, unloading crates from the trailer. The sky was turning grey. She breathed again.

She could see them now on the hillside above her. Crouching down, she headed for the security of the nearby trees; they were thick with leaves. She would be invisible among them.

Head torches were switched on. Clutching ladders, the workers spread out through the line of plum trees.

It was still too dark to see who whey were. She would have to wait. Not long, though. She needed to head back before daylight.

But the light was starting to turn blacks to grey, and then, slowly, the grey to green.

The first worker had already filled a bucket with plums. He climbed down from the tree and carefully poured the fruit into one of the plastic crates on the waiting trailer.

But the brightness of the torch on his forehead made it impossible to see his face.

The fourth person to arrive at the trailer was a small woman. No. Not a woman, she realised. A girl.

An intake of breath.

About Zoe's age. Lighter skinned than some of the others.

Cupidi realised she could see because it was starting to get dangerously light. She could make out the figures. The day shift were Europeans; documented workers. These were a ragtag bunch. Old men. Children.

She took out her phone to take a single photograph as evidence; aimed and clicked. She would go now. She had seen enough.

But just as she was about to move, one of the men broke away from the crowd, took off his bucket, and started walking swiftly down the hill towards her.

He can't have seen her, surely? There was nothing urgent in his pace.

She crouched down as low as she could, hoping she was invisible.

He was in his thirties; gaunt-faced and unshaven. He wore jeans that were a little too short, and a tartan shirt rolled up at the sleeves.

He was only three metres away when he turned right, into the trees she was hiding amongst, turned his back to her and lowered his trousers.

He squatted above the grass for a long time, close to her. This was a ridiculous position to find herself in.

He heart thumped so loud he must be able to hear it. He was so near to her she could smell everything. She held her breath. She imagined telling Zoë this. She would laugh.

Her daughter was not happy. A child shouldn't be so sad all the time.

The man pulled some scraps of newspaper from his pocket and started to wipe himself. She could hear every crinkle of the paper.

And then he stood in one swift moment, hitching up his trousers, and turned.

And he was looking straight at her. His mouth opened wide.

FORTY-THREE

She raised her finger to her lips.

He stood, belt undone in front of her, one hand still holding up his trousers.

'Shh.'

He turned to see if anyone was looking at them. Up the hill behind him, they were all busy picking.

'Please,' she said, not knowing if he even spoke English. 'Don't let people know I am here.'

His open mouth; his big eyes. He was scared, she realised. Frightened of her.

Holding up her palms in front of her, she said, 'It's OK. It's OK. My name is Alex.'

He said nothing; looked round again, as if he were contemplating running.

Why had she given up smoking? Cigarettes were perfect for a time like this. Something simple and non-verbal you could give to another adult. What else did she have in her bag that she could offer him?

And then she remembered what she had carried with her since the start of all this.

'Wait,' she said.

And she pulled out the brown envelope, now worn.

There were several photos inside. She picked the one of the dead man first.

He reached forward and took it, mouth still open. 'Salem.'

'That is his name?' she said.

He nodded. 'Salem.'

He held the photograph close.

'He worked here?'

The man didn't answer. He was staring at it, a puzzled look on his face, as if trying to work out why she had Salem's picture, or what it was about it him that looked so strange.

She could see the shock emerging as he realised what he was seeing. 'He is dead?' He looked up at her.

'I'm afraid so. I'm very sorry.'

The man looked round again, more anxiously this time. He was breathing rapidly now, panic rising.

'Who killed him?' His English was accented, but clear.

'I don't know. I am trying to find out.'

Again, he swivelled to check no one has seen them.

'But I think you know,' she hazarded.

He shook his head. 'How?'

'They drowned him. On a farm very near here.'

It was like she had punched him. She saw his misery. 'No,' he said. 'No.'

'You didn't know Salem was dead?'

'I have to go to work,' he said.

'Who killed him?'

He turned.

'Wait. Wait. Please. What about this woman?'

He looked back just as she was pulling out Freya's photo. Again, the pain on his face was obvious. '*Ya ilahi.* She is dead as well?'

'You knew her?'

'Yes. She was one of them.' He looked round and nodded towards the workers.

'She worked on the farm?'

Taking the photograph, he shook his head. 'One of the bosses.'

'A gangmaster?'

He nodded.

So Freya Brindley had been a gangmaster. That was how she had earned the money that had ended up stolen in Stanley Eason's freezer. The first rays of the sun lit the top of the hill behind the man. Any minute now they would become visible to the rest of the party, above.

'A good gangmaster,' he said. 'Not like them.'

'She worked with them, though?'

'Yes. Yes. But she left. She didn't like it anymore.'

'She used to be a gangmaster, but she didn't like the way they ran it?' On paper, though, she had had no job.

He looked at her. 'Who are you?'

'What about Najiba?'

His lips tightened.

'She's dead too.'

A shout came from the hillside above them. The man turned, ducked down.

'Shit.'

She looked down. Her feet were in sunlight now. They were visible.

'Oi. Yusuf.' A man's voice. 'Who you talking to?'

Yusuf thrust the photograph back at Cupidi, a look of panic on his face. He paused for a second, as if trying to work out which direction he should run in. Then he turned and started running back up the hill towards the pickers, away from her.

'Can I help you?' A man in a black T-shirt shouted down at her.

'I lost my dog,' said Cupidi. 'It's OK. I'll just go back. She'll be down there somewhere.'

The man was sixty metres away, looking down. The other workers had stopped and were staring at her too.

She turned and began walking back to the gate. An engine started up; it revved twice. She looked round and the man in the black T-shirt was on a quad bike, bouncing down the slope towards her.

There was no point running. It would only convince him that she was snooping. So she stood and waited for the bike to arrive.

'What are you doing?'

'My dog's lost. I was on a bridleway . . .'

'At night? You're walking around here?'

She couldn't place his accent; but not anyone who had grown up round here, that's for sure. From his belt, he picked up a walkie-talkie. '*Hunaka imra'aton huna. Kan hina sayedda tehki ma'a Yousef.*'

She recognised the name Yusuf in there. The man was telling someone from his team that a woman was on the farm and she had been talking to Yusuf. The walkie-talkie crackled back. Was it Arabic?

'Are they plums? Do you sell them?' she said, smiling. Distract; confuse. 'I adore Kent plums. I'm told they're the finest in the world.'

He looked at her nervously, not knowing what to make of her. 'What were you showing to Yusuf?'

'Just a map. I was lost. I wanted him to help me see where I was.'

'Show me. I will help you.'

She needed to extricate herself from this fast.

'It's OK. I'll find my own way, thank you.' She smiled and turned her back and started walking quickly down the hill to the gate.

The walkie-talkie chattered back again.

She heard the engine rev; the quad bike was coming after her. There was no point running; she just kept on moving, one step after another.

In a second, the man sped past her. Before she knew it, she was on the ground, screaming in pain. The world turned white as the nerves on her right side rang out. All breath seemed to leave her.

For a moment, all thought left her beyond the hurting. Then she started to surface from the whiteness.

Fuck. Get a grip. She sucked in air.

Think. What had happened?

She looked. The man on the bike had braked five metres away and was holding her bag.

He had stolen it, she realised. She had had it under her elbow, strap over her shoulder, but as he had passed, he had literally ripped its sturdy leather strap from her arm. Was the limb broken? Or dislocated? It hurt like hell.

She looked up. For a moment he looked as shocked as she was by what he had done.

Fighting back tears she said, 'I am a police officer. Assaulting a police officer is a very serious crime.'

But as she stood, gingerly pushing herself up on her left arm, he was already tipping out the contents of the bag. Her phone tumbled onto the grass. Then Freya's picture fell, face up in front of him.

'Do you understand what kind of trouble you are in?' she said.

He looked down at the photograph, then back up at her. Then around, to see where her colleagues were. But there weren't any, because she had been unbelievably stupid and come here on her own.

He spoke once more into the radio. He sounded upset, panicky, unsure of what he should do. '*Laddyha sura lihilari.*'

Stepping off his bike, he strode towards her.

It was one of those calculations she had to make. Normally she would stand her ground. The odds of getting away were not good. But the look on his face was terrifying.

It wasn't just that he was angry; he was scared. She had told him she was a police officer. Now he knew he had made a terrible mistake by assaulting her. But from the look on his face, she guessed he'd also made the calculation that there was only one way to fix this.

When he was almost on her she dummied by raising her left arm. It was a trick she had used before on London streets. In response, the man lifted his own right to deflect the blow, leaving his lower body unguarded.

Swiftly, she brought up her right leg, swinging her whole body behind it and catching him directly in the groin, hard. Her knee met soft flesh.

She heard him squeal, but didn't wait to see if he fell. She was running away towards the gate hoping that the adrenalin coursing round her body would soon dull the pain in her right shoulder.

FORTY-FOUR

This time she vaulted the gate, swinging over on her good arm, landing hard.

Her first thought was to run for Moon's car to get away. They wouldn't know where she was heading, which would give her the advantage.

Then she stopped dead. Shit.

The keys to the car were in her handbag and her handbag was in the plum orchard with her phone. She would have to get away on foot. What a mess.

She set off running again, ducking off the main track into the trees so she would be less visible, dodging branches thick with apples, skittering over fallen fruit. The ground between the trunks was uneven, the grass longer. It was harder work.

She had gone fifty metres when she stumbled and fell, yelping in pain. Reflexes had made her thrust her arms out; the pain from sudden jolt in her injured shoulder was much worse than the fall itself. Looking round she saw what had tripped her; a bloody molehill.

She lay on the grass, silent, left hand clasping her throbbing right shoulder, terrified that someone had heard her. Testing the joint with her fingers, she winced. The limb felt wrong. It wasn't moving properly.

For a minute, after all the action, everything seemed still. Birdsong reasserted itself. Prostrate, she caught her breath. There was no point just running away. She had to know where she was running towards.

Think, for once, for pity's sake.

Her best option would be to find a local; get them to phone the police. But at this time of early morning there would be no one around. The lanes were still empty of cars.

Simply retracing her steps would bring her to the meadow and the lane. The bridleway itself would afford her some cover if she could make it there, but to reach it she would have to cross open ground. She would be more visible in the growing light. Could she risk that route?

If there were no cars around, how far would it be to the nearest house? The marsh was so sparsely peopled; besides, not all of the old houses were even occupied. The kind of rich folk who owned them only visited at weekends.

Second option. Find somewhere to hide to give her time to think. Better. Where? The trees above her here were still young, not tall enough to climb – and with only one arm she doubted she'd be able to do it.

She listened. Far away she heard the sound of an engine. The same quad bike, or another?

She thought of the man, Salem. Had he been running away too like she was now? They had found him and killed him. There had been several people involved; she had no doubt that her pursuer would not be alone.

What was that? Noises from higher up the hill.

The sound of thumping feet heading down towards her from the top of the orchard, the place she'd been running from. She pressed herself flat in the wet long grass.

More people were chasing her already? No. Just one person. It was too late to run now. That would just give herself away. All she could do was lie as still as she could, face close to the earth.

The footfalls were heavy; she could hear breathing too. It was a man, running fast. Would he notice where she had left the main path? The grass would be flattened there.

But he ran on, down the hill. She raised her head slightly to look. It wasn't the person she had felled; this one was stockier, older.

So her guess was right. There was definitely more than one man after her.

Think.

She was on unfamiliar ground and she was injured. She needed information. Simply running away was not enough. She couldn't stay where she was because eventually they'd be back, retracing her route again, she guessed. But she had a minute or two in which to decide what to do and she had to use it.

Think.

What facts did she already have? The farmyard had a farmhouse next to it. There would be a phone there. It might seem stupid to head towards danger instead of running away from it, but there were advantages.

Firstly, she would be going to somewhere where she knew the lie of the land, rather than into the unknown. Secondly, they would be expecting her to run away, not come back.

Carefully she got up and moved west this time, keeping low, not running now. The western side of the apple orchard was hedged, but at high summer the hawthorn was too thick to get through, let alone see through.

If she wanted to make it to the farmyard, she would have to find a way round it.

A stick cracked. More people moving behind her through the trees. She dropped down again into, falling into nettles.

The stocky man who had run down through the orchard, chasing her, was now retracing his steps back up the hill. This time there was a third person with him.

Soon they would reach the place where she had left the main track. As she looked back she could see the path she'd taken clearly visible in the growing morning light, marked by the flattened grass. There was no way they would miss it.

They were so close now. How could she take two of them on? The younger one first, maybe, then the fat one? The odds were not in her favour. She lowered herself back onto the nettles. The stinging was a distraction from the throbbing pain in her shoulder, at least.

'What are you doing?' another voice, speaking in an English accent, called from the top of the field.

'Looking,' said the fatter man. Squinting through the grass, she recognised him now. He had been one of the people in the caravans parked on Connie Reed's land, one of the men who had attacked Ferriter, who had got away from the far side of the ditch she'd been trapped in. He was wearing black jeans with deliberate cuts at the knees; the sort that might look all right on a slim teenager.

'She's not here. Go back. Get her before she gets to the road.'

And, miraculously, before she was discovered, they turned and headed back down the track away from her.

She waited another minute before she dared move, then crawled out of the nettles and stood again.

If they were sure she had gone down the hill, her best option would be to head back up to the top again and loop round to the farmhouse that way.

Cautiously, staying close to the hedge this time, she worked her way up to the corner of the field and then on to the gate she had leaped over what seemed like an age ago – though it couldn't have been any more than ten minutes.

Leaning over it first, she peered up the fields. Work hadn't stopped. Men and women were busy in the early light, plucking fruit off the tree, loading it into the trailers.

A third time she clambered over the locked gate. This time she crouched low, keeping to the other side of the hedge she had just walked along. After a few metres she was behind trees and harder to spot, so could move faster. She peered back to see if her bag had been abandoned where the man had dropped it, but it had gone.

The hedge ended where it joined the lane that they had driven up two days ago. It led back to the yard, she knew. Again, checking to see if there was anyone in sight first, she turned left and cautiously headed back down the track.

She was, she reckoned, about halfway down when she heard

a vehicle coming up towards her. The lane was hedged on both sides, there was nowhere to hide.

Looking round frantically, she spotted a small break in the hedge on the orchard side, roughly opposite where she had been hiding earlier. A hole in the green. It didn't go all the way through, but there was a dark gap in the shrubs where something had died back and not yet been replaced.

She threw herself into it, feeling pain erupt all over her body. Blackthorn bushes, she realised too late; she had impaled herself on thorns as long as a little finger. But she couldn't cry out or move. There was no time. She must not be caught.

A crunching on the gravel, a revving of the throttle, and the tractor passed, hauling a trailer full of empty crates to be filled with fruit. On the trailer, legs dangling over the back, another man, with a walkie-talkie, speaking into it over the roar of the engine.

He looked backwards as he went by and his eyes went straight to the hole in the hedge.

But it must have been dark enough in there; he didn't seem to see her. The tractor carried on up the hill, the man bouncing along behind it.

When it was quiet again, she disentangled herself painfully from the thorns, trying to pull her limbs off the branches without tearing her skin. Fresh red blood stained her suit. There was no time to think about how much she hurt now, all over. She moved again, knowing she had to find cover somewhere.

And then, rounding the bend, there was the yard.

She pressed herself into the hedge again, taking a few seconds to look at it, to get her bearings. The closest building was the equipment barn she had looked into before. The door was on the side. It was only thirty metres away, but to reach it she would expose herself to anyone who was in the yard – and from here, most of the yard was hidden.

With cautious steps she moved forward.

She was ten metres from the barn door when she saw, to her right, the man she had attacked in the plum orchard, the one who had stolen her bag. He was standing facing the big farmhouse, talking to someone she couldn't see. His back was towards her. How long before he turned around?

She realised she must be completely exposed here, with her back against the hedge, a short run from safety.

And now she heard another tractor coming back down the same lane she was lingering in.

She had no choice. She had to move. She made a break for the dark, open door of the barn.

And made it inside just as the tractor rounded the bend into the yard.

Panting, she leaned her back against the metal wall, listening to the sound of the engine trundling slowly past, metres away.

Made it, she thought in the darkness. Bloody made it. She panted, pretty sure the men hadn't seen her.

She was there amongst the hedge trimmers and tractors and crop-sprayers, and it was cool and still. There was a smell of engine oil and dust.

She was not out of danger, but at least here was somewhere she could hide. And, as her eyes got used to the gloom, she saw the perfect place. A stack of grey fruit crates, large enough to climb into.

Until from behind one of the tractors a man stepped out. 'Hello?'

He had obviously been trying to start one of the quad bikes, she realised, to join the wider search. Now he looked around to see the source of a noise – he must have heard her coming in – and there she was, standing still as she could, clothes torn, wishing she were invisible.

'Kent Police,' she said, exhausted.

It was the same big man she had seen earlier; the one from the caravan site.

He looked for a second, as if he could not quite believe what he was seeing. Then shouted, 'Hey!'

From outside, the roar of the tractor revving in the yard covered his voice.

'There are more police on the way,' she lied.

He stepped forward. There was a hopper of some kind between them. He moved one way, to come round it and catch her. She darted the other way, away from the door, almost falling. She looked down. The floor was dark, slippery with oil.

'Hey!' he shouted again, trying to get the attention of the men outside, but the tractor was still working.

Christ.

He held his arms wide, as if somehow that was going to catch her. And then, glancing to his left, he saw a stack of hay forks and darted in that direction to grab one.

Shit.

Swiftly he lifted it, swung it, prong forward towards her, and jabbed. Jolting backwards, she slipped again, tripping on something, fell hard, pain screaming through her back. He ran towards her, fork raised.

She had fallen on an open tin of oil, she realised, knocking it over. Thick gold liquid was pouring out of it onto the floor.

With her good hand she grabbed the can's handle, swinging it up just in time. It still had enough weight to slam into the fork's prongs just as they were coming towards her, knocking them sideways as they closed in on her.

Pulling the fork back again, he was now on top of her, one leg on either side, lifting it high. She reached up and grabbed the tines with her good hand before he could force it down again, this time yanking it to her right just as he threw his weight behind it to stab her. The fork hit the concrete next to her. It was his turn to be surprised by the slipperiness of the oil-covered floor. The man stumbled, losing his balance.

He fell hard on top of her. He was bigger than her, and stronger; she was one-armed.

She wriggled and kicked, to try to prevent him pinning her down, but it was one-sided.

He grabbed her right arm and tugged it above her head. The pain was severe. She screamed, knowing she must not pass out.

Now he was going for her left. She waved it up and down, trying to avoid his grasp. If he had both arms, he would be in total control.

'Hey,' he shouted again. 'Come!'

Somebody must have heard them by now, surely. And there they were: voices shouting back. He looked up.

'In here!'

In the moment he was distracted by the others, her hand touched the fork. It had fallen, handle away, spikes towards her.

Her fingers curved around metal; the base of the tines. Pivoting it in her elbow, she swung the fork, prongs forward, straight at the man's round belly.

FORTY-FIVE

The prongs sank deep into the skin just below his ribs.

He squealed, looked down, shocked, releasing her left arm.

She jerked her body; temporarily stunned by her attack, he fell sideways, bloody tines emerging from his shirt.

He began to scream.

Sliding on the oily floor, she wriggled away, struggling to her feet.

Men were pouring into the shed now, looking around to find the source of the shouting. They had seen her by now. She ran to the opposite corner, grabbed the handle of the door there, and yanked.

Locked.

Somebody laughed.

She turned, and saw three men approaching. One was the man she had kneed in the groin. Now he was holding a knife.

'I am a police officer,' she said. 'Kent Police.'

Her suit was ripped, bloody and covered with oil.

'I am a police officer,' she said again.

'Hey,' said the wounded man. 'Help me.'

They ignored him, closing in on her. The man waved the knife, closer now, deadly serious, face nervous. It was large, with a serrated top; the kind of weapon designed to do as much damage on the way out as on the way in. She thought of the wound in Najiba's neck.

'Police,' she said again.

It made no difference. Like the man she had interrogated, it was as if they had so little to lose. She was literally cornered. She weighed the men up, trying to figure out which of them would be the weakest. Knife Man was in the middle; the others on either side were young and fit-looking.

And then she was suddenly so tired of it all. Exhausted. It was taking so long. It took so little to kill someone with a blade. She had witnessed it in London, the lives of people slipping away in no time.

What a fuck-up she was. Too impulsive. Always shooting her mouth off without thinking. And now she was going to die because of it. She had wanted so badly to find the people who had killed Freya Brindley; now they were going to kill her instead.

The man with the blade stepped forward. The other men encouraged him. 'Go on. Do it.'

He lifted it high; he had done it before, she realised. This was the man who had killed Najiba. He was going to kill her in the same way.

'Please,' she said, crying.

And then she heard another voice. 'Stop.'

The men looked round.

'What the bloody hell do you think you are doing?'

Connie Reed, in jeans and grubby sweatshirt, standing at the open door, hands on her hips.

'Run, Connie! Call the police,' Cupidi shouted. Or tried to. Her voice was barely a croak.

'Step away from her.'

'Don't get involved, Connie. They're armed and dangerous.'

'Get back.'

And amazingly, sheepishly, the men did as they were told.

'Wow,' said Cupidi, her voice cracking. 'You bloody star.' She breathed in for what felt like the first time in minutes. She laughed. 'How do you bloody do that?'

But when she looked around, she realised something was very wrong.

The men looked vaguely concerned, not frightened by what was about to happen to them. She looked from Connie Reed to the men and back again and it suddenly dawned on her. She had been doubly stupid.

That's why these men had been in Connie Reed's field.

'Catch hold of her,' said Reed calmly. 'But do it carefully, for God's sake. Don't leave any more marks.'

Connie Reed was the gangmaster; it was she who had been working with Freya Brindley. And presumably she who had killed Freya.

The man on the ground groaned, more loudly now. 'I'm bleeding,' he complained. 'Help me.'

The three men surrounding her closed in.

She backed away.

'Stop,' she said. 'Think about what you're doing.'

When they grabbed both arms, the agony was unbearable. She screamed loudly until a hand was placed over her face.

Something happens when you know you're beaten. The struggle goes out of you. The agony of her arm was enough to sap her will. Someone was stuffing a rough oily cloth into her mouth; she could no longer speak. One on each shoulder, one at her feet, they lifted her and took her out into the July sunshine. She howled from the pain, but it was muted by her gag to a whine.

As her head lolled sideways she saw workers from the orchard standing around, staring, sullen and silent. Frightened. Some still had buckets strapped to their fronts. They were young and old, men and women. The man who had spoken to her in the field was there. She thought she recognised the girl she had seen, too; maybe she was the girl Zoë had met, out in the fields.

She stared at Cupidi, eyes wide and frightened. Poor young girl.

'Get them out of here,' said Connie Reed evenly. 'Take them far away. Everyone needs to be gone before the next shift comes in.'

And, silently, the hidden people started to move. Nobody was supposed to know they were here. Cupidi pushed at the cloth in her mouth with her tongue but couldn't get it to budge.

Connie Reed led the way out of the yard. The three men followed, carrying Cupidi, past the barn they had caught her in, towards the smaller sheds she had seen before. Eventually material started to emerge from behind her teeth. It was dry and coarse. A man swung his arm round to push it back inside.

'Careful. You've hurt her enough already.'

Finally Cupidi spat the cloth out.

'In here.'

Reed led the way into the second apple store; the one that had been empty.

She shook her head, trying to clear it. 'You killed Freya Brindley, didn't you?'

'Who?' Reed looked puzzled. 'No.'

'Hilary Keen. Her real name was Freya Brindley.'

Reed paused. 'Oh. I didn't know that.'

The men dropped her onto the hard floor.

'I said, *careful*,' said Reed, irritated.

Bruises would add to the record on her body.

'Who else knows about Hilary Keen?' Reed asked.

'So you did kill her?'

'Who else knew?'

'We were closing in on it,' said Cupidi. 'You'd do better to give yourself up now.'

Connie looked at her, frowning for a second. The floor of the apple shed was rough but cool. It felt good to lie still for a while.

'I rather doubt it,' Connie Reed said eventually. 'Otherwise it wouldn't just be you here. There would be a whole team. You're on your own.'

Cupidi smiled. 'You don't know that, though. You don't know, do you? They might be just around the corner.'

'Yes. They might.'

'Why did you kill her?'

'No comment.'

'How? I'm curious.'

'Killed the cat,' said Connie.

'What about Salem? Drowned in cow shit. And Najiba? Stabbed to death.'

The men shuffled. Connie turned to the men who stood around, obediently waiting for their next order. 'Go,' she said brusquely. 'Clear up here. We'll pay off the contract. It's useless now. Get the workers out of here.'

'What about Rasa Petrauska? Did she know she was being used by you? What was it? Some cute matchmaking agency, to get legitimate workers pregnant so illegitimate ones can stay?'

She should shut up. Connie Reed was ignoring her, anyway. 'Get everybody as far away from here as you can,' she was saying. 'Get them out of the county.'

'Where?' asked the man who had stolen her handbag.

'Doesn't matter. Get them out,' she snapped. 'Don't worry. I'll give you money. You all need to disappear for a while. Clean out the houses thoroughly. Make sure they leave nothing behind, no documents, no phones, nothing.'

The men nodded.

'We're taking a massive loss on all this, you realise,' she said, turning to Cupidi and shaking her head.

'Nice job. Living off the back of people who can't argue back.'

'I'm not living off the back of anybody,' said Connie Reed. 'Don't you understand? These people want the work. They beg me for it. I'm the one putting myself out to find them paid jobs. I'm the one taking all the risks here for them.'

'You're practically a saint.'

'Excuse me,' said Connie Reed. 'I'm not the one voting for the greedy politicians' parties who make these people illegal. I'm not the nationalist building walls. "England for the English." I'm the one struggling to give them a fair fucking crack of the whip. And the farms round here . . .' She waved her arms. 'Do you think half of this would survive if it wasn't for people like this? The harder you people clamp down on them, the more they have to exist like this. What do you expect them to live off?'

'I had no idea you were a social worker.'

'I don't find you funny.'

'I don't find me funny,' Cupidi said exhaustedly. 'Nobody does.'

Connie Reed stepped towards the door. It didn't seem worth trying to beat her to it. She was too tired, but she had figured it all out, at least. She was relieved that Reed hadn't ordered her men to kill her right here. Maybe she wasn't going to kill her after all. She was a police officer; nobody would kill a police officer. She would lock her up for long enough to get away.

'Who was Salem? Someone who stood up to you? Somebody who didn't like what he saw you were doing?'

Reed didn't answer. It would be OK, being locked in here. She could make a noise; someone would find her.

Reed took one last look at Cupidi before she closed the door. Cupidi met her eyes, but there was nothing to see in them, and then the room was suddenly black. Cupidi heard Reed turning a handle on the outside, sealing it.

What about oxygen?

The room was quite big; surely there was plenty of air in here. She could survive several hours. That would be enough time for her to get out.

Wouldn't it?

They were just making sure they had time to get away. Probably.

She relaxed. She would find something and start banging on the metal soon. It would be OK.

And then came a gentle whirr, and a cool breeze hit her face from the vents above. It felt nice; soothing.

And then she realised it wasn't air. She had not been thinking straight. What had the farmer said? They stored apples in here; they pumped in nitrogen to preserve them.

Nitrogen would replace the oxygen in the room.

She was going to suffocate. Panic cleared her mind, focusing her. She had been so stupid. It was suddenly clear how Freya Brindley had been killed; she had been asphyxiated in nitrogen. It would not have looked abnormal in Brindley's blood.

Atomic number 7, she thought, obscurely. The commonest element in the universe. That's why the pathologist had not been able to find out what killed her.

How could she think so coldly, so plainly, at a time like this, she wondered, when she was already starting slowly to die?

FORTY-SIX

She scrabbled around, feeling with her fingers in the darkness. In the middle of the room she found the shelves. She tugged at their cool metal, trying to shift them, or break them apart to see if she could turn them into some kind of weapon or tool, but they were very solid, well screwed down.

She dropped down onto her knees. Arm throbbing, she padded around the floor, hoping to find anything that she could bash on the door with, but again found nothing.

Unsteadily she stood, realising that she had become disorientated already. Where was the door?

How long did she have. An hour?

Or less maybe.

The gas was cold, chilling the room.

Gingerly she felt her way forwards until she reached a wall, then moved sideways around the room, trying to find the door.

Connie Reed, the independent woman living alone with her horses, had been the one behind this all the time. A gangmaster hiding behind gangmasters; a dark business concealed behind a shady one, using a hidden army of unofficial workers who were always there. Every year, more migrants were deemed non-people. If the world was being divided between people who had rights and those who didn't, that was a business opportunity.

Freya, a ghost herself, had died in here, she guessed. A woman who had disappeared, living a half-life, pretending to be the friend whose life she had ruined. She would have known this world of gangmasters and surreptitious work.

Freya must have survived, hiding in caravans, working on farms, just as the real Hilary had done for so many years. She had been too good for that kind of work when Hilary had known her, but after killing the children, she had no choice. She had stolen Hilary's identity, keeping under the radar, taking jobs where she left no trace, where no one would question her. It was not clear why Connie had ended up killing her. Because she was sure now it was all Connie. She was the one giving the orders.

Connie had killed Freya. And Najiba and Salem.

Najiba had been a whistleblower; perhaps Salem, too.

Her fingertips had found a corner. Now she continued to inch left, bumping into shelves, and working her way around it back to the wall.

No light made it into the room. After another agonisingly slow minute she discovered the handle at waist height. The door had opened inwards, she remembered. She tugged on it knowing that it would not open. It would have been firmly bolted: DANGER. DO NOT ENTER.

With the flat of her right hand she thumped. 'Let me out.'

Again. Thump. 'Let me out.'

Thump. 'Let me out.'

She kept it up for a minute until the palm of her hand stung. But the shouting would be exhausting her supply of oxygen, wouldn't it? Would it be better to wait for longer?

She stopped. The next shift would arrive at what time? Eight? Nine? What time was it now? Six, maybe? Six-thirty? How long could she last?

She slid down to the floor. Connie Reed would have made that calculation.

If she died here, how would they find her? No. Reed's plan would be to return to collect her body, to dump it somewhere.

She thought of Yusuf, drowning in shit. Of Najiba, bleeding out. At least her death would not be as ugly as theirs.

Suffocation was quite a gentle way to go, anyway, compared to what they had gone through. She was already feeling light-headed. She guessed she did not have long at all.

Zoë.

Poor girl. Poor, fragile, brilliant girl.

That was the worst of it. She would not have a chance to talk to her again.

She should have spent more time with her. It was not fair to have left a girl her age with so much time and only her own, teenage thoughts.

She was crying now. Her beautiful, clever daughter. Troubled, yes, but so bloody smart and sensitive. If she had just another year with her, she could have made it all right with her. They wouldn't drift apart the way she and her mother had done. Just a little more time, looking after her, helping her pass through a difficult time. Which she didn't have now.

All she had wanted to do was prove to her daughter that she wasn't just a mother. She was the woman who found the killers. It was meant to be a kind of gift to her. She had never wanted a girl who thought mothers were supposed to be at home, baking pies. This was something she had learned from her own mother.

She wished she had been nicer to her mother, too. She should have been proud of her, going to Greenham, being fierce, being different from the other mums. Why was it so hard to admit?

Stupid Alex Cupidi. Always getting into shit. Always acting, always speaking, but never thinking it through before it was too late. Stupid, stupid, stupid.

And now it was killing her.

She lay down on the cold concrete floor and spread out her arms. Would it be better to be standing up? Was nitrogen heavier than air, or lighter? Lighter, she thought.

Shivering gently now, she realised that the pain in her arm was not as bad. Was that the lack of oxygen, she wondered? She should relax. Try and use as little energy as possible. Try and last an hour.

She thought she saw a light.

A fine bright ray reaching her from up above.

But it was just her brain playing tricks as she died. She knew that.

She is a policewoman. It is a bright sunny day; she sweats in her uniform as she marches in the passing-out parade. Her mum and dad have come to Hendon to watch.

When they have finished, and all the friends and parents have gathered around, her father salutes her; she laughs. Don't be stupid, Dad. He is so proud.

I'm going to be a detective, just like you, Dad.

Mum wears a huge yellow polyester coat and big round dark glasses, like she is some kind of film star. It's embarrassing.

'I did this once,' her mum says. 'Just like this. Down in Bristol. I was a policewoman too,' she announces, loud enough for other mums and dads to hear.

'You're always saying that,' scoffs her daughter. 'That was bloody ages ago.'

She is a little girl, back from school. Her mother is cooking her tea, slapping down pans. There is rock music on the record player. He mother can't sing but she is trying to.

Dad must be working still, she realises. Mum is in a mood because he is working late. But he is a policeman. A detective. It is a really important job.

Alex knows that.

One day she will be a detective too. She won't stay at home and get angry at the cooker and sing bad rock songs.

Shut up with those pans, Mum, for goodness' sake.

Just let me sleep.

Because you had to give up being a policewoman and become a mother instead. You don't have to be furious all your life. Her mother lifts a pan and throws it onto the floor with a loud bang.

Her mother turns to her, cigarette in hand, and smiles. 'It was something I had to do at the time,' she says.

Bang bang bang. Bloody hell, Mum. You'll break the cooker.

And she wasn't even hungry. She never wanted to eat again. There was no point in eating, was there? Because she was dead.

She opened her eyes. It seemed like an effort in itself.

The banging was real. Someone was battering the door.

She rolled onto her side.

'Help,' she called, but her voice was weak. It was as if there were not enough oxygen to carry her syllables in the air.

Shaking her head, she crawled slowly to the door, felt for the handle, grabbed it, pulled herself up on it.

Pressing her ear to the door she heard shouts. More banging. Someone was screaming.

There was a fight going on outside.

She thumped her palm back on the door, then slid downwards again.

This time she really was going to go. Her brain was closing down. A big dark curtain was being drawn around her. The thumping became a muffled noise and disappeared and then all was silence. And blackness.

It seemed like an age later.

A man lifted her gently in his arms. 'Safe,' he said.

She winced as he carried her into the sunshine. It was so absurdly bright, she could not see anything at all.

'My arm,' she croaked. The pain was back now, ugly and real.

'Sorry, sorry.'

Carefully the man laid her down on the ground outside and knelt beside her. She realised that she recognised him. It took her a few seconds to figure out that he was the worker, Yusuf, who had spoken to her in the field, the one who had taken his trousers down in front of her. Now he smiled at her; she noticed that there was a graze on his cheek, trickling blood. He had been fighting. 'You are safe.'

She sucked in clean air. People stood around, looking at her, chattering anxiously.

The girl she had seen watching her earlier arrived at her side with a bottle of water and held it to her lips. Liquid spilled down the side of her face.

Everything seemed so still. Cupidi tried to struggle to her feet to look around, but she was too weak. Her head spun. She looked around.

The minibus was still parked at one side of the yard. The man who had assaulted her, riding on his quad bike, was sitting against the rear wheel, blood dripping from his head. He seemed dazed. He had been attacked and beaten.

'What happened?'

Yusuf smiled. 'Fuck them.'

'You saved my life.'

He shrugged; grinned. 'They were trying to kill you. We saw them. They killed Salem and Najiba. And Miss Keen.'

'Yes. They did, Yusuf.'

He shook his head. 'No no. No name,' he said.

'Because you're a ghost?'

'A ghost?'

'You are an invisible man.'

He smiled. 'Yes. We are ghosts.'

She looked around slowly and put the pieces together. From behind the metal door, the fighting she had heard was this ragged group of workers, overpowering the gangmasters who were leaving her to die.

'You did this?'

'Yes,' said the man. 'Of course.'

From far away came the sound of sirens. Yusuf's face changed. He clapped his hands. The people in the farmyard began running in several directions at once.

'Why?'

'Because they were bad.' The simplest explanation possible.

The teenage girl joined them, squatting down at Cupidi's side. She reached out and put her hand on Cupidi's bruised head.

'Thank you,' Cupidi said.

'Run,' the man told the girl, but he stayed next to her, not moving. 'You should go now.'

'Bus,' someone else was bawling. 'Into the bus.'

Another man was yanking the bloody-headed man clear of the vehicle, dragging him away from it so the wheels could move and the migrants could escape.

A woman had got behind the steering wheel and was trying to start the engine as people pushed towards the door.

Another grabbed the teenage girl's hand and yanked her away from Cupidi. The workers were panicking, scattering everywhere. It was chaos.

But the man who had saved her life stayed kneeling by her side.

'They'll catch you,' she said.

He looked around for somewhere to run. 'It is too late. The police are coming now.'

'What happens to you if you are caught?'

He didn't answer.

'Lean close,' she said.

He did; she smelt the sweat of the morning's work, and the blood of a man who had just fought other men. And she whispered something into his ear. She said it twice to make sure he understood. And he smiled, nodded, raised his palms as a goodbye, and then sprang up and ran.

And then there was the sound of tyres spinning on loose gravel and engines roaring and sirens wailing, and the yard was full of uniforms. 'Grab them. Get the bastards.'

Men and women, scattering everywhere.

'No,' Cupidi was trying to shout. 'You don't understand. You don't understand. It's not them.' But her lungs were weak still, her voice was thin.

For coppers, it was instinctive. When people run, they must be guilty. So the police officers chased after the people who had just saved her, tackling them, throwing them to the ground as they screamed in fear.

FORTY-SEVEN

It was a nice bungalow in Tunbridge Wells, with neatly trimmed bushes and a careful lawn. The interpreter had arrived before them and was standing outside on the pavement, waiting. She was young and plump and wore a loose cotton dress. Cupidi had found her name on the contact list that Serious Crime kept for times like this. They had been keeping them all busy these last few days, interviewing witnesses from the fruit farm.

'Hurt your arm?' the interpreter asked Cupidi.

'Yes. Dislocated.' It was in a blue sling.

'Ouch,' said the woman. She turned to Cupidi's daughter. 'You must be Zoë,' she said. 'Do I need to know what this is about?'

'No,' said Zoë firmly.

'OK,' she said in a sing-song voice. 'Are we ready?'

'I guess,' said Zoë. She looked nervous.

'Are you not coming in too?' the interpreter asked Cupidi.

'No. It's Zoë who needs to do this. I'd only start asking police-y questions. I shoot my mouth off.'

'She does. It's true,' said Zoë. She turned to her mother, took her good hand and said, 'Thanks, Mum.'

Everything Zoë did these days made Cupidi tear up. She knew all about that kind of thing. Post-trauma. She had thought she would never see her daughter again.

The local authority had handed over the contact details of the emergency foster family. The girl Zoë had met in the field was seventeen years old and was called Esin; she had come from Afghanistan. It had been Zoë's idea to come here. Right away, Esin had agreed to meet.

Cupidi went back to the car and watched her daughter walk up to the front door and ring the bell. A middle-aged Asian woman came to the door and welcomed her in, and then she was gone.

Jill Ferriter said, 'I brought some biscuits, if you want. They're home-made.'

'You fight crime and bake too?'

'Actually, Peter Moon's mum made them.' She laughed out loud. 'They're a bit weird.'

Cupidi took one.

'It's all a bit weird.' She giggled.

'You finally went out with him?'

'We went to Cameo at the weekend. You know, the nightclub? Worst dancer I've ever seen.' Ferriter had offered to drive. Cupidi couldn't, with her arm.

'How is it going?'

'It's OK. I mean, he's good-looking, but . . .'

'But what?'

'A bit up his own arse, really.'

It hurt to laugh. When Cupidi stopped, she said, 'Did you bring the photograph too?'

'God. Yeah.' Ferriter dug in her bag and pulled out a brown envelope. Cupidi pulled out the old photograph and looked at it. Two long-haired boys in a meadow, sitting in front of a caravan.

'You all right?' said Ferriter.

She nodded slowly, then put it back in the envelope.

'She's one of the lucky ones, that girl,' said Ferriter, nodding towards the house.

'Lucky?' said Cupidi.

'Well. You know what I mean. Maybe they won't repatriate her.'

Ferriter had been part of the team who arrested Connie Reed on the same day that she had tried to kill Cupidi. She had been at home, brushing down her horses, as if nothing was wrong with the world.

She had refused to talk, denying any involvement with the killings of Freya, Salem or Najiba. However, interviewing the illegal workers they had caught on the farm over the last week, officers from the Serious Crime Directorate had put together much of the story and, on her PC, they had found log-ins for four bank accounts, each holding tens of thousands of pounds. Tracing back the exact pattern of payments would be a matter of time. It was still not clear exactly what had happened – maybe it would never be – but they had enough to charge her. The man whom Cupidi had stabbed in the gut accused Reed of ordering all the killings. Other workers backed him up. The other man, the one who had been beaten up by the other migrants and left by the minibus, had been one of Reed's inner circle for years, and added more to the story.

It seemed that Freya Brindley had run an informal agency, providing work for undocumented labourers like herself. From years of working that way herself, she had known the ropes. She must have been there at the beginning of it all, when most workers were just a mix of drifters and local misfits.

At some point around ten years ago, Connie Reed had become involved in the business as a partner. But as it had grown more and more profitable, and more regulated, Connie had taken over. As the foreign gangs had come in, instead of giving up to them, Connie had learned from their tactics. And when the laws regulating gangmasters tightened, forcing the traffickers aside, she had gradually moved into the space they had vacated. Copying the gangs, Connie had developed a knack for picking out men who had come from difficult places; those who had already witnessed violence, or taken part in it. They became Connie's bodyguards, her enforcers.

The workers had liked Freya, though. Maybe Freya, who had exploited people for drug money when she was younger, had changed. Maybe she had become a better person. Cupidi would like to have thought so. They would never know why she had kept the picture of the two boys she had killed, Jacob and Finn Olsson; perhaps that had been part of it.

More was emerging, too. Alongside the illegal gangmaster agency, it was now becoming clear that Connie had run a kind of dating agency. Seeking out young single women among the documented labourers, she had set up clandestine meetings between them and the undocumented male labourers she controlled. The women were often lonely and vulnerable, like Rasa Petrauska. The men were desperate to find a way to remain in the country and would pay Connie thousands just to find the right girl; a girl whom they could marry; or better, in terms of immigration law, make pregnant. So that when the baby was born, it became much harder to send them home.

So far the investigation had turned up two other women like Petrauska – one Polish, the other Lithuanian – who said Reed had acted as a matchmaker, pairing them up with young men. Both had given birth but been abandoned by the fathers. It seemed likely there were more.

From what some witnesses had said, it appeared that Connie and Freya had started to argue over the summer. Some witnesses had said it was over money. Others had said it was because Freya had not approved of the increasingly severe regime that Connie was running. If you were overheard criticising her, you would find you weren't paid, or your bed would be given to another worker, leaving you only the floor to sleep on.

And then, one day at the tail-end of June, Freya had simply disappeared.

By then, nobody had asked questions. Everybody had just kept their head down, saying nothing.

Without Freya there, things had quickly become worse. It was clear that some of the workers were loyal to Connie. Others weren't. Nobody was sure whom to trust, who was passing information to Connie in exchange for better treatment, who was spying for her. Everyone had been terrified of talking, of saying anything critical, in case word got back. It was a Libyan man called Salem who had broken ranks first. He was the first one to whisper the suggestion that Freya hadn't just left, she had been killed by Connie.

As a warning to the rest of them, they had come for him in broad daylight, brandishing sticks. Salem had run, escaping them.

Everyone had hoped he had got away, vanishing into the city, perhaps.

Until Najiba turned up to work one morning saying she had seen a photograph of Salem, dead; beaten and drowned in shit. Connie had killed him, too, Najiba had said. At first, few wanted to believe it.

And then, last week, there had been a raid of some kind. The police – Cupidi and Ferriter – had turned up on Connie's land. Connie was now convinced that somebody had talked. Which they had, of course.

Najiba had already given herself away by telling people she had seen a photograph of the dead man. They had come for her at the end of a late shift, dragging her from the seat in the minibus and killing her in front of a handful of witnesses, including Esin.

Cupidi did not know exactly what Esin had seen that night; she could only guess. Maybe she was talking about it now with Zoë.

Connie Reed was tough. Session after session she had sat in the interview room saying nothing.

Except once.

At Cupidi's suggestion, Moon had asked Reed if, when she was out riding along the Royal Military Canal, she had ever had a confrontation with a man in his sixties.

Puzzled by the question, she had answered yes. It was the only thing she admitted to.

It had been a summer evening two years ago. She had been riding along the path when her horse had been startled by a fisherman on the banks who was blocking her way. They had argued. She told him to move. He refused. When she had tried to ride on, he had slapped her horse's neck with stick, forcing her back, threatening to hit her with it too.

The incident had happened a few hundred metres from Stanley Eason's house.

Cupidi could imagine it: Connie Reed, the animal-lover, squaring up to Stanley Eason, the temperamental loner.

When she had returned home, Reed had rung the police and complained that she had been threatened with a stick; she described the fisherman, but had refused to give her own name.

Whether the incident had occurred as Reed had claimed or not was academic. The Complaints Commission would have to concede that the account was enough to support McAdam's decision to assume that he was going to react violently to any attempt to arrest him.

'Another biscuit?' said Ferriter.

Cupidi shook her head. 'Still no sign of my man? The one who pulled me out of the apple store?'

'No,' said Ferriter. 'It appears he got clean away.'

Cupidi smiled.

At the farm, as a paramedic had been preparing to inject her with morphine, Sergeant Moon and Ferriter had arrived from the murder scene.

'Bloody hell,' Moon had said. 'You look like shit.'

Cupidi had told the paramedic to wait. 'Leave me alone, I need to speak to the officer confidentially.'

The young man had stepped back and Cupid had beckoned Moon close. 'See the equipment barn? Over there?'

'Yes.'

She had told the medics about the wounded man in there, the one she had stabbed with a fork. They had pulled him out, still conscious, on a stretcher.

'Get in there. Guard it. Any copper goes in there, tell them it's a crime scene and to keep out.'

'What crime?'

'A man tried to kill me in there. I stabbed him.'

'Jesus.'

'Quick. Get it done.'

'Right. The whole barn?'

'Yep. Keep them out, OK?'

And he had gone off, eager to do his job.

It was true. It was a crime scene. But Cupidi had told Yusuf, the ghost-man who had saved her life, about the grey crates she had been about to hide in. If he had done as she had told him, he would have been in there, waiting for the police to leave.

But then it had been time to get in the ambulance, and she hadn't heard any more about it.

The ghost-man must have taken her advice, because he had disappeared again. He had not been caught. Though they had helped save her life, the rest were already in detention centres and, for them, the removal process would be beginning. Some would be prosecuted, others simply put on planes. All except for Esin; as a parentless child, they couldn't lock her up.

She was in emergency foster care now, her future uncertain.

*

'What about you, Jill?' Cupidi asked Ferriter. 'You OK?'

'Me? I'm fine.'

'Good.'

She looked at her and thought she probably wasn't. Only Cupidi knew how she had tried to win Najiba's confidence. She had told Ferriter it would be better to keep the story to herself. It had cost Najiba her life; a second death following police contact was something they were both going to have to live with.

They sat together in the front of the car, side by side. 'I was thinking of doing a course in digital intelligence,' she said. 'We're going to be able to solve ninety-nine per cent of crime before it even happens.'

'Yeah, yeah,' said Cupidi.

'Serious. Algorithms. All the stuff people leave on social media. Add that to number-plate recognition. And facial recognition. We'll just be wearing bits on our lapels soon and it'll tell us everything we need to know about whoever we're talking to.'

'Fascinating.'

Which Ferriter took as an encouragement to tell her more. 'Just the way you use a phrase on Facebook can be an indicator of criminal behaviour. Did you know that?'

She did her best to nod every now and again, but she was thinking about the ghosts. The growing army of the hidden. The more people thought they knew, the less they did.

She was still talking an hour later, when Zoë emerged from the house. At the door, she and Esin hugged, holding on for at least a minute before they dared release each other.

Two fragile girls.

In the back seat, Zoë was silent.

'Well?' said Ferriter, eagerly. 'What did she say?'

'Nothing much,' said Zoë.

'Did she talk about how she'd witnessed Najiba's murder?'

'Not really.'

Ferriter looked a little disappointed.

Cupidi smiled. Her daughter was a keeper of secrets. All Cupidi knew about Esin was what she'd put in her asylum appeal. She was seventeen and her parents were dead. She had come to England to find an uncle, but she didn't have an address for him. Nothing more.

She would be told, at some point in the months ahead, whether she could stay, or whether they would remove her when she was old enough to return there.

Zoë didn't speak until they were almost home.

'I'm going to teach her English,' said Zoë. 'We're going to message each other.'

'That's great.' Cupidi turned in her seat towards her. 'Just don't take on too much. Go carefully. She might not be here for ever.'

'Mum! I am actually old enough to know what I'm doing.'

'I'm sorry. It's a great thing to do. You're amazing.'

'You are,' agreed Ferriter from the driving seat. 'Bloody amazing.'

'And it's for me, too,' Zoë said. 'Something for me to concentrate on. Apart from myself.'

'That's good. Really good.' Cupidi smiled.

She was nervous about her daughter; she still seemed so fragile. They would get through this; there were three of them now. Her, her mother and her daughter. It wasn't something you could just solve; she understood that. But they could do their best here. It would be autumn soon. The birds would be coming through again. Cupidi was still on sick leave and had some holiday coming too.

They drove down into the flatland. On Denge Marsh, approaching Dungeness, temporary traffic lights slowed their journey. A pump was straining to pour water from one ditch into another culvert.

She recognised one of the men she had spoken to from the Drainage Board, standing in a reflective work coat.

He greeted her as they crawled by. 'Sluice failed,' he explained.

Trying to hold back water, she thought. How long can you do that for? 'We are water,' she said, half out loud.

'What?' said Ferriter.

'The photograph you gave me. The children who were killed in the fire. I was just thinking about that.'

They drove on. The giant power station loomed in front of them.

'Whose is that car?' asked Zoë as they approached the cottage.

'I'm not sure.'

Outside Arum Cottage there was a hire car. They slowed as they approached. Julian was at the door and Lulu was with him, holding Teo in her arms. They must have just arrived.

'They came, then. I didn't think they would.'

An older woman stood by them, almost unrecognisable now. Julian must have bought new clothes for his mother. She seemed to be doing well. She had put on weight, at least, even if Zoë hadn't yet.

Helen was with them. She was setting up a picnic table on the land by the house.

'Is that Julian's wife?' Zoë asked from the back seat.

'Yes,' answered Ferriter. 'Piece of work.'

'They're doing their best,' said Cupidi.

'Maybe.'

'Drop me. I want to tell Nan about Esin. Are you staying for supper?' Zoë asked Ferriter.

'I should get back,' she said.

'No,' said Cupidi. 'You're very welcome. Please join us.'

'You mind?'

'There will be loads,' said Zoë, getting out. 'They keep trying to feed me up.'

They parked the car at the back of the house. Cupidi looked at her watch. It was almost one. 'I need to make that call,' she said.

'Go for it,' said Ferriter.

As they walked up to the front door, Cupidi saw a Tesco's bag hanging from the handle. Poking out of the bag was a small bunch of asters. At the bottom of the bag was a copy of the paperback the book group had finally agreed to: a non-fiction popular science book about physics. She would enjoy that. Tucked inside the book was a note:

Thank you so much for EVERYTHING. (Sorry about last time.)

Colette McAdam. x

'Nice flowers,' said Ferriter. 'Want me to put them in a jug?'

Leaving Ferriter in the kitchen making a salad, Cupidi took her notebook and the brown envelope out of her bag and went to the living room.

One-handed, she flicked through the notebook until she found the telephone number she needed, put it on the coffee table in front of her, then took out the photograph and laid it alongside. She checked her watch, waited another minute. At exactly one o'clock, she took a breath, then dialled.

The telephone rang for a long time before it was picked up.

'*Hej?*' The faraway voice was cautious.

'Olivia Olsson? My name is Detective Sergeant Alexandra Cupidi.'

A pause. 'Yes. My husband said you were going to call.'

It had taken a few days for Cupidi to track down the mother of the dead boys, Jacob and Finn. She no longer lived in the UK. Olivia Olsson was a lecturer in Applied Climatology now, at the University of Gothenburg.

'I have some news about Freya Brindley.'

Did she hear, or did she just imagine, the gulp of air on the other end of the line?

'Yes,' the woman said. 'Please go ahead.'

Slowly, piece by piece, Cupidi told the story about the woman who had killed Jacob and Finn; about how she, in the end, had been murdered and left in cold water.

As she talked, she could hear Ferriter bustling in the kitchen, chopping vegetables.

Olivia Olsson asked few questions; and when she did, they were curt, and almost whispered. 'Would she have suffered?'

Cupidi said, 'No. Not much. Did you want her to have?'

'Naturally,' she said, in the voice of a quiet, contained woman, someone who had become used to not letting her emotions get the better of her.

'If it's any consolation, she did not have a good life after she killed your children. I think she was very troubled by what she had done.'

Olivia Olsson didn't respond.

'I found a photograph of your boys. They were playing in front of your caravan.'

'Royale,' the voice breathed.

Cupidi struggled to understand what Olsson had just said. 'Sorry?'

'Nothing.'

'Would you like me to send it to you?'

'Where did you find it?'

'Freya Brindley had it pinned above her bed. In her own caravan that she lived in until she was murdered. I think she put it there as a way of reminding herself of the awful thing she was responsible for.'

This time the intake of breath was audible. 'I don't want it,' said the mother of the dead boys.

'Was that OK?' asks Ferriter, as they walk slowly back to Arum Cottage, arms full with the salad and bottles of wine.

'Pretty bad,' answers Cupidi.

Ferriter says, 'Do you need a hug?'

'No.'

'I've been having nightmares,' says Ferriter. 'Not sleeping that well, be honest.'

'About Najiba?'

'Kind of. Men with knives. I mean, it's not like I'm going crazy or anything.'

'Normal, given what we went through.'

'What about you? Christ. You were almost dead.'

Cupidi doesn't answer. 'Get a bit drunk. Talk about it. Stay over,' says Cupidi. 'I've got a sofa bed.'

'How can life be so fucking hard for some people? I mean, Peter's nice. But he lives with his mum, for God's sake.'

'Don't fancy him any more now you slept with him, then?'

'I have not! I'm not the one who goes round shagging policemen.'

'Ouch.'

'Sorry.'

They sit on benches and chairs around two tables of different heights. Helen sits down between Cupidi and Hilary. 'Are you OK if we drink?' she says.

Hilary is cleaning up. No drugs, no alcohol. Instead she smokes almost constantly. 'Go ahead. Mind if I hold Teo?' she asks Lulu, with a black-toothed smile.

Lulu is standing on the other side of the long table, with Teo asleep on her shoulder. She has brought a lot of food, including a whole baked salmon with oranges, and laid it out on tinfoil. Pouring wine, Julian pauses. Lulu stands, gently rocking the boy for a little while more, and pretends she hasn't heard.

Hilary busies herself instead, laying out cutlery.

'Zoë's been telling me all about Esin,' says Helen.

'Has she?' Her daughter didn't say much about her in the car.

'She's seen terrible things, that girl. It's a lot for Zoë to take on.'

'I know.'

'Death changes you at that age. It makes you hard.'

Cupidi looks at her mother, holding a glass of wine. 'You're talking about Esin, or yourself?' she asks quietly.

'Both.'

She raises her glass. 'To Alexandra,' she says.

Her mother nods, raises her own glass. It is a solemn moment, shared between the two of them. A strange kind of closeness.

The others look up, unsure what they are toasting.

Zoë will be back at school soon; she's dreading it, but Helen is staying on now indefinitely. They have bought new curtains for her room.

As the warm day turns to evening, they eat. Cupidi watches Zoë talking to Lulu about birds. Julian is trying to explain to Hilary what Lulu does for a living. Ferriter gets drunk and begs Helen to tell stories about what it was like when she was in the police. And as she's talking about how she met Cupidi's father, Helen reaches out and takes Alex's hand and holds it, squeezing it tightly.

A north wind is rising. The tablecloth flutters in the wind, catching a glass which falls and smashes on the shingle. Still they sit, determined to stay out as long as they can in the last of the summer heat until the candles Helen has put in jamjars blow out, one by one.

ACKNOWLEDGEMENTS

This book is the result of my sloppy reading habits. I'm fortunate to be among those whom C. J. Sansom gives early drafts of his novels. Last year he gave me the early pages of his forthcoming Shardlake novel, *Tombland.* It's a wonderful book; I hope he won't mind the spoiler, but it opens with with the ghoulish discovery of the body of a woman; a few pages later, the same dead woman is knocking at the door of her son's house. Instantly I was captivated by the idea of a mother, horribly murdered, reappearing from the dead. Simultaneously baffled and electrified, I skimmed back again to discover I had raced through the first chapters so eagerly I completely missed a vital time-shift. Only when I read it again did I realise that the second part was not an event that happened after her death but a flashback. But I had found the opening to my next book. Is stealing a mistaken idea plagiarism? C. J. Sansom is a lawyer; he says I'll find out soon.

Thanks, too, for help with research to the writer and activist Hsiao-Hung Pai, and to Barbara Storey of SOS Polonia, an excellent charity that helps East European migrant workers in the UK: <www.sospolonia.net>. Gratitude also to Nick Botting and Rob Monje of the Romney Marshes Area Internal Drainage Board. Graham Bartlett's very generous advice on police procedure was invaluable. Also, for their help with research, to Linda Gaunt, Marion McMorrow, Joy Summers, Derick Sharkey, Awatef Samara, Kareem Samara, Jamie Koi, Lisa Cutts and Clare Mackintosh. Lis Hensman helped me with a name and some extremely useful information on the immigration system. Massive thanks to Sue MacLaine for helping me find a heroine.

Much gratitude to those who have given me support along the way. Too many to name, and apologies for those left out: Susan Riaz, Bec Stokes, Barry Forshaw, Simon Cooper, Raven Crime, Llainy Swanson, Terry Halligan, Mystery People, One Tree Books, Heywood Hill Books, and in particular to Rich at Waterstones, Brighton.

Thanks as ever to Jon Riley and Rose Tomaszewska at riverrun, who did so much to craft this book, and also to Joshua Kendal and Nicky Guerreiro at Mulholland. And to the team: Roz Brody, Mike Holmes, Jan King and Chris Sansom for their enthusiasm, diligence and intelligence. Also to Ron Beard and David Murphy of Quercus for doing the impossible.

And, as always, to Jane McMorrow.

Read on for the first chapter of *Deadland*,
the thrilling next investigation for DS Alexandra Cupidi

ONE

The first time they tried stealing a phone, it went arse-tit. The second time, much worse.

It was a Friday. Two boys, both aged seventeen, sitting on a borrowed scooter, one behind the other, helmets on. The first time they waited twenty metres away from the entrance to the town's poshest hotel; not so close that people would notice what they were up to. Amazing how many people walk out of a hotel door with their phones right in their hands for everyone to see.

'What about him?'

'Nope. Shit phone.'

'You can't even see it.'

'I can. iPhone 5. Wouldn't get twenty for it.'

'That one. There.'

'She's got a baby with her, douche.'

'What?' With helmets on, neither could hear much the other said unless they shouted.

'You can't do people if they've got a baby.'

Right. 'Him?'

'Scary-looking one? You mad?'

'We're on a bike. He'll never catch us.'

Enough hesitation for the man to disappear again, out of view, behind a crowd of hen party girls.

Sloth sat at the front of the scooter, Tap on the pillion.

'I'm bored,' said Tap after ten minutes. 'This is pointless.'

'You've got no ambition, bro. No aspiration.'

'Kind of thing your mum says, Sloth.'

'Shut up. Her?' said Sloth. Woman, maybe forty, quite posh in heels and shades, hair still wet from a shower, coming out of the hotel.

'Let's do it.'

'Sure?' They had been sat on the bike outside Snack Box for what felt like ages now, hyped and twitchy. Way too long. Now or never.

'Samsung Galaxy. S9.'

'Reckon?'

'OK. Her.'

Sloth kick-started the engine. 'We doing this?'

'Serious.'

'We sure?'

'Frick sake. Go, you'll miss her,' urged Tap and slapped Sloth's helmet.

Sloth kicked the scooter into gear, releasing the clutch so quickly Tap almost tipped off the back.

''Kin' hell.'

The tiny engine screamed. Way too fast. They were on the woman so soon Tap had no time to think. She was negotiating the brick paving of the pedestrian zone with careful high-heel steps. Tap had just time to glimpse her open mouth as she looked up at the noise of the bike, phone still at her ear as his outstretched arm sped towards her.

But Sloth was riding so hard Tap didn't have a hope of getting his gloved fingers round the phone. Next thing they were past her and, through his visor, Tap could see the shiny device spinning in the air in a long arc.

Never saw where it fell.

Already, Sloth was zig-zagging, avoiding startled pedestrians with buggies and shopping trollies on the narrow street, and Tap was clinging on to his waist again, until they could cut down Market Place and get a bit of real speed up for the getaway.

Sloth wove through cars crazily, leaning this way and that, finally skidding a left into the dead end lane beside the disused video shop. Engine still puttering, he removed his helmet.

'Get it?'

Heart still thumping from the buzz, he slapped Sloth's bare head. 'That was way too fast. Bloody hell.'

Sloth punched Tap back. 'Oh I can't believe you missed it. You're just too slow, bro.'

They burst out laughing.

'I don't know,' said Tap. 'Maybe we call it a day.'

'Douche.'

'Seriously.'

'You give up way too easy, bro. Too hectic there anyway. That was the issue. I know somewhere good we could try,' said Sloth, putting his helmet back on.

*

Second time was definitely a better location. There was no CCTV on the cut-through from the station down to TK Maxx.

'See?' said Sloth.

He was right. They arrived there as a local train pulled in. Coming off the platform, exactly the same thing, everyone pulling out their phones. 'I'm home, love.' 'Need anything from the shop?' Made it easy.

But by the time they'd figured out the area, everyone from the first train had gone, so they had to wait for the next one from London to pull in. They found a spot to hide this time, tucked out of the way beside the Chinese takeaway.

'Spliff?' said Tap after fifteen minutes.

'Nah.'

'Might slow you down a bit.'

'I don't need slowing down, bruv. Stay woke, not broke.'

'Deep. Just keep it nice and subtle this time. All right?'

'Like a girl asking me not to be rough with her.'

''K off. You wouldn't even know what that's like.'

Neither of them would, as a matter of fact.

A train arrived. Sloth started up the motor again. The first commuters were too tightly packed together to bother with. It was like lions, you had to wait to pick off stragglers.

They both saw him at the same time. Ordinary-looking bloke. Jeans and brown jacket. Balding slightly. Earring. Holdall in his left hand, phone at his right ear. The man's face was red, as if he was flustered. From where they sat, out of view, they couldn't make out what he was saying.

'What's he got?'

'Can't see.'

And then, as if just to oblige them, the man held out his phone, looked at his screen, then returned it to his ear and continued talking.

'iPhone X,' said Tap, quietly. 'Look. For sure. Get a few hundred for that. Easy.'

'Reckon?'

'Got to be. Look at the size.'

The man paused by the gate. They could hear him talking now. It sounded like 'Keep your hair on. You still get to keep your half, I just get all the rest.'

'Come this way, come this way,' whispered Sloth.

Tap was suddenly unsure. There was something odd about this man, the tightly wound way he gripped that bag at his shoulder, the redness of his face. Later he would wonder if he should have said something, told Sloth to leave it, but in front of him on the bike, Sloth seemed so sure.

The man ended the call, reached down, opened the bag, and placed the phone inside.

'See that?' said Sloth.

'Yep.'

This time Sloth did everything right. The moment the man was past them, walking across the expanse of litter-strewn tarmac, Sloth kicked hard on the pedal and launched the bike forward off the stand, out of the darkness at the side of the old takeaway restaurant. The man didn't have a chance. In the second that he heard the sound of the motor coming up behind him and stopped to turn, Sloth braked just a touch, slowing the bike just for long enough.

Afterwards, they roared down the ramp onto the pavement,

bumping onto the carriageway, Tap clutching the stolen holdall to his chest and shouting, 'Got it this time, bro.'

And Sloth accelerated round a white BMW 218i Sport, shouting, 'Sweetness.'

The feeling was mad; the fear and thrill like being on the wildest theme park ride, only better.

Uncle Mikey opened the door to his council house, looked at the two grinning teenage boys, one black, one white. An old black moped was parked on its stand, motor still puttering next to his bright red Suzuki GSX.

'Hey, Uncle Mikey,' said the white one.

The other one turned to switch off the engine, not by turning a key, but by plugging in the kill switch, so they'd obviously nicked it.

Mikey shook his head. Benjamin wasn't his real nephew but he had had this on-off thing with his mother for years and liked the lad as if he was his own. Sloth, the black kid, was super-short for his age, only five three. Benjamin was almost a foot taller and milky pale. A right pair.

'Yeah, yeah. What this time?' Mikey, himself six foot tall, an ex-merchant navy man who tapped fags on a packet before he smoked them; still the Paul Weller haircut, though his hair was grey now and thinning at the back.

'iPhone-fuckin'-X. Mint condition.' Sloth held up the holdall like a prize.

Mikey shook his head. 'Oh, boys. Why are you doing this? Get a bloody job.'

'How much?'

'Are you addled? Jesus. Not interested. I'm straight these days. Get out of here.'

'Honest to God, Uncle Mikey,' said Tap. 'It's proper.' They'd called Benjamin 'Tap' at school ever since Year 5 when Mr Parker said he must have been tapped on the head too hard as a baby.

'Don't bloody care. Did you switch the phone off?'

Tap and Sloth looked at each other. 'No.'

'Benjamin Brown. You are unbelievably dense. Beep beep beep. Right now that phone is telling people exactly where it is. The feds can be on you in ten minutes. Bet they're on the way now. Get out of here. I don't want them coming to my door causing me aggravation. I've had enough of it.' He paused, looked them up and down. 'How's your mum, by the way, Benji?'

Sloth yanked Tap by the sleeve. 'Let's go somewhere else. He's not bothered.'

'She's using again, I think,' said Tap. 'Drinking, anyway.'

'Very sorry to hear that. I'll come round. See what I can do. OK, mate?'

'Appreciate it.' Though Tap wondered what Mikey ever saw in his mother.

'You've got to look after her, Benji. I know you think she's a pain, with all that. The thing about growing up is learning who you care for. OK, mate?'

Tap nodded.

'Deep,' mocked Sloth.

'Yeah, yeah,' said Mikey. 'True, though. You'll figure that out one day. Took me long enough. You got to learn it, Benji.

Nobody tells you the rules in this game. You got to work them out for yourself.'

'Very, very deep.'

'Get lost.'

'Can't you wipe it? iPhone X. Mint. Worth hundreds,' said Sloth. 'Show him, Tap.'

Tap delved in and pulled out a small black Alcatel.

'You are such failures,' scoffed Mikey. 'That's some cheap pay-as-you-go shitbrick. Is that some kind of attempt at a joke?'

'Yeah,' said Sloth, smiling. He took the phone and put it in his pocket. 'Now show him the other one, Tap.'

Tap pulled out the second device: a brand new iPhone. When they had stopped to examine the bag, there had been two phones in it. One worthless, the other a top-of-the-range device, barely used.

Mikey hesitated, looking at the device, then said, 'Bollocks. I don't want it. Take it away.'

But, as Tap held it, the screen lit up and the phone vibrated. A message appeared on the lock screen. Mikey reached out and took the handset.

Tap leaned forward to read the words '*Pls give what you stole back £5000 reward no questions*', followed by a phone number.

'Christ in a bucket,' Mikey said eventually.

Sloth pushed past and read what was there too.

'Frickin' hell.'

'Is that five grand?'

'Yeah.'

'Five grand? You could get another five frickin' iPhones for that.'

Sloth giggled. 'He's going to pay us five grand?'

'Sure there's nothing else in the bag?'asked Mikey.

Tap shook his head. 'Nothing. Searched it.'

'Must be something extra-bloody-special on the phone.'

Tap held out his hand. 'Give us it back. It's ours.'

'Actually, technically speaking, not,' said Mikey, holding on to the phone.

'It's our phone. It's our money.'

Mikey smiled. 'Yeah? OK. I'll give it back to you.' But he didn't. 'And what if it's a trick? What if the police put the message on there and when you turn up to get your reward –' pronouncing the word 'reward' with heavy irony – 'they're all waiting for you? Bloke knows two lads on a shit moped nicked it from him. I can say I just found it, accidental. They can't prove anything, can they?'

Tap hesitated. 'Five hundred for you. If you go instead of us.'

'Nope. Fifty-fifty.'

'You are joking? Two-and-a-half grand for being a delivery man? We took the risk nicking it.'

'And I'll take the risk taking it back.'

'That's shit,' said Sloth.

'That's business. Don't I always tell you, lads? Think about the weekend you'll have.'

They thought about that for a second. 'What you reckon?' muttered Sloth.

'Five grand, man. We did the work.'

Mikey shrugged. 'Ten minutes ago you'd have been over the moon if I'd given you a hundred for it.'

'True.'

'I think it's shit,' Sloth complained.

They stood for another minute on the doorstep, before Mikey called the number on the screen.

'Here's a thing. I found this phone,' he said. 'Apparently there's a reward.'

The voice at the other end of the phone spoke.

'Yeah. I know it. Up by the river.'

Tap looked at Sloth; he had that frown on his face, lips pursed tight, like when he was about to start going off. 'It's OK, bro,' he whispered. 'I trust him.'

'Make it twenty minutes. I'll be there. Yeah . . . and the bag. I'll bring it.'

When he'd ended the call, Mikey said, 'Come back this evening. If he's on the level, I'll give you half.'

'Right,' Tap said. 'Two point five?'

'If that's what I get.'

Sloth rolled his eyes.

Helmets off, they rode a little way to the edge of the estate, then stopped, puttering on the footpath.

'Don't believe him,' said Sloth.

'He's OK. He'll give us the money. I promise.'

'Yeah, but reckon the one we stole it off is going to give him the money for real?'

Tap shrugged. 'I'm over it, anyway.'

'How can you be over it? You just give up so easily. Douche.' He thumped his friend on the arm.

Tap dug in his jacket and pulled out tobacco and some spliff. 'Don't know, mate. Just need weed.'

'We should follow him,' said Sloth. 'See if he gets the money.'

'Give us a break, mate. You're always on it. Just relax. It'll be fine.' It's why they had called him 'Sloth' at school. Because he wasn't one. It was better than the one he had before, which had been 'Donnie Darko', or mostly just 'Darko'.

Sloth revved the throttle in neutral, making the little engine whine. He pushed the scooter back a little, down the alleyway.

'I'm going if you're not.'

'Fuck sake,' said Tap, replacing his weed in his pocket and putting his helmet back on. 'He'll be mad if he sees us spying on him.'

'Won't see us,' said Sloth.

And they waited until the red motorbike roared past them, and then Sloth nudged the scooter back into gear and started to follow it down the A106.

But the 50cc engine was so useless they lost him in five minutes.